WANDERING STAR

A ZODIAC NOVEL

WANDERING STAR

A ZODIAC NOVEL

ROMINA RUSSELL

razor
bill

An Imprint of Penguin Random House

Razorbill, an Imprint of Penguin Random House
Penguin.com

Copyright © 2015 Penguin Random House LLC

ISBN: 978-1-59514-743-1

Printed in the United States of America

1 3 5 7 9 10 8 6 4 2

Interior design by Vanessa Han

320140708

Para mi abuelo, Berek el Sabio
Nunca serás olvidado

For my grandpa, Sage Berek
You will never be forgotten

HOUSE PISCES

HOUSE SAGITTARIUS

HOUSE LEO

HOUSE ARIES

HOUSE CANCER

H

HOUSE VIRGO

HOUSE CAPRICORN

HOUSE TAURUS

HOUSE GEMINI

HOUSE LIBRA

HOUSE AQUARIUS

PIO

THE HOUSES OF THE ZODIAC GALAXY

THE FIRST HOUSE:
ARIES, _THE RAM_
CONSTELLATION
Strength: Military
Guardian: General Eurek

THE FIFTH HOUSE:
LEO, _THE LION_
CONSTELLATION
Strength: Passion
Guardian: Holy Leader Aurelius

THE SECOND HOUSE:
TAURUS, _THE BULL_
CONSTELLATION
Strength: Industry
Guardian: Chief Executive Purecell

THE SIXTH HOUSE:
VIRGO, _THE TRIPLE VIRGIN_
CONSTELLATION
Strength: Sustenance
Guardian: Empress Moira
(in critical condition)

THE THIRD HOUSE:
GEMINI, _THE DOUBLE_
CONSTELLATION
Strength: Imagination
Guardians: Twins
Caaseum (deceased) and Rubidum

THE SEVENTH HOUSE:
LIBRA, _THE SCALES OF_
JUSTICE CONSTELLATION
Strength: Justice
Guardian: Lord Neith

THE FOURTH HOUSE:
CANCER, _THE CRAB_
CONSTELLATION
Strength: Nurture
Guardian: Holy Mother Agatha
(Interim)

THE EIGHTH HOUSE:
SCORPIO, _THE SCORPION_
CONSTELLATION
Strength: Innovation
Guardian: Chieftain Skiff

THE NINTH HOUSE:
SAGITTARIUS, *THE ARCHER* CONSTELLATION
Strength: Curiosity
Guardian: Guardian Brynda

~~THE THIRTEENTH HOUSE:~~
~~OPHIUCHUS, *THE SERPENT BEARER* CONSTELLATION~~
~~*Strength: Unity*~~
~~*Guardian: Master Ophiuchus*~~

THE TENTH HOUSE:
CAPRICORN, *THE SEAGOAT* CONSTELLATION
Strength: Wisdom
Guardian: Sage Ferez

THE ELEVENTH HOUSE:
AQUARIUS, *THE WATER BEARER* CONSTELLATION
Strength: Philosophy
Guardian: Supreme Guardian Gortheaux the Thirty-Third

THE TWELFTH HOUSE:
PISCES, *THE FISH* CONSTELLATION
Strength: Spirituality
Guardian: Prophet Marinda

PROLOGUE

WHEN I THINK OF MOM, I think of the day she abandoned us. There are dozens of memories that still haunt me, but that one always shoves its way to the surface first, submerging all other thoughts with its power.

I remember knowing something was wrong when Helios's rays—and not Mom's whistle—roused me. Every day, I'd awoken to the low-pitched call of the black seashell Dad had found for Mom on their first date; she kept it buried in her hair, pinning up her long locks, and plucked it out only for our daily drills.

But this morning dawned unannounced. I clambered out of bed, changed into my school uniform, and searched the bungalow for my parents.

The first person I spotted was Stanton. He was in his room across the hall, one side of his face glued to the wall. "Why are you—?"

"*Shhh.*" He pointed to the crack in the sand-and-seashell wall through which he could listen into our parents' room. "Something's up," he mouthed.

I dutifully froze and awaited my big brother's next cue. Stanton was ten, so he attended school on a pod city with our neighbor, Jewel Belger. Her mom would arrive any moment to pick him up, and Stanton was still in his nightclothes.

The seconds of silence were agony, during which I imagined every possible scenario, from Mom being diagnosed with a deadly disease to Dad discovering a priceless pearl that would make us rich. When at last Stan backed away from the crack, he pulled me into the hallway with him right as Mom barreled out from her bedroom.

"Stanton, come with me, please," she said as she strode past. Lately whenever she and Dad fought, she sought solace in my brother. He eagerly bounded behind her, and though I longed to follow, I knew she wouldn't approve. If she wanted me there, she would have said so.

I looked out through one of the bungalow's many windows as Mom led Stan into the crystal reading room Dad had built for her on the banks of the inner lagoon near his nar-clams; a miniature version of the crystal dome on Elara, it fit three people at most. I'd watch Mom go in there every night, her figure blurring into misty shadow behind the thick walls as she read her Ephemeris in the starlight.

A small schooner pulled up to our dock, and Jewel jumped out, her frizzy curls blowing in the salty breeze. As she ran to our front door, Dad's footsteps slapped down the stairs to meet her. I padded softly after him and hung on the staircase landing to listen.

Dad traded the hand touch with Jewel and waved to Mrs. Belger in the distance. "Stan isn't going in today," he said as Mrs. Belger honked back a greeting from her schooner.

"Oh," said Jewel, sounding supremely disappointed. "Is he sick?"

I crept out a little farther from behind the banister, and Jewel's piercing periwinkle eyes flashed to me. Her chestnut cheeks darkened, and she looked away, either from shyness or to keep Dad from noticing I was there.

"A little," said Dad.

I nearly gasped in shock—I'd never heard one of my parents tell a lie before. Cancrians don't deceive.

"Can I . . . can you tell him I hope he gets better?"

I stared at the back of Dad's prematurely balding head as he nodded. "I will. Have a good day at school, Jewel." As he waved again to Mrs. Belger, I soundlessly slipped behind him and went out a side door.

Tracing the outer walls of our bungalow, I found Jewel waiting for me by a small pond of water lilies that Mom tended to so much, she always smelled of them.

"Is Stanton okay?" she blurted as I came closer. Her skin flushed darker in embarrassment again.

"Yeah," I said, shrugging.

"He told me your parents are fighting a lot. . . ." She let her sentence hang gently between us, an invitation to talk to her as a friend, even though I was only seven and she was Stanton's age. Her attention made me feel important, so I wanted to share something special—a *secret*.

"Stanton's not really sick. He's with my mom. She and my dad just fought."

This seemed to mean more to Jewel than me, because her chestnut features pulled together with concern, and she said, "I don't think it's good for him . . . being brought into their arguments. I think it's making him old."

Then she ran off to her mom's schooner, and as they sailed away, Jewel's face pressed into the glass window, staring back longingly at our bungalow. Her words worried me, even if I didn't fully get their meaning, and I looked toward the crystal reading room, wondering.

I found myself moving closer to the place, the thick sparkly walls reflecting me in the sunlight instead of illuminating what was going on inside. I edged around it, careful to stay low in case Mom or Stanton looked out, and then I peeked in, cupping my eyes and squinting so I could see.

Stanton had just received his first Wave at school, and he was sitting on the reading room's floor, recording information into it. Mom had switched on her Ephemeris, and she was orbiting the space while rattling words off to Stanton, words I couldn't hear.

I took a chance and opened the door a crack, as slowly and carefully as possible.

"After you've cleaned the three changelings, toss them on the griller with a sprinkling of sea salt and sweet-water honeysuckles from the garden. I think that should be plenty of recipes. Let's move on to Rho's morning drills."

"Mom, but *why* are you telling me this?" Stanton spoke in the whiny tone of repetition. Even though he sounded unhappy, his fingers obediently ticked away on his Wave's holographic screen, logging the information.

"I like to wake Rho three hours early with rapid-fire drills about the Houses," continued Mom, as though Stanton hadn't interrupted. "After cycling through all twelve Yarrot poses, she must Center herself and commune with the stars for at least one hour—"

Mom stopped speaking suddenly, and every molecule of my being liquefied beneath her glacial glare. Through the sliver of a gap in the doorway, she was staring straight at me.

The door swept inward, and I nearly fell inside. Scrambling upright, I snuck a quick glance at my brother, who was looking from Mom to me with bated breath. I braced myself for Mom's fury at my eavesdropping—only she didn't look upset.

"You should be on your way to class, Rho." She searched behind me for a sign of Dad. I turned, too, but he was still inside the bungalow. When I looked back at Mom, she wore the same intense stare I'd seen on her face a week ago, when she warned me my fears were real.

They certainly felt real in that moment. Every fearful possibility I'd dreaded earlier swam in my head once more, and I wondered what could have made Mom decide to dictate the details of her daily life to Stanton. Something was happening—something awful. My gut churned and sizzled, like I'd eaten too much sugared seaweed at once, and I couldn't stand the not-knowing.

Mom reached out and caressed my face, her touch more whisper than words. "Your teachers are wrong, you know." It was one of her favorite phrases. "There aren't twelve types of people in the universe—there are two." She stared at the pearl necklace on my chest, which I hadn't taken off all week. Cancer's pearl wasn't centered, but for the first time, she didn't reach out to adjust it. "The ones that stand still and try to fit in . . . and the ones that go seek out where they belong."

That's the last thing my mother ever said to me. When Dad sailed me to school that morning on the Strider—late—neither of us knew he would return to find Mom gone.

Dad lived life mostly inside his head, so he wasn't a big talker. But that morning he broke our usual silence by saying, "Rho . . . your mom and I love you very much. If we argue, it has nothing to do with you or your brother. You know that?"

I nodded. He was speaking softly, in the comforting tone he always adopted post-fight. So I took a chance. "Dad . . . why did you lie to Jewel? What's really happening with Stanton and Mom?"

I could see from Dad's face he would rather not answer, but he was always more forthcoming post-fight. With a slight sigh, he said, "I shouldn't have lied, Rho. I'm sorry you heard that. I'm also sorry I can't give you an answer, because I don't have one. You know how your mom is . . . she's having a spell. She'll be fine when you get home."

It was then I understood what Jewel meant about too much information making someone old. I wanted to believe Dad—to push off the doubt and worry and the queasiness in my stomach that still hadn't gone away. But the absence of the black seashell's song that morning felt more like an omen.

Mom was right.

(She usually was.)

Fears are real.

1

TWELVE FLAGS, EACH BEARING THE symbol of a Zodiac House, lie in tatters before me, on a barren field that extends endlessly in every direction.

I can just make out a crest neatly sewn beneath each House name—a dark blue Crab, a royal purple Lion, an inky black Scorpion. Caked in blood and grime, the defeated fabrics sprawl across the lifeless land like corpses from a forgotten battle.

There are no sounds; nothing moves in the dusty distance. Even the sky is devoid of expression—it's just a constant colorless expanse. But the stillness in the air is far from calm. It feels like the day is holding its breath.

I turn in a small circle to survey my surroundings, and in the eastern distance I see a steep hill that's the only disruption to the flat landscape. I concentrate hard on the hill, envisioning myself cresting it to survey the valley below, and soon my view begins to transform. As the vast valley sharpens into focus, I choke on a horrified gasp—

Thousands of dead bodies litter the powdery earth below, their uniforms a rainbow of colors. Like a gruesome quilt made from people parts.

I slump to the floor, nearly crushing the glass orb in my hand, and shut my eyes, forgetting that nightmares thrive in darkness. Corpses crowd my view in here, too.

Hundreds of frozen Cancrian teens in flashy suits float through the black space of my mind, forever suspended there. I shake my head, and the vision flips to Virgo's ships going up in flames, the air almost thick with the stench of burning flesh and metal.

Then the tiny burned bodies of the once-lively Geminin people.

The wreckage of vessels from what was once our united armada.

I suck in a ragged breath as the next picture forms: the familiar wavy black locks, alabaster face, indigo blue—

My eyes snap open, and I squeeze the glowing glass orb in my fist. The valley of bodies vanishes as the sights and sounds of reality rush into my head, as if I've just broken the sea's surface after a deep dive.

The barren field has transformed back into a large, sterile room lined with floor-to-ceiling shelves that house hundreds of thousands of identical glass orbs. They're called Snow Globes, and each one stores a re-creation of a moment in time.

I replace the memory I was just reviewing in its spot on the shelf:

House Capricorn
Trinary Axis

Sage Huxler's recollections

After a moment, the orb's white light dims out.

I've been coming to Membrex 1206 for two weeks, combing through House Capricorn's memories of the Trinary Axis, searching for answers to any of my millions of questions. I'm desperate for any signs that could lead me to Ophiuchus, or help us defeat the Marad, or bring back hope to the Zodiac.

So far, I've found none of the above.

My Wave buzzes on the table, and I snap it open, anxious for news. A twenty-year-old guy with my identical blond curls, sun-kissed skin, and pale green eyes beams his hologram into the room.

"Rho—where are you?"

Stanton looks confusedly at the Membrex (a room outfitted with the technology to unlock Snow Globes) surrounding us. He's wearing his wet suit and squinting against Helios's rays, so he must still be at the beach helping out.

"I'm in the Zodiax . . . just looking something up."

I haven't told my brother what I'm really up to here—deep within the earth of House Capricorn's sole planet, Tierre—while he volunteers at the Cancrian settlement on the surface. "Any sign of his ship yet?" I ask before I can stop myself.

"Like I told you twelve times this hour, I'll let you know when he's here. You shouldn't worry so much." Stanton looks like he wants to say more, but he glances off to the side, to something happening on the beach. "Gotta go; last ark of the day's just dropped off more crates. When are you heading over?"

"On my way." Capricorns have been shuttling our people back and forth from here to Cancer on their arks, braving the planet's stormy surface to save our world's wildlife. The Cancrians on the settlement have been helping our species adapt to Tierre's smaller ocean.

Stanton's hologram winks out, and I pull up the ledger on my Wave where I've been keeping track of the Snow Globes I've examined, and input today's updates. To exit the room, I pass through a biometric body scan that ensures the only memories I'm taking with me are my own.

Out in the dimly lit passage, I brush my hand along the smooth stone wall until my fingers close on a square metal latch. I pull on it to open a hidden door, and when I slip through, the ground falls away.

My stomach tickles as I glide down a steep, narrow tube that shoots me out onto the springy floor of a train platform. Its bounciness reminds me of my drum mat, except this one's riddled with rows of symmetrical circles that light up either red or green, depending on whether that spot on the train is available.

I stand inside one of the green circles, and almost immediately there's a rush of wind and the hissing of pistons beneath my feet—then the circle I'm standing on opens.

A gust of air pressure sucks me down, and I've tapped into the Vein, the train system that tunnels through the Zodiax.

"*Zodiac art from the first millennium,*" announces a cool female voice. I grab onto the handrail above me as the wind changes direction, and a stray curl falls into my face as we shoot upward.

The Zodiax is an underground vault that contains what the Tenth House calls a *treasure trove of truths*: the collective wisdom of the Zodiac. Down here, there are museums, galleries, theaters, Membrexes, auditoriums, restaurants, reading rooms, research labs, hotels, shopping malls, and more. When Mom described it to me once, she said the Zodiax is like a brain, and the Vein is its neuron network, zooming people around as fast as firing synapses, its route mapped by subject matter rather than geography.

A couple of Capricorn women in black robes share my compartment— one is tall with dark features, the other short with a ruddy complexion. We slow down for half a moment at "*Notable Zodai from this century,*" and the smaller woman is sucked up to a train platform.

"*Surface, Cancrian settlement.*"

I click a button on the handrail and let go. I'm blown up to the bouncy bed of another train station, and biometric body scans search me again as I leave the Zodiax.

Outside, I instinctively raise a hand to shield my eyes from Helios's light. Echoing silence is instantly replaced with the sounds of crashing waves and animal calls and distant conversations. As my vision adjusts, I make out herds of seagoats (House Capricorn's sacred symbol) feeding and roughhousing at the water's edge, and long-bodied terrasaurs flicking in and out of the rocks along the seashore, their scaly skin shiny in the daylight. High above us, horned hawks flap across the sun-bleached sky, circling the air in hopes of picking off the pocket pigs feeding in the weeds.

Tierre is the largest inhabited planet in our galaxy, and it has a single massive landmass, Verity. Up ahead, the planet's pink sand beach spills into the blue of its ocean, and behind me, wild forests grow right up to the ridges of volcanoes, giving way in the distance to snowcapped mountains that pierce the sky. The view is occasionally interrupted by the long neck of a fluffy giraffe reaching up for a fresh tree leaf.

This place is a land lover's paradise—which makes sense, given that Capricorn is a Cardinal House, representing the element Earth. People here live in modest homes on vast plots of land with multiple pets that live free-range.

Cancer's colony is being built along Verity's western coastline, our people predictably opting to settle near our preferred cardinal element, Water. As I walk into our settlement, clusters of Cancrians are working on their respective tasks. Some are building pink sand-and-seashell bungalows, some are chopping seafood for sushi on flat stones, and some—including Stanton—are knee-deep in the ocean wearing wet suits, tending to the newly arrived species. As I walk past each group of people, they don't stare anymore. Not like they did at first.

A month ago, the Cancrians I met on Gemini insisted on my innocence and vowed the other Houses wouldn't get away with this insult to Cancer. Then three weeks ago, we came to Capricorn, and the Cancrians here have barely spoken to me. Their glares and pointed silence have made it clear they're not interested in my political failings—their sole concern is saving what's left of our world.

I wade toward Stanton through a shallow sea of crawling hookcrabs, miniature sea horses, schools of flashing changelings (blue fish that turn red when they sense danger), and a few just-released baby crab-sharks. My brother is with Aryll, a seventeen-year-old Cancrian who came here with us from Gemini. They're in the process of releasing another school of changelings into the ocean.

Rather than disturb them, I hang back and scour the sky for the telltale metallic glint of an approaching spaceship. It's getting close to sunset. He should be here by now.

"You look nice today," says Stanton, spotting me. Only he says it less like a compliment and more like a question. His gaze searches my turquoise dress for clues before landing back on the water.

Aryll turns, and his electric-blue eye roves over my outfit; a gray patch covers the spot where his left eye used to be. He flashes me a boyish smile before rearranging his expression into a Stanton-like look of disapproval. Even though I know he cares for us both, he takes my brother's side on pretty much everything.

"It doesn't matter, I can still help you guys." I come closer, letting the bottom of my dress get wet to show Stanton I'm not fussy.

"Rho, don't," he says with a bite of impatience. "We're nearly finished. Just hang back."

I do as my brother says, watching as he and Aryll set the fish free. The changelings look radioactive, their fiery bodies staining the blue water red, but soon their coloring begins to cool, and they disappear into the ocean's depths. Changelings, being small and low-maintenance, have had the easiest time adapting to Capricorn so far.

Stanton opens up the last closed crate floating beside him, and he and Aryll start releasing hookcrabs into the ocean. "That's good, but watch for its pincers," says Stanton, deftly taking the crab from Aryll before it snaps his finger off.

When he talks to Aryll, my brother sounds different than when he addresses me. With Aryll, his voice dips lower, adopting a comforting tone that's painfully familiar. "See this part of the shell back here, where it curves in a little?" Aryll nods obediently. "That's always the best place to grip them."

Stanton's words sweep me back to Kalymnos, where I learned how to handle the hookcrabs that constantly clawed at our nar-clams, and I realize who my brother is acting like. He's being *Dad*.

It shouldn't bother me. After all that's happened, I should be mature and understanding and compassionate. I should be grateful my brother's alive at all. Some people lost everything.

Aryll was at school on a Cancrian pod city when pieces of our moons started shooting through our planet's atmosphere. The explosion took out his left eye. By the time he made it home, his whole family and house had drowned in the Cancer Sea. Like Stanton, he was herded together with other survivors and transported to House Gemini's planet Hydragyr.

Then Ophiuchus attacked Gemini.

Earthquakes ransacked the rocky planet right as the Cancrian settlement was being built. Stanton was ushering a family to safety when he lost his balance and slipped off the rock face. Aryll caught him just as he was going over.

He saved my brother's life.

"We're going to change," Stanton calls out as he and Aryll duck behind a privacy curtain to shed their wet suits.

I study the horizon again for a sign of the ship I've been anxiously awaiting all day. Ophiuchus hasn't destroyed another planet since Argyr, but the Marad attacks a different House every week. The army has also been linked to pirate ships that have been intercepting travelers and inter-House supply shipments all across the galaxy. Zodai on every House are cautioning citizens to avoid Space travel, encouraging us to travel by holo-ghost whenever possible.

What if something's happened? How will I know? Maybe I should try his Ring, just in case—

"There!" shouts Aryll, his red hair flickering like fire under Helios's rays. He points to a dot in the sky.

My heart skips several beats as the dot zooms closer, sunlight catching its gleaming surface. The ship grows bigger on its approach, until the full form of the familiar bullet-shaped craft is visible.

Hysan is here at last.

2

'*NOX* LANDS ON A PLOT of pink sand far enough away not to disturb our camp. Stanton, Aryll, and I march toward the ship, and in the distance, Hysan's golden figure leaps onto the beach, carrying a black case with him.

I exhale in relief, realizing as I do that I've been holding my breath since Hysan and I parted. In a way, I've been lonelier these past few weeks than I was our whole time on *Equinox*.

Hysan's lips twist into his centaur smile as he approaches, and my mouth mirrors the movement effortlessly. I'd forgotten how relaxing a real smile could feel.

He looks taller, and his golden hair has outgrown its Zodai cut. The white streaks are gone, and so are the expensive clothes—he's dressed in a simple gray space suit that he's filling out with more muscle than I remember.

"My lady." His lively, leaf-green eyes rest on my face and travel to my turquoise dress. "Memory did not do you justice."

"You should have been here hours ago," I say, the flush in my cheeks undercutting my rebuke.

"I apologize if I worried you." Hysan brings my hand to his lips, his kiss activating a million Snow Globes stored inside my body. My skin tingles as the ghosts of his touch echo tauntingly through me.

"Hysan. Thanks for coming. Hope all is well."

The choppiness in Stanton's speech means he's still wary of Hysan. When they met on Gemini, I introduced him as a friend and nothing more. Even though that's technically true, I'm still lying to my brother . . . and apparently not even well.

"Happy to be of service," says Hysan, flashing Stanton one of his winning grins and bumping fists with him. After exchanging the hand touch with Aryll, he says, "I can't stay long. I only came to deliver the Bobbler, then I must report to the Plenum on House Taurus. An emergency session has been called."

"What's happened?" I ask, the alarm in my chest going off.

"Nothing like that. I'll explain later." He opens the black case he's been carrying and holds up what looks like a deflated hot-air balloon attached to a pump. "This is a Bobbler—it's what our scientists use to explore Kythera's surface. As soon as you hit *Inflate*, it will activate, and the navigational system will launch an instructional holographic feed. You can use it to send someone to explore the surface of Cancer—or even into the Cancer Sea, up to a pressure point—and it will withstand the harshest atmospheric conditions."

The Bobbler looks like a person-sized version of the membranes surrounding Libra's flying cities. "*Transparent nanocarbon fused with silica,*" I recite, recalling Hysan's words.

He beams at me. "Exactly."

"What about the species down in the Rift?" Being unpleasant isn't in my brother's nature, so the hardness in his tone is so slight that anyone but a Libran would miss it. "We don't have watercraft that can penetrate deep enough to know how they've been affected or whether we need to move them."

"I've reached out to my contacts on Scorpio," says Hysan, his smile faltering but his manner still pleasant. "It's the only House with ships that can descend to those depths. They're not feeling particularly warm toward Cancer right now"—his eyes flit to mine but don't quite connect—"still, I'm hopeful they'll come through."

Around us the sun is setting, and a few stars are already peeking out in the darkening sky. As Hysan stores the Bobbler back inside its case, the night glows suddenly white. We look up to see silver holographic letters forming high above Tierre:

DINNER.

"Can you stay?" I ask Hysan hopefully.

There's a slight hesitation before he says, "It would be my pleasure, my lady."

Though he's smiling, I sensed something worrisome in his pause. Whatever's going on, it's worse than he's letting on.

✦ ✦ ✦

Dinner for the sector of Capricorn we're residing in takes place in the vast valley of a steep hill—the same one from Sage Huxler's recollections. Herds of black-robed Capricorns make their way there with us, each holding what looks like a magical wand. It's their Wave-like device, a Sensethyser.

Since Capricorns believe in quantifying and containing knowledge, they use a Sensethyser to capture and create holographic versions of anything new they stumble across. When pointed at something—a rare item, a new technology, an unknown mineral or plant or animal species—the Sensethyser digests every detail and creates a holographic replica that's downloaded in a terminal of the Zodiax for review and classification.

When we reach the valley, parallel processions of people pad along both sides of one extra-extra-long table, filling their plates with small servings from every platter. Each person brings his own plate and silverware, and every Capricorn household contributes a dish to the meal. For our part, the Cancrians who were chopping up seafood earlier now deposit a tray of sushi at one end of the table.

There's a stack of extra plates for those who forgot theirs, so Hysan pulls one from there, and once we've piled on some food, the four of us find a patch of grass to sit on. Most Capricorns gather in groups, holding huddled discussions and debates about a variety of subjects, and often people choose where to sit not based on whom they know but what topic is being discussed. As I thread through the groups, heads snap up to look at me.

The Cancrians here may want nothing to do with me, but the Chroniclers—Capricorn Zodai—have taken an avid interest in me since I arrived. They've encouraged my visits to their Membrexes and still regularly invite me to discussions across the Zodiax about the current political climate. They've even requested to create a Snow Globe of my experience leading the armada—but those memories are dangerous enough inside my head. Giving them physical form would only make them more destructive.

After a while, most Capricorns left me alone, probably realizing I wasn't ready to be a full person yet. But now that there's trouble in the news again, they've taken to staring at me like I've been holding out on them.

At last we find a quiet place to sit, in the shadow of a twisty tree. As I look around me, I try to ignore the ghosts of the Zodai who died on this very land . . . but it's hard to forget a quilt of broken bodies.

"What is it?" asks Hysan. His large eyes run across my face like Sensethysers, deconstructing and reconstructing me inside his mind.

There was a time Stanton and I could decode each other like that . . . and now the people who know me best are a Sagittarian and a Libran. "What *isn't* it?"

Hysan and I trade small, nostalgic smiles. I catch Stanton's eyes narrowing, so I add, "What held you up?"

"I found out one of my—one of Lord Neith's—Advisors was a Riser." Since Stanton and Aryll don't know Hysan is Libra's true Guardian, we have to be careful around them.

"But Risers can't help being Risers," I argue, surprised that Hysan would hold a prejudice against any group of people. "It's not their fault—"

"We caught him sabotaging Aeolus's Psy shield. And it's not just him—Lord Neith has been in touch with Guardians from the other Houses, and we've confirmed a spike in the population of Risers everywhere. Which means—"

"An imbalance in the Zodiac," I finish, recalling Mom's lessons.

A person becomes a Riser when her exterior persona conflicts so strongly with her internal identity that she begins to develop the personality and physical traits of another House—and it can happen at any age. Most Risers only shift signs once or twice in their lifetimes, and with each shift they try to build a new life for themselves on their new House. But there are some Risers for whom the shift doesn't take well, leaving them with an imbalance of traits from their old and new Houses. These Risers keep shifting signs throughout their lives, until their souls regain their balance.

But some never do.

Eventually, the transformations begin to wear on the bodies of imbalanced Risers, and they develop permanent deformities, making them look like the monsters of children's stories. Excessive shifting also affects the mind, which can sometimes turn imbalanced Risers into real-life monsters.

"Risers come from unstable Houses. A surge in their numbers now, in the midst of attacks from Ophiuchus and the Marad and the master . . ." Doubt casts a shadow across Hysan's usually sunny glow. "It's getting darker out there every day."

Our conversation is interrupted by the appearance of a girl my brother's age with frizzy curls, chestnut skin, and periwinkle eyes. "Can I join you?"

asks Jewel Belger. Hers is the family Stanton was shuttling to safety on Hydragyr when Aryll saved him.

"Of course," I say. She smiles shyly and sits next to Stanton. Right as Hysan is greeting her, a tall Capricorn Acolyte approaches us.

"Hysan Dax? Sage Ferez has requested your presence." Her tourmaline eyes turn to me next. "Yours as well, Rhoma Grace."

Stanton and I exchange questioning looks. "I'll come with you," he says, his protectiveness reminding me of Mathias.

Pushing away the pain, I shake my head. "I'll be fine, Stan. I'll find you after." Hysan and I leave our still-full plates behind and follow the Capricorn Acolyte underground, where we tap into the Vein. Since the whole House is having dinner, the train is empty.

As they age, Capricorns unlock higher levels of wisdom and uncover more of the Zodiax's secrets. Only young people ride the Vein—those over fifty have a different way of traveling no one else even knows about.

"*Guardian's chambers*," announces the cool female voice, and we click our handrails and are blown up to a station platform. The Acolyte holds her thumb over a hidden sensor on the wall, and the whole thing slides open like a door.

On its other side is a crystalline cave with walls of amber agate. The room's bands of color are so luminous that it feels like we're aboveground on a brilliantly sunny day. The only furniture in the cavernous space is a simple wooden desk with three chairs; behind the desk sits a stooped old man who must be nearing his centennial.

He wears the same black robes as everyone else, the only distinction a lead pendant that hangs from a silver chain. It looks like House Aquarius's Philosopher's Stone.

"Ah, welcome." Sage Ferez nods kindly at the Acolyte who escorted us. "Thank you, Tavia."

He gestures for us to come closer, and as we settle into the chairs across from him, I notice a gold star in his right iris. On his wrist is a heavy Tracker, in the palm of his hand a Tattoo, and on the desk before him are a Sensethyser, a Wave, and—

"I also have an Earpiece, a Perfectionary, a Paintbrush, a Lighter, and a Blotter," he says, smiling at the growing surprise on my face.

"But why?" I blurt before I can think of more polite phrasing.

Far from offended, he pleasantly folds his hands together and asks, "Given the choice between possessing five senses and one, which would you choose?"

"Five."

"Precisely."

The confusion on my face only grows, but Hysan smirks.

"I apologize, Mother Rhoma, for not meeting with you sooner," says Sage Ferez, "but, alas, I have been busy with troubles of my own. I suspect Lord Hysan will understand." He slides his wrinkled gaze over to him. "I believe we have been facing the same transformations among our former friends."

Hysan shifts uncomfortably in his seat. "How do you—"

"Know that you are the true Libran Guardian?" Sage Ferez smiles at him fondly. "Aging may weaken the body, but when done right, it strengthens the senses. There are few veils left my eyes cannot see through."

Hysan looks speechless for the first time.

"Lord Vaz was a dear friend of mine, and on my many visits to him in his final year of life, I observed how deeply he cared for you. Since his passing, I've watched you zip in and out of Houses nearly as often as I. Though they don't know it yet, your people are lucky to have you. Like your Cancrian colleague, you have proven yourself to be a unifier of the Zodiac."

Ferez's black irises glisten like they're filled with swirling ink. "My old friend would be so proud."

Hysan bows his head, averting his face from view, and I have to fight the urge to reach for his hand.

"Dark Matter and the Thirteenth House."

I snap my gaze to Sage Ferez, who's now smiling at me. Against the darkness of his skin, his teeth glow like stars. "Those veils, I'm sad to say, even I never saw through. You have a powerful gift—that alone would be enough to prove you are Cancer's Holy Mother. Yet you have shown you have more than star-sight: Your vision for a united Zodiac isn't a future you've forecasted in the sky, but rather a plan you've undertaken on the ground. That is quite wise for one so young."

"I led us into a massacre," I say, shaking my head, unable to accept so much kindness. "I failed."

"Failure is not an end—it is the means to an end. Study your failures, for they are the scrambled secrets of success." His black eyes crinkle in a mischievous, childlike grin. "There's an old saying about the Cardinal Houses that asserts we are not only masters of our own elements, but we also possess an invincibility to another. *Fire can't be shaken. The grounded can't be blown away. Air can't be drowned. And water can't be* burned."

I bite down on my lower lip as Mathias's words whisper through me. *You're an everlasting flame that can't be put out.*

"Your mother's abandonment did not destroy you. Nor did your father's passing. Even Ophiuchus could not kill you. You are strong and resilient, impermeable to fire or water: You will rise and re-form from the ashes of this defeat."

Now I'm the one silenced by Sage Ferez's words. But while his generosity moves and humbles me . . . I know I'm not worthy of his praise. So does the Plenum, and so does the rest of the Zodiac. I appreciate the few friends I have left, but I'm not kidding myself any longer—I should have refused the role of Holy Mother in the first place. I'm not—nor was I ever—Guardian material.

"I have requested your presence to ask a favor," says the aged Guardian, looking from me to Hysan again. "I'm leaving immediately after this meeting to visit Moira. She is a dear friend, one of the last I have left since Origene's passing, and I fear for her future. Before I go, I would ask something of you. We represent three of the four Cardinal Houses, and as such, we are owners of Cardinal Stones."

"I don't have the black opal anymore," I interrupt. "It was returned to Agatha when she became the interim Guardian."

"The Talisman will only answer to a true Guardian—it remains in your service, whether it is physically with you or not. Once you are reunited with it, I must ask you and Hysan to seek out General Eurek on House Aries with your Talismans in hand. He will explain the rest."

"What will uniting the stones do?" asks Hysan, his speedy processing reminding me of Nishi.

"I believe you may have guessed by now what strength the Thirteenth House once brought to the Zodiac."

"Unity," I supply, the word sour on my tongue.

"Precisely. I have hope that uniting the four stones will help us locate the Thirteenth Talisman, the one lost to time. Perhaps we can access its knowledge and discover the path to reuniting our galaxy."

Hysan and I are so awed by the notion that neither of us speaks for a moment. I still haven't moved past the fact that Sage Ferez believes me—believes in me—and doesn't think the Thirteenth House is my own fabrication. Then Hysan asks, "What about yourself?"

The Guardian shakes his bald head, and the shadows on his face grow longer. "Only the stars know my fate, dear boy . . . but if I should have joined them by then, do not fret, for Eurek will know what to do."

Then his wrinkled features break into a genial smile, as though we were discussing happier subjects. "One more thing."

Sage Ferez leans into his desk, and Hysan and I instinctively come closer, too. "You will hear a lot about Risers in the coming war—and yes," he adds, seeing my expression, "a war is coming. But there is something you must know before it starts. Risers are not a plague . . . they are part of the future."

He turns his glittering dark eyes to me. "You asked why I possess eleven technologies when one would suffice—can you now think of the reason?"

For a moment I'm stumped, and I feel my cheeks heating with embarrassment—but then the answer bubbles forth from my mouth, like it's been trapped there all along. "*Choice*. Because you have the freedom to choose."

He breaks into his childlike grin again. "Precisely. Each House operates a different way because it's shaped according to the preferences of its people. Yet you both know better than most that we cannot control the circumstances of our birth. Not which family we are born into, nor which House. The truth is, our parents are but part of the equation that forms us—because the only thing more powerful than fate is free will.

"Our *choices* define us: The stars may set us on a given path, but it is we who must decide whether we take it."

He gives us a moment to process what he's said so far, but I'm still stuck on the bit about Risers being the future.

"This wave of Risers is only the beginning."

His demeanor grows heavy again, and for a moment all one hundred years seem to be bearing down on him at once. "I know this is difficult to understand, but since you will lead us, you need to hear it. There may well be a time . . . in the not-too-distant future . . . when our House affiliation will no longer be determined by birth."

His inky eyes lock on mine, and I can't even blink.

"When our Zodiac sign will be a matter of choice."

3

I'M STILL STARING AT SAGE Ferez in unblinking disbelief when a couple of black-robed Chroniclers billow into the room from a back door. "Your transport is ready," one of them says to Ferez, offering the elderly Guardian a supporting arm.

The Sage rises on his own, and Hysan and I stand, too. "Until we meet again," he says, "good fortune to you both."

✦ ✦ ✦

Hysan and I ride the Vein in silence.

"*Cancrian sleeping quarters*," says the cool female voice. Since we're still building our bungalows, Cancrians have been given lodging at one of the Zodiax's numerous hotels.

I look at Hysan. "Do you want to come—?"

"Yes," he says quickly, and we both press the button on our handrails. We're blown onto the bouncy train platform, and after I flash my thumbprint over a wall sensor, a hidden door opens into the glossy golden lobby of the Fluffy Giraffe Resort.

Stanton, Aryll, and I share a suite on one of the lowest levels, a three-pronged circular room with offshoots to each bedroom. The round room is spacious and surrounded by books, wallscreens, a teaching crown, and all kinds of games and exercises for mental workouts. There's also a small kitchen, and tucked behind the floor-to-ceiling temperator, which stores food at multiple temperatures, is a tiny table that barely fits two people.

I boil us a pot of brainberry tea. Brainberries, a fruit that grow abundantly on Tierre's trees, are believed to possess nourishing mental properties and are a preferred treat among people and pocket pigs.

Hysan and I squeeze around the square table, and each time one of us takes a sip from our clay teacups, our elbows brush. Goose bumps continually race up my arms.

"Things are rough out there, Rho." Concern shines through Hysan's expression. "The Marad is growing stronger, attacking more often. They seem to be everywhere at once—explosions on a Leonine Pride that killed hundreds, sabotaging the air supply on a Scorp waterworld that drowned dozens, assassinations of high-ranking Clan Elders on Aquarius . . ."

Faint lines press into his skin, making him look older. "The worst part isn't even the violence—it's the *fear*. Anyone could be working for the Marad, so people have stopped trusting each other—especially if they're from different Houses. It's what always happens: The greater our need to unite, the deeper we divide."

I can't think of anything comforting to say. I've seen reports about this already, but it's harder on Hysan, who still has to worry about protecting his people. The news is playing on a small kitchen wallscreen, and it grows louder in our silence. An Aquarian man with glassy eyes the color of a pink sunset (Aquarians' irises reflect the sky at one's time of birth) is addressing a crowd of Zodai University students. A holographic headline scrolls beneath him: *Aquarius—struggling "superpower" already spending beyond its means.*

I look at Hysan, and before I can ask, he answers: "That's Morscerta's replacement, Ambassador Crompton. I haven't met him yet."

Morscerta died in the armada. My hand trembles as I bring the empty teacup to my mouth.

"Since they have the largest store of freshwater in the Zodiac, Aquarius has taken up the charge to coordinate donations among the Houses. But as usual, their idealism exceeds their finances. One of the issues the Plenum is debating this session is whether to bail them out of their debt, which they incurred helping the Houses."

I nod, and we both grow interested in the faint patterns of the wooden table, until Hysan says, "My lady, though I'd rather stay, I should go. I'm expected on House Taurus to discuss the Riser situation."

Getting to our feet is a clumsy process in the small space. Once we're upright, we're concealed behind the tall temperator, our faces a foot apart.

"It's really great to see you, Rho." Hysan's voice is lower and huskier.

"You too," I whisper, my heartbeat speeding up. My back is against the kitchen counter, the space between us so tiny that it makes his mouth's magnetic pull impossible to ignore.

"On Libra," he murmurs, his cedary scent tickling my face, "we're taught to think of every being as a galaxy. We can only see as much of a person as we're equipped to see."

He leans closer, and I'm suddenly aware our clothes are touching, which makes it hard to focus on anything else. "The better our telescope, the more light we can reveal. The more constellations we can uncover."

The weight of his body presses into mine, and my muscles buzz in anticipation, my gaze growing too heavy to lift from his lips. "But I think even the most powerful telescope couldn't come close to capturing all your light," he whispers, "or unearthing all your wonders."

The impulse to kiss him grows too strong, and I close my eyes and reach up—but a stab of pain cleaves my chest.

Guilt, heartache, regret. A warning shot sent by the Mathias sector of my heart. I swallow back my emotions and look away from Hysan, breaking our moment. Neither of us says anything for a few breaths.

"Rho."

When I meet his gaze again, Hysan seems more worried than hurt. "Be careful who you trust. Sage Ferez may be right about Risers in the long run, but if this wave is truly the start of a new evolution, the first generation will likely be unstable and unpredictable. Nature will need time to work out the kinks."

I nod. "Take care of yourself, too." I see again the vision of the battlefield from Sage Huxler's recollections, the body parts that were once people. "I'm worried about what's coming. For all of us."

Hysan reaches out to touch me just as the door to the suite swings open. My brother and Aryll are back. Hysan reads the alarm on my face, and with a quick flick of his wrist, he vanishes. He's wearing his Veil collar.

"Thank you," I whisper into the air.

"Always, my lady." His words blow into my ear, and then his muffled footsteps recede across the round room.

I make a lot of noise greeting Stanton and Aryll while Hysan slips out the door. "Did you deliver the Bobbler to the Lodestars?"

"Yeah," says Stanton, dropping the bag with his wet suit and silverware on the floor. "What did Ferez want?"

"He told me . . . he said he believes I'm the true Holy Mother."

My cheeks blaze bright red the moment I say it. I hadn't meant to tell Stanton that part—in fact, I hadn't worked out what I was going to say at all—but just like when we were younger, I can't help seeking his validation.

Funny how of all the remarkable things Ferez revealed, this is the one I can't shake.

"He shouldn't be meddling with Cancrian affairs," bursts out Stanton, surprising me with the force of his anger. "This isn't your fight anymore."

"But if there's anything I can do to help—"

"You already tried to help," he says, cutting me off. "Besides, it's not up to Ferez to predict Cancer's rightful Guardian. It's the way of the stars."

"But the stars are still saying 'Rho,'" says a soft voice.

It's hard to tell who's most shocked by Aryll's interjection: Stanton, me, or Aryll himself.

"The stars aren't saying *anyone* yet," corrects Stanton, now using a new tone to address Aryll—the same impatient one he's been reserving for me.

"I just mean it's people who kicked her out, not stars." Aryll sounds like he wishes he could take back his support of me. "Anyway, Ferez should really stay out of this stuff. I think I left my . . . back at the settlement—"

Aryll darts out the door midway through his own sentence. Any time Stanton and I start to argue, he runs away. And then once he's gone, Stanton and I lose our conviction. It's hard to care about most things when we're reminded how much worse off we could be. Aryll used to have a sister, too.

I duck into the kitchen to wash the teacups before Stanton notices there are two of them. Zodai across the galaxy are of two minds as to why the stars haven't pointed to a new Holy Mother. Some, like Sage Ferez, think it's because I'm still the rightful leader. Others think it means our planet will never heal, and House Cancer is gone for good.

Like Stanton, I think our fate is still being decided.

When I'm done cleaning, I find my brother on the couch watching the latest newsfeed, his back to me. My hand is already on the door to my room when his voice cuts through the thick air.

"How well do you know the Libran?"

"He saved my life several times last month," I remind him.

"That's not an answer," he says, twisting to face me.

I want to tell him the truth—until now, I've never lied to my brother about anything—but Stanton's Cancrian pride runs Rift-deep. "I just trust him, Stan. He's been a friend to our House."

Without a word, my brother turns back to the wallscreen, and like all our conversations since reuniting, this one's over before it's even begun.

✦ ✦ ✦

Alone in my room, Hysan's presence feels more pronounced than when he was actually here. It feels like the sun stopped by for a visit, and I kept to the shade.

Part of me was hoping I'd discover that our attraction had been a fleeting, adrenaline-fueled thing—but seeing him again drove that delusion from my mind.

Still, his presence made Mathias's absence unavoidable. Hysan and I were like two stars orbiting a black hole, our life forces drawing attention to the place where Mathias's light had once shone.

I lie back on my bed in the dark room, the pale face and midnight eyes projecting in my mind's Membrex. Mathias died because of me—because I was too stubborn to listen—because I was a stupid girl who thought she was ready to lead. Stanton is right: I had my chance to make things better and only made them worse. Now it's someone else's turn.

I dry my eyes and sit up in bed, pushing the bad thoughts away. Crying and moping won't help—I have work to do. I snap open my Wave—which Hysan repaired on Gemini—and call up the tutorial Ephemeris.

My black room comes alive with color. I don't have to focus on the blue orb of Cancer to find its strength within me anymore. I feel home in my every molecule, having at last understood the lesson Sirna and Leyla tried to impart: We don't merely make up Cancer—Cancer makes us.

Celestial objects expand around me, and I walk through the spectral stars, the Ring's core of Abyssthe making it easier to stay Centered. A whirl of light unexpectedly explodes in front of me, like two star systems colliding, and as the brightness dims, I make out a ghostly image forming in the fading light.

Stars are connecting in the shape of a girl's face, like it's a new constellation in the Zodiac galaxy. My *face*.

Except my features are shifting. I seem to be transforming into someone else—my cheekbones are jutting out more, and my chin is lengthening. My blond curls lighten and elongate, becoming straighter, wispier—

The image vanishes so quickly, it might never have appeared at all. Except my pulse is still echoing in my ears. Was that *me* . . . as a *Riser*?

It couldn't be—I'm completely Cancrian—I was even *Guardian*—

I gasp as another horrible theory flits into my mind. The one that won't stay away no matter how hard I refuse to see it.

Maybe it isn't just me . . . maybe *every* Cancrian is changing House.

Maybe Cancer is gone.

I search the pinpricks of lights for the face, but there's nothing left. I've never seen an omen this clear in the Ephemeris before. I just wish I knew if it was a real warning or a manifestation of my worries. Sage Ferez's foretelling of a future of Risers definitely shook me—but was this omen a message from the stars or a cry of the soul?

Suddenly the lights surrounding me start shaking in their orbits, and half the Zodiac—Houses one through six—sinks lower, while the other half—seven through twelve—rises higher.

The galaxy is imbalanced, orbiting a tilted ellipse. Our Zodiac's stars are out of alignment. I feel the energy that binds the Houses together trembling against my skin. Our bonds are being tested.

There's another burst of light, farther out than the first. Once the brightness dims, an image projects past Pisces, where the Thirteenth House used to be. Only instead of a girl's face, a man's shape is forming.

A monstrous hulking man made of ice.

My heart drums louder against my ribs—after weeks of searching, I've finally done it. I've found Ophiuchus.

Almost immediately, his form begins to fracture and fade, just as a frosty chill comes over me, and I feel the Psynergy connecting me to the Thirteenth Guardian.

My mouth freezes in a silent scream. Ophiuchus is in agonizing pain, and even though I've gotten better at focusing in this realm, I still can't push off the unwanted Psynergy, as Moira did when her Ephemeris screeched with his presence. Whoever is hurting Ophiuchus is even more powerful than he is, and yet Ophiuchus seems to be resisting his master's commands. As they fight, the Zodiac teeters on edge, the constellations' shaking growing more violent, like the slightest flick could blow our whole universe apart.

As the image of Ochus fully vanishes, so does the phantom pain. When it's gone, I feel no aftermath of its effects—but the memory is intact.

A brand-new Snow Globe for my collection.

4

I WAKE UP IN THE morning when my Wave goes off. I open it, noticing it's the third time the same person has called. When I hit *Accept*, Nishi's holographic form blasts into the room.

Her holo-ghost hovers over my bed, and the first thing I notice is the new fringe of black bangs falling in a sharp line across her forehead.

She smiles and chirps, "Rise for mighty Helios!" Something our parents used to say when they'd wake us up early.

"M-morning," I say mid-yawn, sitting up and pulling my curls into a sloppy bun over my head. "Love the new 'do."

"Thanks!" she says after a brief delay. "I'm so happy I finally caught you. Deke's here, too."

"Hey, Deke! Sorry I missed your calls yesterday. It wound up being a really . . . unusual day."

I wait the obligatory few minutes for my message to be received, and then Deke's hologram pops into existence, floating next to Nishi's. Since Sagittarius is the House next door, the ghosting effect isn't too bad—their holograms are only slightly out of sync, and our responses lag only a little.

But they're probably using Nishi's Tracker or Deke's Wave rather than a more powerful transmitter, because their forms are pretty pixelated, and the bottom halves of their bodies are faint.

"Rho Rho!" Deke grins at me and sings, *"Rho Rho Rho your Strider, gently along the sea!"* I used to hate it when he and his friend Xander would break into that ditty back at the Academy, but now it makes me laugh out loud. "How are my changelings?" They're his favorite fish for sushi.

"The changelings are adapting better than anyone else. I miss you guys . . . are you still staying with Nishi's family?"

"Our update can wait," says Nishi, trading nervous looks with Deke. "First, tell us about yesterday. What was unusual about it?"

I shrug to downplay my earlier comment even as the truth spills out of me. "I saw Hysan. He came to drop off equipment for our scientists."

A few minutes later, Nishi gasps and clasps her hands to her mouth, while Deke flashes me a roguish smile and says, "And did you help him with *his* equipment, Rho Rho?" Their holograms freeze just as Nishi turns to glower at him.

Nishi and Deke are the only people who know the truth about Hysan and me. Inter-House dating isn't forbidden, but it's frowned upon—enough so that some Houses don't even extend full legal protections to mixed-House couples.

"How was the hookup?" asks Deke when their holograms reactivate. "And no skimping on the details."

Nishi elbows Deke so hard in the ribs that his hologram flickers and vanishes. "I'm sorry, Rho. I can kick him off if you want."

When Deke's holo-ghost returns, his expression is exaggeratedly remorseful. "No, come on, I'll be good, I promise."

"Nothing happened," I say, embarrassed to hear the disappointment in my tone. "I don't know what I was expecting. . . . I mean, I was the one who pushed him away. Besides, we were barely alone—Stanton was watching us like a horned hawk."

"Rho, Hysan's feelings aren't the ones in question. Yours are." Nishi's manner is gentle, but her words sting more than Deke's.

"My feelings for him aren't the problem, Nish. The problem is that being with him hurts. It feels like a betrayal to Mathias." I've told them this before, and each time I can feel their disapproval, as if my emotions are falling short of their expectations.

"Rho . . . it's okay to let go," says Deke. "Mathias wouldn't want to be responsible for you not living your life."

"Even if I wanted to move on"—and as I consider the possibility, a weight seems to lift from my chest—"there are still other issues. The Taboo doesn't exactly extend to us, since I'm no longer Guardian and no one knows the truth about him, but the news would still rile people up. Hysan has a role at the Plenum to protect. What if Charon spins a new tale about how we collaborated to kill Mathias, and then Hysan ends up facing charges like I did?"

"If that's what it takes," says Deke gruffly. "If he loves you, he'll love you no matter the consequences."

"Deke, darling," says Nishi, "do you hear the gentle tone I'm using right now? Even though I want to jab you in the ribs again? If you want to stay on this call, *this* is how you need to speak—"

I have to wait a few minutes to hear the rest of Nishi's rebuke, and when the holograms catch up with their transmission, Deke says, "I'm sorry if that was harsh, Rho. What I meant was, you got it right the first time when you raised the alarm about the Thirteenth House. The only way to change the norm is to break it. Acceptance won't come without a fight."

"I don't know that I have another fight in me, Deke." I wish I didn't sound so defeated. "I just want to stay out of the newsfeeds and keep helping Cancer."

When their next transmission comes in, Nishi is alone. "Deke's fixing the refresher. It just started spitting soap."

She seems nervous, and I'm reminded of the look she shared with Deke earlier. Then I think of the fact that she's been trying to call me since yesterday, including three times this morning before I answered. I've spent this whole conversation talking about my love life when something far more important is obviously on Nishi's mind.

"What's going on, Nish?"

She takes a shaky breath and begins. "I don't know how much you've seen in the news, but the unrest on Sagittarius has intensified. The labor disputes have become violent, and there's still no sign of a truce between our government and the migrant workers from Scorpio."

A knot forms in my stomach. While I wait for the next installment, I replay Hysan's and Ferez's warnings and the visions I saw in the Ephemeris. Hysan's right. It's all connected.

"—which is only made worse by the Marad," continues Nishi when the transmission resumes. "Teenage soldiers seem to be the ones doing the footwork, but no one knows who's running things, or who's a member, or how it got started—or, above all, what they want."

An invisible army, a surge in Risers, the Thirteenth Guardian . . . the Zodiac's boogeymen are coming to life.

The way the Marad operates reminds me of Ophiuchus and everything that happened last month. The axiom *Trust Only What You Can Touch* has always kept the people of the Zodiac safe, but now the things we can't touch are touching us. The Marad feels as ephemeral as anything in the Psy, yet it's killing our people, and we can't strike back at it. Just like Ophiuchus and his Dark Matter.

"There's more you should know," I say, right as Deke's hologram returns. I launch into everything that happened yesterday, from Hysan's updates, to our meeting with Ferez, to what I saw in the Ephemeris—though I skip the omen of my face shifting features. It takes a long time to relay everything, and once I'm done, Nishi looks resolved and Deke's dumbstruck.

"Rho," says Nishi tentatively, "I think Ferez is right about you. Deke and I—we want you to come to Sagittarius. We need your help."

"What are you talking about?" I ask through my shock. "How can I help?"

"Deke and I have sort of done something. We've just been so inspired by everything you did last month, and, well, we wanted to be part of it. It's like Deke said: To change the norm, you have to break it."

I wait through a handful of excruciating minutes for the rest of her story, and then she says, "We've started an underground resistance group to bring together others who want to unite the Zodiac and fight the Marad. To continue what you started—"

"Nish, I can't—I'm sorry," I sputter, my mind seizing with terror at the thought of Nishi and Deke making themselves targets for Ophiuchus on purpose. "You guys shouldn't—I mean, just be careful, *please*. I know you feel strongly that you're doing the right thing, but it's dangerous. You're using the Psy shields Hysan gave you on Gemini, right?"

"Rho, relax, we're being smart. Look, I don't want to pressure you, but I have to tell you how I feel," says Nishi, her amber gaze heavy. "You're hurting right now, and you have every right to be—you're being vilified by the people responsible for the armada, and you feel guilty for what happened with Mathias. But those are two separate things. Don't let the guilt you feel over Mathias confuse your feelings about what the Plenum did. They're the true cowards, not you. You risked your life spreading the word about Ophiuchus, and you did it again going out on that Wasp. That kind of courage creates ripples—and being Cancrian, you know ripples become waves."

"I'm sorry," I say, lowering my face from their holograms. "I think I'd only make things worse for you if I came, especially if you're trying to stay off the radar. Besides, one of the few things the Houses agree on is their distaste for anyone who defies the stars—and if I do this, people will think I'm doing just that. They'll be convinced the lies Charon spread were true.

That I was just some fame-hungry Acolyte looking to create controversy and gain followers, and they'd think I'm now doing it all over again."

"Rho, who cares what they think?" spits Deke, his turquoise eyes flashing. "Forget them. What you did changed things. There are people who believe in you and who will rally to your side."

"Right now I just want to help Cancer however I can. Stanton and I are doing good here. That's all I want to focus on."

"I understand," says Nishi, cutting Deke off before he can argue. "You know how we feel. If you change your mind, we'd love to have you."

"What she said." Deke's shoulders slump forward, and his sandy curls fall over his eyes. "Stay safe, Rho." He takes Nishi's hand, and their holograms vanish.

In the sudden silence, I hear Stanton's voice from the living room and leave to investigate. I don't need to be alone with my thoughts after that conversation.

Stanton is standing next to the kitchen counter, drinking from a clay teacup. His wet suit is only halfway on. "I'll meet you on the surface," he tells Aryll as soon as I emerge. Aryll doesn't speak, but he nods at me from the doorway before ducking out.

"I'm sorry I was crabby yesterday," my brother tells me when we're alone. He sets his cup on the counter to finish zipping up his suit. "You were right—Hysan's been good to our House, and I shouldn't be so hard on him." Next he crouches down to seal his bag shut, and all I can see of him are the close-cropped blond curls along the back of his head. He's avoiding my gaze. "I just don't like the way he looks at you. Like he's . . . *hungry* or something."

Face flaming, I spin around and start rubbing out a nonexistent smudge on the wallscreen behind me. "I-I don't know what you mean—"

"Like he can't wait to get you alone."

"That's just . . ." I start straightening the couch cushions next so I won't have to look at him. "You don't have to be so protective of me."

"Don't you think I know that by now?"

I stop shuffling pillows and stare at him, startled by the sadness in his tone. Stanton's face is expressionless, and his curls look unusually limp on his head. "Stan . . . what is it?"

He shakes his head and slings his bag over his shoulder. "There's no time now. I have to head up."

"No," I say, marching over so that I'm blocking his way to the door. "Talk to me already."

He turns to the wall next to him. "I can't."

"But you can talk to *Aryll*?" I cross my arms and glower at him. "Stan, I'm your sister, and you treat him like he's the one who's family."

"That's not it, Rho." Stanton sets his bag back down and stares at it on the floor. "I love you—it's just . . . he needs me right now."

"I need you, too."

He finally faces me, and I'm silenced by the shininess in his eyes. My brother's never cried in front of me, not even when Mom left.

"When you were little," he says, his voice almost adopting its old softness, "you used to get these awful nightmares. I would hear you screaming and run into your room, and we'd make up stories together until you fell back asleep."

"I know." I remember every nightmare and every story.

"I never said this aloud, at the time or after, because I'm worried it makes me an awful person, but, deep down, I kind of liked it when you had nightmares." His pale eyes don't meet mine. "Because I could come in and rescue you from them."

"Stan, you're the furthest thing from awful—"

"Mom leaving was the first nightmare I couldn't spring you from," he goes on, without letting me interrupt. "Even though I was devastated, I felt sorrier for you. A Cancrian girl losing her mom so young . . . it was practically unheard of. I was afraid you'd miss out on something important. I wanted to rescue you again."

He leans against the wall, like he's deflating as he speaks, and I stay silent and still so I won't disrupt the magic of the moment. "I resolved to be everything you needed—I taught you how to cook, how to dance, how to sailboard . . . even explained how baby Cancrians are made." We flash quick smiles.

"But last month, you faced real horrors," he says, the ends of his mouth falling, "and I wasn't there, Rho. I couldn't rescue you." His voice goes scratchy, and he clears his throat, the words a broken whisper. "Just like when we were little, and I couldn't save you from *her*."

"Stan, stop." The statement startles me because I didn't authorize it. Even the tone of my voice is strange and unfamiliar. There's a knot in my stomach that wasn't there an instant ago, and suddenly I realize why we've both been avoiding this conversation.

He takes my hand and squeezes my fingers. "You were a kid, Rho, and she was training you like an Ariean soldier. I should have stood up to her for you. But Dad didn't say anything, and there I was, convinced Mom was holier than Helios, and . . . I don't know. I just let it happen."

I just let it happen. My brother, who rescued me from imaginary monsters in the dark, couldn't save me from the one that preyed on me in the light.

I still remember the braid of emotions I felt every day from age four to seven, the interplay of dread and readiness I'd wake up to every morning, not knowing if I would See enough to impress her. A single disappointment, one wrong answer, and her mood would crumple for the rest of the day. That could mean up to three extra hours of training.

The truth is, it's not Stanton's fault, or even Dad's—it's mine. For following her orders. Maybe they would have said something if I'd ever given them an opening, but I wanted too much to prove myself to Mom. To show her she was right to invest so much time in me. To make her love me as much as she loved my brother.

I was jealous of the relationship Stanton had with her. I thought by doing everything she asked, I would one day be her favorite. It's only now I know I wanted to be rescued.

"I'm so sorry, Rho." Stanton pulls and crushes me to him, and all of a sudden I'm sobbing into his chest, releasing a tidal wave of emotions I didn't realize I'd been holding on to. When we pull apart, there are tear-lines on his cheeks, and at last, the heaviness that hung between us is gone.

5

BY THE TIME STANTON HEADS up to the settlement, my mood has completely lifted. I'm still really worried for Nishi and Deke, but at least I'm not alone anymore.

Once I'm dressed, I ride the Vein to the surface, but instead of the beach, I head into the woods. About a kilometer into the forest, I step into the patch of sunlight I found my first week here—a small clearing amid Capricorn's giant, gnarled trees. Birds and flutterbys (the insects that inspired Libra's transportation system) flap around me, their wings spanning all colors, shapes, and designs. Horned hawks screech to each other from overhanging tree branches, and small rustles in the flowering bushes tell me pocket pigs are nearby, nibbling on fallen brainberries.

I've been coming to this same spot every day to train. Lying back on the wild grass, I spend four uninterrupted hours cycling through Yarrot poses. Stanton thinks I'm continuing my Zodai lessons using the Wave tutorials Sirna sent me, but the truth nobody knows—not even Nishi and Deke—is that I came to Capricorn on my own mission.

I made myself a promise when the Plenum impeached me. A promise to find Ochus and his master and to avenge Dad and Mathias. And I haven't turned my back on that oath.

Yesterday was the first time I saw Ophiuchus since our last battle, but all I got was a glimpse of his predicament, with no indication of where he is or how to find him. Since I need to be stronger when I face him next, I've gone back to Mom's obsessive training schedule from my youth. The only goal driving me now is vengeance.

I come out of my trancelike dance just in time for the House-wide lunch call. The overexposed sky turns velvety black, like someone's flipped an *off* switch, letting the sun shine through only in select slivers. The light spells:

LUNCH.

I often skip the midday meal to go indoors and study the Ephemeris, but today I want to spend more time with Stanton, so I grab the plate and utensils I brought with me and cut across to the valley. I find him with Aryll at the end of the food line, and the sudden sight of my brother's giddy grin reminds me of when we were little kids on Kalymnos. There's a matching smile on my face as I join them.

"Rho!" Stanton sounds surprised. "You're lunching with us common folk?"

"Every star falls eventually," I say dramatically, and Aryll snorts so loudly that the Capricorns walking along the other side of the table snap their heads up to look at us.

I smile apologetically at the teenage girl across from me, who's watching us with a strange expression. When I meet her gaze, she just stares at me coldly.

My grin falls off my face, and I focus on the food on the table. As I'm reaching for the bowl of hawk wings, I spy only silverware in the girl's hands and no plate. I chance a glance at her again, and this time she's smiling at me.

Then, in a flash of silver, she sinks her knife and fork into her neighbor's neck.

A bloodcurdling scream rends the air as the middle-aged man falls forward onto the food, and the girl melts into the mass of black robes around us.

Aryll drops his plate, and Stanton grips us both by the shoulder as more screams join the first. The shouts seem to be coming from all over the valley, confusing the crowd of Cancrians and Capricorns around us. No one knows which way to go.

"This way!" says Stanton, pushing us toward the steep hill—but moments later we're pulled back by the current of the crowd.

Every direction we push in pushes back. People are moving closer together instead of farther apart, as if we're herding ourselves.

The acrid smell of smoke invades the air, and I finally understand—there's a fire encircling us. It's blazing on every side of the valley, sending puffs of black clouds over our heads. There's no way out. "Rho!" Stanton shakes my shoulder, speaking loudly over all the noise. We're crammed amid so many people and so much smoke that it's hard to get air. "Are you okay?"

At first I don't know why he's asking, then I realize he and Aryll have been dragging me along with them this whole time. I haven't been able to work my legs since that stabbing.

"Yeah," I say shakily. But I'm not. That girl wasn't a hulking man made of ice. She's a teen from a peaceful society, a House that prizes wisdom and collaboration above all. And she just murdered someone without hesitation.

A loud, booming voice thunders down to us from the sky: *"Stand silent and still!"*

A hush falls over the valley as everyone looks to the top of the steep hill, where twelve young Capricorns in black robes are standing over us. Fire flickers in every direction. The flames crackle louder in our silence, black smoke filling so much of the sky that Helios's rays can barely break through it.

"We are the Marad."

Gasps and screams sweep through the crowd, and I grip Stanton tighter, flashing to the morbid scene from Sage Huxler's Snow Globe. Is this how that battle began? Will we be nothing more than a pile of ash tomorrow?

"We are broadcasting to the Zodiac with a message: The age of the Twelve Houses is over. A new sign is rising—we are all Marad."

The teen girl must be up there, I realize, suddenly understanding what Hysan meant about the Marad's tactics. They're sowing fear from the inside. If that girl is Marad, anyone is suspect.

A holographic army of masked soldiers suddenly materializes behind the twelve teens, and a Capricorn baby begins to wail. The soldiers are dressed all in white, and their featureless faces look like they're made of white porcelain. They have no eyes, nose, or ears—just a mouth.

"We demand that every Guardian renounce their position and denounce their House's allegiance to the Zodiac. Every House that does not comply will suffer Cancer's fate."

At the mention of my House, my gut hardens with something solid. It feels like hate.

"We will begin with Sagittarius. The fighting between the government and the Scorp workers is just one more example of the Zodiac system failing us. Guardian, hear us well: You have five galactic days to pledge your allegiance to the Marad. On the fifth day, we will descend upon your planet Centaurion, and we will depart with your head."

All at once, the army vanishes into the daylight, along with the twelve Capricorns. The Marad must have Veils of its own. When they're gone, even the heat of the surrounding flames can't cut through the lingering chill.

Stanton, Aryll, and I run to the long food table and join a group of Capricorns that's throwing drinking water at the fire. Rain starts to sprinkle down on us, and we look up to see an ark flying through the smoke, showering the valley with water.

Soon the fires have been put out, and healers arrive to tend to the wounded. Five are dead, including the man murdered in front of me.

That girl knew who I was. She was waiting for me to look. The Marad wanted to send me a message—and I'm starting to feel like I want to send one of my own.

✦ ✦ ✦

We spend the rest of the day holed up in our hotel's round room, flipping through various newsfeeds, trying to glean more information about the attack. It turns out we weren't the only ones the army visited today—ours was one in a string of simultaneous terrorist attacks on every House.

When the Marad threatened Sagittarius, the thunderous voice was also broadcasting to every inhabited planet of the Zodiac. No single voice has ever addressed all our worlds at once before. There hasn't been any reason to—at least not for a millennium, since the Houses became sovereign territories. We haven't had access to one another's security, satellite, or communications systems since—which means the Marad isn't just violent and unpredictable. It's also technologically superior.

And now it's targeted Nishi's home next.

The faceless porcelain head haunts my mind. I think of what Ferez said about choosing one sense over five, or one technology over eleven (Piscenes don't have their own House-specific device). The Marad chose just one facial feature: a *mouth*. They aren't interested in seeing or hearing their victims. They just want their will to be done.

Brynda Wazel, the twenty-three-year-old Sagittarian Guardian, is now on the news, standing at a podium with the Archer crest hanging behind her. I met her briefly on Phaetonis, at an armada meeting, but we didn't get a chance to talk. As she faces the Zodiac, her long-cut amber eyes are clear, and her hair is in a black braid that hangs down her back. She looks like an older version of Nishi.

"House Sagittarius has heard the Marad's threat, and I am here to say we will *never* renounce our allegiance to the Zodiac. The Ninth House will not bow down to terror: We will stand our ground and protect our people against the Marad and anyone else who attacks us. We ask the other Houses to stand with us by protecting their own worlds and sending us whatever help they can spare."

When the image cuts back to the newscaster, I think again of Ophiuchus and how I could never prove his existence. The Marad seems to operate a lot like him. Even now, when the army has directly addressed us, it's just as impossible to prove it's real, or pinpoint its members, or strike back in any way.

Next, the newscaster interviews an aged Chronicler who's studied all the major conflicts in Zodiac history. He looks as old as Sage Ferez, and he's transmitting from a Membrex. There are more than five thousand in the Zodiax in all.

"This army is the greatest threat to our galaxy since the Trinary Axis."

At the mention of the Axis, the air in our round room hardens, making it difficult to breathe. Stanton, Aryll, and I look away from the wallscreen but avoid one another. It's always the same reaction when that war is brought up in a room full of Cancrians. Because even though a thousand years have passed, we haven't gotten past our guilt—Cancer was one of the three Houses that started the war.

"It's clear to me that the person or people behind the Marad knows their history," continues the Chronicler. "In particular, they've studied the Axis well, and they are replicating the parts that worked—riling up the public with dramatics, operating in secrecy where we can't prosecute them, and launching their war with coordinated attacks on every House that are reminiscent of the uprisings that launched the war a millennium ago."

I reach for my Wave just as it starts going off. Nishi's hologram pops out, her eyes bright with terror. "Rho! Are you watching—?"

"I saw," I say as the newscaster starts reviewing Guardian Brynda's leadership record. He cites her support for what's referred to as "my" armada as a sign of her youthful impulsiveness. He calls it her most grievous failure.

I don't know how I can help Guardian Brynda or Nishi and Deke, but I'm starting to think that if the Marad is on Sagittarius, Ophiuchus will be nearby. I no longer doubt that they're working for the same master—their methods are too similar and their attacks too coordinated. What I want to know is what the master is after. And to find out, I have to be where the action is.

"I'm coming to Sagittarius, Nish. I'll be in touch later."

Stanton's head spins when he hears my declaration, and I snap my Wave shut, ending the call.

"Rho, this isn't your fight anymore—"

"It'll always be my fight, Stan," I say, seeing the image that remains branded in my brain: a small pink space suit, frost covering what was once a girl's face.

"It doesn't have to be." My brother takes my hand. "You're not alone. We still have each other. We can live anywhere, start over—"

"Where, Stan? Where won't the Marad and Ophiuchus and the master be able to reach us?" I hear the volume of my voice rising. I glance at Aryll, still sitting on the couch, and expect him to scurry off to his room as he always does when things get tense. But now he stays put. What happened at lunch seems to have toughened him.

"There are Zodai on every House who've trained their whole lives to fight a threat like this one," says Stanton, his voice soft and parental and inviting. "Let them handle it, Rho."

"It's not just that." I furrow my brow, trying to think of the right words to explain what I feel—the same sense of purpose that seeped into my skin the moment I became Guardian. Taking off the coronet may have changed Cancer's feelings toward me, but it didn't change mine toward Cancer.

"I'm only alive because I was inside a crystal dome on Elara when the blast hit, and somehow it was a strong enough barrier to protect me from the power outage. But my friends and classmates and teachers are gone. *Dad's gone.* And I can't let them all become casualties of evil when I have the chance to make their deaths stand for something greater."

"Like what?" asks Stanton.

"*Change.* If the Twelve Houses come together and fight back as one Zodiac, Cancer won't be just a name on a long list of worlds Ophiuchus destroyed. Our people will have died to bring us something better. They'll be martyrs in the triumph of unity over hatred!" By the time I stop speaking, my face is flaming like a small sun, and I'm mortified at how passionate I got—I sounded just like a Leo.

So I'm startled to see the small smile spreading across Stanton's face. "You just reminded me so much of Mom."

The statement is as gratifying as it is terrifying. Seeing my mixed reaction, his grin widens. "She used to get just as worked up with Dad whenever he didn't want me to skip a day of school to help her with her latest cause. Remember how she was always trying to save a community from something? Poverty, pollution, natural disasters?"

I nod. I was rarely around for those discussions because I was in the midst of Yarrot or Centering or reading the Ephemeris. On those days, Mom would leave me to train alone, while she'd set off with Stanton to work on her newest project, and when she got home she would test me.

"The speech she used to convince Dad to let her take me to Naxos Island after Hurricane Hebe must've been amazing," says Stanton thoughtfully. "And she was right. I found a baby in the wreckage."

Aryll nods reverently, and I get the sense he's heard this story before, and it's maybe even why he worships my brother so much.

Stanton looks from Aryll to me. "You're right, Rho. You and I want the same thing: We want to save Cancer. Only you're doing it by rescuing its people, and I'm taking care of our wildlife."

He pulls me in for a hug, and my heart falls as I realize he's not coming with me. "Promise you won't do anything daring or brave," he whispers in my ear.

"I'm a coward," I say when we pull apart. "It's official, the Plenum held a ceremony and everything."

"It would've been nice to have been invited—"

"I'm going, too."

The grin freezes on Stanton's face, and he turns from me to Aryll.

"I've never liked this planet, you know that," says Aryll nervously. "And I'm no good with wildlife—if anything, Stan, I'm slowing you down." He holds up his hands, which are covered with nicks and cuts. "Look, I've never known what I'm good at. I don't have any talents or skills that make me special. I just want to fight back. I want to be a part of this."

His electric-blue eye looks directly into mine, as if committed to the assumption that this is my decision and not his or Stanton's. This is the first time I've seen Aryll so animated.

"Are you sure?" I ask. "You've been through so much . . . don't you want to get away from the violence?"

"Don't *you*?" he shoots back.

I sigh and turn to my brother, who's still staring at Aryll. Somehow, his shock seems to have already settled into resignation. "What if you came with us, too?" I ask hopefully.

He shakes his head. "That's not me, Rho. My place is here."

"I'm going to bed," announces Aryll, turning around. "We can talk tomorrow . . . or something," he throws back as he slips into his room.

Stanton and I stay up watching the newsfeeds late into the night, neither of us saying much until we're ready for bed. "Can't you talk Aryll out of coming with me?" I ask.

My brother shakes his head. "Just . . . give him a chance. I'm starting to think there's more than choice and chance at play in everything that's happening here."

"What do you mean?"

"You know . . . like in the story of Hurricane Hebe." I shake my head and arch my brow, completely lost. Stanton sighs in frustration. "You're going to make me spell it out?" I nod. "Fine. I think *the stars* may have put Aryll on our path *for a reason*."

He rolls his eyes at himself, and he sounds so much like Mom that I can't tell if he's being serious. Stanton's never been big on fortune-telling—like Dad, he's spent his life looking down more than up. He pecks me on the forehead and walks toward his room.

"I still don't know what you're actually saying," I call after him.

"Aryll saved my life once." He looks back at me from his doorway. "Maybe this time he'll save yours."

6

BEFORE GOING TO SLEEP, I hail *Equinox* from my room. Hysan checked in with me on my Ring earlier to make sure I was okay, but we didn't have time to really talk.

Since he's programmed 'Nox to patch me right in whenever I call, I hologram myself into the ship's front nose using the hotel room's transmitter, which is more powerful than my Wave. I stand in front of the wall device, and it beams a holographic replica of 'Nox's crystal-capped front nose into my room just as it scans a holographic replica of me into the ship.

My mouth curves at the sight of the last place that felt like home. Hysan must be near the Seagoat constellation, because the transmission signal is so clear that the time lag is barely perceptible.

"Rho Grace. A pleasure."

My smile wilts at the sight of a buxom, blond-haired bombshell at the control helm. I'm so taken aback by her presence I don't immediately say anything.

She watches me mysteriously, undisturbed by my sudden appearance or muteness. Her immaculate beauty has an ageless quality—she could just as easily be a teenager as a forty-year-old—and her stare is admirably inscrutable.

"Don't think I packed enough pistols," says Hysan, striding into the nose from the back of the ship. He's barefoot and wearing only boxers, baring a more cut upper body than the one I knew a month ago.

"*Rho!*"

He freezes upon spotting me, his demeanor uncharacteristically frazzled. "I didn't expect—it's lovely to see you, my lady." He pulls on the gray coveralls, which are dangling over a chair. "How may I be of service?"

I realize my arms are crossed and unfold them. "I was just—I didn't mean to intrude." I look again at the blonde, who's so stationary she might not be breathing. She's still watching me.

"You're not—you never are." His voice softens on the second half of the sentence. "Miss Trii and I were just going over supplies."

"*Miss Trii?*" I stare at her in astounded disbelief. "You're—I mean—*oh*, nice to meet you!"

"Yes, I'm an android," she says, her voice and expression exceptionally pleasant. She seems to have completed her examination of me, and I can't help wondering how much of his face-reading talent Hysan programmed into her.

"Would you like to sit a moment?" she asks, turning to him. "Your heart is beating unusually fast."

"I'm fine, Miss Trii," he says quickly, his ears going pink. "Actually, if I could have a private moment with Lady Rho—"

"Of course, but first, she has so many questions for me. They're bubbling up all over her face. It would be rude to leave before answering some." She flashes me a conspiratorial smile full of Libran charm. Turns out she's even more clairvoyant than he is.

"Hysan's parents were Knights in the service of Lord Vaz's Royal Guard, and they died on duty the very year Hysan was born." I look at him when she says this, but he's busied himself with one of the ship's holographic screens, averting his face from my view.

"His father was a very clever inventor." Miss Trii moves closer to regain my attention, and I focus back on her. "He built me while his wife was pregnant, to have someone to watch over Hysan during their working hours, programming me with the lessons he wanted to pass on to his son. You see, Librans write their first will at age twelve and are legally obligated to review and update it every year. In theirs, Knights Horace and Helen Dax stipulated I would continue bringing up Hysan if they should pass."

Her quartz irises have a crystallized texture, and they reflect back a million fractured versions of myself. "He was lucky to have you," I say.

"I've always been the lucky one." Her expression fills with so much warmth that I can't believe she isn't human. "As I began imparting his father's lessons, Hysan quickly surpassed him. By then I was becoming an outdated model, so Hysan used me to test out his theories and ideas, making me one of the most advanced robots of our time." She looks at him like a proud parent, and even though his face is still turned away, his ears are pink again.

"When he was eleven, he and Lord Vaz finished building Lord Neith, and I asked Hysan to fashion me a human form from Kartex, like his. Not only did he do an exceptional job, but he even let me design myself." She does a slow twirl to show off her enviable figure. "Nice, right?"

"Stunning," I say, resisting the sudden urge to laugh at her human-like pride.

"I now have a question for you," she tells me, and though her manner is still amiable, there's something dangerous in her sharp expression. Even Hysan comes over to join us, looking more alert. "If you're so afraid to give in to your feelings for my Hysan, why do you keep reaching out to him?"

"Miss Trii, *please*," says Hysan, his voice gentle but firm, "I would really like to speak with Rho alone."

"Hysan Dax, I'm the android who raised you; show some respect," she chides him. "I have every right to get to know the woman you—"

Something flashes from Hysan's Scan, and Miss Trii stops speaking mid-sentence, her face relaxing into a placid expression.

"Sorry about that," he says, avoiding my eyes. "It's what happens when you give your robots too much freedom. First it was designing her own body, then she wanted access to her programming, now she's making her own personality adjustments, overriding my behavioral modifications, and—"

"She's amazing," I say, my focus now completely on the handsome golden face before me. Hysan's close enough that if he were really here my skin would sizzle from the proximity. "*You're* amazing."

This time he accepts the compliment in true Libran fashion, his dimpled centaur smile resurfacing. "She was recharging on the ship when we landed on Capricorn; otherwise, I would have introduced you. I'm sending her back to Libra as soon as we land on Sagittarius. Is that what you're calling about?"

I nod. "I wanted to see what you were doing."

"I changed headings mid-flight the moment I heard the Marad's message. Guardian Brynda is a friend of mine."

"I'm meeting Nishi and Deke. It sounds like they've tapped into a network of people who want to fight. If we can get organized, and if we can get support from Guardian Brynda, maybe we can actually help."

"I've spoken with Nishi and am meeting her as well." His gold-green eyes gleam. "Would you like a lift?"

"No, we'll just hitch a ride with the Capricorns. There are shuttles to and from Sagittarius here daily." It's a mutually beneficial relationship: Since Sagittarians are curious about everything, they're in and out of the Zodiax constantly, and since Capricorns love amassing wisdom, they're always intrigued by the new gadgets and ideas the Sagittarians bring with them.

My gaze veers away from Hysan, toward the ship's familiar surroundings, and I bite down on my inner lip. I suddenly see Mathias everywhere. By the helm, the teaching crown, the curving glass windows. When I meet Hysan's eyes again, he's watching me.

"I like talking to you this way," he says, though he sounds sad. "It feels honest."

"Honest how?"

He trails a finger across my cheek, and though I can't sense his caress, I feel its memory. "I can look, but I can't touch."

✦ ✦ ✦

In the morning, Aryll and I manage to secure passage on a ship to Sagittarius that leaves the next day. In the meantime, he's helping out at the settlement with Stanton, and I'm in my room, consulting my tutorial Ephemeris.

The moment I'm Centered, I hear the screeching sound and feel the distortion of Psynergy that means Ophiuchus is approaching.

This time, I manage to endure the high-pitched shrill the way Moira did, by receding into the deepest recess of my mind and steadying myself in the Psy. Then I'm ready to face him.

As Ophiuchus takes his full icy form, the stars around me start spinning wildly, transforming into the slipstream where we met before. We're in the astral plane.

The Thirteenth Guardian towers over me, a giant carved from ice with black-hole eyes, his hulking body at its fullest strength. *At last you start to understand*, says the gravelly voice. *You are beginning to believe in your power.*

I don't waste energy speaking—there's nothing left to be said between us. Instead, I prepare to attack him by anchoring myself in my Center, tunneling deep into my soul, until I'm absorbing waves of Psynergy from people all across the Zodiac. The force of energy strengthens my presence and makes me powerful in the Psy—only this time, it's a jittery and unstable kind of power.

Psynergy is how a Zodai taps into her Center: The more we access, the more Centered we become. But the more Psynergy I'm allowing in, the less steady I feel. When I've reached capacity, I swing my arm and unleash a shaky blow into Ochus's stomach—the highest part of him I can reach.

He's not expecting my punch, so the impact blasts him backward, creating a massive crater in his midsection and causing him to stumble. My fist sears with pain, but I press past it. When he regains his balance, he bellows out a deafening laugh that burns my ears.

I am not your enemy, child. Do not repeat your previous mistakes by letting your emotions overrule you. Today, we fight on the same side.

You and I will never be on the same side, I snarl, breathing heavily from my exertion.

Ochus's torso repairs itself, and he shrinks down to human size, so that our heights somewhat match. I've never faced him as an equal before, and the gesture is the only reason I listen to him.

You can feel the instability of the Zodiac in the very Psynergy feeding your presence here, he says, making even his voice sound human-sized. *This is my master's plan at work—he is using the Marad as he used me. He seeks to stir up enough chaos for the Houses to destroy each other. I no longer believe he has any plan to restore the glory of the Thirteenth House.*

Then stop him, I spit back. *What do you want with me?*

I have tried and failed. I believe if we combine forces, we can take him down together.

My laugh is mirthless and cold, and I cut it off when I realize who I sound like. *Us work together? You ruined my life,* murderer. *You killed my father. You killed Mathias. I hate you—understand? I will never, ever work with you.*

Ophiuchus reassumes his immortal shape, growing into a mountainous form. His icy body chills the air, making my every breath frigid and cutting. I clench my fists to mask my trembling.

Even the lowest scum in the universe deserves redemption for his mistakes, he thunders in a voice that could belong to Helios. *There is good and bad in the Zodiac—the point is not to eradicate one but to find the balance of both that yields the greatest harmony.*

Is this a lesson from your Talisman? My words are low and whispery, the icy air stabbing me every time I draw breath. *Where did it end up? If the Zodiac needs to unite, what better way to teach us than the Talisman that stored the power of Unity?*

Even though the physical change hasn't come over him yet, Ophiuchus seems to grow emotionally older and wearier at the mention of his stone, and the temperature rises a few degrees. *The Talisman was lost when I suffered this state, half-alive and half-dead, trapped in the spirit world with no agency of my own.*

You don't have a body?

I exist only in the Psy. My master said he would return me to the physical realm, but I now believe that too was a lie. You must help me either to live again or die completely. After all, my enemy's enemy is my ally, and that is you.

I cross my arms, his weakening state filling me with strength. *Why would I believe you?*

Because you are me now.

My body chills again as his voice grows quieter than I've ever heard it, his breath a snaky stream of vapor. *After everything you did, the Zodiac still refuses to believe in me, but they revile you. You have dethroned me as the new boogeyman. Now that you know disgrace, you know the way people can twist the truth and manipulate stories to further their agenda.*

He cocks his head curiously, a gesture so human that for a moment I glimpse the mortal behind the immortal. *The universe has cast you as a liar without a trial, Rhoma Grace . . . can you so quickly do the same to me?*

The anger tastes like bile in my mouth. *How dare you compare me to you? You're a murderer.*

I will prove to you my new allegiance by betraying the old. The Marad will not strike Sagittarius, as they claim. They will select their true target on the day of the attack, so that no Zodai can foresee it—but my Sight tells me it will be Capricorn.

His eyes grow larger and deeper, twin black holes that seem to be sucking my soul within their whirlpools.

The question is, Acolyte, will you trust me in time to save this world?

7

WHEN OPHIUCHUS DISAPPEARS, I STAND by my half-packed bag, wondering where to go. The first thing I do is try reaching Hysan on his Ring, but he must have his Psy shield up, because I can't get through. I can't hail him by hologram either. He's veiled and shielded; 'Nox must be flying through a dangerous pocket of Space.

Ophiuchus destroyed Cancer—and nearly did away with Virgo and Gemini, too—so why in the Zodiac would he warn me about Sagittarius?

Unless he's really turned on his master.

I sensed their battle in the Ephemeris just the other night. And even now, Ochus did seem different . . . more restrained. The violence had vanished from his voice, replaced by something else, something far too familiar to me. *Defeat.*

And yet he's played me this way before. I've always done everything he wanted, since the first time we met when he threatened my life if I spoke of his existence. That very day, he summoned all the Guardians to the Plenum so they could witness my humiliation firsthand. He knew I would defy him, so he and his master set me up to be a pawn for their schemes. I had a part in their plan. My whole journey was a diversion.

Ophiuchus knows Cancrians, knows our greatest power—our unparalleled ability to love and forgive—can easily become our greatest flaw. Is that what he's playing on now?

What if he's telling the truth?

When I leave my room, I'm surprised to find Aryll flipping through newsfeeds on the couch. "Where's Stanton?"

"Surface. I wasn't able to help much"—he holds up his hand, which boasts a bulky bandage over a new injury—"so he told me to hang out. I was checking the latest."

I slump beside him on the cushions. He smells like the earthy moisturizing lotion provided by the hotel.

After being here a few weeks, Stanton's and my sun-kissed tans are back, but Aryll's skin has turned as red as his hair, and his nose looks like it might start peeling. He pulls away from the developing story on Sagittarius to stare at me. "Are you okay? You have a funny look on your face."

I shake my head, blowing out a hard breath. "I-I just saw Ophiuchus," I blurt out quickly.

Aryll's face goes slack with horrified shock, his electric stare setting my hair on end. "He was—*here?*"

"No, in the astral plane. He . . . he said the Marad's true plan isn't to attack Sagittarius but Capricorn."

"Capricorn?" Aryll furrows his brow thoughtfully, rubbing the bronze locket that hangs off a black strap of levlan around his neck. It's his only possession, and I've never seen him take it off. "Rho . . . promise you won't go off on me," he says tentatively, not meeting my gaze, "if I say something you don't like?"

"Yeah. What is it?"

"It's just . . ." He's still holding his locket and avoiding my eyes. "Even after everything that's happened, you never actually proved Ophiuchus's existence."

I suck in a gasp, a million angry thoughts jostling for first place in my mouth—

"Just . . . don't yell, okay?" he says quickly, raising both hands like a shield.

Guilt clamps my mouth shut.

"How did the master trick you last time?" he asks.

I frown. "He used a feint—while we went after Ophiuchus, his army came after us."

"Exactly. Look, I believe you saw Ochus. But can I throw out another possibility?"

He waits for my approval, and, grudgingly, I give a quick, sharp nod. "If Ochus has no body and can do things in the Psy no human can . . . and we've just seen proof that the Marad has technology that outmatches ours . . . don't you think Ophiuchus could be an—an *invention*?"

"*What?*" I blurt, caught between a laugh and an eye roll. "How? That's—"

"Just listen," says Aryll, swinging his legs onto the couch and facing me, his expression openly eager. "The master is obviously a master at manipulating the Psy, right? So what if he invented Ophiuchus to distract you? People mess with their Psynergy signatures all the time—think of this as a more advanced form of identity fraud."

"Why *Ophiuchus*?" I ask, freeing my curls from a sloppy bun so I can wrestle them into a tighter one. "Why not just a white-masked scary person like those soldiers?"

From the way he can't wait to speak, I can tell he's already considered the *why*. "We know two important things about the master," says Aryll, holding up two fingers. "One, he likes to play games, and two, he's a student of history. Just as he studied the Trinary Axis for the Marad's attacks, he could have learned about Ochus by studying Zodiac lore and adopting him as a dramatic disguise. Can you think of a better way to distract our whole universe than revealing a hidden House?"

I'm shaking my head, like I still want to argue with him, even though the words don't come. Aryll's unconventional thinking reminds me of the way the Libran jury arrives at decisions: He's considering the problem from every possibility. I never realized he was so bright. It makes me wish he'd speak up more often.

I can't produce an argument against Aryll, so he goes on. "He sent you zooming through the Zodiac with an urgent warning he knew no one else would believe, something sensational enough to capture the attention of every House—doesn't that sound exactly like what he's trying to do now? So that you'll direct everyone's attention this way . . . while he goes the other?"

Even though my emotions are writhing and whirring, wanting to be heard, I push them down and follow Aryll's logic. This is the kind of thoughtful analysis Mathias would have urged me to do before bursting into action.

"You're right," I say, sighing. "I can't let him keep using me—whatever he is, he's the opposite of me."

We're silent a while, Aryll probably still thinking through his theory, while I'm wondering what I'd do—what *Stanton* would do—if Aryll didn't make it back.

I steal a glance at him, and he's still fingering his bronze locket. I recognize that kind of attachment to an object; without having to ask, I can tell it's Aryll's last memory of home.

"Are you sure you want to do this?" I whisper.

He doesn't immediately answer, his gaze still adrift. "Not really," he admits.

My voice flush with relief, I say, "Great! Then *stay*—"

"I also don't want to be on Capricorn. I don't want to be watching the news waiting to hear how many others have died. I don't want to be in a war. I don't want to be an orphan." He's squeezing the locket so tight, I'm worried he'll cut himself. "They've taken everything from me. My family, my home, even half my vision. I have nothing left."

I rest my hand on his, and he finally looks at me, his grip on the locket relaxing. His blue eye is shiny with tears. "You have us," I whisper. "We're your family now."

He wipes the tears with the back of his bandaged hand. "My older sister and I used to fight all the time. We could barely be in the same room without competing for the same game or the same person's attention." He shakes his head like he doesn't like remembering.

"I wanted a brother. Like Stanton." More tears run down his cheek, but he doesn't wipe them. "Do you hate me now?"

"No," I murmur, squeezing his hand. Then I pass him a tissue, and while he dries his face, I try one last time. "Stanton really loves you. He'd be thrilled if you stayed."

Aryll surveys the room, as though his decision depends on these very walls. "I can't stay. I don't like it here, Rho. I'm not sure what it is . . ."

Watching him now, I spot the discomfort in his expression. His sunburn is looking worse today, and I start to wonder if maybe it's just this place that doesn't agree with him.

"Too much land," I say, nodding decisively. "I think we're going to like Sagittarius."

✦ ✦ ✦

The next morning, Stanton accompanies Aryll and me to the spaceport. Aryll boards the shuttle first and saves us seats so that I can say a longer goodbye to Stanton. As I look into my brother's face, I think of the flickering of Thebe in the Ephemeris and how I stayed silent while Stanton was in danger. My mind travels back a decade, and I see the bubbles in the Cancer Sea that foreshadowed the Maw's attack. I stayed silent then, too.

"Come with us," I say, taking his hand.

He frowns. "This is *your* calling, Rho . . . mine's here."

"I saw Ophiuchus in the Psy yesterday. He told me Capricorn is the true target, not Sagittarius." I say it real quick so that I don't have to hear the words or consider their meaning.

"I know."

I blink. "You *know*?"

"Aryll told me. He also told me his theory about Ochus being an invention, and I think it's worth considering. I'm happy you can talk to him, Rho."

Stanton's gentle tone sounds like Dad's again, and I realize how much I wish we still had someone to tell us what to do right now and take care of us and shield us from our fears—a *parent*. Only as I think of the word's meaning, it's not Mom or Dad who come to mind.

Stanton's right. He's always been more than a brother—he raised me. And now, to both of our dismays, I've outgrown his protection.

"I love you," I say, pulling him in for a bone-crushing hug.

"Love you, too," he whispers, and then I step up to the shuttle, refusing to look back, so I won't cry. I feel like I'm twelve years old again, boarding the ship to Elara and deserting the person I love most in the Zodiac.

Just as I'm stepping through the door, a Chronicler calls my name. "Rhoma Grace! A package for you from Sage Ferez."

I accept the small box and step inside the ship, which is a long cylinder lined with reclining levlan seats on both sides. It's built for speed, not comfort; we'll get to Sagittarius in under a day.

I spot Aryll's red hair and make for the seat next to his, suddenly stricken by how much even he's reminding me of myself from five years ago, when I left home for the first time. How lonely it felt to leave behind everything I loved. Only in Aryll's case, everything he loved left him.

An offer of friendship was the only way I got through that trip to Elara.

"Aryll," I say, sitting down beside him, "I know you have an easier time talking to my brother, and that's totally fine. But I want you to know I'm here for you. I'm going to look out for you like Stanton did. You're not alone."

Aryll's gaze grows glassy, and he nods at me without speaking. He's clasping the locket in his fingers again, like it's for good fortune. I give him some privacy by looking down at my lap and focusing on the box from Sage Ferez.

When I pop the lid, the first thing I find is a note:

> *Until you are reunited with your true Ephemeris, this one is on loan to you from the Zodiax. It is said to have belonged to Vecily Matador of House Taurus before she became Guardian and a member of the Trinary Axis. Should you find time to indulge in the mind's most sacred act, I Waved you a text on Guardian Matador that I think you will find most illuminating. Safe travels.*

I set the note aside and find a heart-shaped device that looks like it's been carved from bone. Rolling the Ephemeris around in my hand, I feel the buzzing of the Abyssthe in its core responding to the Abyssthe in my Ring.

"You really made an impression on him," says Aryll, reading over my shoulder.

Since we're taking off, I put the Ephemeris back in the box and stuff it in my bag. After buckling in, I say, "Aryll . . . if, for whatever reason, I don't make it—"

"I'll return the stone to Ferez," he says in a low tone. "But only if you never bring that up again."

I nod just as an automated voice speaks through the ship. *"This shuttle is now taking off. Please enjoy your trip. We will be landing on Sagittarius in nineteen galactic hours."*

The engine vibrates across the cylindrical ship, and I look through the windows across from us as the spaceport grows smaller. Tierre has the widest range of topography and animal species of any planet. It's so vast that the higher we go, the more land I see—forests, mountain ranges, grassy fields, swamps, beaches—until, with a jolt, we escape Tierre's gravity, and I can make out the edges of the colorful globe. The tapestry of textures is undeniably impressive . . . but I miss the blending blues of home.

Once the ship jumps to hyperspeed, Aryll takes an eighteen-hour sleeping powder from the seat's side pouch and promptly passes out. But sleep doesn't appeal to me—I'm in a thinking mood.

I open my Wave and pull up the file from Ferez. It's a report dated almost eighty years back, which he wrote when he was a university student. Blue holographic text unfolds before me.

> It's been almost a millennium since the Trinary Axis, and yet we have never forgotten the greatest love story in Zodiac history: the forbidden romance of Cancrian Holy Mother Brianella Amarise and Leonine Holy Leader Blazon Logax. Their story is the basis for the universally popular nursery rhyme "Ballad of Bria and Blaze" as well as the inspiration for the two most famously star-crossed lovers in Zodiac fiction, Nella and Lazon. The legend of these two ancient Guardians has even crept into modern-day idioms: When someone says his relationship or marriage "blazes on," he is alluding to the eternal flame between Blazon and Brianella.

I stop to consider the legendary love story about the Cancrian and Leonine Guardians. Even today, the galaxy's most popular holographic series—holoshow—is shot on House Leo, and it follows the love triangle of three Zodai—the last human survivors after the Zodiac's been wiped out—who adventure to unknown reaches of Space searching for a new home. The characters are named Amara, Logax, and Velia, after the three Guardians of the Trinary Axis.

The thought brings Hysan and the Taboo to my mind. I can't even consider how people would react if they found out we broke that law, especially given how much closer the Zodiac is coming to war . . . and the worst war we ever had was triggered by the same breach. I refocus on Ferez's report.

However, the person about whom the least is known is the Axis's mysterious third member, Vecily Matador of House Taurus. Vecily never told her people why she joined the Axis, and she rarely spoke at any rallies. Yet, after reviewing the details of her early life, I believe that I have stumbled upon three crucial moments that point to her state of mind and reveal her reasons for taking on this fight.

The first moment occurred when Vecily was a seventeen-year-old Acolyte at the Taurian Academy. She had a best friend, Datsby, from whom she was inseparable. They were top of their class, the best star-readers at the school, and their instructors and classmates were certain both girls would make it into the Royal Guard. Until one day, a few months shy of graduating, the stars diverted their paths.

Vecily and Datsby were sun-soaking in a corner of the Academy's grazing grounds between classes when a couple of male friends dumped water on them from a fifth-story window. Vecily's initial shock gave way to laughter as soon as the young men ran over with towels, but Datsby's shrieks would not be soothed. When Vecily and the boys tried to help, they discovered something strange about Datsby's appearance. Her makeup had washed off, unmasking a deep, tawny tone far darker than the caramel color of her face paint.

Datsby was changing Houses. The young men's playful, flirting words changed to outbursts of disgust, and they shouted ugly names at her: Riser! Deviant! Freak! Soon a crowd formed around them. All Vecily could do was shield her crying friend from the gawking glares and vicious voices.

At last, a Promisary intervened. Vecily was taken to the dean's office, where her mental and emotional health was thoroughly assessed, and where she was assured and reassured that the situation would be handled.

Later, it was noted that, earlier that same year, Datsby had started wearing long, sweeping bangs to conceal her eyes, which were no longer hazel but dark brown. And though her hair color hadn't changed, it had started growing so fast that she had to trim it at her chin every week to keep it at the traditional Taurian length. In Datsby's day, the Zodiac's stance on Risers was even more narrow-minded than it is today, which means they invariably became outcasts.

Vecily is said to have spoken only once in the dean's office, to ask if Datsby was okay and if she could see her. Nothing else is known about that day, but it has been documented that Vecily and Datsby never saw each other again. For the rest of her recorded life, Vecily rarely spoke, and when she did, she chose her words sparingly and wisely.

I let my eyes drift from my Wave, too distraught over Datsby's fate and my renewed thoughts of the Trinary Axis to read on.

A thousand years ago, the Houses didn't operate as separate, sovereign entities, the way they do now. Back then, the Guardians passed universal legislation that superseded the Houses' own laws. Universal rights versus House rights was a constant source of tension and debate, and one universal law in particular was creating controversy: a ban on inter-House marriage.

The ban had been around a few centuries, but there were rumbles that some Houses wanted to reverse it. A court case on House Libra was working its way up the ranks to a universal trial at the Plenum, and when it was finally brought before the Guardians, it was struck down, seven to five.

Two Guardians had been hoping the law would be overturned—Brianella and Blazon. Their outrage over the case's outcome transformed their unbridled passion and unconditional love into something fearsome. They decided to secede from the Zodiac and convinced Vecily to join them. They called themselves the Trinary Axis, and they declared themselves free of Zodiac rule and able to run their Houses however they wanted.

The other Guardians didn't honor their secession, but the Trinary Axis continued their work underground, recruiting members from every world to their cause. By the time they launched their choreographed attack on the Houses, it was no longer an issue of inter-House marriage; it was a crisis of universal rights versus House rights, and it had awoken a monster.

For one hundred years, civil war raged on in every House. The Guardians eventually stopped convening, too busy with the situations in their own worlds. By the time the war was over, new Guardians had replaced the old, and they all agreed to govern their Houses independently—with the exception of one galactic rule, which the Guardians swore always to follow in order to prevent the destruction caused by the Trinary Axis from ever happening again and to ensure no two Houses would ever get too close and gain too much power. It's the Taboo—the Zodiac's only unbreakable law.

And I broke it.

8

I WAKE UP WITH MY Wave still in my hand. The lights of the Archer constellation wink through the windows across the aisle. We've dropped out of hyperspeed, so the trip will be over soon.

House Sagittarius has four planets—all inhabited—and five moons. Centaurion is its largest and most populated world, and the Capital is where the government meets and also where Nishi's family lives. Sagittarians call their capital city simply the Capital, for the same reason they refer to their Guardian as Guardian. I sometimes think they're the only people who use language how it was originally meant to be used—literally.

"We there yet?" asks Aryll, popping open his cerulean eye.

"Soon. I'll wake you when it's time." He nods and goes back to sleep.

"You're Rho Grace."

I turn around to see a Sagittarian Acolyte with blue-black hair and honey-colored eyes, also just waking up. "I'm Nova Ken," she says, reaching out to trade the hand touch with me. As soon as our fists bump, she pulls hers back to stifle a yawn. "A-are you coming to Centaurion to fight the Marad?"

"To help, if I can."

"Your Sagittarian friend who was spreading the word about the Thirteenth House—is she why you're helping?"

"She's one of the reasons, yes."

Her honey gaze is so direct it's like staring into Helios. "How did you convince her that Ophiuchus was real when you couldn't convince the people in your own House?"

"She trusts me."

When I first met Nishi at the Academy, I found the clipped, back-and-forth pace of her conversational style off-putting. I couldn't believe the way she skipped small talk and went straight to satisfying her curiosity. But after getting to know some of the other Acolytes, I realized I preferred the purity of Nishi's speech. It was a luxury, not having to wonder what was truly on someone's mind.

Nova looks ready to fire off more questions, so I steer her to safer topics. "Why were you on Capricorn?"

"Conducting research in the Zodiax for my graduation project. My parents want me to stay there, but they're not evacuating, so I'm joining them."

"I'm sorry," I murmur. I'll never forget what it felt like to witness the devastation of my home. That kind of horror stays with you.

"I'm sorry for you, too. After everything that's happened to you . . . if it were me, I'd have stopped helping by now." Her brow dips quizzically. "Either you're incredibly committed to converting the Houses to your Ophius cult"—she uses the Sagittarian word for Ophiuchus—"or you've been telling the truth all along, and now you're risking your life again, even when it's no longer expected of you."

I don't say anything, and her honey eyes hold mine in their glow. "What scares me is I think you're telling the truth . . . but I really wish you weren't."

We stare at each other a moment longer, and then the shuttle's automated voice cuts through the air. *"Prepare for landing."*

I wake Aryll up, and then my body grows heavy as we cross the invisible barrier into Centaurion's gravity. From this distance, the planet looks as if it's infested with metallic insects: Every variety of aircraft is buzzing in and out of the atmosphere, swarming the surface with activity. It's easy to see why Sagittarians are called the Zodiac's wanderers—even from way out here, they look restless.

"Good fortune, Rho," says Nova when we land, steepling her fingertips and touching her forehead. I return the Sagittarian gesture, and as we rise to disembark, she surprises me by pressing a galactic gold coin into my palm. "And thank you."

She rushes off, and I pocket the money, shrugging at Aryll's raised eyebrow. "It's nothing," I mumble, moved and humbled by Nova's gift.

It's rare for people to carry coins anymore—nowadays they're mostly used for off-the-books payments and bribes. For everything legal, we swipe our thumbprints, and the sum transfers from our accounts automatically. But for some Houses, galactic gold coins have taken up a symbolic significance.

Capricorns collect currency from every galactic year to see how far into the past they can touch. The Geminin have dream wells where they toss a coin and make a wish, and Imaginarium-type technology shows them what the world would look like if that wish were to come true. Sagittarians use them literally, to pay people praise: If someone does something truly worth commending, they give her a coin. They call it a *fair trade*—exchanging gold for gold.

"RHO!"

At almost the exact moment Aryll and I step onto the crowded spaceport, I'm pulled into a body-binding hug. Nishi and I cling to each other, and I flash to Ferez's story about Vecily and Datsby. My hold on her tightens as I remember I've come here to *fight*. Last time I fought, some of my friends didn't make it back.

What if this time it's Nishi or Deke or Aryll or Hysan?

"Come on, leave some Rho for the rest of us," says Deke after he's greeted Aryll, whom he met on Gemini. Deke peels Nishi and me apart and lifts my feet off the floor with his hug.

Despite the warmth of their welcome, the atmosphere in this spaceport is bleak. Sagittarians are vying for seats on any transport going almost anywhere, while holographic wallscreens scroll through the never-ending columns of names on the waiting lists for every flight. The screens that aren't crammed with words are blasting images of wounded Sagittarians from the fighting that's broken out between them and the migrant Scorp workers on Wayfare, one of the House's moons. The sight brings to my mind the burned bodies on Gemini, and I have to swallow to clear the taste of ash from my throat.

As Nishi nimbly leads us to the exit, I'm jostled on every side by the tizzy of travelers tunneling in the opposite direction, all desperate for a way off this planet. We seem to be the only ones trying to get in.

Once we've left the spaceport, I get my first view of Centaurion's capital city—and it's like nothing I've ever seen before. The Capital is a vast Imaginarium come to life.

The buildings here are bizarre shapes and colors, their outer walls covered with diagrams, drawings, and questions: *If the universe has a beginning, what came before the universe? If the future isn't written, how is it we can predict it? If the stars guide us, what guides the stars?*

There are no cars on the ground, so there are no streets, just one large, lavender landing pad in the center of the city for intraplanetary flying vehicles. All around the pad are millions of narrow pathways that wind in curving patterns through the city's jumble of buildings, storefronts, and curiosities. I can't discern a design in the pathways—it seems they just meander through downtown, at times abruptly ending at various destinations, though some seem more direct than others.

"Depends if you're walking or wandering," says Nishi, observing me observe her city. "When we're in a wandering mood, we take a more roundabout path; but when we have a target, we'll take the quickest route to our destination."

I nod as I scour all the activity blooming around me. Metallic-bodied androids bustle alongside dark-haired Sagittarians in the crowds, and though I don't see any names on the piles of pathways, everyone seems to know where they're going. High above us is a different picture altogether.

Rows of traffic ripple the sky as vehicles imported from all over the Zodiac and spanning every time period stop at holographic traffic lights, waiting. Whenever a green light blinks on, the next vehicle shoots off. They fly so fast they vanish from view almost immediately. Sagittarians may sometimes wander on the ground, but in the air they're like arrows: When they pick a mark, they hit it.

Nishi and Deke lead us down one of the wider pathways, past a display of decorative centaur sculptures and shops with names like Robotic Reset (a spa for androids), Startastic Tastings (a market with foreign foods from across the galaxy), and Absolutely Abyssthe (the Sagittarian economy is export-based, and Abyssthe makes up 95 percent of the exports).

Every few minutes, we come across another overstuffed souvenir station—tents filled with strange trinkets and gadgets that span everything from antiquated technologies to innovative inventions. Nishi told me Sagittarians like to collect tokens from their travels and often donate them to their city to share their curiosities with their neighbors. But today's wanderers are hurrying up and down the street with purpose, too preoccupied to pay the stations any attention. The mood is as grim as the leaden sky.

Our pathway weaves around a triangular hotel and past an arrow-shaped archery supply store. Holographic graffiti covers the structures' surfaces, and my gaze darts in every direction to take it all in. I think I glimpse a girl's face drawn onto the archery store's wall, but when I look back we've already turned the corner. I'm probably just seeing things, but she looked just like me.

"With everyone trying to leave the planet, we didn't dare fly here in Dad's *Icarus*," Nishi explains, gesturing to the clogged airways above us.

"So how'd you get here?" I ask as we pass an ancient cannon, behind which a line of Sagittarians has gathered. Nishi stops walking, and we all turn to watch a girl wearing a helmet and protective gear step inside the cannon.

A moment later, fire flames out from the cannon's backside, and I gasp as the girl rockets out—hugging her knees tight like a ball—and disappears into the far-off horizon.

Deke looks at me. "It's really not as bad as—"

"Oh, don't *even!*" I snap, shaking my head. "There is *no way* I'm doing that!"

"Come on, Rho," pleads Aryll. He seems to be teeming with excitement at the concept of being launched through the air like a missile. "It looks fun!"

I point to his injured hand. "If being maimed once again is your idea of a good time." Despite my panic, I'm relieved to see Aryll looking less sad. As I watch him in this new world, I realize for the first time how little he liked Capricorn.

"Rho, you don't have a choice," says Nishi, shoving me in line. "It's the only way to get home, and we need to go. People are waiting on us."

My panic intensifies, and I feel a line of sweat forming on my forehead. I don't say anything because she's right, but every cell in my body is urging me to run. This is the riskiest thing I've ever done—and I've done some deadly things, especially lately.

"Sweetzer Suburb," says Nishi to the cannon's operator when it's our turn. She faces me. "You should go first—just get it over with." My mouth is too dry to form words. "Tuck everything in," she says, helping me into protective gear, "and roll up tight."

She snaps on my helmet, and then a tall Sagittarian ushers me through a side door into the cannon. I tuck myself in tightly, like Nishi said, my heart bashing so violently against my rib cage that my pulse seems to echo through the chamber. Then, before I can dread it for one more second, a blast of force thrusts me through the air, and the whole world looks like the stars at hyperspeed: threads of light and a blur of textures.

I grip my knees tightly and dig my chin in, like a crab in its shell. The wind whips against the exposed skin of my neck, and my whole body aches from the strain of being so clamped up. The flight seems to last forever, and then I start to feel a falling sensation that builds until there's a tickle in my stomach that won't go away.

I land in a vast meadow, on a lavender bed of the most comfortable, foam-soft material I've ever felt. I'm helped to my feet by another tall Sagittarian, and as I'm handing him the protective gear, Aryll lands in the lavender, looking delighted, followed by Nishi and Deke.

"Wasn't so bad, right, Rho Rho?" asks Deke, giving my arm a squeeze.

My joints are still sore from crushing everything to my chest, and my neck spasms with pain each time I move it. "Never . . . again." My knees wobble as I speak the words.

"We're close," says Nishi encouragingly, and we follow a pathway far less crowded than the main route through downtown, into what looks like a residential area. On either side of us are single- and multi-family homes, each structure so strikingly different from the next in color and shape and design that the effect is dizzying.

Some homes are painted with polka dots, some with stripes; some change color depending on where you stand. Some flash films from their windows, some have chimneys branching from chimneys, and some have see-through walls. Some are built underground, some wear their staircases on the outside like exoskeletons, and some are so skinny they become almost invisible when looked at from certain angles.

After a while, we turn a corner and enter a quiet area surrounded by a sky-high hedge. We can't see what's on the other side, but the sight of so much gentle green soothes my eyes. I'm about to ask how much farther when Nishi turns and then vanishes into the hedge.

"It's a hologram," says Deke, following Nishi through.

Aryll and I inspect the greenery. The leaves look real, smell real, even feel real . . . until I touch the spot where Nishi and Deke disappeared, and my hand goes right through the green. It's a small holographic doorway hidden within the hedge. I step through it to the other side and find myself standing before a sprawling palatial estate.

Aryll's mouth hangs open, and I look at Nishi in awe. "That's *home?*"

She shrugs. "I hated this place growing up," she admits, a gust of wind tossing her hair back as she stares up at her palace. "My parents were always traveling for work, and I don't have any siblings, so to me it seemed the embodiment of loneliness." She looks at me with sadness glinting in her amber eyes. "The Academy was my home, Rho."

Deke and Aryll awkwardly amble away as she and I pull each other in for another hug. I don't think I fully appreciated until now that when Ophiuchus destroyed Cancer, Nishi lost part of her home, too.

Nishi lets us into the mansion, which is just as majestic on the inside: It's vast and echoing and glossy, and it seems to have an endless supply of kitchens and bedrooms and bathrooms and common rooms and reading rooms and White Rooms and more. White Rooms are traditional in Sagittarian homes—completely and literally white and empty of everything, they're places where Sagittarians can go when their thoughts or surroundings grow too loud. The starkness helps them Center.

"I need to Wave Hysan."

"He already knows you're here," says Nishi. "He checked in last night and said he'd come over as soon as he can."

"How soon?"

"I don't know, but don't worry about him. He knows what he's doing." She links her elbow with mine and steers me into a big, open sitting area in the center of the mansion, filled with long paneled windows and a circle of creamy levlan couches that could seat a small army.

"Hysan's arranged for a fleet of bullet-ships to transport people to Verity," explains Nishi. "Guardian Ferez said all are welcome. Most Sagittarians are evacuating to our other planets and moons, but some have taken Ferez up on his offer."

Ophiuchus's warning thunders through my mind, and I wonder whether I should tell Nishi. I'd love to share the weight of his words with her—if only the action didn't feel so cowardly. I have no way of knowing if Ophiuchus is telling the truth, and neither does she. The two of us raising the alarm once more would be the perfect way for him to wreak more damage to our already fragile House bonds. Once again, he's wound me up like a toy set to self-destruct.

But this time I'm not playing Ochus's games. I'm going to help Sagittarius.

Nishi fetches a carafe of water and some glasses, and Aryll and Deke sprawl out on separate couches. Deke rests his dirty boots on the light-colored cushions.

"Nish, where are your parents?" I ask.

"That's sort of . . . the thing," she says, trading a nervous look with Deke, like the one from the other day. "See, they were on House Libra the past week, so when the Marad made its threat, I kind of told them to stay there—because I was evacuating with Deke to Gryphon."

"*Nish!*"

"I know it's wrong, but I don't want to put them in danger," she says quickly, avoiding my gaze. "And I want to fight."

"What about your Tracker? Won't it give you away?" I stare pointedly at the flint device around her wrist designed to ping out her location wherever she goes, so loved ones can find her.

"Hysan taught me how to disable it," she mutters under her breath, pouring each of us a glass of water.

I don't know what to say. I want to yell at Nishi about family being too important to gamble with, and how this isn't fair to her parents, and they'll feel so awful if anything happens to her. But Nishi's the smartest person in this room. She already knows everything I'm not saying, and she still made this decision.

My best friend is making sacrifices for this war, and I'd be a hypocrite if I didn't understand why. I put my arm around her as she sits down beside me. "It must be hard lying to them."

"It is," she admits, her eyes downcast beneath her heavy black bangs. "But it makes it easier, knowing they're safe. And anyway, with them gone, we were able to bring everyone together." She looks up, her voice regaining its usual cheeriness. "So we can all be in one place."

"You mean us and Hysan?"

"No, she means *everyone*," says Deke. "Everyone willing to fight—whom we've been able to reach—is crashing the zillions of rooms here."

Nishi nods. "Now you can address us all together, and we can train as a unit for whatever the Marad has planned."

An uneasy feeling prickles my stomach, the start of a panic far worse than the kind I felt inside the cannon. I look from Nishi's eager face to Deke's determined one, and I flash back to the moment Rubidum nominated me to lead the armada. I came to Sagittarius to help—but Nishi and Deke asked me here to lead.

Before I can say anything, the swooshing sound of doors opening fills the air, and soon about fifty Acolytes are crowding the bright space. A flurry of dark faces and long-cut, wide eyes blur before me as I trade touches with each one. Like Nova on the flight over, they all ask questions after introducing themselves.

"Hi, I'm Mina. Do you still believe in Ophiuchus?"

"I do."

"Thanks for coming. My name is Wynn. Do you think Ophius is involved with the Marad?"

"Yes."

"Chan; nice to meet you. Do you know how we're going to defeat the Marad in just three days?"

"Not yet, but I came to help figure it out together."

"I'm Gyzer," says a guy with soulful eyes, a mournful voice, and coal-black skin. It's early morning on Sagittarius, and while most of the students are still in their bed clothes, he's one of the few who is already in his lavender uniform. "If you consider only what was within your control, where did you go wrong last time?"

"Accepting leadership," I say without hesitation. I knew nothing of governance or war or politics. I wasn't ready then—and I'm still not.

"Did you come here to help us or to get revenge?" asks the youngest in the group. She looks to be about fifteen. "I'm Ezra," she adds, tossing back her hair, which is in hundreds of tiny braids.

After a beat, I admit, "Both."

Once I've met everyone, they all take a seat while Nishi stays standing. "Okay, now that Rho is here, let's launch into our progress report so we can bring her up to date."

"What about the Libran? Has he returned?" asks Ezra.

"Not yet," Nishi tells her. "And, guys, please hold on to all your questions for later. Updates first. Deke, you start."

Deke springs to his feet and Waves a blue holographic diagram of the Capital into the air. "So far, the Marad has targeted the richest and most powerful parts of each House it's attacked: Leo, Scorpio, and Aquarius. Given that, and the fact that it's threatened to leave Sagittarius with Guardian Brynda's head, we can expect it to strike somewhere within this radius, right here in the Capital." He enlarges the diagram so that we're seeing only the sector most likely to be in danger.

Nishi's Tracker beams out a red holographic overlay that lines up with Deke's and adds a new layer to his diagram. Now there are concentrations of red dots dispersed throughout the city. "This is the latest Stargazer defensive formation, sent to us by our contact in the Royal Guard," says Nishi. "The Sagittarian government can't legally endorse our participation in military actions, Rho, but unofficially they're feeding us details."

"Most of us aren't combat fighters, nor do we have access to or experience with weapons," says Deke. "Which is why violence is not our primary objective." Gyzer and a few other guys grow disgruntled when they hear this, but they don't argue, so it's clear this subject has already been settled.

"We're going to be using invisibility Veils that will conceal us from others but are networked so we'll be able to see each other." Nishi holds up one of the collars Hysan gave her back on Gemini. "Once the fighting starts, we will back up the Stargazers, supplying weapons reloads, transporting the wounded, and bringing back reconnaissance updates on the Marad's positions. *That's all.*"

Deke shuts off his hologram. "Today and tomorrow, we will continue training in combat and weapons so that if the worst should happen, we can defend ourselves."

"There are vials of Abyssthe available for anyone who wants to do readings," offers Nishi.

"What happens if they attack us with Dark Matter?" asks Ezra, her elaborate braids practically swallowing her small face. "How will we defend ourselves then?"

Until now, the Marad has been attacking with brute force and advanced weaponry—not Psynergy. There's been no evidence of any Dark Matter assaults since the armada, and with Charon back in power and still spreading his fabrications about cosmic rays from the Sufianic Clouds, most question the existence of the Psy weapon altogether. Despite the evidence Lord

Neith and Ambassador Sirna presented to the Plenum on Aries, no one wants to believe in a superweapon . . . just as they don't want to believe in a supervillain.

"The city will be shielded."

My heart recognizes the voice before my ears do, and a torrent of blood floods my face.

"And this time, I can assure you the shields will work, because I built them all myself."

Hysan strides into the room in an inconspicuous all-black getup and casts his green gaze around the group. He stops on my face.

"My lady . . . it's good to see you." A strange silence follows, but Hysan seems to be the only person in the room who doesn't hear it.

"Great to see you again, Hysan," says Deke, dispersing the cloud of discomfort. "How do we shield the city?"

"I've spoken with Guardian Brynda, and we agreed that I will deliver the shields today," answers Hysan, who still hasn't broken eye contact with me.

Everyone murmurs, clearly impressed by his high reach. "That's perfect," says Nishi. "Rho, you should go with him and talk to Brynda since you've met her before. But first," she says, gesturing to the rest of the room, "do you want to say anything—?"

"Well, we really should go now," I say, as anxious about addressing the group as I am eager to be alone with Hysan. "The sooner we touch base with Guardian Brynda and find out what's going on, the better."

"Agreed," says Deke, and a few others nod with him. Nishi's the only one who looks disappointed with this plan. "Rho, you and Hysan should head out now so you can be back before dark. There's been a curfew imposed until the threat's over."

Aryll looks at me like he might pull a Stanton and ask to come with us, so I head him off. "Stay and let Stanton know we got here safely? Nishi will help you get settled until I'm back. I won't be long, I promise."

Nishi walks over to Aryll while I join Hysan in the hall. I offer him my hand for the traditional greeting, and he kisses my skin softly. He doesn't release my fingers as he leads me out the front door. "Wait—how are we getting there?" I ask, freezing in place for fear of his answer.

"We're not going far—we'll take one of the moving pathways."

Since I don't hear the word *cannon*, I follow him through the hedge. "What's—?"

"This way." Instead of stepping onto the wide pathway I walked down earlier, Hysan cuts to a small alley between Nishi's mansion and the adjoining one, where the road is a river of polished stone. The street looks as if it's squeezing itself through the suburb's mismatched homes in a deliberate direction that leads toward the tall buildings on the horizon.

The moment we step onto the smooth stone, it starts to move. I grip Hysan's hand tighter in surprise.

He grins at me. "High-powered Sagittarians who work together often also live near each other so they can install these moving pathways for a speedy commute. It appears Nishi's parents are pretty powerful Stargazers. Does she ever talk to you about them?"

"Nishi's better with questions than answers, especially when it comes to her family." Since I don't like talking about Mom either, that's always worked out fine for us. It's one thing Nishi and I have always agreed on—leaving the past in the past.

The day's heavy sheet of clouds has broken up, and rays of sunlight pierce through the sky like spotlights. I don't think Hysan likes revisiting his past much either, and I can see why. I sneak a glance up at him as we cross through a sunray, the light making his hair glimmer like gold. Meeting Miss Trii made his childhood seem less lonely, but it also made it sound less *child*like. Hysan didn't just grow up without parents—he had to build his own.

When our silence starts to grow noticeably long, I ask, "How's Miss Trii?"

"Same as ever. Probably a day from landing on Aeolus. She ingested a few thousand files on Risers, so when she arrives she'll be able to advise Lord Neith." The pathway moves us forward at a surprisingly clipped pace. I'm secretly relieved for the extra security of our interlocked hands.

I wait for Hysan to offer more, or to ask me a question back, but he seems to have finally run out of conversation. His brow is faintly furrowed, and his irises have faded, the way they do when he's deep in thought. Today it feels like we're both keeping secrets.

"Rho," he says gravely.

He shifts to face me, his fingers still laced with mine. "I know you need space after everything that's happened, and I've been trying to give it to you. But this distance between us is starting to feel forced."

I nod in agreement.

"I know you have a lot on your mind, but you don't have to endure it alone. If you want to talk—about *anything*—I promise I'll listen. Without judgment." Even though he doesn't say his name, I know he's talking about Mathias. But the mere thought of him sucks me back inside my shell, and my fingers fidget involuntarily inside Hysan's grasp.

He must feel my reaction, because he gently releases my hand. I'm too embarrassed to meet his gaze, so I silently stare into the colorful buildings ahead that are growing larger on our approach.

"Tell me how you're feeling," he pleads into my ear, his voice husky and soft.

My muscles clamp with discomfort. I don't know how to ask Hysan what even I don't understand: How can I still be so torn between him and Mathias when Mathias is gone forever?

"I'll take a one-word answer, if necessary." His tone is more insistent now. "Just don't abandon me here. Please, Rho."

Abandon tugs at something in my gut. It's an action I associate with Mom, yet Hysan just used it about me. I wonder if I've been wrong about that word all my life.

Mom didn't abandon us when she left home. She abandoned us long before that, by shutting us out. By never letting us get to know her.

"I'm sorry," I say at last. Stanton already compared me to Mom once this week; that's not a pathway I'm curious to explore.

"I do want to talk, it's just—I don't want to do any soul-searching right now, because it's a mess in there. Besides, I can't indulge in stuff like this right now, not with everything that's going on." As the words spill out, I hear the relief in my own voice at releasing them. "There are so many people you and I are responsible for. All I know is I have really strong feelings for you, and I've never met anyone like you, and I miss you when you're not around, but I'm not over—"

Hysan presses his mouth to mine, stopping my sentence, thoughts, heartbeat.

The Abyssthe-like effect of his lips is addictive, and once we've started kissing I can't even think of stopping. His hands hug my waist tightly, as if he's afraid to lose me. The more I give myself over to the moment, the more it seems to be stripping us of our identities, removing layer after painful layer, until every obstacle standing between us has floated away.

I feel weightless and tingly and *alive*.

When we pull apart, Hysan whispers, "I understand this changes nothing for you, my lady." Our hearts hammer in unison against our chests. "But I can't apologize, because I'm not sorry. All I can do is promise not to kiss you again."

With a flicker of his centaur smile, he adds, "Unless you ask me to."

9

I'M STILL LIGHTHEADED FROM OUR kiss when the moving pathway comes to an end at the Capital's government square, four starscrapers that look like they're facing off against each other. Each represents one of the Sagittarian planets: Interron, Millium, Gryphon, and Centaurion. The Sagittarian Guardian acts as an advisor to the government—same as on Cancer—and her offices are in the Centaurion building.

When we walk inside the structure, I feel like I've returned to the Academy on Elara—only instead of deans and instructors, the students are in charge.

Dozens of young professionals in official Stargazer uniforms bustle across the lobby, their faces buried in red holographic screens. Everyone is so distracted that nobody notices us. Unlike the Lodestar suits on Cancer, these lavender uniforms are covered in pockets packed with basic essentials so that Sagittarians are ready to travel at all times.

Sagittarius's leaders are the youngest in the Zodiac. After Stargazers complete their Zodai training, mostly in foreign Houses, they usually turn a curious eye toward home. Since they've already traveled extensively during school, they're ready to test themselves other ways, primarily politically. Even though anyone can run for office, it's rare for those over thirty to do so, since by that age a Sagittarian's interest in home begins to wane again, and she starts itching to explore the corners of the universe she has yet to see.

Wallscreens and framed holograms of celebrities who've visited the Centaurion building decorate the lobby, and prepackaged foods cover every surface—snacks for on-the-go Sagittarians. Hysan taps me on the shoulder, and we step into an elevator crammed with more Stargazers. The lift stops on what feels like every floor, but by the time we get to the higher stories, the crowd surrounding us begins to thin. Eventually, it's just Hysan and me left.

As always, he knows where he's leading us. "Is there any world you *haven't* visited?"

He grins. "The Thirteenth."

Once we reach the top floor, we walk down a long hallway filled with doors, each one featuring a digital message tablet like the ones we had in our dorm-pods at the Academy. When we get to the last room, it's already open.

Guardian Brynda sits at a round table with a dozen young diplomats arguing about strategy. I'm immediately reminded of my meetings with my Advisors on Oceon 6.

"Hysan!" Brynda springs to her feet, silencing the diplomats, who all at once turn to look at us. "'Gazers, our Knight has arrived!" she squeals, leaping up to hug him. Hysan twirls Brynda around, and when they pull away they're both radiating so much happiness that suddenly I feel sullen and self-conscious.

My handful of reunions with Hysan have all been heavy-hearted and laden with mixed signals, but somehow Brynda is able to bring out his sunlight.

"I come bearing shields," says Hysan, brandishing a stack of thin metal plates from his pocket. One of her Advisors accepts the devices while Brynda reaches up to squeeze Hysan's dimples.

"That centaur smile . . . I keep telling you, there's a Sagittarian somewhere in your bloodline." Then she turns to survey me. "And, of course, Rho."

"Hi," I say as she comes closer, examining me like I'm an item up for sale. "Nice to see you again."

"I'm sorry for the way things went down at the Plenum. It was wrong. I may think you're crazy to resist Dimples here"—she winks at Hysan—"but I think you're right about the Zodiac having to unite to defeat Ophiuchus. And whoever else is out there."

"Thanks," I say, liking her more with every frank word she speaks.

"Why don't you two hang out for a while? You can listen in and take an update back to your troop." She settles back into her seat at the head of the table, and Hysan pulls over two extra chairs. Looking at him, she says, "Your fleet of bullet-ships and these Psy shields are the best resources we've gotten from the Houses. We'll activate the shields later tonight. First we need our Stargazers to finish consulting the Psy."

"Tomorrow we're cutting off all transportation in and out of Sagittarius," says a spiky-haired Advisor, jumping in the moment Brynda pauses for breath. "Stargazers are orbiting the planet already, to alert us at the first sign of the Marad."

"Why aren't the other Houses doing more to help you?" I ask, unable to repress the question. I guess curiosity is contagious.

"No one's seeing an oncoming attack," says Brynda, shrugging. "Zodai on every House have been searching the stars. I spent all yesterday consulting the Psy myself, and I didn't see any signs of trouble either."

"They think the Marad may be faking," says the spiky-haired Advisor. "No one wants to send their own Zodai away when their House might be the true target."

A distant drumming grows louder, drowning out the sounds of voices, and I realize it's my heartbeat. Ophiuchus was right—we won't see the attack until the master decides on a target. We won't have any way of knowing which House is getting hit.

What if he's also right that it'll be Capricorn?

"Maybe no one can see the attack because it will be perpetrated with Dark Matter," suggests Hysan. "No one could foresee what happened to Cancer, Argyr, or Tethys either." He looks at me and adds, "*Almost* no one."

Every face at the table turns toward me, and I feel my cheeks heating with nerves. Hysan has a point. So either Ophiuchus is a turncoat—or he's the one leading the charge.

And I'm the only one who can see him.

The only one who can judge.

"Still, we don't know for certain that those were actual targeted strikes," says the spiky-haired Advisor, her voice lower this time, as if she's embarrassed to be so blunt before me. "Charon's character may be questionable, but scientists haven't ruled out his theory that those three disasters could have been triggered by cosmic rays from the Sufianic Clouds. Even Lord Neith's proof of a Psynergy attack on his ship can't be verified because it's the first proof of its kind anyone has seen—there's nothing to compare it to. Ambassador Sirna's claims of a Psynergy attack on Thebe were equally nebulous—the influx of Psynergy that coincided with the explosion could've been a correlation and not the source. There's simply no reliable evidence to prove Dark Matter did any of this."

Hysan's chest expands, but Brynda intervenes before he unleashes his outburst. "Whatever the stars are saying, we can't risk the attack, so we're taking it seriously. As Hysan just reminded us, human Sight isn't star-proof. We're stationing our Stargazers all over the Capital. We've already evacuated most of downtown, but we left your friends alone since they're staying to fight."

From her Tracker, she beams a diagram of the city, like the one Deke showed us earlier, only this one is blanketed with so many extra layers that it would take weeks to review them all. Brynda's Advisors run us through their lead theories on how the Marad might strike, but they have such a surplus of schematics and projections that it takes hours to get through them all.

Their overwhelming curiosity makes it easy for Sagittarians to brainstorm possibilities and look at situations from multiple perspectives, so they seem to have thought through every single potential outcome. What they're missing are the Arieans' military grasp, and the Scorps' advanced weaponry, and the Capricorns' patience for planning, and the Taurians' diligent teamwork, and so on. The Marad have those strengths because the army is made up of all the Houses. They'll have the advantage.

"Rho, have you consulted the Psy since the armada?" asks Brynda. Her spiky-haired Advisor turns to me as though this is the point she'd been hoping Brynda would press. It reminds me that the last time the universe heard from me, I was too afraid of the boogeyman to open an Ephemeris or wear my Ring.

"I have."

I watch the effect of these two short words ripple down the table, and to my bewilderment, everyone is suddenly alert and focused on me again.

"Have you seen anything in the stars about the Marad's attack?" asks Brynda.

"I've seen a steep imbalance in our galaxy, and that a war is coming"— their downcast eyes tell me they've seen that, too—"but nothing clear on Sagittarius."

I don't bring up Ophiuchus because I have nothing real to offer her about him. Every time I interfere with governance, people pay with their lives. I won't make that mistake again.

"I can look again tonight," I offer.

"Thank you, Rho."

When I attended these kinds of meetings before, my participation was met with condescension, impatience, and disinterest. I was more symbol than person. But in this room, I can feel the curious eyes watching me with wonder, as if they're genuinely interested in my insights. And for a moment I catch a glimpse of what it would feel like to be vindicated in the eyes of the Zodiac—and I realize how much I want it.

"Lady Brynda, Rho and I should go before it gets darker out," says Hysan, rising to his feet. "Do you need any assistance with the shields before we leave?"

A lanky male Advisor turns to him with questions, and Brynda walks me out. "Hysan does have exquisite taste," she says when we get to the hallway. She wraps me in a hug and says into my ear, "You know he's in love with you, right? That's the only reason I haven't hit on you myself."

My chin drops, and my cheeks flare red. Thank Helios she can't see my face.

"But in the future," she says before pulling away, "if you should ever develop any curiosities you'd like to satisfy . . ."

She doesn't finish her thought; she merely winks as she walks over to Hysan, who's just stepped out of her office. As he and I head into the elevator, my face is still afire with flattered flames.

✦ ✦ ✦

By the time we make it to Nishi's, it's already curfew. The Sagittarians have been training all day, and Nishi and Deke gather them in the sitting area with its circle of creamy couches so Hysan and I can report what we learned from Brynda. Afterward, Deke brings out trays of the mushroom sushi he invented on Gemini, and a pleasant atmosphere falls over the house as we eat and chat and wonder.

Nishi and I are sharing a love seat in a corner of the room, catching each other up on our days. "How was being alone with Hysan?" she asks.

My eyes automatically find him at the other end of the room, flirting with a group of Sagittarian girls, Ezra and Gyzer glued to his sides. They glommed onto him during dinner and haven't stopped peppering him with questions all night. Gyzer's are mainly philosophical, and Ezra's all practical—apparently, like Hysan, she likes to invent things.

"Hard," I admit. "My guilt over Mathias had been a strong enough barrier until now. It's kept me from having to dig too deep into my feelings for Hysan. But today . . . we . . ."

Nishi's eyes gleam with impatient curiosity. "You *did* say he was an incredible kisser. . . ."

A smile breaks through my expression, pulled to the surface by the memory of that kiss. "But I still don't know what I want, Nish," I say, pushing back down on my feelings. "I mean, even if . . . we're just so *different*. Before, we could have died at any moment—every aspect of life, every emotion, was so heightened that we grew close really, *really* fast—but we still know so little about each other."

I look to him again, noticing how comfortable he seems, engaging and entertaining new people. Unlike Mathias, who would be sitting beside me all night, Hysan likes to work his way around a room.

Dating Hysan wouldn't be like having a Cancrian boyfriend, who would be quiet, committed, devoted. Hysan likes his freedom. He even told me so himself the day we discovered he was Libra's true Guardian. He said he uses Neith because he doesn't like to be *tied down*.

"Rho . . . you love him. You're just afraid of giving in to something so big. I'm sorry, but it's true," she says, reacting to my glare. "It's like you're here, but you're not *here* here. You've had this wall up since last month . . . and it makes you unreachable."

Even as I flinch from her words, I know she's right. Stanton broke through his shell, but I've yet to puncture mine. Dad's and Mathias's deaths are too fresh, and I still can't forgive myself for the part I played in them.

If I'd refused the Guardianship and gone straight to find Stanton and Dad, Mathias might be alive. Dad, too. Along with everyone from the armada.

"I'm not a leader, Nish. I know what you want me to do here, but I can't. I only came to look out for you and Deke. Your faith in me during Ophiuchus's attacks got me through my worst defeats—I owe you too much gold for this friendship to be a fair trade, and I'm here to start repaying my debt."

"I love you, Rho," says Nishi, resting a hand on my shoulder. "But you're wrong."

My Wave buzzes in my pocket, and Nishi goes to check on Deke while I head into the quiet foyer to talk. When I snap the golden clamshell open, Stanton's hologram beams out. "Hey, hero. How's the war effort?"

"Unclear." I nestle into a window seat overlooking the front garden. "How's the rescue effort?"

His hologram hovers beside me. "Bunch of Sagittarians arrived seeking refuge. Ferez put them up in rooms at our hotel."

"Who are you hanging out with now that Aryll and I are gone?"

"Jewel, mostly."

I smile. At least one person is happier for our separation. Jewel is too shy to talk to Stanton in front of others, and he's too oblivious to realize she's in love with him, so maybe now that they're alone they'll finally get the chance to connect.

"Aryll doing okay?" he asks.

"He spent all dinner chatting with two cute Sagittarian sisters. I was going to go over and talk to him, but I figured he'd like me better if I didn't."

"I've taught you well."

"Stan . . . I'm worried. Zodai can't predict where the next attack is going to happen. What if Ochus is right?"

Stanton stares at me tenderly. "Rho, *all* the Houses are in just as much danger—Sagittarius probably most of all."

I shake my head, annoyed. "Please don't stay on Capricorn."

"Have you always been such a worrier?" My brother grins at me. "What did Mom used to say when we worried about something that hadn't even happened yet?"

The memory emerges before I can stifle it, and I recite, "*If you choose to live in yesterday or tomorrow, you'll miss out on today.*"

"*The present's a present,*" adds Stanton, quoting a line from a children's holoshow we used to watch. I smile back, thinking to myself, *But tomorrow would be an even greater gift.*

✦ ✦ ✦

When we disconnect, I don't rejoin the group. Instead, I wander into the mansion's shadows.

Nishi wrote the name of each room's guest on their door with an erasable paint Deke's family used to produce. I'm one of the few people without a roommate. I stare at my name above the door handle, the letters a blend of blues drawn in Nishi's curlicue lettering.

"You look troubled, my lady."

I see Hysan's outline, moving toward me in the semidarkness. "Is there anything I can do?"

I lean against the door and dig deep for any way to keep myself from swinging it open and inviting him in. "I . . . I saw Ophiuchus in my Ephemeris before coming here."

Hysan's eyes widen, and I tell him everything Ophiuchus told me. His brow burrows down as I speak, his clever mind probably already sorting through meanings and possibilities and ramifications. When he meets my gaze again, his eyes are distant, still working through the problem.

"I'll consult my reading room on Libra and see if there are any new portents for the Houses, particularly Capricorn. I suggest you read your Ephemeris again, too. The Psy shields will be fully activated within a few hours, so we only have tonight."

"Good idea."

We fall silent, the same forced quiet that slinked its way between us on Capricorn and has entombed us ever since. It's a heavy hush, weighted down with unspoken feelings and inappropriate thoughts, and I know if he kissed me now I wouldn't stop him.

Only he won't do it unless I ask, and I won't ask because I can't.

"I'm only a few doors down," he says. "If you need anything." He leaves looking troubled, and I slip into my room wishing he were still with me.

When I've washed my face and changed into bed clothing, I flip off the lights and switch on Guardian Matador's stone. A twinkling carousel of colors drowns the darkness, and I see the universe rendered in much more detail than with my Wave's tutorial Ephemeris, though not as vast and all-encompassing as the black opal shows.

Once I'm Centered, the spectral map expands until its light reaches every corner of the room. I tune into the innermost beat of the Zodiac, trying to read what's coming for us.

The fire Houses—Aries, Sagittarius, Leo—are still flaming brighter than the others, as they have been for weeks, heralding the coming war. But I don't sense anything beyond that. I search for Ophiuchus. If he's truly switched sides and wants to gain my trust, he should be eager to talk to me again. But, somehow, I feel disconnected from the deeper Psy.

My first thought is that the shield has gone up, but it can't have—I'm still attuned to the Psynergy feeding my presence here. Maybe it's this new Ephemeris. I switch to my Wave's tutorial version instead, but I still can't See. I'm blocked.

Everything feels wrong.

Sagittarius is about to be attacked, and we're its best line of defense. No one's coming to help, and that's my fault for deepening the dividing lines between the Houses. Sirna and Mathias tried to warn me, but I wouldn't listen. I had a chance to unite the galaxy, and I wasted it on my obsessive pursuit of the Thirteenth Guardian when I could have made a real and lasting difference in our world.

I pull on a robe and wander the black halls of the mansion to work off my frustration. The moons' light pools on the floor, illuminating my path. In the distance, red holographic beams flicker like flames; moving closer, I spot several Sagittarians spread out in a reading room reviewing holographic texts. In the entrance hall I come across more Sagittarians sleepily going through the motions of Yarrot. Ezra and another girl are in a kitchen examining one of Hysan's Veils while picking through leftover sushi.

Even though it's the dead of night, there's a restless energy bouncing in the air, keeping sleep away. By now I can identify the feeling as the brewing of fear and adrenaline that precedes battle, intensified by the Sagittarians' curiosity about what it will be like to fight.

On my way back to bed, I stop by Hysan's door. Like me, he's rooming alone, and more than anything, I ache to step inside and into his arms.

But I don't.

10

I DON'T FALL ASLEEP UNTIL early morning, so I miss the day's first meeting. As soon as I wake, I peek through the wide windows into the garden, where the Sagittarians have gathered for target practice. They're using the pistols Hysan supplied. When they fire, all the Archers hit their marks.

This guest room is easily the biggest, most luxurious place I've ever stayed in. The canopy bed is double the size of even the one from the Libran embassy, and there are two closets—one for clothes, the second for shoes. Beside the bed is a controller with a button for *everything*: opening or darkening the windows, a holographic feed of every room of the house, adjusting the temperature of the stone floor to make it toasty or cool, and more.

I should be checking in with the group instead of admiring the room's quirks, but I'm not ready. I don't know how to face everyone when I can't contribute what's supposed to be my best skill. I can't see what's coming tomorrow.

Looking for some inspiration, I grab my Wave and beam Ferez's holographic report, picking up Vecily's story after Datsby was sent away.

The second moment that unearthed to me Vecily's sense of purpose in joining the Axis is one very few people know about. It revealed itself to me when I was in the Zodiax transferring outdated memories to the newer Snow Globe technology, and I found a Taurian recording that I believe to have been deliberately misfiled centuries ago. The memory is as follows.

Vecily was nineteen and only a few months into her Guardianship. She was performing her nightly readings when she saw an omen so great, she couldn't wait until morning to tell her cabinet, so she awoke her Guide and had him assemble her Advisors. "The Zodiac's unity is tainted," she told them, then revealed the rest of the omen. She had seen that, long ago, one Guardian had deceived all the others in an act of unprecedented treason. Until this deception was brought to light, she said, there would be no true trust among the Houses.

Vecily asked her Advisors to create a Zodai task force to surreptitiously investigate the past Guardians and discover the snake in their ranks. Yet their readings revealed nothing, and, furthermore, her council despised the idea of stirring up controversy when relations between the Houses were growing more fragile every day. Eventually, they disbanded and persuaded Vecily away from her plans.

As a Taurian, Vecily had been brought up to follow rules and respect her elders, even if she was the Guardian and they her Advisors, so she never argued or mentioned the omen again. Yet, as I am about to demonstrate by recounting a third crucial moment in Vecily's life, I have reason to believe she never stopped seeing it.

I reread the blue text a few times. Though she didn't know it, Vecily saw Ophiuchus. She foresaw his threat a millennium before I did—and no one believed her either. Even worse, the people of her House hid her vision, stashed it away as if it was something shameful.

How many other Guardians through history have seen Ophiuchus only to be thwarted from revealing his treachery by their own people? I've come the furthest—at least I managed to convince the universe for a whole galactic minute. But just as it was done to Vecily before me, those in power drowned out my warnings.

I let myself think of Mom for the first time in a while, specifically her Ochus tale about the Guardians who were too afraid to believe in their fears. I had to become Holy Mother to learn a truth she taught me a decade ago with a children's story: Those in power are so afraid of losing it, they will do anything to keep the world under their control. Even when "anything" means ignoring dangerous truths that threaten to grow more powerful the longer they're unaddressed.

I glimpse out the window. Gyzer is running his students through Yarrot training. It's what Mathias would be doing if he were here. The thought is a knife stabbing my heart, and I look away.

My luggage is on the polished stone dressing table, and lined up next to it are my most prized possessions: my Wave, a parting gift from Dad when I moved to Elara; Mathias's mother-of-pearl Astralator; Vecily's Ephemeris; Hysan's turquoise crab-shaped Psy shield; and the four silver moons from the suit the sisters made me. I touch the pink pearl on my chest that was a gift from Sirna, then pad over and search the pockets of my Lodestar suit for the galactic gold coin from Nova, adding it to my collection on the dresser.

Tokens of trust.

The phrase enters my mind unbidden, and I consider what it means. The people who gave me these items each did so because they believe in me and wanted to contribute proof of that trust—proof that I can touch. It's something Vecily didn't have. *These are my true Talismans.*

"Rho?" calls Nishi from outside the door.

"Come in, Nish."

She bursts inside wearing a Cancrian blue suit that looks like our Acolyte uniforms, the ones we lost on Elara. Only instead of *House Cancer*, the tunic says *House Helios*—a nod to the ancient expression *Houses of Helios*. In addition to the Crab crest, there's the Archer, the Lion, the Scorpion, the Triple Virgin, the Seagoat, the Ram, the Water Bearer, the Double, the Fish, the Bull, and the Scales of Justice.

My throat closes as I think of the bloodied flags from Sage Huxler's Trinary Axis recollections.

"Guardian Brynda," starts Nishi, breathless, "wants everyone who's fighting to report now." In her hands, she's holding a suit just like hers. "I had only a couple of these made. I understand if you prefer to wear your Lodestar suit," she says as she sets it down on my dresser, beside my Talismans, "but I wanted you to have the option."

"Thanks," I say, and as she leaves, I inspect the twelve colorful crests. This time, my mind flashes to a different Capricorn Guardian. I think of Sage Ferez and his collection of devices from every House. Maybe a millennium apart has been enough, and now it's time for the Zodiac to come together.

I change into Nishi's new suit and meet everyone in the creamy Ievian sitting area. The students are a sea of lavender, with a smattering of blue and a spot of gold.

"Morning," says Aryll. He's wearing blue like me, but his suit is like Stanton's—one of the Lodestar uniforms they handed out to survivors on the Geminin settlement. When he notices the added symbols on my tunic, his eyebrows draw together, as if in disappointment. His hardcore devotion to Cancer reminds me of my brother. "Did you talk to Stanton last night?"

"I did. How are you doing?"

He shrugs, and I catch his gaze straying to those Sagittarian sisters. "Better than on Capricorn."

"I see." I smile at him, and his blush is concealed by his already sun-burned skin. He's as red as a hookcrab's shell.

Nishi and Deke are at the front of the room with Hysan, and when she sees I've donned her outfit, she smiles. "I count everyone," I hear her tell him. In his golden Knight suit, Hysan looks like hope personified.

He says something to Nishi, and she nods and gazes out at all of us. "Tomorrow is the Marad's deadline. Guardian Brynda wants everyone to convene to discuss final plans. Let's stay together and move quickly."

We file out, and I fall back toward the tail end of the group, still not ready to reveal my failure. We take the same moving pathway, swiftly wind-ing through the clashing colors of our Sagittarian surroundings, but when we reach the government square we pass the four starscrapers and cut onto a new pathway. Hysan hangs back to join me, leaving Nishi and Deke in the lead. "Morning, my lady. Did you See?"

"Nothing," I say quickly. Then I realize he said *sleep*, not *See*. "Oh, I mean . . . yes, some."

"I didn't See anything either." Up close, he looks just as worried as he did last night. We don't say anything else, and soon the busy structures sur-rounding us melt into a sweeping Gemstone Park that stretches far into the flickering horizon. The vast plaza is a sparkling expanse of stones, glinting in elaborate patterns and brilliant hues.

Gathered on the rolling landscape is a crowd of Stargazers huddled beneath the floating hologram of an Archer. Looming behind them are six very different-looking ships, each waving its own holographic flag: the yellow Scales of Justice, the blue Crab, the orange Double, the brown Seagoat, the green Triple Virgin, and the silver Fish.

Other Houses came.

In the ships' shadows, dozens of Zodai gather in groups. The leaders of each delegation stand apart from the crowd, conferring with Brynda and her Advisors. When Brynda spots Hysan and me, she calls us over, and the rest of our troop joins the Stargazers.

As we approach, my mouth turns to sandpaper. What will I say when she asks what I read in the stars last night?

Suddenly I feel a pair of small hands clasp around my waist, and I look down to see a startlingly pretty girl with skin as pale as the inside of a cantaloupe and deep, tunnel-like eyes.

"Rubi!"

"How exciting it is to be part of the encore," she says with a big, youthful smile. "Let's hope we survive again!"

Looking closer, I notice she's not the same childlike mischief-maker from a few weeks ago—she's aged. Her expression is weary, and there are faint lines beneath her eyes. It seems that ever since Caasy died, Rubi's years have been catching up with her.

Even though Gemini is ruled in pairs, Caasy remains Guardian in spirit, and his reign doesn't end until his Twin's does.

While it's jarring to see Rubi looking so downtrodden, my mood lifts at the sight of her. I survey the other House leaders, and they stare at me with wide eyes. As I look into their faces, I'm paralyzed with dread. I was expecting Zodai. Military leaders. *Adults.*

Not teenagers.

I look to Hysan in alarm, but he's not surprised or upset.

"Hysan, you've been holding out on us," says Brynda, sounding absolutely thrilled by his deception. "Thank Helios you warned us this morning; otherwise our Stargazers would have shot their ships down," she adds with a laugh, as our new allies look on in horror.

Hysan turns to me and explains. "These are students I know from my travels, and they wanted to be part of the fight. I didn't tell you about them because I didn't want to risk giving our plan away to any potential Marad spies. They came on their own chartered planes. They're not here as representatives from their governments. They're here as private citizens, of their own accord."

The dead bodies from Sage Huxler's memories continue to grow more pronounced in my mind, along with the panic that's been brewing in my belly all morning. "Excuse us," I say, pulling Hysan aside to speak privately. Though not invited, Rubi happily tags along with us.

"How'd you convince these people to come?" I ask when we're out of earshot.

"I didn't have to convince them, Rho," he says, clearly surprised by my question. "All I had to say was that you would probably be leading the charge."

"For Helios's sake, why do you think I came?" interjects Rubi.

"Right, because things went so well the last time I led us into battle," I snap at them.

"Rho . . . you don't get it." Hysan steps up to me so that I'm forced to focus on his face. "The Plenum is yesterday; these students are tomorrow— and they're here because they believe in your vision for the Zodiac. Today is our chance to unite our universe, and it starts with them."

"Hysan, I had my chance. I'm responsible for enough deaths. The armada is known as mine, and what happened to it will be my fault forever. . . ." Thoughts of the Trinary Axis crowd my mind, and I shake my head to clear it. Everyone here wants me to lead, but I seem to be the only one who doesn't know where I'm going.

"You're the one who doesn't get it," I say, my sudden anger surprising even me. "Cancer is already responsible for the Axis, and a thousand years haven't been long enough for us to move past that guilt. Thanks to me, we're now going down for the armada, and if anyone ever found out I broke the Tab—"

I stop speaking, not just because Rubi's listening, but because of Hysan's face. It appears that I just confirmed something for him, something he suspected—and he looks hurt.

"I'm sorry," I say, no longer even sure what I'm apologizing for. "I can't make Cancer the face of another war."

"It's a little late for that," says Rubi, pointing to the sky.

I squint as my gaze follows her finger to a holographic image that looks like the serpent from the old Ophiuchus glyph . . . only there's something else there. A girl is wrangling the snake into submission, and she looks a lot like—

"Rho!"

Aryll runs over, pointing at the moving image overhead. The snake writhes and struggles against the girl's powerful hold. "You're in the sky!"

"What is that?" I ask.

"A glyph. It's the sign brandished by your supporters, and it's been popping up everywhere," says Brynda, joining us. "I'm surprised you didn't see it stamped on the walls of the Capital. It's you kicking Ophiuchus's ass. Now, can we please get back to the meeting, and can you save your personal dramas for when we're not at war?"

Aryll sticks by me as we rejoin the others—I can see Stanton written all over this gesture—and Hysan looks disgruntled about it. The crew leaders from each House introduce themselves and exchange the hand touch with me.

"I'm Candela Snowe," says the Cancrian. She has crunchy curls and a heart-shaped face.

"Thank you so much for coming, Candela." We bump fists—and then I notice she's wearing a Zodai University uniform.

"I was also on Elara when we were attacked," she says quietly, seeing where my eyes have strayed. "The ship I boarded landed on Oceon 4, and by the time I got to Oceon 6, you had already taken off for Gemini.

I watched you on the newsfeeds addressing the Plenum after Virgo was attacked, and I can't agree with you more—we have to unite to survive."

"Thank you," I repeat, and we bump fists again.

The olive-skinned Virgo touches hands with me next, introducing himself as Twain. He has windswept auburn hair and, like all Virgos, eyes the color of moss. "Thank you for staying with Empress Moira when she was wounded," he says, bowing and touching his heart in the Virgo sign of friendship. I mimic the gesture. "You must be a rare talent to have detected Dark Matter in the Psy when our Empress did not."

His words remind me of how useless I am to them now, so I don't say anything. "I'm sorry," he goes on, filling the silence. "I know we Virgos aren't exactly beloved. We hide behind mirage walls and rarely interact with the other Houses. I can see how we might not come off as the friendliest. But my friends and I came because we believe our isolationism isn't right anymore, and the attack on our House proves it."

He smirks, and it suddenly strikes me that he's handsome. "Alone, we're not perfect, but together, we can be."

The openness and sincerity in his mossy gaze somehow pierces past my shell to the real me—perhaps the effect of a Virgo admitting fault, a rare occurrence in our galaxy. Nishi was right: Only part of me came to join the fight on Sagittarius. The other part hasn't woken up yet.

"Well, you're here now," I say, to both of us. "When Cancer was attacked, Empress Moira sent us twelve ships of grain. We haven't forgotten Virgo's generosity."

Before Twain can say more, a Geminin girl with lustrous tawny skin sticks her hand out to touch mine. "I'm Imogen." Her elaborately choreographed greeting involves a long sequence of knocking knuckles, bumping elbows, and slapping hands.

"What you did was so brave." Unlike her House's artificially youthful centenarians, teenage Imogen seems to ooze sexuality, from her pouty red lips to her curve-hugging suit to her high, spindly heels.

"Thanks—and thanks for coming."

"I believed you from the start, you know." Her copper-flecked eyes sparkle in the light, like the gemstones we're standing on. "I mean, even the most imaginative Dreamcaster couldn't have devised an immortal Thirteenth Guardian carved from ice who attacks through the Psy. No offense."

"None taken," I say, nearly grinning.

"You knew the Plenum would laugh at your tale, but you stuck with it. That takes more than Aerian bravery or Leonine passion . . . it takes Cancrian heart."

I give her a hug because there are no words.

Once I've met the Capricorn, Libran, and Piscene leaders, Brynda quiets the group and gives us our orders.

"This is how we're breaking things down. Capricorn, Libra, and Virgo will study strategy with me to see if we've missed anything. Cancer, Sagittarius, and Gemini will train for combat with our Stargazers. Pisces will focus on reading the stars' forecast for tomorrow. We're lifting the Psy shield over this sector of the Capital for a few hours. We'll work in the Centaurion building."

While the captains update their crews, Rubi takes my arm and strolls me away from the noise and activity. "So. How are you, Rho?"

"I saw Ophiuchus again," I say. Since Rubi believes in Ophiuchus, I know she's a good person to consult. "He claims he's turned against his master, and to prove it he said the Marad is going to attack Capricorn, not Sagittarius. I don't know whether to trust him and warn Capricorn, or treat him just like the liar and butcher I know him to be."

"A few months ago, you saw an impossible vision in your Ephemeris, and you fought against me and every other Guardian in our galaxy to reveal it—and now you're asking for *advice*?" Her eyes are so deep and dark they almost look like Ochus's black holes. "Rho, you're looking outward for answers you'll only find within. To learn the truth about Ophiuchus, you have to find your voice again."

I sigh. "And how do I do that, Rubi?"

"What the Helios did they teach you kids at the Academy? All holograms and no common sense!"

She gestures to the students surrounding us, as if the answer couldn't be more obvious. "Look around you: These people heard your voice and committed their lives to your cause. You start right here, with them. Visit with the crews. You'll give them confidence—and if you let yourself believe that, you might even catch some yourself."

11

EACH GROUP MEETS IN ITS designated area of the Centaurion building and grounds. While the Stargazers train their troops outdoors, Brynda's
Advisors meet with the teams from Libra, Virgo, and Capricorn in her
office, and I join the Piscenes in Brynda's reading room, where we'll access
the astral plane.

The silver-veiled students gather around the lights, and a charge fills the
air as we tap into our Centers and activate the Psynergy surrounding us.
The Piscenes hold out their Astralators to take measurements, and one by
one their bodies fold down to the floor to work out the math. They look like
puddles of silver gleaming in the dappled dark.

Only I remain standing.

Mom once told me that Piscenes, who only travel beyond their House
when they're on altruistic missions, wrap themselves in fabrics of woven
silver because they believe that, in order to be truly selfless, one must not
show off one's self. Beneath the veils, Piscenes of both genders have delicate, feminine features with small frames and statures.

It's easy to Center myself in this crowd, with so much Psynergy buzzing in the air. As the balls of light around me ascend and decline, I focus my read on the Archer constellation. I dig down into my deepest depths and reach into the Psy for a glimpse of tomorrow, focusing so hard that a headache blossoms, but nothing else happens. I still can't access the stars' secrets.

When the sharp pain in my frontal lobe grows too strong to ignore, I pull away from the lights of House Sagittarius. I don't know how long I was staring—could have been seconds, minutes, hours. I bury my burning eyes in my hands, massaging my forehead until the worst of the effects pass. When I open my eyelids, twenty Piscene faces are looking up from their math at me.

"What do you See?" whispers Hexel, the leader.

I don't answer.

"You can tell us. We won't turn on you," she assures me. "We believe you."

I shake my head and whisper, "Nothing."

"*Please.* Trust us. Whatever it is, we can handle it."

"No, that's what I saw," I say, a little louder this time. "*Nothing.*" I drop my gaze to the floor, feeling powerless and angry and betrayed by the stars. I'm a complete fraud for even being here. Rubi said my mere presence would inspire confidence, but these students risked their lives to follow a true seer, and now they'll know they've been duped.

I'm supposed to be better than this—the stars *said so,* they *chose* me to be Guardian. So why are they punishing me this way?

"Well . . . you have been through a lot."

I glance up. Rather than angry or hurt, Hexel looks sympathetic, and her voice is gentle.

"What . . . what does that have to do with my reads?" I ask, sitting down among them.

"Everything," she says, sounding every bit like the spiritual being she is. "Piscenes are taught that our reads come from our souls. The more honest we are with ourselves, the more we can See. When your life was smaller, it was probably easier to see concepts clearly, as either black or white. But everything you've lived through has confused your inner compass. And when your own vision of yourself becomes unclear, your Sight suffers."

"How am I supposed to fix that?" I'm embarrassed by how fragile I sound, when not so long ago I felt I was strong enough to take on the whole Zodiac.

"By being honest," says a guy named Jox. "If you face the things you're avoiding instead of putting up more walls, you'll find yourself again."

I think of who I became the last time I led others. I was blind, stubborn, careless—and people who didn't deserve it paid a far worse price for my decisions. "What if I don't like who I find?"

"You'll like her because we like her," Jox says kindly. "Enough to give our lives for her."

I smile at him gratefully and think of my trust Talismans, and Vecily's story, and what Nishi, Hysan, Rubi, and now the Piscenes have said. And it all boils down to the same conclusion: If I'm going to help the Zodiac, I need to come out from this shell. I need to forgive myself for Dad's and Mathias's deaths. And then I need to let them go.

Brynda's spiky-haired Advisor walks in carrying a tray of spongy-looking cakes, and the hungry Piscenes leap up to sample the sweets. I use the distraction of food to slip out. The reading room is on the ground floor, and I cross the lobby, busy with government workers, to the training zone behind the building. This time, the harried Stargazers know who I am and pay curious attention as I walk past them.

Outside, Sagittarians, Cancrians, and Geminin are learning how to handle an Arclight, the Ninth House's signature weapon. It shoots out bullets that burst into flames on contact. Every Stargazer has the metallic device implanted into his or her Tracker, and now these new troops have them on their wrists as well.

"Third House!" shouts a Stargazer. He's calling the students up in teams to practice hitting human-sized holographic targets.

The Geminin group lines up. About half of them hit near or on their marks; the other half miss theirs completely. The Cancrians are next. They're all wearing blue university suits—like Candela, Nishi, Deke, and myself, they're survivors of the attack on Elara. When they fire, only Aryll comes close to grazing his target, but none of the bullets connect. We're not natural fighters—not by far.

Deke takes his turn with Nishi and the Sagittarians. Before the attack on Cancer, Deke's devotion to the Cancrian way of life was as ardent as Stanton's and Aryll's. But now he's living on Sagittarius, in love with a Sagittarian, and wearing a House Helios suit—only instead of being sad because our House is losing him, I feel proud of his courage. He's changing the norm by breaking it.

Every person in the Sagittarian group hits their mark—even Deke. Nishi's been training him. But Ezra and Gyzer are easily the best shots of them all. Even the Stargazers look impressed by their marksmanship. They call a five-minute break, and as everyone disperses, they pull Gyzer and Ezra aside, no doubt to discuss their Zodai ambitions.

Nishi, Deke, and Candela run up to me. "How were the Piscenes?" asks Deke, taking a swig from his water canteen. "You show them what a real seer looks like?"

"No, actually . . . they showed me."

"You look different," says Nishi, scrutinizing my face. "More . . . *aware*. Did they make you drink one of their Piscene tonics, Kappa what's-it-called?"

I laugh, and then the spiky-haired Advisor bounces into the training space with another platter of cakes. Deke grabs Nishi's hand, mumbles something that sounds like "food first," and together they join the stampede toward the Advisor, whose face is growing increasingly alarmed at the oncoming rush.

Candela hangs back with me. "I'm sorry Cancer didn't stand with you," she says, her curls pulled up in a puff atop her head. "Ambassador Sirna should have been as brave as you."

"She did what she had to do to save me from worse. Don't judge her harshly—she was actually helping me." Just beyond Candela, I watch Deke raise Nishi onto his shoulders so she can reach over the crowd for cakes.

"Then if you're not upset with our House, why are you avoiding us?"

"I'm not avoiding anyone," I say, focusing back on her heart-shaped face. "I'm just doing what the Plenum wants and staying away from politics . . . and keeping to myself."

"Forget politics," snaps Candela, her voice full of fight. "We need *leadership*."

In her sea-colored eyes, I see the same idealism and hope that sent me all over the Zodiac. The belief that I could change worlds. "I once thought leadership could exist without politics, too. But that's just not the way it works, Candela. I'm proof of that."

"Then change the way it works!" she says fiercely. "Otherwise, *why the Helios are we here?*"

"Break's over!" shouts one of the Stargazers. Candela bows at me stiffly, then walks away and joins the Cancrians, who are lining up in front of their targets. I'm happy to be spared from having to respond to Candela's accusation, but I can't escape the truth of her words. I asked for the Zodiac's support, and when the Plenum turned its back on me, I turned my back on the Zodiac.

I'm guilty of the same crime as the ambassadors: I put my pride ahead of what's best for my people.

✦ ✦ ✦

I leave the training area and head up the elevator to the building's top floor. Brynda's door is open, and she and Hysan are in the front of the room projecting holograms, while the Libran, Capricorn, and Virgo students sprawl across the floor on pillows and take notes.

Hysan's face lights up when he sees me. "My lady. Welcome."

Students straighten and stare as I thread through them. Twain springs to his feet and offers me his spot on a plush pillow, but I smile and shake my head, joining Hysan and Brynda instead. Hysan frowns at the Virgo.

"You're just in time to see our new attack scenario," says Brynda brightly. "Stargazer reads project this one at seventy-two percent probability. It involves the Marad striking our Abyssthe factories. Our whole economy depends on them, so if they really want to bring us down, they'd be a good place to hit."

The Virgos are the first to jump in and offer feedback.

"Have you stationed Stargazers there?"

"Have your Zodai completed focused reads in the Psy for the future of those factories?"

"Have you presented this scenario to Zodai from other Houses, to compare it with what they've seen?"

Brynda answers yes to all three questions, but soon there are three more and then another three, and so on. Like Sagittarians, Virgos prefer a spitfire questioning approach for solving problems—but where the former use curiosity as fuel for their inquiries, Virgos use their pragmatism.

Once the Virgos have exhausted themselves, the Librans begin offering their feedback. "Have you contacted the factory managers to see if they've noticed strange behavior among their employees, in case the Marad have been working with people on the inside?" asks blond-haired Numen, whom I met at the park. She's in charge of the Libran crew.

Instead of examining the plan under a microscope—like the Virgos— the Librans seem to take a wide step back so they can assess the full picture—along with its framing and the wall it's hanging on—before speaking. The Capricorns haven't contributed yet because most are consulting the holographic data they're screening from their Sensethysers. They're reviewing information from the Zodiax, searching for stored wisdom that might apply to this latest scenario. A few of the Librans are intrigued by the Capricorns' texts and are leaning over to read along with them.

Numen turns to me suddenly and flashes me a charming smile. "But we have a first-rate fortune-teller right in this room! What have you seen in your reads, Lady Rho?"

Hearing my name makes me feel suddenly and fully *here*, as if I've been yanked from my slow awakening into complete consciousness. And I hear myself say, *"I've seen a warning for Capricorn."*

I freeze in shock at my own words, my eyes locked on the brown-suited students. Speaking up now might be a mistake, but instinct compelled me to do it.

I remember this feeling.

"I don't know if the source of this omen is reliable," I caution everyone, breaking the resounding silence. "But I think we should warn Sage Ferez, just in case. Tierre might be the Marad's true target."

Brynda nods and flicks on her Tracker to send the message. She doesn't doubt me or ask follow-up questions or consult her Advisors. She just trusts.

It's Brynda's reaction more than anything else that makes me realize I'm not weak and broken. The Plenum just wants me to *feel* like I am.

Vecily's experience proves the same thing that mine has: Change will not start at the top. As Hysan said, it starts right here, with these students . . . *my army*. My Sight on its own won't make a difference, but coupled with believers, it just might. My voice is my weapon—and its reach is the true power I wield.

It all comes down to what Hysan said just a few hours ago, about the very reason the Plenum fears me even now. The ambassadors control the agenda today, but we will control it tomorrow.

Suddenly Brynda's spiky-haired Advisor bursts into the office and turns on the largest wallscreen, which broadcasts images of a massive explosion that happened moments ago.

My trust in myself came too late.

The Marad has struck Capricorn.

12

THE EXPLOSION ON TIERRE WAS close to our Cancrian settlement, and now I can't get in touch with Stanton on his Wave. This nightmare feels too frighteningly familiar.

The Psy shield isn't down yet, but I'm testing my Ring compulsively. Brynda said she'd deactivate the shields, so access to the Psy could return at any moment. I *need* to know Stan's okay . . . after everything we've survived, he has to make it through this.

The Marad duped us all. Everything they said was a lie—the deadline, the target, the mission. They did exactly what Ophiuchus said they would: tricked the masses by faking left and going right, leaving Sagittarius evacuated and locked down, while Capricorn was overcrowded and vulnerable.

I knew. I knew, and I didn't say anything.

Ferez trusted me, and this is how I repaid his faith. Hundreds of Capricorns are dead—an estimate that keeps rising—and a wing of the Zodiax was obliterated. If I'd spoken up, they could have taken precautions. Ferez could have searched the stars for a sign of the threat. Chroniclers could have more intensely monitored travel in and out of Tierre.

But I stayed silent. Just like I didn't mention the threat to Thebe. Or the bubbles in the water before the Maw attacked Stanton.

He has to be alive.

At the Centaurion building, every student, Advisor, and Stargazer crowds the dining hall—the largest gathering place—our eyes glued to the massive wallscreen. There's a gaping crater in Verity's earth, exposing not sedimentary rock but broken layers of the Zodiax.

When we disband, leaving the officials to bring Sagittarius back online, the Capricorns and Piscenes take off almost immediately to Tierre to help. The other Houses haven't decided what they're doing yet.

I return to Nishi's house with the Sagittarians and lock myself up in my room, waiting to hear from Stanton and for the Psy shield to come down. Hysan promised to fly Aryll and me to Capricorn first thing in the morning, but until then, only one being knows what's coming for the Zodiac. And while he's the last face I want to see, I have to find him.

Now that he's been proven right, Ophiuchus will be furious I didn't believe him. Maybe he even returned to the master after I refused to join him—or maybe he knew I wouldn't believe him all along, and his warning was just part of a plan to gain my trust so he can set me up for something worse.

Maybe Aryll is right, and Ophiuchus and the master are one and the same. He could have sent me that vision of himself struggling against someone stronger just to mislead me.

My Wave starts buzzing in my hand, and I frantically crack it open.

"Rho—I'm okay." Stanton's hologram blooms out on the bed beside me.

"*Thank Helios,*" I breathe, the air finally reaching my lungs. I survey his image closely. He's wearing a white medical robe, and his hologram is hazy and flickering. "You're injured—your chest—"

"Just a burn, it'll heal," he says, tightening the robe around him to cover it up. "I'm about to get treated, but first they're letting me use a transmitter to call you. The blast happened at night, so the Cancrians were sleeping in the Zodiax. Our hotel wasn't hit, and none of them were hurt."

"What about you?"

He goes quiet, and blood rushes to his face. "Jewel and I . . . we'd gone on a midnight swim."

I feel myself going red, too. On Cancer, a *midnight swim* is when a couple gets together for the first time. Since we can't bring our significant others back to our parents' house, it usually happens at night, in or near the Cancer Sea.

"She's fine and with her family right now," he says quickly, eager to fast-forward. "I would have reached out to you sooner, but I lost my Wave in the ocean in the attack. Again."

"You should really think about trading it in for a Scan this time."

"Maybe I'm a Rising Leo."

I laugh, more from relief than humor. The average Leo runs through ninety-nine Lighters in his lifetime.

Stanton grows serious again, concern pooling in his pale green eyes. "Rho . . . I know you. I know what you're thinking, and it's not true."

My spine goes as rigid as a Sensethyser. "What am I thinking, Stan?"

"That this is your fault. That you should have said something to Ferez. That this confirms you're not a real leader—and it's not true. Because if anything, this proves you're everything Ferez said you are: our true Holy Mother, the one the stars have charged to protect us. Only I don't think it's just Cancer you're protecting anymore."

"Stan—"

"Just listen." His voice takes on Dad's comforting tone, and it hurts that I can't reach out and touch him. "If the Plenum had trusted you—if *I'd* trusted you—you could have made a difference. I get that now. We're holding you back, Rho. You don't belong on Sagittarius, hiding from the Plenum, and you don't belong on Capricorn, hiding from the Zodiac. You belong in the world—in all the worlds—leading, inspiring, and healing us."

I shake my head even as my heart soars to hear my big brother say these words to me. Tears sting my eyes, but I resist them. "I belong with *you*, Stan. I'm going back to Capricorn first chance."

"I knew that's what you were planning—that's why I had to reach you." He stares steadily into my eyes. "That's exactly what the Marad is counting on. It wants to slow you down and distract you, to make you doubt yourself. So don't let it. You said it yourself, Rho. This is your chance to unite the Zodiac, to make the war that started with the destruction of our House end in light and not darkness."

The tears are now streaming down my face because I can feel the decision firming up in my soul before my mind can consider it. Stanton is the only person I've ever wanted to make proud—and now that I've finally earned his faith, I can't lose it.

"But we just found each other," I say in a weak, whiny whisper.

"And we'll find each other again," he says, his eyes growing shiny. "I swear it, sis."

✦ ✦ ✦

After talking to Stanton, I feel at once overwhelmingly relieved and intensely determined. I test my Ring again, and, at last, the Psy shield's down.

Since my vision has been so blocked, I decide to do my reading from a White Room. Most of the group is huddled around the largest wallscreen in the heart of Nishi's parents' mansion, so I take a roundabout path to avoid running into anyone. On my way, I overhear two people arguing in one of the smaller kitchens.

"I'm just wondering why your astrological fingerprint registers *two* records." It's Hysan speaking.

I press into the wall, staying in the hallway's shadow. "Why are you look-ing into my records?" That sounds like Aryll.

"I look into everyone who I'm going to be working with."

"Right, I'm sure this is about *work*—"

"Meaning *what*? Speak plainly."

"Rho's been through a lot, okay? She needs her space. If you can't deal with that, leave. Just don't come to me looking for a fight, because I won't get sucked into your drama."

I don't stick around to hear Hysan's answer. New identities are only adopted for protection or because the person's running from the law, and as far as I know, Aryll doesn't fall into either of those categories. So why would he have two records?

I'm beyond curious, but I don't want to spy. I'll ask him tomorrow. Right now, there are more important things.

When I get to the dark White Room, I sit on the floor and try to clear my head of the ferocious guilt gnawing at me so I can See, but the room's emptiness does nothing to influence my mind.

I flick on the star map. Our twelve constellations encircle Helios, and once I've accessed my Center, I stare at the pulsing Dark Matter covering parts of planets Cancer, Tethys, and Argyr. I move closer to the place where our four moons once shone, now patches of writhing blackness.

Darkness is spreading, drowning out the lights of our solar system. A chill races down my spine, and as I'm turning away from Cancer to inspect the other Houses, a light blazes bright above our constellation. And for a fleeting flicker of an instant, I see a familiar face in the stars.

Mathias?

The vision disappears before I can identify it with certainty, but I can't stop staring at the spot where it had been. My heart swells up so much I think it might crack my rib cage. Could the Cancrian myth about the dead be true? Do those who pass on with unsettled souls really become constellations in the sky? Does that mean there's a chance Mathias could *come back?*

I scour the whole galaxy for him. I practice Yarrot for hours to deepen my Center, and search every corner of the map for a hint of his midnight eyes. If the Thirteenth Guardian is real, why can't Mathias be?

It's the dead of night when I return to my room, no restless Sagittarians wandering along my path. After all the time I spent in the White Room, I didn't meet Mathias or Ophiuchus in the Psy, nor did I see any omens. I'm still blocked.

I pull on my bed clothes—too frustrated to be sleepy but determined to force it—and as I'm climbing onto the mattress, there's a knock on my door. The last thing I want is to see anyone, until I hear his voice.

"My lady?"

"Come in!" I sit up on the foamy lavender bedspread, feeling around for the controller to turn on the lights.

"I've got it," says Hysan, pulling a lighter from his pocket. A small blue flame bursts to life in his hands, and he sticks it into a recess in the room's stone walls, lighting the first in a string of connected candles tucked within the stone. The recess forms a pocket that encircles the room, so when the fire catches, the blue blaze spans the whole perimeter, releasing a soft lavender scent.

"Thought you might be hungry." A pulsing glow illuminates Hysan's face and gray coveralls as he moves closer to set a plate of food on the dresser.

"What's the latest death toll?" I ask in a somber voice.

He perches at the edge of the vast bed. "You didn't kill those people."

"I should've told Ferez. He would have listened. He would have known what to do."

"*How?* He's never seen Ophiuchus. You've entered Psy territory no Zodai can explain or has experienced. You're figuring this out as you go, Rho."

I throw off the covers and pad across the heated stone floor to the dressing table to check out the treats he brought. "Aryll has a theory that Ophiuchus and the master are the same person. He thinks maybe the master is masking his own Psynergy signature to deceive me."

"When did he say that?" Hysan's voice is tight.

"On Capricorn, after I spoke with Ophiuchus." I lean against the dresser and bite into a spongy cake. I like its soft texture, but the purple frosting is a tad too sweet.

"He never mentioned this theory before then?" presses Hysan.

"No . . . but it's not like Ophiuchus was a frequent subject of discussion." I finish the pastry in two bites. "Why, what's up?"

"I don't trust him."

I already know what this is about, so I don't ask for specifics. "I'm sorry you feel that way, but I do trust him. He saved Stanton's life on Gemini."

"Rho, there's something *off* about him. First he tells you his theory about Ophiuchus just when your decision was most likely to be swayed. Then, at the park today, he attends a meeting to which he wasn't invited—"

"He wasn't snooping, if that's what you're suggesting," I say, knowing that Stanton probably instructed Aryll to stay close to me during this trip.

"Earlier tonight," Hysan goes on, his voice dipping, "I accessed his records. I found a second, inaccessible file under his astrological finger-print." He rises to his feet and steps toward me. "Rho . . . that only happens if someone has altered their identity."

I nod and say, "I'll ask him about it." Then I shove another cake in my mouth just to have something else to focus on.

"You're not concerned?" asks Hysan, his eyes widening significantly, as if he doesn't think I've heard him correctly.

"That's why I said I'll ask him," I repeat, irked by the way Hysan is condemning Aryll without knowing the whole story—it's not very Libran of him. "He's my friend, you don't know him, and you're already judging—"

"I know how to make fair judgments," Hysan cuts in, his voice sharp. "I'm a skilled reader of people, and I'm telling you it's my opinion that he may not be trustworthy."

I cross my arms, fed up with Hysan's jealousy. First he thought Mathias seemed untrustworthy, so he secretly searched his cabin, and now he's picking on Aryll. "You don't have to trust him if you don't want to," I snap, my voice almost cold, "but *I'm* not pushing him away. He doesn't have anybody else."

Hysan frowns and stares at the candles surrounding us, looking lost in thought. Then he turns to me with newfound resolve. "Fine. Let's be certain you're right. We'll feed Aryll false information that would appeal to the master and see what he does with it."

"Aryll is not working for the master!" I say incredulously. "And I am *not* deceiving a friend, especially when this has more to do with the conversation I overheard you two having in the kitchen than with anything real. It's not *him* you're upset with, Hysan. You're upset because he was trying to protect me, and you think that's a job that only belongs to you."

Hysan's eyes flash, and the darkness deep within him, the counterbalance to his sunniness, rises closer to the surface. In a voice devoid of light, he says, "My lady, do not mistake my adoration of you for servitude. You may be the better seer, but I am the better judge of people. I will act as I feel is right, as I've sworn to do as a Guardian of the Zodiac."

There's nothing I can say. Hysan is right. So I just stare at him in defiant silence, my arms crossed.

"You're still so determined not to trust me." His voice is suddenly low and sad. "Can't you remember how you felt when Mathias wouldn't listen to you?"

I look down to the stone ground, my neck unable to hold my head up. I can't believe he would bring up Mathias now. And yet, once I move past the sting, I realize Hysan is right again. While I don't think Aryll is a double

118

agent, if Hysan has a doubt, I owe it to him to investigate it. After all, a mind closed to other possibilities here would be just like the stubborn mind-set that led to the armada.

"Hysan . . ." I meet his gold-green gaze, and I'm startled by the pain painted on his features. "There's enough going on without us fighting each other. Can I just talk to him first and see what I think before we do anything?"

He nods after a moment. "As you wish, my lady."

With that, we're out of words; silence brings out the sharpness of the stings our argument has caused.

"I'll leave you to sleep," murmurs Hysan. "Good night." As he moves toward the door, I reach for his hand.

He turns and looks at me, and in the flickering blue light, I see the hunger Stanton spotted in Hysan's eyes. But I think what truly bothered my brother was seeing my own hunger reflected back whenever I look at Hysan.

I slowly lead him toward the bed. Desire spreads to Hysan's face and body, until I can feel it emanating from him like a physical force, making my blood buzz. I pull down the zipper of his coveralls, and he steps out from them until he's left wearing only boxers.

The new muscles in his chest make me think of Mathias, but I jettison the thought from my mind. "Stay with me," I whisper to Hysan, moving close enough to inhale his cedary scent. I pull off my long sleeping shirt so I'm also in my underwear.

"Ask me first," he says, his voice husky as he moves closer, pressing into me. His skin is smooth and firm against mine, triggering goose bumps wher-ever he touches me. He feels warm and strong and safe—exactly how I want to feel.

"Hysan," I whisper, circling my hands around his neck. "Kiss me?"

He dives for my mouth, and we fall into bed. He's everywhere all at once, wrapping my body in his, consuming me with his appetite. I want him so much, want to feel him all over me, to lose myself in him—but to my horror, tears burn my eyes and a sob bubbles up my throat.

"Rho—" Hysan pulls away as I cocoon into myself, rolling onto my side in embarrassment. "What is it?" he asks, stroking my hair as I cry into the mattress.

When I bring my face up to catch my breath, covered in tears and snot, Hysan wipes the wetness away with his thumbs. "Don't be ashamed," he whispers, as I try to turn away again. "I'm not judging you."

I shake my head, feeling my cheeks burn. "I don't know," I whisper back, even though it's not true.

Being with Hysan makes me feel too much like I've let Mathias go—and I'm not yet ready to. Especially after tricking myself into seeing him in the Ephemeris tonight. "Do you think we could just . . . lie here?" I ask, staring at the high ceiling to avoid his gaze.

"We can do anything you want." Hysan softly kisses my cheeks and forehead and chin and earlobes and nose and neck until I'm smiling and breathing again.

"I'm sorry I'm such a mess," I say, rubbing my eyes. "It's been such a crazy trip—we worked so hard, brought so many people together . . . and all for nothing."

"Not for nothing," he says, cupping my face with his hand. "You got to cross Sagittarius off your Zodiac Dozen."

I laugh, and the sound is so sudden and brazen it startles me. The Zodiac Dozen is an old universal joke, a checklist of the twelve things a person is supposed to do—one on each House—before dying. "I bet you've done a Full Orbit," I say.

"Never checked, actually." He sits up and rests his back against the bed's headboard, interlocking his hands behind his hair. "Let's find out."

I nestle into his chest and say, "Okay—we've obviously both wandered through Sagittarius already. But did you ever swim with a Scorpion whale, sun sail on Leo, or tour the Aquarian royal palace?"

"Yes, yes, and yes."

I tilt my head back to look up at him. *"You swam with a Scorpion whale? What was that like?"*

"Indescribable." He plants a kiss on the top of my head. "They have six flippers on each side and swim faster than you would believe. The trick is keeping your feet away from the flippers so the whale doesn't sting you with its whip tail."

"What else?" I ask, curious to know everything I can about him.

"Well, I've obviously befriended a Libran . . . touched my imagination on Gemini . . . impressed a Virgo . . . what's that so far?"

"Seven out of twelve. I think I'm only at, like, three." I trace the number with my finger on Hysan's chest.

"I hope you're not counting the Libran one," he murmurs, "because technically *I* befriended *you*."

Ignoring him, I press on. "Have you opened a Bull's Head bank account on Taurus?"

"Yes."

"Sought wisdom from a Capricorn?" The thought of the Tenth House makes my grin fade a little.

"Think we can both cross that one off," says Hysan, sounding sad, too.

"Had your stars read by a Piscene?"

"Yes."

"Slept with an Ariean?"

He goes quiet, and I look up at his face. "Since you're turning Ariean red, I'll take that as a resounding yes—"

"A gentleman doesn't speak of such things," he murmurs, glowing scarlet.

"Guess I picked the right *House* to do that in, but the wrong *guy*—"

I burst into laughter as Hysan starts tickling me, and we roll around on the bed until he's on top and has me pinned down. We're both breathing heavily from our laughter and closeness.

"But what about the Taboo?" I blurt, and as soon as I ask it, my gaze drifts from his face to the ceiling as I feel my cheeks flood with color. "I mean—if the Aerian you were with—even if she wasn't a Guardian . . . it's still *wrong*, isn't it? Whether or not anyone knows, you're still a Guardian."

I know saying this makes me the ultimate hypocrite, but I also don't understand how he breaks that rule so casually when I've done it once and am still brimming with guilt.

"I don't believe in the Taboo," he says simply, as if his opinion nullifies the law. I meet his eyes in surprise. "Though I would rather not discuss this with you yet, since I feel you should come to your own conclusion once you've seen all the worlds of the Zodiac. You should gather the facts for yourself."

I stare into the small golden star of the Scan in his right iris until I'm no longer seeing it. Even though I shouldn't be, I'm thinking of Mathias and the wall that stood between us. He wanted me to see the universe his way, but Hysan just wants me to *see* it.

"If I promise not to let you bias me," I whisper, "will you tell me what you think?"

When he smiles, the candles around us seem to brighten, as if they're extensions of his light. "I've visited every House of the Zodiac, and I have the overwhelming sensation that not everyone would be happiest where they are."

A sense of unease settles in my belly, his words reminding me of Ferez and his future of Risers. "The universe is unending, but we aren't," whispers Hysan. "No matter what happens to our souls, our physical lives do end." He strokes my cheek, as if he can tell my thoughts have strayed into the shadows and he's trying to pull me back to the present. "Should we let things we have no control over determine our destiny? Or, as Ferez said, do we deserve a choice?"

"I . . . I don't know." I'm proud of being a Cancrian. It's not that I don't want a choice . . . it's just that I don't want to lose my identity amid so much freedom.

"We forgot something," says Hysan, his tone now lighter again. "Last item on the Zodiac Dozen—fall in love with a Cancrian."

His gaze smolders, and my mouth goes dry. Hysan hasn't used the word *love* with me yet.

"You were right after all," he whispers, his lips brushing mine. "Full Orbit."

13

I WAKE UP IN THE morning with my head on Hysan's chest. Now that I'm alone, I spend a long time admiring his golden face without worrying about anyone catching me. Asleep, the new concerns he's been carrying disappear, and he looks more like the light-hearted Libran I first met at my swearing-in ceremony.

The longer I stare at him, the more certain I am that Nishi's right. I do love him. The problem is, I'm still in love with Mathias, too.

Not that it can matter. I'm a Cancrian who can't think about love. My focus must be on war, like an Ariean.

I consider waking Hysan, but now that I've seen him so unburdened, I don't want to bring him back to the imbalance of the present. He doesn't stir as I slip out of the room with my Wave.

Sunlight spills through the mansion's many windows, and everything is bright and quiet in the early hours. I step outdoors to stroll around the back of the sprawling estate, which I haven't explored yet. After weaving through an intricate hedge maze, I come upon a field of firebursts—red-orange flowers that absorb so much heat from Helios they occasionally spit out firework-like sparks.

The cool air becomes balmy as I walk through the blossoms. They all face the sun, their petals glowing like embers, and every few minutes, fiery sparks spurt into the air. Once I pass them, the balmy heat becomes cool again, and I pop out in a sitting area dotted with outdoor furniture and fire pits.

I lean back in a reclining seat and hear a rustling sound in the bushes behind me. From a tangle of branches emerges a four-legged animal with a velvety violet hide and facial features that are startlingly human.

It's a centaurion, the creature this planet was named after. They're all over Sagittarius, but it's impossible to tell. They show themselves only when they want to be seen.

This one isn't very big, so it must be a doe. She sniffs curiously at my feet and then turns her wide Sagittarian eyes up to me. Her face is round, and she doesn't have a snout or whiskers, just a small velvet bump for a nose and a mane of lustrous black hair.

"Hi there," I whisper. She whinnies in response, and I slowly stretch my hand out so I won't scare her. When the centaurion doesn't move away, I pet her soft fur. Eventually the creature clomps closer and rests her head on my lap. I keep stroking her head with one hand, and with the other I pry open my Wave and pull up Ferez's report. Time to finish Vecily's story.

> *The final time Vecily spoke in public was after the Houses struck down the Trinary Axis's decision to secede from the Zodiac. The Taurian, Cancrian, and Leonine Guardians returned to their homes in disgrace and appealed to their people. Below is a transcript of Vecily's speech from that day.*
>
> *The Zodiac is not one. We are twelve. To unite the Houses as one requires a special type of bond, one missing from our universe: trust.*

None of us believe our neighbor has our best interests at heart. This is why the Fire Houses ally and vote together on most issues. It's why Scorpio and Virgo turn inward and close themselves off from their brethren. It's why Sage Huxler has such a hard time coaxing us to contribute the secrets of our worlds for preservation in the Zodiax. It's why I'm here before you today.

There can be no unity until there is trust. And trust will not come until we can speak openly and accept all lifestyles. We are too focused on the stars above and not paying enough attention to the people below. Rather than enforce rules and beliefs that divide us— such as the ban on inter-House marriage, and our institutionalized prejudices against Risers—we should be seeking ways to bring the Zodiac together. How can we call ourselves one galaxy when our own laws forbid us from truly uniting?

In the galaxy's current state, there can be no trust. The air is too full of fear, which keeps us from reaching out to each other and revealing our true selves. We are too concerned with fitting into an existing system rather than modifying that system to fit us.

My fellow Taurians, I am asking you to listen to me. I am not perfect, but I have a Guardian's Sight, and I have Seen a terrible tragedy in our stars if we do not make a change. I beg you to stand with me so that we may be the first House to step into a future where everyone is equal and all ways of life are accepted. Let us light the way so the other Houses may follow.

The Second House has always led the Zodiac in teamwork, and we are the natural choice to bring unity back to our galaxy. Let us begin by seceding and forming a new and more perfect union with Cancer and Leo, so that the other Houses may eventually join us in a new order, one that encourages true harmony and acceptance.

When it came time to vote, the Taurians impeached Vecily, just as Cancer did Brianella. Only House Leo stood by its Leader, so Blazon offered Vecily and Brianella refuge, and the three carried their rebellion underground, recruiting members from every House to their cause. Yet Vecily never spoke again, nor did her heart ever recover.

It's my opinion that after Vecily saw what happened to Datsby, she began to fear anything that might make her stand out from her peers. She first faced this fear when she was a new Guardian and saw the omen in her Ephemeris, and after her Advisors rejected her insight, she shut herself down for a long time. When she finally gathered the courage to try again, she put all the fight she had left into the appeal to her House, and, once again, she lost. And this final failure is what broke her. She was abandoned by her people, just as Datsby was, and so Vecily gave up. She never again found her voice.

While it could be argued that the Cancrian and Leonine Guardians wanted to go to war for personal gain, I believe Vecily's motives were pure. She was trying to prevent the oncoming bloodshed that was to persist for the next one hundred years. In the end, she was proven right: Once the existing system was breached and the Houses were able to create a new one, they chose to become independent, sovereign worlds. Yet it's clear from her speech to her House that this was not her end goal. Her true hope was for the Houses to ultimately reunite in acceptance.

*Every day, the Zodiac moves further away from that goal.
We are forgetting each other. Each House may be its own
world, but Helios traps us all within her gravity.*

*Our orbit around our galactic sun is a delicate balance of
unity and space. If the energy that binds us were to pull our
planets tighter together, we would burn. If it slackened and
moved our orbit farther out, we would freeze. I believe the
same can be said of the Zodiac people.*

*The air is growing chilly out here. It's time to make good
on the second part of Vecily's vision by getting to know our
neighbors and remembering that we are part of a larger whole.*

When I'm done reading, there are tears in my eyes. The centaurion picks
her head up and looks at me, as if she senses the shift in my mood. Ferez
is right, and so was Vecily: This fight isn't about unity versus freedom. It's
about striking the right balance of both.

The thought reminds me of what Ochus said the last time we met, about
good and evil. The point, he said, is not to eradicate one and salvage the
other but to find the harmony between them. I have to speak to him again.
I need to find out what he knows.

I give the centaurion a last pet and stand up. Within seconds, the doe
vanishes into the hedge and out of sight. I cut across the field of hot firebursts, slip inside the mansion, and head into one of the White Rooms,
where I switch on Vecily Matador's Ephemeris.

As soon as I'm Centered, a vision manifests, as if it's been waiting impa-
tiently for me to regain my Sight. I see my face in the sky again, and I'm
transforming into a Riser. I watch my hair thinning, face narrowing, eyes
going glassy . . . I'm becoming Aquarian.

Of all the Houses, Aquarius is one of the last I'd expect to fit into. They're
cerebral and bookish, whereas I rely far more on instinct and emotion than

logic. I move closer to inspect the omen, and it vanishes. In its place is an icy giant.

Ochus's gargantuan body is already fully formed, his menacing sneer freezing my blood. *I told you Capricorn was the true target.*

I tether myself more tightly to the Psy, becoming attuned to the deeper plane, and now that I'm unblocked, I can once again sense the shakiness in the Psynergy surrounding me. The universe is becoming less stable by the moment.

Who's the master, and what's his next move? I ask, faking a confidence I don't feel.

Ophiuchus's frigid stare is emotionless, and I can practically see the thoughts running through his transparent head. Every time we meet, he could just as easily decide to kill me as help me. I see him mulling over that choice again now . . . and it hits me that there's a reason he hasn't ended me yet.

He wants something from me.

When I offered my aid before, you were revolted, he says testily.

I didn't trust you.

That hasn't changed. So what has?

I'm going to have to give answers to receive them. *I realized not everything is as black and white as it seems. I know now that sometimes you have to become allies with the wrong people for the right reasons.*

He nods approvingly, as if this is the answer he's been seeking. *You have grown wiser since our last encounter.*

I hate being complimented by this murderer. *Does that mean you'll answer my damn question now?* I snap.

Ochus's icy body glistens and grows, until his Psynergy is pressing in on me from all sides. The invisible pressure grows so intense that it constricts my neck and chest, and for an instant I think he might finally finish me off—

I don't know the master's true identity, but I know how you can find out. The Psynergy retreats back into him, and at last I can catch my breath again.

I try pulling in the air subtly, so he won't see how much he hurt me. My throat burns as oxygen blows through it.

There is an old piece of Capricorn wisdom from my day: Only through Death's hand is our true enemy revealed. *You will notice that even though I could kill you right here where we stand—and could have killed you many times before—I've refrained.*

I'm not interested in his perverse bit of wisdom, but I know better than to set him off again. *How does that show me the master's identity?*

Ophiuchus's stare turns calculating, as if a new thought, one I can't read, has suddenly entered his mind. *First . . . you must swear to do something for me once the master is exposed.*

He does want something from me. But just like I can't imagine actually doing anything for him, I can't imagine there's anything I have that he could possibly need. *What is it?* I ask tentatively.

Free me from the everlasting coils of time.

What? I ask in a tone full of incredulous disgust. *You're asking me . . . you want me to make you mortal?*

No. I want you to give me the death I have craved for so long.

I glare at him, even more confused and repulsed. The last time Ochus claimed to want to die, it was just to manipulate me so he could kill more of my people. I don't trust he means it any more now than he did then.

You needn't be wary, little crab, he goes on when I don't answer. *I am only asking you to swear to do the very thing you have long longed to do.*

I already swore as much to myself when I set out to avenge Dad and Mathias. I might as well renew my vow to my target himself if it'll get me to the master.

I swear it.

On your Mother's life.

I stare straight into Ophiuchus's black-hole eyes as I reaffirm my solemn oath to murder him. *On my Mother's life.*

Then you have my word as well. Take a ship to the asteroid belt between Houses Libra and Scorpio. The Marad uses Psy shields, so their headquarters are hidden, but one of their cells is located near there; they're using the asteroid activity for cover. If you don't appear to pose a threat, they probably will not shoot you on sight, but they will most definitely stop you mid-flight and board your ship. Once they identify you, they will capture you and tag you as a high-priority hostage, and it's likely they will take you to their headquarters. Unless they decide to kill you outright.

This sounds more like a suicide mission than a plan. I can't help you if I'm dead.

Exactly. We're both risking everything. This is my only plan—the master is as skilled in games of the Psy as I am. He clouds my eye.

Say I live long enough to meet the master. What's the point of knowing his identity if he kills me before I can tell anyone?

Surely your friends will be tracking your location as soon as the Marad captures you. I believe you are familiar with the concept of bait—you have played the role before, to much acclaim.

His icy form glints like a blade, and in its reflection I see the wreckage from the armada: *Firebird* plummeting into the Piscene planet Icthys, Mathias pummeling the airlock door, begging me not to abandon him—

I hate you, I spit, my breathing growing shallow.

His body melts into a wintry wind, and as he gusts past me, I pluck meaning from his whispered breeze. Your anger is a searing flame . . . but you have not yet lost as much as you think.

✦ ✦ ✦

I leave the White Room, darting down the hall to find Nishi. I tell her to get Deke, Hysan, and Aryll and bring them to my room. When we're all gathered, I tell them about my visit to the Psy.

"Which is why I need a ship to take," I say quickly, not giving them time to react to my story. "Hysan, do you have access to a Wasp?"

"*Equinox* is yours, my lady," he says, his expression so somber it dampens his golden glow. "We can depart as soon as you wish."

"I'm doing this alone," I say, my voice firm. "I'm the bait; it has to be that way. You guys will be tracking me, and if anything goes wrong, you can—"

"Are you crazy? You're not going alone. We're either coming with you or you're not going," says Nishi flatly, her arms crossed and a small wrinkle in the center of her forehead.

The anger I felt for Ochus in the Ephemeris comes rushing back to me now. "Nish, do you realize how dangerous this trip is? I *might* have a chance of surviving because the master *might* find me useful politically, but you guys have *no* chance—"

"Rho, a Wasp won't fly to coordinates that distant, and you don't know how to pilot '*Nox* or any other ship," says Hysan, his manner more matter-of-fact than confrontational. "Not to mention the asteroid belt is dangerous and only an experienced pilot can navigate through it. You need help, whether you want it or not."

I release a hard, exasperated breath. "Fine. Hysan, you and I—"

"No way!" roars Deke. "If he goes, we go. We've been your friends for longer."

"You know you're not going anywhere without me," adds Aryll. Hysan clenches his jaw but doesn't say anything.

I ignore the sinking feeling in my chest warning me this is a terrible idea. I know in my gut Ophiuchus is right—this is our best chance to intercept the master before he strikes again. There's nothing about this plan that feels sturdy or reliable, but, like Ophiuchus, I don't have another. The Marad already murdered so many people, and there's no doubt they'll keep slaughtering more. If I can possibly help put a stop to it, I have to try.

I just wish I knew how to keep my friends safe in the process.

"Let's tell the others," says Deke, and before I can say more, he and Nishi leave to corral the other Sagittarians into the creamy levlan sitting area. Hysan and I meet each other's eyes.

"Do you mind giving me a moment with Aryll?" I ask him.

"Of course," he says, almost too happily, and leaves.

"Let me guess: You don't want me to come?" asks Aryll glumly. I survey his sunburned features before answering. He stares at me anxiously, scratching his peeling nose, and all I see is a sad little boy.

I look from Aryll's electric-blue eye to the gray patch on the opposite side and sigh. "It's not that I don't want you around . . . but you know you can't come on this trip."

His features pull together, as if he's tasted something sour, and he crosses his arms over his chest. He looks like he might pull a tantrum or maybe run away, and his pouty expression reminds me so much of a Cancrian child that it's hard to remember we're the same age.

"Why are there two records for your astrological fingerprint?"

Aryll dramatically drops his arms to his sides. "*That's* what this is about? Your boyfriend doesn't like me, so now you're taking his side—"

"Aryll, cut it out," I say, gripping his shoulders. "This is life and death— you can't be a child anymore. You saved my brother's life. Act like the hero you are."

Rather than empower him, my words seem to hit a sore spot. He looks ashamed, and the reaction reminds me of the way Twain's compliments affected me. There's something uneasy in Aryll's expression, something unknown . . . I see it now.

"*Why do you have two records?*" I repeat.

"Because this isn't the first time I lost my family, Rho."

I stare at him blankly, my grip on his shoulders loosening.

"When your brother was two," he says softly, in a soothing tone that's at odds with his uneasy expression, "he and your mom went to Naxos Island to help the victims of Hurricane Hebe. They found an infant in the wreckage."

Aryll's eye starts to sparkle overly bright. "*Me.*"

14

MY HANDS FALL FROM HIS shoulders. "I-I don't understand—"

"Your mother became a legend on Naxos," he says, still speaking in that gentle voice. "She never told us her name, so we started calling her the White Dove. She just showed up with the morning, like a miracle."

I can hardly hear his words past the beating of my heart. Even though his revelation is too extreme for me to fathom, I still picture the scene as he describes it. Mom's looks were already striking, but she must have been a vision on Naxos: pregnant, with a two-year-old by her side, emerging from the depths of the Cancer Sea like the day's first ray of light.

"When you became Holy Mother, the newsfeeds ran all kinds of stories about you," he goes on. "I watched from the settlement on Gemini. They showed an image of your parents on their wedding day, and after seeing hundreds of drawings of the White Dove, I recognized her. So when they ran pictures of your brother, I knew he was the person I owed my life to."

I flash back to what Stanton told me, about how us meeting Aryll was written in the stars. "Does Stanton know?"

Aryll nods sheepishly. "I asked him to keep it a secret. . . . I honestly wasn't sure until this moment that he actually had."

"Stanton is true to his word." I hear the defensiveness in my voice, even though I'm stung my brother didn't trust me enough to share something so powerful. "Why didn't you want me to know?"

Aryll looks uncomfortable again and starts running his bronze pendant along the black strap of levlan. "I thought . . . maybe you wouldn't like me as much."

"What are you talking about?"

"You were just so nice to me. You were so grateful to me for saving Stanton—you kept thanking me and looking after me as if I was someone . . . *admirable*. I worried that if you learned the truth, you wouldn't welcome me to your family so quickly. We'd already be . . . *even*."

"Aryll!" I start laughing suddenly, surprising us both. "We don't love you just because you saved Stanton! We love you because you're our friend, and we care about you." I pull him in for a hug, but he pushes me off, suddenly angry.

"You don't get it—I'm not a *hero*." His brow furrows down. "I was following Stanton around the settlement like a coward, too scared to tell him who I was, afraid he wouldn't believe me or that he'd somehow let me down. Then the earthquakes started and I saw him outside—not running to shelter like the rest of us, but hanging out in the rockiest parts helping the people who hadn't made it yet.

"I saw the danger he was putting himself in, and I—*I didn't want to help him*. I wanted to go with the others. I wanted to be safe."

Aryll turns fully away from me, and his back is a hard shell between us, keeping me out. "But you didn't go," I whisper. "Why?"

He sniffles but doesn't spin back around. "I thought, *What if he dies? And I had the chance to save him?*" He turns around again, and half his face is striped with tears. "I'm not brave, or sent by the stars, like Stanton thinks.

I only saved him because I'm *selfish*. Because otherwise I couldn't live with myself."

I wrap my arms around Aryll, ignoring his resistance, and we sink into a huge hug. "That's *exactly* what makes you a hero," I whisper into his ear. "You chose to do the right thing, even when it was your worst option."

When we pull away, he pries open the pendant hanging around his neck. Inside is a single pure-white nar-clam pearl that could have only come from the Cancer Sea.

"I couldn't save my first family, and I couldn't save my second one . . . but I will save their memory. I'm doing this for Cancer."

✦ ✦ ✦

Aryll and I go into the main room to join the rest of the group, who are already gathered and waiting expectantly. Aryll plops down on a couch, and I remain standing in front of the Sagittarian sea of more than fifty faces. "Thanks for meeting, everyone. We have a new plan—"

A door bangs open deep inside the mansion, and more people wearing a range of new colors rush into the room. "Sorry we're late!" calls Brynda, who is walking arm-in-arm with Rubi.

"Curiosity and Imagination do not make the fastest traveling companions," chirps the diminutive Geminin Twin.

Behind them are Imogen and the Geminin students, Twain and the Virgos, Numen and the Librans, and Candela and the Cancrians. The Capricorns and Piscenes must be landing on Tierre soon. The sight of all the colors pouring in fills me with strength.

Everyone finds a place to sit, and the leaders from each House greet Hysan. He must have organized this. As they all settle down, the room gradually falls silent, and every face finds mine.

"Close your eyes," I say.

The group complies with my command.

"Raise your hand if you think at least *some* people are still peeking." Every hand shoots up.

"Look at your neighbor." Hands lower to half-mast as people blink open their eyes and look around at each other.

"We want to unify our universe, and we don't even trust the people we're going to be fighting beside."

Amid the murmur of reactions, I catch a glimpse of Hysan's approving face, and it bolsters my confidence. "A few months ago, I saw a vision in my Ephemeris, and very few people believed me. So when Ophiuchus spoke to me again last week, *I* didn't believe me. My distrust cost Capricorn countless lives that should have been spared. I'm sorry for that."

I pause to look at them all, trying to connect with every pair of eyes the way I've seen Hysan do.

"We all want to bring the Zodiac together. But before we can make a change out there, we have to make one in here. We have to start trusting ourselves and each other. We can't immediately jump to doubt and suspicion anymore."

"Hear, hear," says Rubi, nodding along. She takes Brynda's hand, and Brynda takes Imogen's hand, who takes Gyzer's hand, and so forth, until the whole room is physically connected.

"I spoke with Ophiuchus again." His name is like a glacial gust, and it snuffs out the warmth my words had just kindled. I try to ignore the uneasiness in the room as I go on to share the details of the expedition. "This is the only way to get close to the master," I finish.

Ezra raises her hand but doesn't wait to be called on to speak. "Who's on your crew?"

Hysan, Nishi, Deke, and Aryll raise their hands. Hysan furrows his brow at me when he sees Aryll's hand shoot up, but he doesn't contradict me out loud.

"I want to go," says Twain, shooting to his feet.

"Me too," says Ezra, who stands up as well.

Imogen and Gyzer also rise, and soon there are people talking over each other all across the room until I can't hear any of them.

"Shut your Maws!" shouts Deke. "Rho's the leader, and this is her plan. The rest of you need to outfit your ships and get ready, because if the Marad kills us, you'll get your turn."

Everything goes silent and cold.

"Rubi, Brynda, Twain, and Numen, if it's okay," I say, "I'd like to ask you four to start crewing up ships to come after us." They all nod, and immediately Gyzer, Ezra, and Imogen line up behind their Guardians to volunteer for their Houses.

"Candela," I say, and she rises. "Please go to Tierre and get in touch with Mother Agatha to see how Cancer can help. Sage Ferez has been exceedingly kind to our House, and we need to stand by him and Capricorn."

Candela nods, and as the rest of the Cancrians file out, she comes up to me and extends her hand for the traditional greeting. "I'm sorry if I spoke harshly before."

"I'm glad you did," I say, bumping fists with her. "I needed to hear it."

"We're going, too," says Brynda, walking over with Rubi on her arm. The Geminin troop follows behind them. "We'll be in touch once we've worked out logistics."

Nodding, I catch sight of Twain and the Virgos out of the corner of my eye, huddled apart from everyone on the other side of the room. Even though Twain said his House was ready to open up and reach out to the others, change is a slow process. I know he's hurt to be excluded from the trip, but I didn't want to bring anyone with me in the first place. And besides, I wasn't selecting Houses—I was choosing *people*.

I watch Hysan approach Twain and then follow his lead.

"I can help," Twain's telling Hysan as I get close.

"I know, and that's why we need you here, ready to pursue us if we're taken."

"We want to be part of this mission, Hysan," insists Twain. "We don't want to be punished for having isolated ourselves in the past. Give us a chance."

"That's not what we're doing," I say, startling them both with my quiet arrival. "We need to keep the first group small so we don't pose a threat to the Marad. We need our best fighters and flyers to come after us—we're depending on you."

Once the Virgos and Librans file out, the room is a lot quieter. I'm left parched, my head already pounding with pressure. I wish I could fly out alone. Agreeing to lead means accepting the possibility of more blood on my hands, and a week ago I couldn't have handled it. But today, quitting means letting down Vecily and Ferez. And House Cancer, and the entire Zodiac—and that weighs even heavier.

I excuse myself from the group to send an encrypted message to Ambassador Sirna. She's the only person in the Cancrian government I'm entrusting with the details of this expedition—when the time comes, she'll fill in Agatha and the others on what we're doing here. For now, though, I want to keep our circle small.

When I come back out to the common space, everyone is eating mushroom sushi.

"Rho!" Nishi calls out from across the crowded room as soon as she sees me. The whole place quiets down. "Should we burn some energy?"

Everyone sits up with excitement, and before I know what's going on, Nishi declares, "If we're dying tomorrow, then I say let's make like Leos and live for a night!"

15

EVERYONE APPLAUDS IN ASSENT, AND soon the whole place is getting ready to go out and revel. My face has gone slack with disbelief, but Deke bounds over to me happily. "That's why I love her!"

"She's not serious—"

"Why not? Let people have some fun before the sea rises." *Before the sea rises* is a Cancrian expression that means before things go bad. "It'll feel good to celebrate after so much tension."

The word *celebrate* triggers flashbacks to the last celebration I attended, the night of Helios's Halo. I flash not to the celebration itself, but to days later, when the new friends I made turned on me on the village streets, their love contorted to hate, their cheers twisted to jeers. The day the Zodiac abandoned me.

What if the Sagittarians lose their faith in me, too?

What if Nishi and Deke do?

"Rho, are you okay? We don't have to do this if you think it's a bad idea," says Deke, his grin falling off. He slings a comforting arm around my shoulder and narrows his gaze on my face.

I shake my head dismissively. "No, no, you guys are right. We all deserve a night off."

His roguish smile resurfaces. "Excellent." Then he scans the room, and from the excitement on his face, I can tell he's searching for Nishi in the crowd.

"I love seeing you this way," I tell him. Most Cancrians love openly, their hearts on full display. But Deke and I have always had thicker shells than others. . . . I think that's partly why we understand each other so well. I knew why my walls were up, but until recently, I'd only ever suspected Deke's reasoning.

There's no easy path to falling in love with someone from another House.

"Thanks. And what about you, Rho Rho?" His turquoise eyes glint with playful mysteriousness. "Now you *know* I would *never* intrude on your private life . . ."

"Oh, of *course* not."

". . . however, the other night, when I was on my way to the kitchen for some refreshments, I happened to notice a certain *gentleman* slipping inside a *gentlelady's* room. . . ."

"Deke!" I punch his arm, and he starts laughing.

"*What?* I'm happy for you! This is good news all around—you're getting some, I'm getting some, Nishi's getting some—"

"Listen up!" shouts Nishi, quieting the room and saving Deke from my fists. "The Capital is shut down, so we're going to Starry City. Most people there didn't evacuate."

"The Aleph!" shouts Ezra excitedly, and someone whoops with glee.

"How are we getting there?" I ask tentatively.

Deke's fingers close preemptively around my arm. "The cannon is even more fun the second time around, I *promise*."

✦ ✦ ✦

Nishi makes me go first again.

I curl my body into a tight ball inside the echoing chamber, and then a blast of energy shoots me into the air. I keep my head down and eyes squeezed shut for what feels like hours, until I sense myself starting to descend. This time, I loosen my neck just the tiniest bit, and I look down at the rapidly swelling Starry City.

The city has five points, like a geometric star, and unlike the loud, mismatched buildings of the Capital, the structures are all made out of frosted glass. It looks like an ice world, like the Piscene planet Icthys, where *Firebird* crashed.

A shiver of sadness echoes through me, but soon my heart is pounding in my ears as I plummet toward the ice below. I close my eyes and brace myself for the crash—

But the ground is soft, like freshly fallen snow, and it cradles my body securely when I land. A tall Sagittarian offers me his hand, and I rise to see Hysan, Nishi, Deke, Aryll, Gyzer, Ezra, and all the others dropping down behind me.

"Here you go," says the same Sagittarian who helped me up, holding out two steel blades to me.

"Um . . . what—?"

"Like this, Rho," says Nishi, attaching similar blades to the bottoms of her boots. Then she helps me do the same with mine.

"My lady," says Hysan, offering me his arm when he sees me wobbling.

"Thank you," I say with relief, resting most of my weight on him. "Let me guess—you've done this before?"

Hysan draws out his dimples, as Nishi leads us out of the landing pad and onto the icy pathways of Starry City. The landing pad is the largest and highest structure here—everything else is low to the ground, with semi-transparent walls and ceilings. The pathways around the homes and businesses in this city are just as intricate as they are at the Capital, and there are also souvenir stations everywhere.

"This is awesome," says Aryll, coming up on my other side. His wide blue eye reflects the frost surrounding us, and he reminds me of a young Cancrian wading into the Cancer Sea for the first time.

"Follow meeeee," sings Nishi, skating past us hand-in-hand with Deke. We all follow, and soon Hysan and I fall behind everyone else.

"I'm sorry," I huff, trying to stay balanced and also make forward progress.

"For what?" he asks pleasantly, holding both of our weights and seeming undisturbed by having to stop again and again for me to catch my breath or untwist my ankle.

I stare through the walls of a frosted house where two small children and their parents are eating dinner at a large table. And a memory stirs . . . I've heard of this city before. "It's like everyone here is on display," I say, trying to remember.

"This is one of the most ancient cities on House Sagittarius," says Hysan, filling in my mind's blanks. "It's said that Sagittarius himself, the original Guardian, founded this city, and he designed it to look like his home among the stars. In Space, there's no such thing as privacy, so those who live here don't have the same inhibitions as you and I do. It's very liberating."

I can tell from his voice that he really likes it here. Every time we talk, I discover something unexpected about Hysan, something that makes me want to learn more. He's as ever-expanding as Space itself, and I can't help wondering if I'll ever fully know him, or if he'll forever remain just as unknowable.

"We're here!" announces Nishi when we reach the city limit. She starts removing the blades from the bottoms of her boots. All I see in front of us is a sea of snow. *This* is the Aleph?

Suddenly a periscope pops up from the blanket of white beside us, and Nishi presses her thumb against its glass. The rest of us take turns doing the same thing until we all have identified ourselves. The powder surrounding us starts to rise up like a tidal wave about to swallow us—but we're actually descending underground, into a round room surrounded by a dozen closed doors.

"Welcome to the Aleph," says a metallic-bodied android standing in the center of the empty space, holding a silver tray. "Would you like any Abyssthe before entering?"

"No thanks," says Nishi. Then she turns to me in excitement. "Pick a door, Rho."

"Which one?"

She shrugs mysteriously, and I roll my eyes and walk forward to the one directly across from me. When I open it, the room is dark with pulsing holographic lights, and it's packed with people dancing. But I can't hear anything.

Curious, I cross the threshold, and as soon as I step through, the sound blasts on. A percussion-heavy song beats through the room and once everyone else is inside, we thread through the crowd toward the stage, where a tattooed band is performing a high-energy number. Nishi, Deke, and the Sagittarians immediately start moving to the music, and suddenly I find myself next to Hysan, and we're the only two people standing still.

He takes my hand, and we drift to a corner of the room near the back bar, where it's quieter. Neither of us says anything, but there's a new energy between us. It's the first time we've hung out like this, overtly together, in public. His eyes drop to my lips, and tonight, I'm willing to give in to our feelings even here, in front of everyone. It's like Nishi said—if everything ends tomorrow, let's live today.

My lips are centimeters from Hysan's when I hear the voice of a demanding girl.

"I want to talk to you."

Annoyed, I turn to see Ezra, with her hundreds of braids spilling over her mahogany face and her arms crossed over her chest.

"I'll get us drinks," says Hysan, pulling away from me and leaving us alone.

"What's up?" I ask Ezra.

"I want to go with you tomorrow. And don't say I'm too young—you were only sixteen the first time you took on Ophius."

"Ezra, I've already chosen my crew. You know I'm not going to change my mind."

"I won't get in your way."

"I know that, but I said no."

"I'll follow orders, and I can help—"

I clench my hands at my sides but try to keep the anger out of my voice. "*I said no*. Now please drop it." I relax my fingers and reach out to rest a reassuring hand on her arm.

She shoves my touch away and snaps, "Why not?"

"Because this is life and death, Ezra, and I won't have your death on my hands!"

Everyone at the bar looks at us. Ezra's chest is pulsing rapidly with her heavy breathing, as if there's a wild bird in her rib cage.

"I-I'm sorry," I stammer, "I didn't mean to shout—"

She runs off before I can finish my apology, and Hysan returns to my side. "You okay?" His eyes glow in the semidark like the holograms that dance along the walls.

I shake my head, my cheeks burning with regret. "I just blew up at her—I don't know what's wrong with me—"

"Come on," he says, leading us out of the loud room and into the quiet of the threshold.

Soon we're back in the soundless, circular lobby with the android. When we cut across the room, it turns to us as though we just walked in for the first time and says, "Welcome to the Aleph. Would you like any Abyssthe before entering?"

"No thanks," says Hysan. The robot seems satisfied with his answer and turns back around. I stare at it a moment longer, thinking of the sophistication of Lord Neith and Miss Trii. I'm not sure I've heard of an android anywhere in the universe as advanced as those two.

Hysan squeezes my hand, and I meet his gaze. "Rho, the past few months have tested you in ways few people could withstand. You've had to fight down so much—your fears, worries, wants—to do what's best for everyone else. Who could blame you if some of those feelings break the surface every now and then?"

"I know, and you're probably right, but Ezra still didn't deserve that."

"She'll forgive you. She wasn't at her best either—she kept pressing you even though she knows you made the right call. Speaking of . . . do you know what you're going to do about Aryll?"

"Let's not talk about that right now," I say, dropping his hand. Revealing Aryll's secret requires sharing truths about my own childhood, and this isn't the place for that.

"Well, what *can* we talk about?" he asks, a trace of annoyance in his tone.

"Us." The word falls from my lips before I can catch it.

Hysan's expression suddenly relaxes, and I wonder if I've surprised him as much as I have myself. "Okay then," he says, his voice now lower, huskier. "How do you feel about us?"

I inhale deeply, worried if I don't get this out now, I never will. "I know I've been punishing myself. Not just for Mathias but also for breaking the Taboo." Hysan nods along, as if he suspected as much. "But the truth is, I love you."

He stops nodding. I say it just as simply as I feel it, like the inescapable truth it is and not a secret I had to mine the depths of my soul to unearth.

"I don't want to keep running away from myself," I press on. "Mathias is gone." While the words cut me, the blade doesn't dig as deep anymore. "He can no longer be my excuse to stay stuck. I don't think he'd like that." I'm startled to find myself repeating not Nishi's words but Deke's.

Hysan looks like he's going to speak, so I speed up to reach my point. "I'm telling you all of this in case this is my last chance to do it. So, I love you, but I can't offer you anything more right now. My heart is in this war. If we survive it—"

"Rho, even if we weren't at war, one of us could still die tomorrow," says Hysan, taking my hand again. "My parents weren't killed by Ophiuchus or his master or the Marad. A forecasted future can be every bit as hopeless as an invisible one." He cups my face with his hand. "I know your head has to be elsewhere right now. But when we get back from this latest life-or-death adventure, I want something from you."

"What?" I whisper.

"I would like to take you out on a real date, my lady."

"A *date*," I repeat, amused by the modesty of the request.

He smirks and pulls me in for a kiss, and every second I feel Mathias slipping further from me, but in a way that makes me feel lighter rather than heavier. Right now, with Hysan, I see the first hint of a brighter tomorrow, a chance for the happiness I thought I'd lost along with Dad and Mathias.

But only if we survive.

When we pull apart, Hysan's centaur smile lights up the Aleph, and he takes me by the hand to try a new door. I gasp at what I see: a grand hall in which a full orchestra is performing for a packed house. The next room is by far the emptiest—there's a lonely singer belting out what's probably a ballad, and a few couples are swaying slowly to her song. Hysan turns to me, and I know what he's going to ask, and I'm already crossing the threshold into the room when a voice calls out behind us.

"Hello, lovers!"

Deke and Nishi are in the lobby, both pink-cheeked and breathless, the way they used to look whenever one of them got away with breaking a rule on Elara.

"You didn't think we came all the way to Starry City just for a good party?" says Nishi, though it's no surprise a Sagittarian would travel even farther than this for the promise of a great time. "There's something I wanted to share with you. It might be a clue about Ophiuchus. We'll come right back—we're not going far."

I look at Hysan. "Up for another adventure?"

He offers me his arm. "Naturally."

✦ ✦ ✦

Back outside, we skate down a narrow, icy pathway, away from the Aleph, toward the homes of Starry City. "As soon as we got back to the Capital," says Nishi, leading the way while I hold on to Hysan and try to keep up, "I started researching Ophiuchus again. I figured, being in the land of Curiosity, there were bound to be a bunch of questions about him over the ages. But when I looked, I could only find vague references. I think who-ever's been erasing any trace of the Thirteenth House from history has been more meticulous than we thought.

"So instead, I started looking into Guardian Sagittarius—after all, he would have been a peer of Ophiuchus's. And it turns out, like most elder Sagittarians do, he became obsessed with a singular curiosity. The question he most wanted answered was: *What is time?*"

Time . . . the time-worm, Moira and Origene's experiments. I feel Hysan's muscles tense in sync with mine, and I can tell he's just as intrigued as I am by Nishi's discovery.

We come to a stop before a massive memorial carved from crystal. It's a statue of the original Sagittarian Guardian. He looks like a combina-tion of all his people, and in his features I see Nishi, Brynda, Gyzer, Ezra, and all the others. Across his chest is the Archer symbol, as large as his head. "See?" asks Nishi, pointing to the bow and arrow. "Time."

She runs her finger along the arrow and says, "It's either linear"—then she circles the arch of the bow—"or circular."

Hysan moves closer, clearly entranced by Nishi's theory. "Here's where it gets hazy," she goes on, while Hysan traces the symbol just as she did. "Since there are no direct references to Ophiuchus, there's not much in the way of facts. But there's a legend that started in the earliest days of our House, about a magical object that possesses the truth about time, located somewhere in the Zodiac."

My head hurts from the effort of not looking at Hysan. Though she doesn't know it, Nishi is referring to the Guardians' Talismans.

"What if Sagittarius suspected Ophiuchus had it?" she asks eagerly, having reached her main point. "What if Ophiuchus truly was wronged?"

"So what, though?" asks Deke, and Nishi glares at him. "I'm just saying, whatever happened to him doesn't justify all he's done—"

"Of *course* it doesn't justify it; that's not my point—"

My Ring finger buzzes as Hysan's voice whispers in my head. *What if another Guardian did steal Ophiuchus's Talisman?*

I touch my Ring, my eyes tracing the lines and curves of the Archer symbol. *It could have been anyone . . . doesn't even have to be a Guardian.*

And if they stole his secrets, adds Hysan, *they could be immortal, like him. They could be anyone, anywhere.*

I gasp out loud. *The* master.

Hysan nods. *We should share our suspicions with Ferez.*

"What is it?" asks Nishi, obviously aware that Hysan and I are communicating through our Rings. She and Deke immediately quit quibbling.

"I just got chills," I say, which is at least part of the truth. "Nish . . . you're a genius."

Hysan stares at Nishi with an expression of deep admiration. "You are truly brilliant."

"*Genius, brilliant,* really now," says Deke, trying to bite back his own smile. "You fill her head with these grandiose words, and then who has to deal with her massive ego when you both go back home?"

Deke skates away playfully before Nishi can grab him, and suddenly a woman's voice speaks inside my head.

We need to talk. I'll be in touch in an hour. Make sure you're near a transmitter.

I touch the Ring on my buzzing finger. *Sirna? What is it?*

Ochus.

16

AN HOUR LATER, I'M BACK in my room with Hysan, Nishi, and Deke, awaiting Sirna's call. I feel all the magic from earlier in the night disappear as we tensely stand around in a circle, not meeting each other's eyes.

We've watched the feeds but haven't heard anything new. Whatever Sirna knows, it's not public knowledge yet.

Suddenly, the wall transmitter sings out a musical jingle and begins to glow red. The four of us inhale together as Nishi uses her Tracker to accept the transmission. The hologram of a dark-skinned woman in a long, flowing skirt with a coat that bears the four sacred moons beams into the center of the room.

"Rho," says Ambassador Sirna as soon as her sea-blue eyes meet mine.

Despite the circumstances, my mood lightens on seeing her—but, though her gaze softens a little, her expression doesn't match the feeling. She looks worried. "I wanted to wait for more concrete information before reaching out, but when I received the details of your plan, I knew I had to speak with you now."

I nod. "What is it?"

"I'm at the Plenum, where the ambassadors are reconsidering your account of the Thirteenth Guardian."

The air in the room goes from tense to stunned. This sounds like it should be good news, but I can tell by Sirna's expression it isn't. "Initial analysis of Verity shows the destruction might have been triggered through the Psy . . . and Ophiuchus is the only being we've heard of who can do that. The Plenum now believes he may be the master."

My friends turn to me, their faces a mix of surprise and concern, but I stay focused on Sirna. "Thank you for telling me. We will reconsider our plan and let you know if there are any changes."

When her hologram winks out, I turn from the screen and face my friends. "Let's find out as much about this rumor as we can and regroup at dawn with the other Houses. If the plan stays in place, we'll set out immediately after the meeting. For now, I'm going to consult the stars."

✦ ✦ ✦

I've been in my room for hours, reading Vecily's Ephemeris, desperate for a sign of Ophiuchus, when I hear a knock on my door.

"Come in."

It's Hysan, who's changed back into his gray coveralls. I wave him in.

"Hi," I say, switching off the star map. Dawn is a couple of hours away, and still no sign of Ophiuchus.

"Anything?" he asks.

I shake my head. "But I'm not buying it."

The words are a revelation even to myself, and I feel better after expelling them. "I know Ophiuchus is still playing games with me, but I don't get the sense he's lying about the master. I think there's someone else out there, someone much more powerful than him."

"I agree," says Hysan, sitting down on the bed beside me. "The master has been far too careful about hiding Ophiuchus's existence to slip up now. If anything, I believe this news proves Ophiuchus has truly switched sides. I think the master has discovered this fact and is now feeding him to the masses, the way he did you."

Hysan's reasoning mirrors mine, and I smile with relief at the lightness and rightness of conviction. I've missed this feeling—the certainty I can trust myself.

"What do you want to do?" he asks.

"I want to talk to him again. If the master is lying, Ophiuchus will be desperate to prove it."

Hysan nods. "Then I'll leave you to it."

I yank him back by the pocket of his coveralls and bring his mouth to mine. "Thanks," I say. "I needed that."

"Any time, my lady."

✦ ✦ ✦

I keep staring into the Ephemeris as the sun's first rays peek out, willing Ochus to appear. I let my vision unfocus, my eyes aimed at the place where the Thirteenth House once existed, until the area seems to be growing larger, or I'm getting sucked into its darkness. Then, suddenly, I begin to see the Snake constellation through the writhing Dark Matter, as if a black curtain were lifting and the starry serpent starts undulating forward.

When the full, heavenly form of the Thirteenth House is floating before me, it speaks in Ochus's bitter voice.

I've disguised myself to hide from the master. Remember, if I were your enemy, would I not do away with you now instead of waiting?

I believe you, Ophiuchus, I tell him, meaning it.

Even though he no longer has a human face for me to read, I can feel in the Psynergy connecting us that I've stumped him. He expected me to fall for the master's ploy. I guess I haven't given him reason to have more faith.

We're setting off for the asteroid belt today, I continue when he doesn't answer. *I only came to tell you the plan is still on.*

Then there is nothing left to say. There's a change in his tone that reminds me of a performer who's gone blank and is now making up the lines. *Watch yourself, little crab.*

◆ ◆ ◆

"No change in plans," I tell the room once we've gathered. "We're leaving in five."

A door bangs open, and Hysan bursts in, his hair pointing every direction. "I apologize for the interruption—my lady, I must speak with you urgently." He's coming from his bedroom, where he was consulting with Neith before our departure.

I'm immediately terrified by what could rattle Hysan this much that he would break his courteous customs. "Excuse us," I tell everyone as I dart over and follow him into a White Room, shutting the door behind me.

"I can't accompany you," he says.

"*What?*" I blurt, steadying myself against the wall.

"It's Neith. Someone's taken over his controls. They must have found out the truth about who he is . . . and who I am. It has to be the master." Hysan paces the floor, pale and absolutely petrified. "Rho, I might have put my whole House in danger. If they break through my protections, they could do anything—know everything. I *have* to go before they get the chance."

I can see the horror in his face, and I know he's right: His House needs him.

"I'm leaving you *Equinox* and taking a smaller ship to Libra. I'll come find you as soon as I've located Neith and made sure my people aren't compromised. You'll only be a seven-hour flight from Kythera, so that's two hours on one of my engine-enhanced Dragonflys."

"Don't worry, we'll be fine," I say, knowing the concern on his face isn't all about Libra. "Focus on Neith, don't come after us unless—"

"Rho, I'm not Rubi or Brynda or the others. I won't wait until you're in danger to come after you. I'm joining you as soon as I see to Neith—and I'll be stealthy. But you'll have to take Twain. He's a good pilot. He'll get '*Nox* through the asteroids."

I nod, still in too much shock that Hysan isn't coming to be able to do much else.

"You are the first and only person I have ever loved, Rhoma Grace," he says, holding my face in his hands. He kisses me and takes off without saying goodbye to the others.

I recover enough of my own breath to leave the White Room and join the group. "Hysan is needed by Lord Neith," I announce. "Twain, you're replacing him."

Nishi and Deke look alarmed, but Twain beams with silent pride.

"Five minutes then," I say, quickly ducking into the nearest kitchen to steady my nerves in private.

"I'm scheduled to go to the Plenum on Taurus," says Rubi, who has followed me in and is pouring herself a cup of tea. "You sure you don't want me with you?"

I shake my head. "You're the only one stubborn enough to keep this up if I fail."

"Can't argue with you there."

"Rho, I need to go back and meet with my Advisors," says Brynda, striding into the kitchen and setting an empty teacup down on the counter. "I'm sending a group of Stargazers and students to Tierre to help Ferez. I will be tracking your progress and will have a ship outfitted and ready to go the moment there's any danger."

"What if we send one stealthy ship alongside you?" asks Rubi for the thirteenth time. "So someone's close by, just in case?"

"Thank you, Rubi, but the master is just too smart and too powerful. If he suspects a trap, he won't show. He needs to think we're alone."

"You *are* alone," says Brynda, and I don't say anything.

When my crew is gathered, I trade the hand touch with every single person we're leaving behind—except Ezra, who refuses to let me get close—and then Aryll, Nishi, Deke, Twain, and I venture into Space.

17

AT THE SPACEPORT, TWAIN FOLLOWS Hysan's instructions and leads us to 'Nox. As we get closer, I spot a glimpse of golden hair by the bullet-ship.

"Hysan!" I shout, speeding up with relief. It must have been a false alarm, and he's coming with us after all!

But I stop short when I get close enough to see the face that belongs to the hair.

"Stanton?"

My brother stands before me, wearing Cancrian blue and a broad smile. He looks so real . . . but he can't be. He picks his bag up off the floor, proving that he can touch, and I've no choice but to believe my eyes.

"No way!" Aryll calls out.

"What—why are you here?" I ask incredulously as I wrap my brother in a hug.

"I should have come with you in the first place," he says. "Mom and Dad wouldn't want me saving marine life—they'd want me fighting beside you. It's where I want to be, too."

My heart is so soft and swollen that it's hard to recall all the hard-edged emotions that had been stabbing it earlier. I can't imagine anything better than having my brother by my side—but I can't let him come on this trip.

"Rho, don't look at me like that. *I'm going*," he says. "You may be able to boss everyone else around, but I do the bossing around in the Grace family. Now let's go!"

Twain unlocks the ship. Deke and Nishi hold hands as they board, and Stanton steers Aryll by the shoulder. I used to think my biggest fear was being far from my family when the world was under attack.

Now I know it's just the opposite.

✦ ✦ ✦

We each take a different cabin on the ship. I convince Nishi and Deke to take Hysan's, the largest, until he's back, and while everyone settles into their new space, I join Twain in the nose. Through the glass, I watch the Capital grow smaller until we escape Centaurion's gravity and Space swallows us.

"Jumping to hyperspeed," says Twain. Soon the stars are threads of light, and we're tunneling through darkness.

Sitting beside him at the control helm, I'm reminded of the last time I sat here, when the captain was Hysan instead of Twain. I remember how innocent I was as I left the Crab constellation for the first time. I didn't yet understand the weight of the leadership I'd accepted. In that moment, I was just drawn to Hysan's light the way firebursts are drawn to Helios.

"I think you're the first friend Hysan's ever had," says Twain, watching me with a shrewd expression.

"Aren't *you* his friend?"

"I think I'm as close as most people get," he says, looking back down at the screen to monitor our heading. "You ever notice when you talk to him how he'll be so focused on you, he doesn't give up anything about himself?"

"Well, he's been alone a lot of his life," I say defensively.

"True," says Twain. "But I also think it's part of being Libran. They're always expected to be friendly and helpful and put together . . . but no one could feel that way *all the time*. Certainly not on Virgo. I think to be a people person, you probably can't let people get too close."

"You're pretty smart," I say, and he laughs. "So why do you want to risk your life so badly?"

His smile fades and his brow furrows, casting a shadow on his handsome face. "On Cancer, your connection to your family grounds you, right? Don't you have a saying? Something like *Happy families start with happy homes?*"

"Yeah." The mention of the Cancrian axiom brings Mom's face to mind, and I shake my head to dislodge it.

"On Virgo, practicality trumps sentiment. Broken families are common. I come from one. Being so practical prevents us from digging too deep into personal passions, either, or any kind of major movement or organization that requires absolute devotion. We can't love broadly, see. Our curse is our perfect vision. We're forced to live in the details."

I never thought about the Virgo lifestyle that way—from a Virgo's own perspective.

"But being here, away from Virgo," Twain continues, looking steadily into my face, "I believe in something with my whole head and my whole heart for the first time."

Meeting his mossy gaze, I murmur, "Thank you."

"*Shielding from Shadows*, what's that?" calls Aryll, reading from the control helm as he makes his way from the back of the ship, Stanton at his side. He looks to be in far better spirits now that my brother is here. While Twain explains to Aryll what the various menus mean, I join Stanton by the crystal-capped round nose.

"I don't know why, but all of a sudden I can't stop thinking about the day Mom left," he says to me in a low voice.

I hate that memory. If it were a Snow Globe, I would smash it. "A week after you were bitten by the Maw," I say just to say something.

Mom and Dad fought that morning, and they were still mad at each other when it was time for Dad to drop me off at school. Mom gave Stanton permission to skip his classes, and while he was playing in his room, she left the house and disappeared into the Cancer Sea. She didn't take our schooner, so we assume she swam.

"Wish I could forget that Maw bite. Worst tenth birthday ever," says Stanton, staring darkly into Space.

"Remember that black seashell she used as a whistle *and* a hairpin?" I ask, trying to distract him from the pain I know he's reliving.

Stanton chuckles. "I'd forgotten about that thing. I was always mesmerized by how she could twist all those heavy curls over her head and then secure them with something so delicate. I guess you saw a different side of that shell."

"She woke me up with it every morning for drills." I look up at my brother. "Stan . . . why do you think Mom left you all the household responsibilities instead of Dad?"

He sighs. "I think because she knew he would be the most broken by her leaving."

I nod. I always thought the same thing. Being so in sync with Stanton makes me feel brave enough to ask the question I've been wanting to ask him for ten years.

"Why . . . why didn't you make me do those drills every morning, like she told you?" My voice sounds so tiny, I feel seven years old all over again.

"Rho, I never even considered it," he says quickly. "I couldn't do that to you." He swallows, hard. "I never told you this, but when I was four, Mom tried to train me."

I stare at him, aghast.

"I was decent at Centering, but I didn't See much. . . . After about a week, she gave up. I didn't have your talent."

Neither of us says anything for a while. We just stare at the lights through the nose, each lost in our own memories. "The day Mom left," I whisper, "before I followed you guys to her reading room, I talked to Jewel. She told me it was wrong for Mom to keep pulling you into her arguments with Dad. She said it was making you older."

Stanton stares at me curiously. "She said that?"

"Yeah . . . she's a smart girl. You, on the other hand . . . let's just say I can't believe it's taken this long."

"I know that already." He shakes his head and turns away from me, probably still unsure about discussing his love life with his little sister. Without facing me, he says, "She reminds me of home."

"I know." When he looks at me, I pose the other question I've been waiting to bring up, the one we ask each other about once a year, as if it's a ball we're throwing back and forth between us.

"Do you think Mom's alive?"

He shakes his head, as he always does. Stanton has always believed that Mom saw her own death in the stars and set out to die alone. I used to believe that, too, but when Admiral Crius said she was alive—even though it was just a Guardianship test—the spark of possibility was ignited. Once kindled, hope is a hard flame to put out.

Aryll claps a hand on each of our shoulders and announces, "*Nox* plays digital mah-jongg!" as though the fact settles an argument. "Who's in?"

I leave Stanton and Aryll to play with the ship and head to my room, when I hear a scream coming from Hysan's cabin and start running.

"*Nishi? Deke?*"

I open the door to see Nishi sitting at the edge of the bed and Deke on bended knee before her, holding her hand and whispering. Both look near tears.

"Rho!" squeals Nishi. "Get in here!"

Deke's smile widens when he sees me. "We're getting hitched, Rho Rho!"

I shriek with delight and squeeze him tight, and Nishi jumps up and joins us. Deke tips us all over, and we laugh as we fall onto the bed, locked into a mega hug. The three of us roll apart on the mattress and lie side by side, Deke in the middle. We used to do this on Elara whenever one of us wanted to talk about something without having to look anyone in the eye.

"Do you think our kids will turn out Sagittarian or Cancrian, Rho Rho?"

"What if they're half-Crab, half-Archer mutant babies?" I tease.

"Then we'll have to live half the year as Sagittarians and the other half as Cancrians," says Nishi, and Deke and I laugh. Then she adds, in a more serious voice, "I don't care who they are . . . just as long as it's who they want to be. I don't ever want them to have to choose between belonging and being happy."

Deke turns his face toward her and presses his lips to her forehead, whispering, "I love you."

We stare up at the blank ceiling for a while, and then Nishi says, "I miss music."

"I miss home."

Deke mumbles, "I miss my sisters."

Nishi and I curl into his sides to comfort him, and he puts an arm around each of us. "How do you think this all ends?" whispers Nishi.

"Either when we stop the master. Or when the master wins," says Deke, his voice gruff and cold.

"I don't think this ends for a while," I say gently. "Remember what Ferez predicted . . . if Risers are the future, it's going to take a long time for the Zodiac to accept that. I'm not sure we'll see the end of this in our lifetime. How we act on the journey is what matters."

"Did you overdose on Aquarian juice this morning?" asks Deke, and Nishi smiles but rolls her eyes at his false accusation.

I force a smile, but the ghostly face from the Ephemeris floats through my thoughts. Could it be that I'm really becoming a Philosopher? Am I part of the new wave of Risers?

"You okay?" asks Nishi, looking at me across Deke's chest.

I haven't told anyone about that vision yet, and I don't plan to. "Yeah," I say, "I just miss this. I miss being an Acolyte. I never thought I'd feel that way when we were actually on Elara."

"Me too," says Nishi, and Deke nods.

"Where do you guys think Kai is?" I ask. We last saw him on the Cancrian settlement on Gemini, where he'd located an aunt. She had taken custody of him by the time I left for Capricorn.

"His aunt said they were staying on Hydragyr," says Nishi. "It's the largest settlement, so it's where they'd have the best chance of finding other surviving family members."

"Do you think Cancer's coming back, Rho?" Deke's voice sounds more vulnerable than I've ever heard it.

Right now, I don't know what I think. I just know I want to heal him. I want to heal all my friends across the Zodiac. I want to bring them hope.

"I *know* it is."

✦ ✦ ✦

"We're nearly at the location," says Twain, knocking on my cabin door in what would be early morning back on Sagittarius.

"Gather everyone in the nose. I'll be out in a moment." I remain in my cabin, the same one I stayed in the last time I was on this ship, a little while longer. In spite of everything that happened then, I was almost happy here . . . in the company of two men and comrades whom I loved, on a mission I believed in wholeheartedly, fueled by an idealistic certainty that we would prevail. It's the way I know Nishi and Deke must feel now.

I can't let anything happen to them.

I join the others in the nose as we leave hyperspeed. "Let's get as close to the asteroid belt as we can without putting ourselves in danger," I tell Twain. "We'll explore the area until we find someone—or someone finds us."

He nods. "You got it, Captain."

Nishi takes my hand, and the six of us wait in silence for someone to attack.

Three galactic hours and four path variations later, there's still no sign of the master's army. "I don't like this," says Aryll, voicing what we're all feeling. "Maybe we should raise our Psy shield."

I shake my head. "We can't appear as if we're prepared for a fight. The whole point is to seem nonthreatening—we have to keep the channels open."

"There's something on the radar," says Twain. "A ship. It's heading for us at—holy Helios, it's impossibly fast!"

'Nox starts shaking violently. A screeching noise grates my ears, like a Psynergy attack from Ophiuchus. The six of us shuffle from side to side, trying to cling to handrails and each other.

Every screen on the ship goes blank and glows white. Then the same black letters begin to form across all of them—a message from Ophiuchus.

> The master's minions are here. They will board your ship by force. If you want to meet the master, you must face them . . . but remember what I told you. Death's hand will reveal your true enemy—and Death is what you are inviting on board.

18

THE SCREENS GO BACK TO normal, and the shaking and shrieking stop. Everyone faces me with expressions slack and lips parted, awaiting my response to Ochus's warning.

"There are enough escape capsules for all of you," I say quickly and calmly, just as I rehearsed in my cabin this morning. "You've gotten me this far—now please, abandon this ship and reconnect with the others. It should be easy to locate Marad headquarters now that you have a path to follow."

Nobody moves.

"That's an *order*," I say, my voice hard. I glare at Stanton and push against him, but he stays still. I tug on Nishi's arm, but she doesn't budge either.

"Give it up, Rho," says Deke, his face set in a determined Lodestar expression that reminds me of Mathias. "This is what you want. This is *unity*—get used to the sight."

Equinox jolts forward as something hooks onto us. "They're overriding the system," says Twain, feverishly clicking through holographic navigational screens. "I can't stop them!"

Their ship has suctioned onto 'Nox, merging us together. "We'll have to fight," says Deke, raising his Arclight.

"We can't fight," I say, hoping my leadership doesn't kill the people I love. "The plan has always been for them to take me to the master, remember? There's no reason for the rest of you to come. Take the capsules—"

"You're surrounded," says a booming voice, the same one that spoke from the sky on Tierre. It's coming from 'Nox's own sound system.

"We are coming in. If you resist, we will be forced to kill you. Stand back and lay down your arms."

Deke reaches for his weapon. "Deke, don't," I whisper. He seems hesitant, but when no one else follows his lead, he lowers his hand. "We're unarmed," I say in a loud, trembling voice.

Suddenly the ship's door opens, and three people stride in. They're wearing white space suits and holding long, black cylinders—certainly weapons of some sort. All of them wear the porcelain face masks of the Marad, with holes for their mouths and no other features visible.

"Hold out your thumbs," says the same voice, but this time in person instead of over the speakers. It seems to be coming from the smallest of the three.

We do as the Marad soldier commands. When it's my turn, an identity hologram pops up. *Rhoma Grace, Former Guardian of the Fourth House, Cancer.* The soldier who screened me silently gestures to the other two, who join their comrade in front of me.

There's a palpable change in the air as they realize who I am. Then the smallest one—who seems to be in charge—steps up to me and breaks the hesitant atmosphere with one quick, purposeful gesture.

The mask comes off to reveal a teenage girl.

She has features that seem to belong to different faces from all over the Zodiac—and some features that I've never seen before in any other human.

Her eyes are large, dark, and close-set; her lips are pale, thin, and long; and her skin is a gray, ashy color, so dry it looks like levlan. She has all the markings of an imbalanced Riser.

From what I know about Risers, this one seems to be going through the shifting process. Her old skin is molting off to make way for new.

"We've captured Mother Rho," she says, now using her own voice to speak. It's raspy and low, almost reptilian. "And right as we're transporting—" She smiles a cold grin, stopping herself from finishing her thought. "I mean, it's almost enough to make you believe in true love." She runs her tongue over her cracked bottom lip. "Then again, I could just be having a good day."

"Please," I say, my voice low like hers, "take me to see the master."

She laughs. The sound is mousy, as if she's someone who's used to laughing only in the dark. "'The master . . .' You do love your boogeymen, crab." She looks to the two masked soldiers behind her. "We won't have enough air. Keep *her* alive, for now—kill the rest."

"NO!" I shout, holding my arms out to shield my friends. "We have enough air on this ship for all of us!"

"Why would we need the others?" she asks, looking at my friends as though they're expendable. She doesn't see their humanity because she can no longer feel her own. Her soul is so twisted and deformed she probably can't even Center herself. But if I've learned anything from all of this, it's that people who can't see the future are usually the ones who fear it the most.

"I've seen something," I say, trying to sound as ominous as possible. "A *vision*. It involves the people I've brought on this ship. Your master will want to meet them." While speaking, I surreptitiously twist my Ring. *Hysan, are you there?*

I can't feel a connection—the soldiers must have their own Psy shield.

"Well, then," says the Riser, inspecting my face closely. "If *they're* so important, we'll get rid of *you* instead."

I force my features to stay fixed and unflinching. "I think your boss will want to hear the details of what I saw."

"Don't worry, I'll relay your message." She raises the large, cylindrical weapon and points it at Stanton's chest. My whole being freezes, as if I'm trapped in one of Ochus's Psynergy icebergs.

"Start talking, or Blondie dies along with you."

Suddenly, a beam of red light shoots from Deke's wrist. One of the masked soldiers falls over, writhing and screaming with pain. Blood spurts from his knee, soaking his white suit and spilling out onto the floor.

It takes everyone a moment to understand exactly what just happened, and then we all react at once. The Riser girl pivots to aim her weapon at Deke, but he ducks out of the way before she can fire. Yanking on Nishi's hand, they dart deeper into the ship, and Stanton and I chase after them.

Behind us, in the ship's nose, the wounded soldier is shouting unintelligibly, but I'm momentarily relieved that I don't hear the sound of their weapons discharging. As we race toward the escape capsules, Stanton takes my hand, and I hear footsteps falling behind us. I glance back, further relieved to see Twain.

"Stop, or he dies."

The voice is once again coming from 'Nox's own sound system. Around us, every wallscreen powers on and projects the same image: the Riser, pointing her weapon into Aryll's chest. His eyepatch slightly askew, Aryll looks two steps beyond terrified. His chin is trembling, but he's not crying. He looks like he's trying to be tough.

Immediately, Stanton and I turn back.

"No, you can't!" shouts Twain, grabbing my arm. "Our only choice is to take back control of the ship. *We have to fight.*"

"Go with Nishi and Deke. Get inside the capsules," I say, freeing myself from his grip. Nishi and Deke double back to see why we're not with them.

"They hijacked the ship's controls. We can't access the capsules," says Twain, crushing my last hope.

"What's the plan?" asks Nishi. Her cinnamon skin looks pale, and her amber eyes are glassy with fear. She's not the assertive, sharp, quick-reasoning Nishi she is in everyday life. I need to get her through this. I can't make the same mistakes all over again.

"*Tick, tock, tick, tock, little crab . . . come out from your shell. . . .*"

I look up at a screen. Aryll is facedown on the floor, trying to speak. "Rho—don't do it—"

The Riser is sitting on his back, and she pushes down on his head with her weapon until he can't speak. *"Sixty seconds before I'm angry . . . another thirty until I'm really angry—and then Red's time is up."*

I turn back to my friends. "Get into Hysan's cabin and hide. Keep your weapons on the door. The moment it opens, you *fire.*" I look to the screen again. The Riser is brushing Aryll's red hair with the butt of her weapon. "I'm going back for Aryll."

"I'm not leaving you," says Stanton, his first words since the Marad invaded our ship. "And I won't desert Aryll. He saved my life." He looks as frightened as Nishi, but his complexion is regaining color. From a quick glance at the others, I know they're not leaving me either.

Arguing will be useless, and a waste of precious time, so instead I focus on the fight ahead. "Fine. If we're all going back in together, we first need to get a message to Brynda and the others so they'll know we made contact. There's a Psy shield up, and I bet they've cut off hologram transmissions, too. We need to think of something else. *Fast.*"

Immediately, Deke opens his Wave, Nishi flicks on her Tracker, and Stanton clicks menus on a monitor in the wall. Twain pulls me aside.

"Hysan told me about Aryll, how he doubts him," he whispers hurriedly. "I know you think Aryll's your friend, but Hysan is the fairest judge and best reader of people I know. You should trust him."

"I know all about that, and I'm not abandoning Aryll," I say, louder than I intended. I look over at the others and the holographic lights reflecting on their faces. "Any luck?"

They shake their heads without looking up.

"*Say your goodbyes, crab.*" The Riser is standing over Aryll, her weapon pointed at his red head. She looks ready to shoot.

Without any more thought, I rush forward into the nose, followed by my friends. We get there and see the uninjured soldier bandaging his comrade's wound, and then the Riser, who is still standing over Aryll. She laughs softly on seeing me and kicks Aryll in the stomach. He groans in pain and curls into a fetal position, and Stanton dives to the floor to pull him from her reach.

"When we captured you, our orders were to keep you alive," she says to me. She licks her chapped lips, cocking her head as she examines me. "But I don't like you. And since you're going to die soon anyway, it might as well be at my hand."

So quickly that there's no time for me to react, she raises the black cylinder, and a blue light flashes from the end pointed at my chest. I hear my friends' screams and feel a hard shove on my side as I fall to the ground, the searing heat of the blue ray grazing my arm.

I look up and see Twain where I was standing just seconds ago.

The shot hits him in the chest, and for a moment he looks frozen and shocked, suspended in time. I almost think he's okay, that the weapon misfired and he's merely stunned but not wounded. Then his body trembles violently as he falls to the floor, his eyes open but clearly unseeing.

The silence that follows is sickening. This doesn't feel real.

"Another boyfriend of yours?" asks the Riser. She lovingly caresses the polished black surface of the weapon that just stopped Twain's heart forever. No mess, no noise, no collateral damage.

She readies herself to aim at me again, but before she can, the uninjured soldier springs up and wrenches the weapon from her hands. He doesn't speak out loud, but I can tell they're communicating silently.

"Fine," she says at last, all pleasure gone from her voice. "I'll bring her alive. But we can still have fun with her friends."

The soldiers bind our wrists and ankles together and remove our Rings and devices. They toss us to the floor and roughly shove us against the wall. No one speaks or resists—we're barely even breathing.

I can't take my eyes off Twain's body, still lying where he fell. His mossy eyes are shiny and bright, his olive face and windswept hair still beautiful, even in death.

Nishi's sudden sobbing disbands my disbelief. The sound brings the scene into focus, and everything becomes harshly and bracingly real. *Twain gave his life for mine.*

The reality of his death blocks up my throat and crushes my heart and coils around me like a snake, constricting the cells of my soul. He couldn't have been older than nineteen. He knew how dangerous this trip would be, but still he wanted to come. He wanted to die for something worth living for.

"It's time for your close-up," says the Riser now, twisting my arm and dragging me over to 'Nox's transmitter near the controls. She fastens my hands and feet to a chair, paralyzing me. Stanton and the others struggle to free themselves, but the uninjured soldier raises his weapon threateningly. The one with the wounded knee sits at the helm, his weapon trained on me as he plugs in new coordinates. I hope Brynda and Rubi have a way to track us despite all the Marad's shields.

"Let's open with a bang," says the Riser in her reptilian tone, surveying my friends like she's at a buffet line and they're the feast. The soldier watching over them stands beside her, and they seem to be communicating silently again. "Yeah," she says after a moment. "Yeah, she does look like the Sagittarian Guardian."

Nishi's eyes widen, and she edges back against the wall. Deke tips over, trying to block her with his body.

"You don't need any of them!" I call desperately. The injured soldier grips his weapon tighter and aims it at my knee.

"We *did* promise to take their Guardian's head," muses the Riser, still contemplating Nishi. Deke is using the wall to sit upright, his hands moving up and down, as if they're working behind his back. "It would get their attention . . ." continues the Riser, oblivious to Deke.

"Kill *me*!" I shout, ignoring the gun pointed at my leg. *"Leave her alone!"*

The Riser grabs Nishi. Deke bursts forward, his hands suddenly unbound, and head-butts the masked soldier in the stomach, knocking his weapon free. While the soldier tumbles, Deke scrambles forward to grab the black cylinder. He wraps his fingers around the trigger just as the soldier regains his balance.

Deke fires. The soundless blue shot hits the soldier in the chest, and he flops to the floor with a shudder, then lies eerily still.

Screaming, the Riser tosses Nishi at Deke, causing him to drop the gun as she falls on top of him, and they crumple to the ground. Before the Riser can shoot, Stanton slams his head into her midsection, his wrists still tied behind him, and they both fall.

In all the chaos, no one notices the injured soldier dragging his right leg around the control helm and over to Deke, who's helping Nishi use the same screw in the wall to undo her own binds.

Nishi looks up and sees him first. She screams. From where I'm sitting, I can see only the soldier's back as he raises his gun.

I don't know when he fires—all I see is Deke's face in the gap between the soldier's legs.

He's wearing the same expression as Twain.

19

NISHI THROWS HERSELF OVER DEKE'S chest in one final attempt to
protect him, but his eyes are already unblinking and lifeless.

The Zodiac stops spinning. Time isn't cyclical or linear or multidimen-
sional—it isn't anything anymore. All of existence has ended forever, and I
feel like I've been sucked into a Snow Globe from my life, a memory where
I can live out my remaining minutes.

Suddenly I'm twelve again—small body, big hair—and choking back
tears as I part with Dad and Stanton to board a ship to the moon. I was
heading to the Zodai Academy on Elara.

While hugging my brother, I spotted a sandy-haired boy in the distance
bidding his parents and older twin sisters farewell. The women and girls
were weeping, but the boy was in good spirits—he kept making them laugh
through their tears. I couldn't imagine being funny in that moment—this
was the second-worst day of my life.

"You're shivering," said my brother, gazing concernedly into my eyes.
"Are you sure you want to do this, Rho?" He'd been asking the same question ever since I received my acceptance from the Academy.

"I'm sure, Stan."

He took off his favorite gray jacket, the one I was always begging to borrow because my frizzy blond curls fit comfortably inside its oversized hood. Also because it was his.

"I want you to have it," he said, helping me into it.

"But you love it! You never let me—"

"It doesn't fit anymore," he said, even though it looked fine on him. "Now go, before the ship takes off without you." I gave Stanton another hug, and then we both pulled away quickly to avoid tears.

I queued up in line with the other students, forcing myself not to look back as I boarded. Inside, no one was crying, so I bit on my bottom lip hard enough to distract myself from the wound widening in my chest.

In the seat beside me was the sandy-haired boy. Peeking up at him, I was shocked to see tears freely fountaining from his turquoise eyes. He didn't look happy or good-humored anymore, and I realized it was all an act for his family's benefit. He was being strong for them. He reminded me of Stanton.

"I'm Deke," he said, seeing me seeing him. He held out his hand.

"Rho," I said as we bumped fists.

"Is that your brother's jacket?" He must have watched me with my family, too. I nodded. "Is he your best friend?" I nodded again. "My sisters are mine. Want to be substitute siblings?"

"What's that?"

"You be my sister and I'll be your brother while we're at the Academy." He passed me some tissues, and I realized I'd been crying this whole time, too.

I nodded in agreement. He took my hand and held it in his, and suddenly I was no longer alone. Thanks to Deke, within minutes of leaving my family, I found a new one.

The ground shudders beneath me, and a sharp, piercing cry shatters the glass of my Snow Globe.

I try holding on to twelve-year-old Deke's hand, but I'm already old again, and time is moving unmercifully forward. I open my eyes. Nishi is still lying on Deke's body, her limbs nearly as limp as his. A scream cleaves the air—it's my brother.

The Riser jabs him with the butt of her weapon, and the sound of a rib cracking echoes through the ship. When Stanton cries out again, I cry, too.

She hits him again, this time on the head, and I let out a shrill scream as my brother falls to the floor, unconscious. Aryll's bound feet hook around Stanton's arm, and he pulls my brother closer, until he's dragged Stanton's body to him. He holds him protectively.

"Shackle them to the wall this time," the Riser commands the injured soldier. Nishi resists him only a little, as if her life force has been halved. The soldier whacks her across the head with his weapon, and I scream again as Nishi passes out. My throat is so raw I taste blood.

I watch Nishi's placid, unblemished face hang sleepily as the soldier chains her to the wall, and I wish they would knock me out, too. Maybe Nishi resisted on purpose.

Aryll, who didn't do anything aggressively defiant, is the only one who isn't brutally punished. He's in shock, leaning over Stanton like my brother is all he has in the world.

The injured soldier returns to the control helm as the Riser sets up a broadcast and goes over the plan with him. She speaks out loud now, clearly confident in her triumph and not worried that we'll overhear. "Too bad we're down to three expendable hostages. Would've been nice to be able to show off our weapons by offing the Sagittarian on the live feed. We'll save the rest in case the crab gets tongue-tied later. Let's pull the Virgo and Cancrian corpses into the shot. Get rid of the third body."

She doesn't even care enough about her own fallen comrade to give him a proper burial—let alone refer to him by name. I close my eyes as she puts her mask back on, and the transmitter lights up. In the Marad's voice, she starts in on a new proclamation.

"We have captured Rho Grace, the fallen Cancrian Guardian. We have already executed two of her supporters"—Deke and Twain are still right there on the floor before me, but I can't look—*"and we will be executing the rest, live, within one galactic hour. The Zodiac is too fractured to be united, and the House system is on the verge of collapse. A new order must rise. First we will get rid of the Guardians, the last remnants of an old and outdated civilization. This Cancrian, though no longer a Guardian, represents the hopelessness of unity among you. In one hour, that fairytale will end."*

The transmission cuts out. The Riser removes her mask and stares at me, excitement flickering in her close-set eyes. She takes my trembling hand in her scaly one. Her touch is almost tender, reassuring. But then her stare grows cold again—and she yanks off my thumbnail.

I bite down on my tongue, tasting the metallic tang of blood again, my skin searing in agony. But I stay as mute as the dead bodies beside me.

Laughing softly, she plucks off the next nail. Tears stream down my face, the pain so great my head is drowning in it, and I grow too dizzy and nauseated to think clearly.

"If I were to kill you now, you would become a martyr, and that's not the boss's plan," she whispers. "Before you go, you will denounce the House system and the whole Zodiac way of life for the entire galaxy to hear." She turns and looks back at Nishi, Stanton, and Aryll. "If you aren't feeling my message, don't worry—I know how to get you in the mood."

Then she wrenches the nail from my middle finger, and the world goes dark.

20

"YOU THINK THE STARS KEEP you safe at night . . . but they can't protect you from what's coming."

I open my eyes. My vision is bleary, and my face feels wet. There's water on my lips. I lick them thirstily and look around. Something's hurting me. . . .

"You believe there are twelve kinds of people in the universe, but what about me? Where do I fit in, crab?"

The scene on 'Nox is blurry and out of focus. The Riser is still talking to me and seems to have been speaking to me this whole time . . . as if she didn't realize or care that I'd passed out. I look down at my fingers. Every nail on my left hand has been removed.

When I see what the Riser is doing now, I bite back a scream—*I can't react, I can't let her win, I can't fall apart.*

The pain I've been feeling comes into full focus. She's slicing my arm open with a knife. She's carving the twelve House symbols into my skin.

"You won't belong to any House either when I'm done with you." She's already up to my elbow and midway through the Zodiac. The pain is so overwhelming that nausea is rising up again, and I can't cling to the present for very long.

"You're killing her!" screams Aryll, his face red and splotchy. He sounds like he's been shouting himself hoarse for as long as I'd been unconscious.

The Riser holds up her knife, giving me a moment to breathe. "I can take care of that tongue for you, Red. While I'm there, I can pluck out that other eye, too, make you symmetrical again."

She's going to keep torturing me until it's time for the broadcast, even if she kills me first. I can see from the look in her eyes that not even an order from the master can stop her from going too far.

The injured soldier is still at the control helm, watching the Riser closely. Again, they're communicating in silence. After a few moments of this, she grudgingly puts down the knife. "Fine. You have two minutes to recover before I continue, crab."

She takes a drink of water and then splashes some on my face. My only ally now is the time I have left until the broadcast, and all I can do is distract her as long as I can. Everything's riding on the hope that Brynda, Rubi, and the others can get past the Marad's technology and track our location. Before we're all dead.

"H-hey," I manage. "What . . . what House were . . . you from?" My voice is croaky and insubstantial, and it makes me cringe to hear it.

She shrugs disdainfully. "What do you care? I don't. I don't even remember. The Houses have nothing to do with me."

Mom taught me about these kinds of Risers—the ones who shift so many times that they begin to lose their earliest memories, until eventually they can't remember anything before their life in their current House cycle. They forget who they were, and even though they've taken on a new appearance in a new constellation, all that truly remains of them is emptiness. A void so vast they try to fill it with anything—money, sex, violence, power—whatever works.

"Do you have a name?" I chance.

"One I have chosen, not one that was given to me." I note how important the distinction is to her. "I am Corinthe."

"Is . . . is there anything you care about?"

"Killing you. Destroying whatever hope the Houses have left."

"Why? What will that do?"

"Cleanse the planets so we can start anew," she says in her raspy voice. "We won't have to hide behind masks because we won't need your acceptance anymore."

"Corinthe, this isn't the way. If you let us go, I'll still appear on the broadcast with you and plead for your acceptance . . . even after everything you've done."

"Break's over," she snarls. She yanks on my arm, and a spasm of pain shoots through me. I turn my head to the side and vomit on the floor.

"What an idiotic little fool," Corinthe says fiercely. The blade of her knife pierces my skin, and the agony is unbearable. My whole arm is on fire as she carves the Scales of Justice into the crook of my elbow. "Acceptance of the new only comes with the ousting of the old. Just like the Trinary Axis. You have to overthrow the system to build a new one."

"You're . . . wrong," I breathe. "You're being . . . brainwashed."

Corinthe has been ostracized, bullied, despised. Like Vecily's friend Datsby. And now the master is exploiting her pain for his own needs. "Corinthe, you're as much a victim as the rest of us."

The knife digs so deep I can't hold back my cry. I pass out as she starts on the Scorpion.

✦ ✦ ✦

When I come to again, my whole arm is cut up, from wrist to shoulder. I'm pallid and weak, and I've lost a lot of blood. A light is flickering in front of me, and I realize Corinthe is beginning her broadcast.

"Took you three ampoules of wake-up gas," she murmurs in her reptilian tone. "Do as I say, and I promise you a swift death. You're nearly there already."

A message scrolls across the wallscreens in the nose. It takes me a moment to see the words clearly.

> My name is Rhoma Grace. I was a citizen of what was once House Cancer. I'm here to tell you I've realized that the House system is wrong. It must be overthrown. The only way for us to truly unite is to lose the twelve signs and come together under one banner. We are all Marad.

"No," I croak.

Corinthe raises her weapon and points it at Stanton, who's sitting against the wall, half-conscious, watching us. He barely has any strength to react.

"*No.*"

Not my brother.

I have to say what she wants. *But she's going to kill him anyway*, says a small voice in my head. I might as well die staying true to my beliefs. *Doesn't matter*, I argue with myself. I can't do something that will cause Stanton pain.

My eyes fill with tears as I read the Marad's words once more, this time preparing myself to speak them aloud. Charon was right, after all—I am a coward. My Cancrian heart doesn't make me strong; it makes me weak. I'm about to betray everything I hold true, everything I've fought for, because of my irrational, irrepressible love for my brother.

I clear my throat and look into the transmitter. "My name is Rho—"

The transmission cuts out as every light in the ship shuts off. *Equinox* goes dark.

"What's happening?" says Corinthe, sounding nervous for the first time.

"We've lost power," says a man's muffled voice. It takes me a moment to realize it's coming from the injured soldier, who's speaking through his mask. That means their communication system has been affected, too.

The nose is completely black, but I begin to hear faint footsteps nearby. "Try to—"

Corinthe is cut off abruptly, and soon I hear the sound of a scuffle by the control helm, too. Something heavy hits the floor.

For a moment I hold my breath, unsure what's happening.

Then I hear him.

"Look alive, 'Nox."

21

THE SHIP'S LIGHTS BLINK BACK on, and I see Lord Neith's towering, white-haired figure at the control helm, binding the hands and feet of the injured soldier, who's been knocked out. Hysan is tying up an unconscious Corinthe.

"Neith, are you okay?" he asks.

"Yes," booms Lord Neith's sonorous voice.

Hysan surveys the rest of the room, and our eyes meet. *"Rho."*

The golden color drains from his skin, and I can only imagine the version of myself that's reflected in his horrified gaze. He rushes over to where I'm sitting and bleeding out. He quickly but carefully undoes my shackles and scoops me up in his arms. In my periphery, I can see Lord Neith and Aryll tending to my brother and Nishi, but I can't speak. Hysan is silent as he carries me into his cabin and sets me on his bed to rest. He hits a few keys on a wallscreen, and the healing pod emerges from a hidden floor compartment.

"I don't want it," I whisper, my voice so frail it splinters.

"Rho, you need to heal." His words are thick with suppressed emotion. *"Please."*

I shake my head, my whole body shivering. Hysan quickly pulls back the sheets so I can burrow in, and I surprise myself by repeating something Mom used to say: *"Erasing a memory from the body doesn't erase it from the mind."*

Hysan pours me a tonic for the pain, and as soon as I take it, I feel a sleepy sensation come over me. I'm still awake, but my muscles feel dormant even when I'm tossing and turning to try to get comfortable. Then he brings over a healing kit and carefully cleans my cuts. Hysan finishes by wrapping a long bandage around my arm, covering it completely. Then he tends to the raw skin beneath my nails and bandages the ends of my fingers.

Once I'm finally sitting up and seeing clearly, Hysan holds my uninjured hand in his and whispers, "I'm sorry, I'm so sorry, Rho. I should have been here. I shouldn't have left—"

"Stop." I wrap my healthy arm around him and let myself fall apart, the way I did when I lost Mathias. Only this time, I lost Deke. My best friend. My second brother.

"H-how did you find us?" I ask when I've calmed down some, my face still buried in the crook of his neck.

"Sirna's necklace."

I stare up at him in surprise. I touch the rose-colored pearl, the token that's become such a part of me I don't even think about it. I owe my life to Sirna—again.

"Neith and I flew a Dragonfly over. It's veiled and docks into a secret port on 'Nox, so the soldiers couldn't detect us."

"But how'd you override the Marad's controls? When we tried to escape, Twain said . . ." My voice breaks on his name, and I forget what I was saying.

"I'm sorry, Rho." Hysan kisses my hair, his heartbeat pounding faster in my ear. "I knew Twain. He was an absolutist—he was seeking something to believe in, and once he found it, he could only believe in it all the way, no compromises. I know he would have considered this a worthy death." Even though his words are soothing, his voice is swimming in sadness. Twain was his friend for far longer than he was mine.

"Remember how I told you I built the Libran Talisman into 'Nox's brain?" asks Hysan, and I nod. "Well, the Talisman is more powerful than anything manmade, and it responds only to me. So once I located you, I had no trouble gaining access."

"What happened with Neith?" I ask, suddenly remembering why Hysan wasn't with us earlier. And it's a good thing he wasn't, or none of us would be here now.

Hysan frowns. "I'm not sure. I have to run some more diagnostics when we land. I found him on the streets of Aeolus, completely disoriented. According to his Royal Guard, he was missing for more than a day, but he doesn't know where he was. He's lost time."

There's a knock on the cabin door. "Come in, Neith," says Hysan.

The android's regal figure shadows the doorway. "Lady Rho, I'm so relieved to see you safe." As always, his quartz irises are strikingly human. "I have secured the hostages in the storage hold. Your friends' wounds have been tended, and they are in their cabins resting. Nishiko might need the healing pod if you're done with it."

I jump to my feet, the movement so quick it disorients me, and Hysan has to steady me. "Easy, Rho. Relax."

"I need to see Nishi." Hysan offers me his arm, and Neith shows us to her new cabin. With a pang, I recall that until today, she'd been sleeping in Hysan's with Deke.

I'm at her door, but I don't immediately go in. I don't know if I can face her. It's my fault Deke is gone. She has to hate me for it, and I can't bear to see that on her face.

"She needs you," whispers Hysan. I nod and open the door.

Nishi is in a ball in the middle of the bed, her blanket of black hair nearly covering her whole body. When she looks up at me, there's no blame in her eyes—only unending despair.

I don't know which one of us moves first. All I know is we're melting together to the floor, sobbing into each other's ears.

The war's over.

We lost.

✦ ✦ ✦

Once I've convinced Nishi to use the healing pod, I check on Stanton and Aryll.

"Rho," breathes my brother, hugging me as soon as I walk into the galley. We stay locked together a few moments, neither of us willing to step away.

"I want to kill her." We pull apart and turn to Aryll. I've never seen his stare so cold before. "She deserves it," he says defiantly.

"We can't," I murmur. "She and her army are our only leads to the master."

"They're *murderers*."

Stanton looks as though he wants to agree with Aryll but knows better than to say so. "Aryll, let's catch our breath first," he says, resting a hand on his shoulder. Aryll doesn't argue with him.

I sit in their silent company until I can't wait any longer, and then I leave and head toward the storage hold.

"You sure that's a good idea?" Hysan's already by the door, having predicted my next stop.

"I have to question them. They're our best way to find the master."

Hysan nods. "I know . . . I just wonder whether you're ready to face the people who, just hours ago, tortured you and murdered your friends."

I flinch at his words, though he's made his point: If I can't handle hearing the facts, how will I handle facing Corinthe?

"What did we do with . . ." I can't say their names, let alone the words *corpses* or *bodies*.

"Neith and I moved them into an empty cabin for now. They're resting peacefully."

"Thank you."

I pull open the door into an echoing chamber that houses extra fuel, spare parts, compressed meals, oxygen tanks, and other necessities. In the middle of the cluttered space are the two Marad soldiers, bound tightly to chairs that are bolted to the floor.

"Why does he still have his mask on?" I ask, looking at the soldier with the bandaged knee. For Deke's sake, I hope the wound hurts worse than Maw poison.

"We couldn't remove it," says Hysan. "The mask is made of organic matter and is attached to his face. Only he knows how to take it off, and he's not speaking."

Thinking of Deke makes me want to shred the mask off the soldier's face with the five fingernails I have left. He killed him. Aryll's right: They should both die.

I suck in a deep breath and take a long time exhaling, trying to push the hatred away so I can think. "Why does he want to hide his face at this point?"

It's easier to talk about the soldiers like they're not here, to make them feel as insignificant and expendable as they made us feel.

"Because his appearance is a clue," says Hysan, confirming my suspicion.

We lock gazes, and I know we're thinking the same thing, only this time neither of us says it. The masks, the brainwashing, the ruthlessness of the attacks . . . they're *all* imbalanced Risers. The master found himself a whole army of sociopaths.

I think of Datsby and Vecily and the injustice that was served to them. Two girls with the same talents and smarts and potential were diverted on opposite paths just because one of them was born into the wrong House.

Ferez is right. Change has to come.

Whoever the master is, he and I have the same power and resource: our young followers. We have believers willing to act on—and even die for—our visions for tomorrow. This war will be between those who trust in his vision and those who believe in mine.

Corinthe's dark, close-set eyes follow me in the dim lighting. We both know she's not going to tell me anything, but that's not why I came in here. I came to show her she didn't break me.

"I'm still going to fight for a world that accepts you," I tell her. "Because whether you know it or not, you're a victim, too." A sneering, too-wide smile splits her levlan face. "The master is manipulating you," I go on. "He's playing on your pain by doing the very thing you hate me so much for doing—giving you *hope*. Only his is a false hope. Murder and destruction will only bring you fear—violence won't make anyone love you. And I know that's what you're really after."

"I don't believe in love," she says, and I feel something like déjà vu coming on—only it isn't that. I heard her say similar words before. When she first stormed onto 'Nox, she said, *"It's almost enough to make me believe in true love."*

What did she mean by that?

Without another word, I spin around and cut through the ship to the nose. Hysan closes the door behind us and hurries to catch up. "I want to board their ship," I tell him when we've reached 'Nox's main doors.

"Neith is trying to break through their access codes. We're nearly there." He joins Neith at the control helm, and I pace the nose until Hysan announces that our communications are back online and the Marad's Psy shield is off. Then the door into their ship opens.

Neith, Hysan, and I enter a cold, hollow hallway that's pitch black. We advance into a larger space that's slightly less dark, its lights hazy and low to the ground, illuminating us up to our waists while leaving our faces in shadow. The circular room is entirely devoted to holographic screens and navigational controls and all kinds of weapons. While Hysan and Neith review the technology, I head down another narrow hallway to the back.

The cabins here are half the size of the ones on 'Nox, and each is furnished with a single bed and nothing else. No closet, no desk, no dresser. There's one lavatory on the ship for everyone to share and a small galley that barely fits one person. All that remains at the end of the hall is a large metal door.

I pull, but it doesn't open. Hysan comes over and punches a series of codes into a screen, until something clicks and the door slides open on its own.

The smell that immediately wafts out makes us cover our mouths and hesitate. It's so much darker in there than the rest of the ship that it takes a moment for my eyes to adjust as we peer inside.

The first thing that becomes clear is a wall bolted with chains and blades and spiky weapons. Down in the corner, I see where the smell is coming from: a metal pot someone has been using as a toilet. This is a torture chamber.

We take a few steps, and then I see them. Two people are huddled on the floor under a thin, stained blanket: a guy who's been severely beaten and a girl who's leaning over him protectively. With her oily hair matted across her face and her ready-to-pounce pose, she looks like a wild animal.

"It's okay," I say softly, "we're not Marad. We're not going to hurt you."

As soon as I speak, the guy looks up, and I see the features in his bruised and hairy face.

I gasp and fall forward to my knees, the breath completely leaving my body. My pulse is a speeding metronome marking off the new racing rhythm of my life, and I can't think or feel or focus. It can't be—

"Mathias?"

22

HYSAN HURRIEDLY FREES THEM FROM their chains, but I'm still on the floor, my eyes still locked on the indigo blue irises that I never thought I'd see again.

How is this possible?

How did he survive?

Who is this girl?

They're both so dirty and bloodied and bruised that it's hard to make out much of their features—if I didn't know Mathias's face like it was my own, I wouldn't have been able to recognize him. I can't even tell what House the girl is from—not that it matters. Right now we have to get them on *Equinox* and take them to healers. I get to my feet and reach down to help Mathias up.

He jerks away and clings closer to the girl. I seal my lips to keep from gasping as a pain worse than Corinthe's knife stabs me in the chest.

"Let's get you out of here," coaxes Hysan, kicking away the chains that had bound them. The girl puts an arm around Mathias, and together they get to their feet. Hysan leads the way through the Marad ship and onto

Equinox. Mathias and the girl go wrapped together, still holding on to their ratty blanket, heads bent down against the light.

Aryll and Stanton's jaws drop when they see us walk in with two badly beaten hostages, and they silently follow us into Hysan's cabin. Nishi has already left the healing pod and must have returned to her room, so Hysan tries to help Mathias into the pod.

"NO!"

His shout is so loud, I can almost feel his voice reverberating through the room long after he's gone quiet. Something's different about it.

His music is gone.

"I'll tend to him," says the girl, her voice scratchy, as if she hasn't had water in days. Hysan immediately fetches them a carafe and a couple of glasses, and Stanton and Aryll carry in a tray piled with food. Meanwhile, the girl gently deposits Mathias on the bed and investigates the contents of the healing kit Hysan used on me earlier.

As the four of us are filing out of the cabin minutes later to give them some privacy, she manages a quiet "Thank you."

In the hallway, I'm conscious of Hysan's eyes drilling into me. Only I can't meet them. Instead, I storm into the storage hold.

Corinthe barely has time to lift her head before I charge my fist into her face. My blow lands on her jaw, and she laughs out loud for the first time.

"You found my gift, then?" she asks in her raspy voice.

In response, I punch her again, this time landing on her nose, and I feel the brittle bone crack. A patch of skin is flayed off where I struck her, as if it's made of actual dried-out levlan. The Marad's advanced technology and special suits hide her inferior makeup: Imbalanced Risers have the highest number of diseases and deformities of anyone in the Zodiac.

I pull back to hit her again, but a hand cinches my wrist and yanks me away.

Hysan drags me out of the room while Corinthe cackles with glee. He pulls me into the galley, where Aryll and Stanton are waiting for us. Holding my bleeding knuckles in his hands, Hysan starts sterilizing the wounds without a word.

"*What's going on?*" Stanton finally asks. "Who are those people? What happened to your hand? And no one has explained what the Guardian of Libra is doing here!"

"Lord Neith personally requested to lead the rescue mission," says Hysan tonelessly, his face focused on my cuts. "Those people are hostages we found on the Marad ship. One of them is Rho's former Guide."

"Your *Guide?*" asks Stanton incredulously. "The person the Plenum practically charged you with killing?"

"I don't get it either," I say, my metronome pulse still racing at its new record speed. Mathias is alive . . . I saw him, but I can hardly believe it. What if it's a trick? The master's technology outmatches ours, so odds are he can build androids as sophisticated as Hysan's. Creating a false Mathias to toy with my emotions sounds just like the kind of twisted torture the master would want to inflict.

"So what now?" asks Aryll, just as Lord Neith appears in the galley doorway.

"The ambassador from House Cancer is calling."

We run into the nose to find Sirna's hologram waiting for us. "Rho, thank Helios—when we lost your signal, we feared the worst."

"Thanks, Sirna—once again, I owe my life to your Tracker."

After a transmission delay, she bows. "I'm relieved you're all right."

"I don't know what we would have done without you. We've taken two soldiers prisoner. They had two hostages with them who are in pretty bad condition. We need to take them to healers." I don't mention Mathias by name in case he's not real—I'd rather Hysan and I find out all we can first, in case this is part of the master's plan.

I especially don't want his parents to have to lose him twice.

"Bring everyone to House Taurus," she says, an unexpected smile breaking through her usually stern face. "We found evidence of an explosive, which means the destruction on Tierre wasn't set off by a Psy attack. What's more, Sage Ferez appeared as a holo-ghost from the undisclosed location of Moira's bedside to tell us that Ophiuchus is real. He advised the Plenum to heed your advice."

My skin tingles with new energy.

"Ferez's revelation has made such an extreme impact that the Houses have split into two polarized factions. Aquarius, Aries, Scorpio, Taurus, and Leo believe the Marad is the true enemy and remain unconvinced of Ophiuchus's existence, but Houses Sagittarius, Gemini, Libra, Virgo, Pisces, Cancer, and Capricorn are behind you. They believe you have been telling the truth, that you are the most gifted seer we've seen in ages, and they have called on you to testify to Ophiuchus's existence. This split in the Plenum is unprecedented in Zodiac history, Rho. Your testimony is vital—it could bring the Houses closer than we've been in centuries."

I look at Hysan, forgetting that I'd been avoiding him, though the vulnerability I sense in his expression immediately reminds me. "I heard the news right before Neith and I found you," he says somberly. "I think Ambassador Sirna is right. This is a huge chance to unify at least half of the Houses."

I nod, and something Hysan said on Capricorn about the Houses flits into my mind: *The greater our need to unite, the deeper we divide.* Hysan and I are guilty of that same crime—right when our worlds are finally communicating, he and I aren't.

We end the call with Sirna after I agree to testify at the Plenum, and Neith charts a new flight path that will get us to Taurus within two days. He and Hysan detach the Marad ship from *Equinox*, and since Brynda and Rubi have already dispatched the rescue craft to these coordinates, their Zodai will study the Marad's equipment for clues once they arrive.

Neith hands back my Ring and the other devices the Marad took from us, and I return everything to the rightful owners, saving Nishi for last. When I open her door, she's asleep. She seems to have raided the sleeping powders in her drawer and ingested more than one variety. I rest her Tracker and Deke's Wave on the desk, then cover her with the blanket and gather up the remaining powders before leaving the room. As I'm depositing them in one of the ship's larger healing kits, I hear my name.

I look up. The girl we rescued is in the hallway with Hysan, waving me over. The cabin door behind her is open only a sliver. The three of us slip inside and shut it behind us. The room's lights have been dimmed to semidarkness.

Now that she's washed her face and hair and changed into the yellow, temperature-controlled Libran suit Hysan loaned her, I can tell she's Aquarian. Her ivory skin and dusky violet eyes give her away.

She perches on the edge of the bed, while Hysan and I stand in the center of the room. Sitting beside her, but hidden in her shadow, is Mathias, his face shaven and clean save for a few bruises and shallow cuts. A long, straight scar runs down the side of his neck, and his wavy black hair is longer than I've seen it. He doesn't meet my eyes, but his midnight blue gaze pierces through the gray air.

"He was there longer than I was," says the Aquarian in her misty voice. Her auburn locks drape down like a waterfall, swallowing her small face but tapering in at the ends, past her shoulders. "He endured . . . unspeakable things. I tried keeping him sane. I'd remind him who he was every night, so he didn't forget and lose himself completely. I'm Pandora, by the way. Of the Nightwing clan."

Aquarians are divided into six clans. Nightwings are the House's star-readers. "Like Mallie," I say, picturing the owl design of her Philosopher's Stone, which I'd admired the night of Helios's Halo.

Pandora nods. "She's partly the reason I'm here . . . though the real reason would be you." Her amethyst eyes watch me, unperturbed by the strangeness of her declaration. Her disarming stare reminds me of Leyla's.

"Then you were at the Plenum on Aries?"

She nods again. Beside her, Mathias is still turned away from us, giving no indication he's even listening.

"I joined the armada," says Pandora. "I was on an Aquarian ship, and when we were attacked, I ejected in an escape capsule . . . same as all the others."

"*Others?*" echoes Hysan.

"The Marad's ships were there, too. We just didn't see them. They used their own Veils. While the armada was being destroyed, their ships snuck in and stole escape capsules and Skiffs without anyone noticing. They took dozens of us hostage. They were waiting for us."

"How do you know that?" My voice sounds suspicious, and I almost regret prying, after everything she's been through. I don't mean to put Pandora through more pain, but I can't dismiss the possibility that she and Mathias might not be who we think they are. That the master could be luring me into another trap.

"If it's okay, Pandora, do you think you could try telling us what you remember?" Hysan's voice is velvety soft and lacks the suspicion that sharpened mine.

"I don't know days or hours anymore," she begins, addressing Hysan. "Time is just one long, run-on sentence. I only know that before the beatings, I was in a kind of detention center with other girls my age. Most of us had been taken in the attack on the armada, but some were abducted earlier—disappearances across the Houses that no one had thought to link. The armada had provided the army with a feast."

She pauses, and when she starts speaking again, her voice is lower. "Once they caged us, the soldiers spoke openly around us. . . . They knew we would be killed soon. Every now and then they'd take a couple of us away, and we'd never see those girls again. One day, it was my turn. I was put in that torture chamber where you found us. When I arrived and saw him," she says, taking Mathias's hand, "he seemed dead. I think he nearly was."

At her touch, Mathias's eyes cut to mine, and this time he holds my gaze. He always seemed so invincible that it's hard seeing him so damaged. It's even harder watching someone else tend to him when I would give anything to be the one touching him. To feel his realness.

If that's really him.

"What's the Marad doing with the people they're taking hostage?" asks Hysan.

"I don't know . . . I only heard vague things." She sounds like she knows more but doesn't want to say.

Hysan moves toward the bed and kneels on the floor, looking up into Pandora's face. "Please . . . if there's a chance what you know can help us save others, we must know the rest of your story."

She shakes her head. "It's . . . it's awful. They've been *studying* us. Running psychological experiments. When we die, they conduct autopsies to see how people from each House differ on the inside." She swallows and blinks rapidly. "They . . . they're organized. They're not just a random group of disgruntled people. They hold seminars and mandatory classes the soldiers have to enroll in. There was one lesson where I watched them strip naked twelve people, one from each House, and talk about them as if they were cuts of meat."

She looks at me then, her amethyst eyes wide. "When I realized who Mathias was, I couldn't believe it. I remember when I first heard they'd captured him. The soldiers were excited to have someone so close to you. They thought he would be a good surprise weapon if they ever needed one. He became a novelty prize—they passed him around among the top officers, torturing and humiliating him. They scoffed at how noble he was. How he wouldn't break, wouldn't denounce you, no matter what they did to him."

Dizziness—not just from my own blood loss, but from Pandora's tales of torture and death—rises up in me again. The painkilling tonic is beginning to wear off. Hysan seems to notice, because he rises to his feet and steadies me with his arm.

Mathias is still watching, and I whisper, "I'm sorry . . . I'm so sorry." He turns away, facing the wall instead, and the renewed rejection is worse than anything Corinthe did or could do to me.

Hysan helps me out of the room, and the last thing I see is Pandora laying a consoling hand on Mathias's shoulder. He doesn't shirk her touch.

"This is a little too hard to believe, Hysan. I'm worried he's an android," I say as soon as we enter my cabin. "The master has sunk to an all-new low, using a Mathias look-alike to unnerve me." Hysan helps me into bed and hands me a glass of water. "I'm not sure we can trust her either," I go on. "She knows too much for a prisoner."

But Hysan isn't looking at me. He's sitting at the far end of my bed staring at the wall. "Rho, *Equinox* does a full-body scan of every person who comes on board. She's really an Aquarian teen believed to have died in the armada . . . and he's really Mathias."

He's really Mathias. Those are the only words that linger in my mind after he's spoken. *He's really Mathias.* He's alive.

Something savage and painful erupts in my chest. I gulp down the water to keep Hysan from seeing my face. The wave of relief spreads to every corner of my being, making even my stinging skin feel soft and sleepy. In spite of all the horrors . . . I'm *happy*.

I'm happy Mathias is alive.

I lie back on the mattress, and I feel myself falling, only I'm lying on the bed. Before Hysan can shut off the lights, I'm swallowed by darkness.

23

I WAKE UP MORE THAN twelve hours later, having slept for the first time since leaving Sagittarius. I wonder if Hysan diluted a sleeping powder in my water or if it was just that my brain couldn't take another conscious second. I leave my room and join the others in the galley for a meal, unsure whether it's lunch or dinner. I'm starting to get what Pandora meant about time feeling like a long, run-on sentence.

"Where are Mathias and Pandora?" I ask, not seeing places for them at the table.

"Eating in their room," says Stanton, who's sitting next to Aryll.

"So is Nishi," says Hysan, arriving last. "I checked on her before injecting the Marad soldiers with nutrients." It's a way for healers to deliver food to patients who can't eat. Hysan keeps stores of those needles on the ship in case of emergencies.

Once he sits, we dine on more of the sandwiches and spongy cakes Brynda's staff packed for us. "How are you feeling, Rho?" asks Hysan.

"Much better. You, Stan?" I say, turning to my brother.

"Good." He piles three sandwiches and two cakes on his plate. There are bandages on his chest and head where Corinthe beat him.

"And you, Aryll?" asks Hysan, who hasn't reached for food yet. "You seem to be the only one who got by unscathed."

"You mean besides you," says Aryll, imitating Hysan's pleasant manner.

"I was the one who *rescued* you," says Hysan, correcting him. "What I don't understand is why everyone else fought for their lives and you didn't."

"Hysan—" I start.

"Aryll had a gun pointed to his head, just like the rest of us," snarls Stanton, his tone so even it's almost icy. Aryll glares menacingly at Hysan but doesn't defend himself.

"Excuse me. I just realized I'm not hungry after all." Hysan gets up and leaves without eating.

Though I don't follow him out, I've lost my appetite, too. Stanton, Aryll, and I don't speak for the rest of the meal. After I've helped them clean up, I knock on Hysan's door. Since Mathias and Pandora have been staying in his cabin, he's taken the room farthest back and closest to the storage hold.

"Drop your war with Aryll," I say as soon as he lets me in. "You're wrong about him. He's not what you think."

I suck in a quick breath, and once he shuts the door, I say the rest in a rush. "Before I was born, when my brother was two, our mom foresaw a hurricane that would strike a neighboring island. She took Stanton with her to deliver resources to the community. He was small, and when he wriggled through a hole in the wreckage, he found an infant still alive. The baby was Aryll."

Hysan doesn't react, and I can't read his expression. He's either waiting to hear more, or he hasn't heard a word.

"Do you hear how crazy that sounds?" he finally says.

"I believe him. Only four people know that story. Two of us are on this ship, two are dead."

"It didn't strike you as *convenient* when he decided to divulge this to you days ago, and not when you first met?"

"Actually, he told Stanton back on Gemini."

"Did Stanton tell you that, or did Aryll?"

"Aryll, but—"

Hysan shakes his head. "Rho, he's not trustworthy. Can't you see—"

"All I see is you taking your frustration with *us* out on Aryll because you don't like him," I snap. "And you're ignoring everything I said on Sagittarius about us needing to trust each other completely to unite."

The green in Hysan's gaze fades, and I know I've lost him. "You have your freedom to trust whomever you want, my lady, and I have mine." He's pulling away from me. "But since I do trust you, I want you to know I've planted false information in *Equinox*'s intelligence files. If Aryll's Marad, he'll find it—and then we'll know the truth about him."

I want to yell at Hysan for treating a friend like this, but he's completely within his rights. He's a Guardian with the duty to protect his people. If he has a suspicion, I can't prevent him from acting on it. "What false information?" I ask with a sigh.

"I got the idea from Nishi and Ferez. I faked a message from myself to Lord Neith alleging that I'd located the Thirteenth Talisman. I claimed that this was the reason I went back to Libra instead of coming with you on this trip. Anyone working for the master will want to get his hands on the stone."

"But that just makes *you* a target—"

"Good thing Aryll's innocent, so I have nothing to worry about."

I open my mouth to retort but instead storm out of the cabin. I look everywhere for Stanton and finally find him coming out of Nishi's room. He closes the door behind him, and I pull him into the empty galley. "How is she?"

He shakes his head, his brow a hard line. "I'm worried about her, Rho. I think she needs to be with family—and far away from this ship."

"I know." Stanton met Nishi when we were thirteen, on our first break from the Academy. Most Cancrian Acolytes can't wait to visit home after a year on the moon, but Nishi asked if she could come back to Cancer with me instead of Centaurion. She said her parents were always traveling and wouldn't be on Sagittarius during the holidays anyway.

"I don't think we should press her, though," I caution. "Would you mind keeping her company when we get to Taurus?"

"Of course, Rho."

Then I voice the question I came to ask. "Stan . . . on Gemini, did Aryll tell you the truth about who he is?"

My brother's tense features abruptly split into a wide grin. "*He told you!* Rho, I'm so sorry I didn't mention it—I swore to keep it secret until he was ready; he had some dumb idea you'd like him less—"

I exhale pure relief. Stanton is still talking, but I'm too excited to listen. "It's okay, I'm not mad," I say, cutting him off. "I think it's incredible—"

"I know! It almost feels like—" His cheeks go pink with discomfort, and the sentence stays suspended.

"Like maybe Mom's still watching over us," I finish for him. He nods, his glassy eyes mirroring mine.

After wishing my brother good night, I crack open the door to Nishi's room. She's sitting up in bed, staring at a hologram floating beside her. It's Deke.

I'm so shocked by the image that I must have audibly gasped, because Nishi turns around to face me before I can say anything.

"The night before we left"—her words startle me, and I look from Deke to her—"Deke said we should record goodbye messages for each other, in case we never got the chance in real life." She's silent a long moment, and my heart aches to see her so agonizingly lost.

"I thought he was joking. He was always only half-serious about anything, wasn't he?" Her voice sounds unnaturally high. "Besides, the thought of doing something like that . . ." She shakes her head. "I was so stupid, Rho. I didn't think it could happen to us."

I close the door and approach the bed, taking her hand in mine. "Nish . . ."

"I didn't record anything, but Deke did. He must have set the message to auto-send at the same time every night unless he manually canceled it . . . and this time it went through." She looks at me, her eyes so watered down I can barely see the amber. "Rho, don't leave me."

"I won't." I squeeze her fingers, and we stare at Deke's ghost as she activates the message and he comes back to life.

"I know this is too morbid for you, so I doubt you'll do it." Ghost Deke grins, the same roguish smile that won Nishi's heart and made him popular at school. "But when my sisters died, all I could think of were the things I didn't say while they were alive. So if I wind up shooting off to Empyrean, I need you to know that my biggest regret will be missing out on a lifetime with you."

Nishi starts crying quietly, and I wrap my arms around her, tears already on my cheeks, too, as Deke's message plays on.

"I also want to say something I should have told you forever ago. I didn't wait this long to make a move because you're not Cancrian. I waited because I knew that if we dated, you'd realize you could do way better. I'm just an ordinary guy, Nish. What makes me special is that *you* picked me. And if I can't be by your side forever, you'll fall in love again—"

Nishi sobs louder, and I clutch her more tightly. "—and that lucky bastard will be made special by your love, too. Just make sure he has Rho's approval. Speaking of which, if I'm gone, I know you're not watching this alone. . . ."

Nishi buries her face in my neck, her whole being devolving into sobs.

"*Rho Rho Rho your Strider*, I'm proud of you. Thanks for leading us. I'm sorry I wasn't supportive when you first became Guardian—I just didn't want to lose the only sister I had left."

By now I'm crying as hard as Nishi. Deke's bouncy energy is subdued, and this no longer seems like a quirky exercise but a real farewell.

"You're the love of my life, Nish. I hope you never see this message, but if you're watching it now . . . tell my parents I love them. And don't forget me."

24

I STAY WITH NISHI UNTIL she falls asleep. When I leave her room, I pad past Mathias and Pandora's cabin, pausing by their door. It's hard to process all that has happened, and all that will come next, when I can't get past the fact that *Mathias is on this ship*.

Maybe it's because he's so different now, but I don't fully feel that he's here. I don't know this person we rescued, nor does he seem to know—or want to know—me.

While everyone rests, I curl up in the ship's crystal-capped nose and look out into Space. Neith works soundlessly at the control helm, and I find his company comforting as I stare into the ever-expanding blackness ahead.

It's my fault Deke and Twain died. I let them—and everyone else—come on board. I led us. And yet, I don't feel the suffocating guilt or the crushing self-doubt or the shattering sadness from the armada. I've grown harder.

On Cancer, we're taught the loss of one life is as unacceptable as the loss of ten thousand, because every life is precious. Yet I can't take on this charge without accepting some losses. I can't let every failure stop me. And even though this semihard shell is what the Zodiac needs me to wear . . . I like myself less for it.

"Lady Rho, I hope I'm not disturbing you." I look up to see Lord Neith towering over my shoulder, his hair silver in the starlight. "May I join you a moment?"

I nod and wipe a tear from my lashes as he lowers himself to the floor. "How are you feeling, Lord Neith? Hysan told me you lost time."

He sits with his back ramrod straight, his quartz eyes cutting a path through the black. "I'm concerned. Anything could have happened that day. We reviewed my central functions and updated my security system, so we know I'm not transmitting or recording. Yet what we cannot know is how much information was compromised during my time away. Hysan refuses to see the gravity of this situation."

"What do you mean?"

Neith's face softens with sympathy. For a moment he feels to me like a real parent, and I want to relax into his protectiveness. "You are all he thinks of, Lady Rho. The moment we lost communication with *Equinox*, he knew you were in danger. We took off before he could complete my examination."

"What can I do to help?" I say, staring at the floor.

"Help me show Hysan he's ready to step forward as Guardian of the Seventh House."

My head shoots up in shock. "*Now?* But—but then what happens to you?"

Lord Neith doesn't answer and instead takes an object from his pocket and holds it out to me. It's a small metal circle the size of one of the finger-nails Corinthe took from me.

"Do you know what this is, Lady Rho?" I shake my head. "*Me*," he says, flashing his sparkly white smile. "It's my first memory drive."

He tips it into my hand, and though practically weightless, it feels heavier than anything I've ever held. "I am not this body or this voice," says Neith. "I am all of the things that are in this chip. A collection of memories."

His voice grows deeper, graver. "I am too great a liability, especially now, when we face an enemy with superior technology. I contain information that's too powerful in the wrong hands. For House Libra's sake, Hysan must destroy me."

"He would never do that," I say, my body rejecting his words wholly. "Lord Neith, this is unnecessary—"

"Miss Trii and I have spoken about this, and she has agreed to dispense with me and scatter my parts if Hysan will not agree. We are aware that, when it comes to me, his emotions cloud his judgment. As do his feelings for you." I look up into his expressive quartz eyes and find I can't pull away from their authority. "I hope, Lady Rho, that I can count on your support when the time comes."

"Lord Neith, I can't—I don't want that for you either."

He reaches out and takes my hand. I'm once again surprised at how warm and alive he feels.

"You are Cancrian, and your emotions make you strong. That is why I know I can trust you to see that I am right." His eyes are so bright, they look like they could produce tears. "After all . . . aren't memories the most a parent can hope to leave his child in the end?"

Lord Neith closes my fingers around the metal chip and rises in one graceful motion. He returns to the control helm, and the darkness falls heavier around me.

◆ ◆ ◆

When we drop out of hyperspeed, I focus on the view of House Taurus to distract myself from what's going on inside the ship—and my head.

The Bull constellation has two planets and one moon, but only one planet is inhabited. Vitulus has twelve landmasses and shallow oceans, and even from this distance its cities are aglow with artificial light. Everything in Taurus is always buzzing with energy—especially its people. They seem to need less sleep than the rest of us and are known for working hard so they can play even harder.

Stanton and Aryll help Neith prepare the ship for landing. Hysan is in his room reaching out to his contacts on Taurus to reserve a runway at the spaceport and make transportation arrangements. This is one of the rare times *Equinox* is arriving somewhere unveiled.

I stop by Nishi's room to tell her we're landing. The light of a hologram quickly extinguishes as I open her door. "We're almost there," I say softly. She nods but doesn't meet my gaze. "Can I get you anything?"

She shakes her head, and after a moment, I ease back into the hallway and shut the door. I hate being so powerless to help her. As I turn back toward the nose, I notice Mathias's door is ajar.

I look around to make sure I'm alone in the hallway, and then I nudge the door a little farther and peek inside. He's wearing the gray suit Hysan loaned him, which only fits now that Mathias has lost so much of his burl and bulk. He's alone at the edge of the bed, Pandora nowhere in sight, pulling on a pair of paint-speckled black boots that look strangely familiar. My breath traps in my lungs as I recognize them.

Mathias spots me and freezes, with only one of Deke's boots on. We stare past each other—he on the bed, me in the doorway—until finally I say, "I don't want to cause you more pain. I-I just want to say I'm sorry . . . that day, I shouldn't have closed the airlock door. Everything that happened—it's my fault, Mathias. I'll never forgive myself, and I don't expect you to either. *I'm so sorry.*"

I turn to go because I'm too choked up to say more, and then I hear it at last—a single musical note.

"Rho."

Without waiting for more of an invitation, I stride in and sit as close to him on the bed as I dare, leaving enough space so he won't shrink from me again. When he doesn't say anything else, I whisper, "We're landing soon. Your parents will be so happy to see you."

His indigo eyes travel up my bandaged fingers and arm. "*She* did that?"

I nod and survey the cuts on his face, my eyes trailing down the thick, straight scar that slices his neck and disappears into his tunic. "Was that Corinthe, too?"

Mathias clenches his jaw, his anger making it too hard to answer. Then goose bumps rise up along my arms as he finally meets my gaze.

"It's not your fault, Rho."

I spy a flicker of recognition in those lost eyes, as if *my* Mathias is in there, trying to reach me. "By the time Pandora found me . . . I thought I was dead. Her touch became proof I still existed." He looks back down at his uneven feet and murmurs, "I know it's hard to understand, but if I let go of her . . . I'll disappear again."

The door opens, and I stand as if on cue. I don't reply to Mathias or greet Pandora as she walks in. I keep my face averted the whole way, so neither one of them will know that I'm breaking.

25

MATHIAS'S WORDS WON'T LEAVE MY head. He's not upset with me. He doesn't blame me. He's just . . . replaced me.

He has a bond with Pandora I can't come between. I don't have a place in his life anymore. He's not my Guide, and he's definitely not my boyfriend, so where does that leave us when *Equinox* touches down?

My body feels heavier as we cross the invisible barrier into Vitulus's gravity, and I join Stanton and Aryll in the nose for a close-up look at the planet. Hysan's with Neith at the control helm, and he keeps his eyes glued to the screens when I stride in.

I wish I could walk over and clear the air between us, but now more than ever, I wouldn't know what to say. If my feelings were jumbled before, that's nothing to what they are now that Mathias is back. And Hysan knows, because he always knows.

I think of Nishi and Deke, Stanton and Jewel. Mathias was right a lifetime ago, when he warned me against falling for him or Hysan, but he was wrong about the reasons. It wasn't about age or rank. Love simply can't thrive in a war—and believing it can is like trying to light a flame in a room without oxygen.

Vitulus now looms larger. Its twelve countries are referred to as Sections, and each one is named for a part of the bull—the Hoof, the Heart, the Shank, the Horn, the Head, the Rib, the Spine, the Flank, the Throat, the Tail, the Belly, and the Leg. When I was younger, I read that the naming system was meant to convey the notion that each Section is part of one organism, and they must all work together for the whole system to function. I always found that beautiful.

The Heart is the House's capital, and it's where the Plenum meets. The Guardian is the House's Chief Executive, and her Advisors are the executives of each Section—together, they form the Taurian Board of Directors. Everything in each Section is privatized in a free market model, down to public services, and, collectively, the businesses in each Section must subscribe to three rules: Employ the full population, ensure environment-friendly operations, and maintain a positive consumer rating—or the Guardian can replace the offending Section's Executive.

As we near the Heart of Vitulus, its cities grow bigger through the glass. The place looks as busy as the Sagittarian Capital, but its architecture is infinitely more modern. There are sleek-walled starscrapers everywhere, blaring huge holographic ads visible from even this altitude. Speeding bullet-shaped cars zoom through white roller-coaster highways that loop around the air and through the buildings like ribbons wrapping the scenery together.

When we land in the spaceport, a line of Promisaries—Taurian Zodai—march onto *Equinox* in their olive green uniforms. They present their orders to Lord Neith, the highest-ranking official on our ship.

"They're in the storage hold, very last door," says Neith, waving the officers on. They file forward, returning straightaway with Corinthe and the masked soldier, both tied up at the hands and feet. Corinthe's close-set eyes glare at me defiantly as she's shuffled off the ship, and I can't help wondering what's going to happen to her.

She murdered a Cancrian and a Virgo, so both Houses will want to bring her to justice through their laws, which makes it a universal case. So she'll face her charges on Libra, where the jury will be made up of twelve people, one from every House, and Lord Neith will preside over the proceedings. However, if hers is declared a wartime crime, she'll go before House Aries, and it's likely we'll never hear from her again.

When the Promisaries disembark, I see two Cancrians run on board toward me—Amanta and Egon Thais.

They pull me into a hug, shocking me with their affection and ready acceptance, and immediately I feel guilty for not reaching out to them. But I was too afraid they blamed me as much as I do. I can't believe they don't.

"I'll show you where he is," I say and lead them to the largest cabin, its door still closed even though we've landed. As soon as Mathias sees Amanta, he leaps up and engulfs her in his arms. As Pandora begins to introduce herself, I quietly leave and head into Nishi's room, only to find it empty. Back in the nose, Lord Neith is perusing another holographic document from another set of Promisaries.

"We're grateful to your Guardian for arranging this," he says, looking up. Then he turns to me. "Chief Executive Purecell has sent these Promisaries to transport Deke and Twain's bodies back to their families."

I nod jerkily and lead them to the cabin where my friends are resting in Space-proof body bags. When I open the door, I find Nishi.

She's lying beside a black body bag, staring through the small square window at Deke's pallid, bluish face.

"No," she says, looking up at me and clinging to Deke.

I push past the Promisaries and cross over to her. "Nish, they've come to bring him home to his parents. He wouldn't want to be launched into Empyrean from here."

She looks down at him, her dark bangs drooping over her eyes. She finally lets her hands drop to her sides. Two Promisaries reach down and scoop Deke up. Another two lift Twain, and then Nishi and I are alone.

"I don't want to move on," she says, her voice cracking. "I want to die with him." She bursts into sobs, and I hold her close to me, brushing her long locks with my fingers.

"You only think that because it sounds easiest," I whisper. "Deke will wait for you in Empyrean . . . but first he wants you to make a life here. Besides, what happens to me if I lose you, too?"

She sniffles and wipes her eyes. "I'm sorry . . . I do want to be here for you, especially now. It's just—Rho, I feel so adrift without him."

"I know. Me too." I take her hands in mine. "So hang on to me, and I'll hang on to you. We'll be each other's lifesavers."

✦ ✦ ✦

When Nishi and I head into the nose, we learn that Mathias and Pandora have already disembarked with his parents.

He's gone.

Ignoring the ache in my chest, I file out with Neith, Hysan, Stanton, Nishi, and Aryll into a vast, open-roofed spaceport with ships of all sizes rising and descending everywhere we look. "Welcome to the Heart," announces a lithe Taurian teen in an olive green Acolyte uniform. She shakes hands with each of us. "I'm Arcadia. Chief Executive Purecell dispatched me to escort you to the Plenum meeting, so please come along. Leave your bags—an attendant will make sure they're delivered to the proper embassies at the International Village. This way, please."

She's articulate, polished, and succinct—in short, very Taurian. We follow her through crowds of people, all with silky hair and earthy complexions. Taurian skin tones range from caramel—like Arcadia's—to dark cocoa, and they tend to keep their fine hair trimmed short.

Women rarely grow theirs past their chin.

Since the Taurians in this spaceport are sporting business attire, I know it must be Monday, Tuesday, or Wednesday. Taurus has four-day weekends.

"Step right in," says Arcadia, ushering us into a bullet-shaped car with dark levlan seats and tinted windows. Arcadia sits up front with the driver, hidden from us by more black glass.

An attractive woman's hologram materializes in the middle of the car. She speaks in a smooth voice, and the text of her speech scrolls beneath her. *"The Bullet Express invites you on board and welcomes you to the Heart. While here, be sure to visit our Heart-Pounding Amusement Park, shop from one of our Hearty Fashions franchises, and dine at a Heart Healthy restaurant. Don't forget to award your driver Star-Stock in the Star-Stock Market to receive a ten percent discount on your next Bullet Express ride."*

The hologram disappears, and I click my seat belt closed. Suddenly, my shoulders slam into the seat back as the car accelerates forward so fast that I'm completely pinned in place. The highway twists and turns and loops, but our vehicle is so outrageously swift that the seat belt is unnecessary—I can't move a muscle.

Across from me, Aryll and Stanton are ogling at the sights speeding past the window, and beside me, Nishi keeps her eyes closed, her mind clearly far from the present. I take her hand, and though she doesn't react, I hold on to it. Sitting farthest back are Neith and Hysan, staring out of their windows in silence.

Even though Hysan and I have a lot to discuss, Mathias is in our way again. I'm no longer sure that the three of us can exist in harmony; I don't know that I can handle both of them in my life.

As I look out at the rapidly passing city sights, I try to picture what this place was like in Vecily Matador's day, one thousand years ago. Something about visiting this House after reading about her life, and while in possession of her Ephemeris, feels almost foretold. As if I'm back on the stars' path.

As I observe the city, I realize that the Heart is tiered, with three stacking layers. The ground level is a vast layout of parks, gardens, and fields, where animals graze and parents play with children. The greenery is interrupted only by the foundations of buildings and the columns that hold up the highway system. The Heart's uppermost level is a series of metal bridges built across all the building tops that pedestrians use to get around the city. Everyone uses these bridges; the skyline is filled with the silhouettes of people walking from rooftop to rooftop.

We're between the ground and the sky, traveling through the middle layer—the roller-coaster highways that thread between the starscrapers, weaving white designs in the air. The only two things that can cross all three levels are spacecraft taking off from and landing in the spaceport, and restaurants that fill up on the ground and float into the sky for meals served with a view.

The Bullet Express comes to a stop at the edge of a vast forest. Until now, everything I've seen in the Heart has been so developed, it's strange to suddenly arrive at a wall of towering trees.

As we climb out of the car, Arcadia hands each of us a small rectangular card. It's a Guest Blotter—a stripped-down version of an actual Blotter, which is House Taurus's primary communication device. The tourist versions lack any holographic functions, but, like real Blotters, they can be swiped at public Bull Feeds to get news or award Star-Stock.

I try meeting Hysan's gaze, but he's projecting out a golden hologram from his Scan, tinkering with an unintelligible code. Arcadia leads us into the woods, and soon Helios's light is blocked out by the canopy of green arcing above us. Insects buzz by, and birdsongs echo through the tree trunks.

At first it's nice to walk and stretch my legs, but eventually I start to feel as if the forest will never end. Then, to my relief, a couple of Promisaries materialize from the greenery, their suits camouflaged to match the foliage. "Thumbs out, please," one of them says, holding a sensor to scan our identities.

Once we've been approved, the horizon of never-ending trees disappears and is replaced by a familiar sight: the International Village.

I turn around to see that only part of the forest—the stretch behind us—is real. The stretch in front of us is a hologram designed to conceal the embassies. We follow Arcadia through the alley between Aquarius and Pisces, until we're standing in the heart of the village. It looks almost exactly as it did on Aries, and I stare longingly at the four bungalows of House Cancer, anxious to get there already.

Instead of the inter-House market from Aries, a big building bearing all twelve symbols of the Zodiac sits at the center of the village. "The Plenum meets in here," explains Arcadia as we hustle toward the front doors. We cut across a rhombus-shaped lobby decked out in rustic wooden furniture with gleaming stone surfaces and feathery accent pillows.

Arcardia parades us past the security desk and into a large hall where the Plenum meeting is being held. Unlike the velvety black box where the Plenum meets on Aries, the room that we enter is bright, with a clear view of Helios shining through a glass-domed ceiling. The twelve ambassadors sit at a long table at the head of the hall, facing the audience. There must be at least a thousand people here.

Between the long table and the audience is an open space where Ambassador Sirna stands, addressing the other representatives. "Excellencies, we all agree the Marad is dangerous and must be stopped— let us at least be united on that. As for whether or not Ophiuchus exists, new evidence has surfaced. Yesterday we voted seven to five to lift the ban on Rhoma Grace, former Guardian of the Fourth House, from addressing this Plenum."

Sirna turns to look at our group, and so does everyone else. "I now call forth Rhoma Grace to testify."

26

I FEEL EVERY PAIR OF eyes taking me in as I walk toward Sirna. Most of the faces staring at me are young, like the crews who came out to Sagittarius. They're here to make sure tomorrow will be better than today.

Wending my way toward the Plenum stage, I recall the walks that came before this one, and I pity the Rho I was on Aries, the young girl who had no idea what she was embarking on. I'm not that person anymore. There aren't many surprises left for those in power to throw at me, because I've seen the worst and best of them. Sage Ferez said our failures aren't an end in and of themselves; rather, they're the scrambled secrets of success. I'm finally starting to understand what he meant.

When I reach the front of the room, the sight of Sirna's warm ebony face relaxes me. She's about to speak when the blade-faced ambassador of Scorpio rises from his seat and announces, "I will interview the witness myself."

Charon's words produce the kind of stillness that sucks even silence from the room, creating a vacuum of air. Since he's more senior, Sirna must step down, but she still spares him a cold look as she hands him the speaker's staff and sweeps back to her seat.

"My dear Rhoma," says Charon in his familiar, greasy voice. "It's good to see you alive and well after your ordeal. I only hope, for your sake, that this time you have come to us with actual proof of your boogeyman."

"I have, Ambassador." I adopt the unflinching focus of a Taurian to show him his jabs lack their usual sting. "Ophiuchus appeared in my Ephemeris when I was on House Capricorn. He told me he had been working for the same master who leads the Marad, but was ready to denounce him and switch sides. To prove it, he warned me the army would strike Capricorn and not Sagittarius. As you can imagine, given recent events, distrust led me to dismiss his warning. I only realized my error once it was too late."

Charon keeps a mask over his face, just like I'm doing, but now his facade breaks into a sharp smile. "Do you really expect us to believe you knew of the attack on Capricorn ahead of time?" His voice projects into every corner of the sunny hall. "*Anyone* could claim to have known *anything* after it's already happened. Once again, you offer us facts with no proof."

"*I'm* proof." I look out at the audience toward the new speaker. Standing in the front row is Guardian Brynda, wearing her Archer coronet. "Rho was in my office when she told us Capricorn was the true target. I sent Sage Ferez a message from my Tracker moments before the attack."

Midway through the room, a row of yellow-uniformed students rises. "We were present as well," shouts Numen proudly.

"As were we," says one of the emerald-green-suited students standing beside the Librans. They're Virgos, members of Twain's crew.

My heart's pounding so mightily I feel like it must be shaking the stage. Then the Capricorn ambassador rises from his seat at the head table. "House Capricorn can confirm that Guardian Brynda sent us warning before we were attacked. I have personally spoken with the Capricorn students who were in the room, and they relayed the same information to me. And, I might add," he says, turning his deep black eyes to me, "they were very taken with you."

"Very well," says Charon roughly, the smugness gone from his tone. "Let's move on—we can't spend all day on this testimony. Even if you knew of the attack ahead of time, how do we know it was this Thirteenth Guardian who alerted you?"

"I met with Ophiuchus again after the attack."

"And . . . ? What did he say?"

"He told me the only way to get close to the master was by attracting the Marad's attention. So I took a small crew where he instructed me, to the asteroid belt between the Eighth and Ninth Houses. That's where the soldiers attacked us."

"That's a fascinating tale, but again, I'm not seeing any *proof*—"

"It's right here," calls Hysan. He's standing at the back of the room, beaming the unintelligible hologram he'd been tinkering with from his Scan. One of the Geminin students in the back row duplicates the image with her Tattoo and beams it forward, a Taurian sitting closer up copies it with her Blotter and projects it, and so on, until copies of the hologram hover all over the hall.

The image shows a series of strange symbols that shift into letters as we watch them. It's the message Ophiuchus sent us through *Equinox*'s screens. The code must prove the message originated in the Psy and not a physical device.

> *The master's minions are here. They will board your ship by force. If you want to meet the master, you must face them . . . but remember what I told you. Death's hand will reveal your true enemy—and Death is what you are inviting on board.*

Everyone studies the text silently, and I study Hysan, who shuts off his Scan now that the information is out. Then, he barely looks at me as he slips out of the Plenum and into the village. It's the first jab on this stage I can't shake off.

A rumble of discussion spreads through the hall and grows loud enough to reach me. Everyone is marveling at the proof Hysan just shared, and explanations of what the codes mean are being repeated from neighbor to neighbor.

The last time we showed proof of a Psy weapon, Charon dismissed it with his more compelling evidence of cosmic rays from the Sufianic Clouds—but he can't explain away this. For the first time, Ochus left a permanent mark. Not with violence, which fades as people heal, but with words that linger.

I hear the new Aquarian ambassador, Crompton, say to his neighbor, "A purely metaphysical being—how fascinating!"

"We will have to verify this data," says Charon, trying to tamp down the excitement in the room. "What happened when the soldiers boarded your transport?"

I recount how the Marad threatened and subdued us, how we fought back and two of our crew members lost their lives, and how, just as the broadcast began, Lord Neith and Hysan rescued us. Everyone is silent throughout my account, and before Charon can ask another question, I say, "What's happening to the soldiers who attacked us?"

"We are not releasing that information at this time," he says haughtily. "Let's continue with your tale. You then boarded their ship and found hostages, did you not? Where are they?"

I smile at him. "We are not releasing that information at this time."

Charon's face looks more than ever like a rapier, but before he can slice into me, Ambassador Crompton rises. He's nearly as tall as Neith, and his silver hair is so long that he's swept it into a neat ponytail. "House Aquarius has been convinced."

He may be the newest Plenum member, but there's power in Crompton's presence. His voice emanates a warm kind of strength, the sort of sound that seems as much from the heart as the mind. "We believe Rhoma Grace's account of Ophiuchus, and we are committed to helping her defeat him and his army."

Cheering breaks out among more than half the room's occupants, making it hard to hear the Taurian ambassador when he springs up and shouts, "House Taurus has also been convinced!" He's followed by the representatives from Leo and Aries, until the only House left in the dissenting faction is Scorpio.

"Scor-pi-o! Scor-pi-o! Scor-pi-o!" The audience chants at Charon, and at last he raises the speaker's staff to hush them.

"House Scorpio will need to examine the evidence firsthand," he says, once the room is silent. "If the proof is indeed legitimate, we will reconsider this tale."

It's not exactly a guarantee, but it's as close to an agreement as proud Charon is likely to give, and from their reaction, the audience knows it. The whole room is on its feet—the Zodiac has united. They believe in the Thirteenth House. They believe in me.

"Thank you," I say to the whole hall as Charon returns to his place at the long table to confer with the other ambassadors. I don't know if I've been given the floor to speak or if I'm expected to wait while the ambassadors finish their discussion, but since I have something to say, I seize the chance.

"Ophiuchus must be dealt with, yes, but he is not the priority. The Marad has a leader, and he is not it. We need to focus on finding the army's hiding place and stopping it from further destruction. Ophiuchus will have his turn, but he's not the immediate threat. The master is."

"Thank you," says Crompton, rising again and taking the speaker's staff. He and the rest of the ambassadors are now all smiles. They don't seem to have heard what I just said . . . in fact, it appears as if the whole room tuned out as soon as the Houses united. They don't want to hear more omens and warnings. They want to hold on to hope.

"We now have an announcement," says Crompton, his pink sunset eyes warmly sweeping across my face. "Rhoma Grace, this Plenum wants to apologize for our treatment of you on House Aries. You are a rare and gifted seer, one of the best in our galaxy, and we want to honor you with a title that hasn't been used in centuries."

The crowd cheers, and Crompton holds up the staff to quiet them. "Before the Trinary Axis, when the Guardians ruled the Zodiac together, there was a thirteenth place at their table, which they held open in cases where a tie-breaker was needed to help sway a vote. As the role was a lifetime appointment, the Guardians chose a Zodai who was beloved among the Houses—a great seer, and most importantly, someone who rose above House affiliations to be a citizen of the Zodiac. As the Houses are now autonomous, this position no longer exists in an official capacity. But we would like to bestow on you the honorary title."

He gives me a low bow.

"Welcome back, Rhoma Grace, our Zodiac's Wandering Star."

27

AS CHEERS ENGULF THE ROOM once more, every muscle within me begins to relax. Here, at last, with the universe's forgiveness, I can finally forgive myself. I may have taken Cancer off course for a moment, but I brought Her back. Our House has risen once more to its rightful role as caregiver of the Zodiac.

The Aquarian ambassador bangs the speaker's staff to end the session, and I'm swarmed by people. Sirna reaches my side first, but soon an ocean of others surrounds me, and I'm swept up in the hall's warmth and excitement and hope as delegates from all over the Zodiac approach to trade the hand touch with me.

"Mother."

I hear the voice and spin around, Rubi and Brynda clasping either arm, and see a familiar pair of misty gray-green eyes. I free myself from the Geminin and Sagittarian Guardians so I can bow to mine. "Holy Mother."

"No," says Agatha, shaking her head of white hair and pulling me upright. "The stars bestowed that title on you." We wrap each other in a long embrace. "I believe our House will soon remember that."

"I've worn so many titles the past few months—Acolyte, Guardian, Coward, and now Wandering Star—but the truth is I've barely mastered being Rho."

"It sounds as though the stars have been whispering to you," she says with a smile. The saying is so Cancrian it hurts to hear it. Her eyes growing mistier, Agatha adds, "I can't believe I once wondered whether you were really Chosen. Watching you now, it's so clear: You're the brightest point in this already brilliant room."

When the tears subside and my vision refocuses, a blurry face sharpens before me. Arcadia.

"Chief Executive Purecell has summoned you for a private meeting in her chambers." She must have just tunneled through the crowd to find me, because her silky, russet hair is tousled, and the fabric of her uniform has a few large snags. "If you wouldn't mind," she says breathlessly, "please come along."

I part with Agatha and the others and follow Arcadia to the Taurian embassy, which is nearly as tall as the Libran embassy and surrounded by flashing lights and holographic advertisements for the planets' twelve sponsoring corporations. It looks like a bustling business district.

"Where are my brother and friends?" I ask Arcadia as the Taurians at the entrance hand us free samples of candies, perfumes, and lipsticks.

"Ambassador Sirna offered everyone accommodations at the Cancrian embassy," says the Taurian. "The Sagittarian is staying there as well, but the Librans respectfully declined."

I picture Hysan alone in his penthouse, in his gray coveralls, making adjustments to one of his amazing inventions. I wish he were with me now. Not because I'm afraid or uncertain of myself, but because I love hearing his mind at work. There's something Ferezian about his superhuman intelligence.

My thoughts are soon drowned out by the noise of the indoor city that is the Taurian embassy. There are shops blaring holographic advertisements, entertainment centers where people can hologram themselves into the world of a virtual reality game, restaurants that float up thirty stories to the building's glass ceiling, nightclubs, Bull Feeds, and more.

Arcadia swipes her Blotter on a door device, and almost as quickly as we entered it, we leave the bright and busy city lobby to slip into an office-like floor that's just as bustling. Taurians in olive green uniforms are staring at a massive holographic representation of the rising and falling Star-Stock Market hovering over their heads. Everyone is soundlessly speaking through their Rings, reporting every minute change in the market to the Psy. It's strange seeing so much activity but not hearing a word.

A few Promisaries pull away from the blinking data to peek at me, but most of them stay focused. Once we get past the crowd, Arcadia and I arrive at Chief Executive Purecell's chambers.

"How may I help you?" asks a young, sharply dressed guy sitting at a desk outside her door.

"Wandering Star Rhoma Grace is here for her appointment," says Arcadia.

"Great," he says pleasantly. "May I see your Guest Blotter?" I pass it to him, and he swipes it on a portable screen, then hands it back to me. "Please go in. Chief Executive Purecell is waiting."

"I'll be here," says Arcadia, pulling out a small mirror to fix her ruffled, boy-cut locks.

"Thanks." Then I open the door and step into a room that's missing a wall.

The office's fourth side is completely open, and a gargantuan tree from the surrounding forest reaches its thick, snaking branches inside. The largest branch has been shaved down to a flat surface that ends in a burst of leaves and petals—that's the Guardian's desk. The next biggest branch has also been filed into a flat surface, and it's smothered with feathery pillows—the couch. Other branches form a table, a coat hanger, and a footstool. No limb touches the ground, but they're so sturdy and solid that they don't seem movable.

"Call me Fernanda." A tall, middle-aged woman with fine, short hair sits at the tree-desk and extends her hand for mine. "I'm so pleased we could meet. Have a seat."

"Thank you." We shake hands, and I sit across from her on the tree-couch's fluffy feather pillows.

She leans forward. "You were holding back today."

"I will not disclose the hostages—"

"The Marad is all Risers."

We stare at each other as though frozen in place. "How do you know that?" I finally venture.

"How much do you know about me?"

I know Fernanda has been Guardian nearly ten years. I know she's the one who established the Taurian four-day weekend. But I don't know much else because she came after Mom's time. "Not much," I admit.

"You must've been eight when the stars promoted me to Chief Executive, so you wouldn't be aware of the scandal it caused." She says *scandal* as if it's something that's good for business. "I'm the first Guardian of Riser parentage."

The shock must show on my face, because she laughs. "My father was born a Geminin, and he was a Zodai University student when the changes began to manifest. Instead of sticking around and suffering inevitable preju-dice, he moved to Taurus and tried starting over. His shift was so smooth that a few months after the changes began, he passed for a natural Taurian, and he stayed that way for the rest of his life." She seems proud of the com-pleteness of his transition. Of course, as Guardian, she can't help but think of him as a true Taurian.

"Still," she goes on, "everywhere he went, his astrological fingerprint betrayed him as a Riser, so he struggled to find employment and worked harder than most parents do to provide for me. Even though the contemporary Zodiac is more accepting of Risers than it was in his day, I still had to fight incredibly hard to win over my detractors. However, I'm happy to report that my leadership has resulted in great progress toward the acceptance of Risers on Taurus and even across all the other Houses. That's why they feel they can talk to me—*Risers*," she explains when she sees my flicker of confusion.

"No one else listens to them, and they don't have a true home in the Zodiac. When I ascended, I think they were happy to know there was someone in power who sympathized with them." Her words remind me of Corinthe and the kind of world the master promised her and the other soldiers.

"A couple of years ago," says Fernanda, her voice now lower and more serious, as if to demonstrate that the pleasantries are over, "I had a troubling experience. My Riser correspondents confided in me that they'd been approached by an activist group. The organization seemed professional and well funded, and my correspondents were thinking of getting involved with them. Within weeks, most of them had cut ties with me.

"This was before the attack on Cancer, back when we thought the mudslides in the Hoof were caused by natural disasters, so I wasn't suspicious. But a few months ago, one of my former Riser correspondents contacted me again. She told me, in confidence, that by the third activism meeting she attended, the tenor of the conversation had changed. The organization's leaders were no longer discussing legal protections and equal pay for Risers. They were enlisting members into combat and weapons training."

"Did you tell the other Guardians?"

She glares at me. "What do you think would have happened if I did? I'd be setting Risers' rights back a thousand years, to the days before the Datsby Decree."

"Datsby Decree?" I can't help my curiosity, even though I'm guessing Fernanda has little patience for tangents. "Is that named after Vecily Matador's friend?"

Fernanda's eyebrows shoot up in gratified delight. "The very same. You know your Taurian history! Before taking part in the Trinary Axis, Chief Executive Matador had been trying to pass the Datsby Decree, which would grant refuge and equal rights to all Risers who came to Taurus. It was only ratified forty years ago, after my predecessor pushed for it." Fernanda's features crinkle with concern. "You kept quiet about the army of Risers because you know as well as I do that those in power only look out for themselves. You did the right thing, and I asked you here to thank you."

I open my mouth to argue, but I can't. The word *Riser* never came out of my mouth, despite the fact that this emergency Plenum session was called due to an abundance of them. Even though Ferez warned me they're the future. I didn't mention them because of what Fernanda said—I wanted to protect that population from further humiliation.

"What about imbalanced Risers?" I ask.

"What about them?" she asks snippily. "The change is as much out of their control as it is for the balanced ones."

"Of course . . . but I think they need more help than we're giving them. I never met an imbalanced Riser until this attack, and though I agree they're victims, many are still violent and unhinged—dangerous—and it doesn't benefit the larger Riser population to ignore that."

Fernanda's small-picture approach to Risers' rights reminds me of how I handled things last time around, when I obsessed over Ophiuchus and ignored the Marad. "There's a saying on Libra," I say. *"When we open our minds too wide, we risk closing them.* We have to look at the situation fairly—not just from the perspective we want. Don't you think?"

I'm worried I've insulted her, but she looks at me almost pityingly. "Rho, your idealism is admirable, but you've seen what popular opinion is like. If we give the masses more reasons to hate and fear Risers, most of them won't pause to make a distinction between balanced and imbalanced—they'll just hear *Riser* and dismiss the whole group."

"Then we educate them," I say, conviction making my voice grow firm. "We can't give up on people anymore. Even if most react like you say, *some* won't. So we start with the hearts we can change. That's how we make a difference—we begin with a ripple to end with a wave."

28

I LEAVE FERNANDA'S OFFICE THINKING a lot about Vecily. Her name will forever be tainted in the Zodiac's eyes for taking part in the Trinary Axis, just as mine will be stained by the blood spilled in the armada. Vecily and I suffered for the same mistake: trusting in others more than ourselves.

We gave control of our voices to older people who we thought were wiser. If I don't want to end up like Vecily, I can't keep relying on my friends' trust to carry me when my strength wanes—I have to become my own biggest believer and start finding that strength within myself.

Candela was right: I can't let *the way things work* guide my behavior, because things aren't working so well. Those *older, wiser* people Vecily and I trusted have already proven they don't always know better. Because there is no better. The Zodiac has twelve worlds, all with unique cultures and governances. If one lifestyle were objectively superior to the others, we would all live by the same systems and sets of rules.

Ferez predicts the worlds of tomorrow will be the ones we choose, not the ones we're born into, and even Hysan believes that's what's best for us.

We've been adhering for one thousand years to laws that applied to people living in primitive times with outdated technology and beliefs. Librans are legally required to update their wills every year of their adult lives—shouldn't we be required to review our laws every century to make sure they're still worth following?

When Arcadia walks me out of the embassy, I'm surprised to realize I'm not ready to go home yet. "I want to learn more about Vecily Matador," I say.

"Then you'll want to see her house," says Arcadia. "Follow me."

✦ ✦ ✦

We hop back on the Bullet Express, zipping past the busy, triple-tiered downtown to what appears to be a quieter suburb. Here the highways unfurl in straight lines, and there are no starscrapers chomping up the horizon.

"Where are we?" I ask Arcadia, who is sitting in the back of the car with me.

"The heart of the Heart," she says, and for the first time, her almond-shaped, sepia eyes grow gentler. "Everyone in each Section of Vitulus lives within a community; this one is called the Professional."

The bullet-car pulls onto a ramp, and we exit the highway and cruise into a cluster of interconnected homes. Our speed has dramatically decreased now that we're in a residential area, and I glue my face to the window to take everything in. The modest, two-story houses have super-thick walls, which they share with adjacent structures, so that the rows of homes appear as though links in one chain. I also don't see any barriers between neighboring properties: Swing sets straddle lawns, tree branches in one yard jut into the next, balconies bump against each other, and so on.

Yet most striking of all is the technology that outfits each home, making every task more efficient. There are elevators waiting at front doors, holographic sensors that trim the grass when it grows too high, roving litter catchers, sliding sidewalks, spinning driveways, and more.

It's evening, and many families seem to be reuniting after a day apart. There are cars pulling into garages, returning home from work, and a collection of big blue buses depositing children done with their daily lessons and activities. "Adults work from morning to night three days a week on Taurus, so on those days kids participate in Selfless Service, which keeps them busy until about now," explains Arcadia.

"Selfless Service is an after-school activity organized by the Education Department of each Section," she adds, though I already know this from Mom's lessons. "Big blue buses pick students up from every school and bring them to communities that could use a hand—the less fortunate, the elderly, the disabled."

Our vehicle comes to a stop in front of a decrepit house that looks nothing like the perfectly manicured ones surrounding it. No modern technology or cars or people are milling around . . . it's just a rough-hewn wooden structure that's barely standing upright.

"This was Vecily's childhood home," says Arcadia when we've exited the car. We stand in front of the cabin, looking up at it somberly.

It looks like a rotting animal carcass, its lawn overgrown, the ceiling partly caved, the paint flaking off the walls. "Why hasn't it been torn down?"

Arcadia runs a hand through her short, silky locks. "Then we would forget."

I turn to her in curiosity, and in the dimming day, her complexion deepens to an even richer shade of brown. "Vecily didn't stand with her House," she explains. "She went astray. So now her home sits here as a relic, a reminder of what happens when you go against your people."

I start walking toward it, but Arcadia yanks on my unbandaged arm. "What are you doing?"

"I'm going inside."

"But it's not safe in there! The structure is a millennium old; it could come down any moment—"

I free my arm from her grip. "I'll be quick." I didn't come all this way to turn around now.

Arcadia hangs back as I walk up the overgrown, weedy garden and reach the creaky, rotting door of the ancient cabin. I recoil when I feel fuzzy moss on the handle, so instead I push the moldy wood with my shoulder. Immediately I have to cover my mouth from the stench that greets my nostrils; it's like the smell of decay from the Marad torture chamber.

The cabin is smothered with dust and dirt and spiderwebs, so much debris that it muffles my footsteps and makes the air taste solid. Smears of mud and graffiti cover the walls, and shards of broken bottles gather like fangs in the room's corners.

There's an archway leading to the back of the house, where there are two bedrooms. I know which one is Vecily's by the rotting V carved into the closed door. I have to shove it twice before it comes to life, and when the door finally swings open, the hinge cracks off, and the whole thing thumps down onto the dusty ground.

When the air clears, I look inside and see a moldy mattress, a three-legged chair, and a slanted wooden desk. I picture Vecily the teenager, perched at that desk on the day she was named Guardian, knowing her life would never be her own again. I think of her lying on the small bed, contemplating her childhood, probably remembering Datsby most of all.

I can see her resolving to make a difference in her friend's name. To do whatever it takes to change the plight of Risers in our worlds.

But her Advisors didn't take Vecily seriously when she came into power. Her own people didn't listen to her. And then along came enigmatic Blazon and beautiful Brianella, and they invited Vecily to be an equal. They whispered to her of a future without divisions—no walls between Houses, no hate toward Risers—and she saw her chance to have an impact. An opportunity to be a true leader of her people—and the Zodiac—and she seized it.

"I'm going to finish what you started," I say out loud, so that maybe this dying house might finally find some peace.

29

IT'S LATE WHEN I GET back to the Cancrian embassy, and Lodestars are about to lift the plank for the night. I hurry into the first bungalow, where there are hammocks outfitted with embassy Waves and a saltwater swimming pool. The Cancrian representative at the reception desk gives me my lodging information and shows me the way.

My room is in the third bungalow, beside Nishi's. I open her door slowly to check on her, and I find her asleep, with Deke's frozen hologram drifting slowly through the room. I close the door quickly, my pulse beating in my throat.

Stanton and Aryll are bunking together on the other side of my room. I'm sure they're already asleep, too, so I resist the urge to knock. I'm too pensive to sleep myself, so I take out Vecily's heart-shaped Ephemeris and turn it over in my hand, thinking of her rotting home. Then, remembering one of my favorite details from the Cancrian embassy on Aries, I head to the top floor of the bungalow to the reading room.

On Cancer, and on most Houses, a reading room is a place for starreading. Since most Cancrians prefer to study their Ephemerii under natural starlight, the room is often built as a planetarium. In this embassy, it takes up the whole top floor of this bungalow. The walls and ceiling are cut from crystal, just like Mom's reading room at home.

I expect it to be dark inside, but when I open the door, I see shimmering lights swirling in black air. A girl walks through them, and in the hollowness of the room, it looks as though she's wading through real Space. I turn to go, but—

"Stay," says Pandora.

"No, that's all right, I was just—"

I spy a gaze as dark as midnight shining from a spot on the floor, watching me. I forget my excuse and stare back at Mathias, who, save for his eyes, is wrapped completely in shadow.

"How are you?" I chance.

No answer.

"He's been a lot better since reuniting with his parents," says Pandora softly.

I walk across the room to the wall Mathias is sitting against, and I join him, leaving a few feet between us. He's still watching me, but at least he doesn't move away. Pandora hangs back, staring at the lights of her Ephemeris, giving us space but not any privacy.

"I heard about what happened at the Plenum." Mathias's voice is so weak, his words might as well be the whistling of wind. He clears his throat and adds, "I'm . . . proud of you."

I wonder whether it's speaking or just my presence that's making him miserable, and I wince. "I didn't do anything."

"Rho." At the sound of my name, my heart releases a sharp punch, and I let myself look up into Mathias's eyes. "You restored Cancer's reputation."

This time the words come out effortlessly, and I think he might mean them. "Thank you." Emboldened but still cautious, I say, "I . . . I was hoping we could talk. You know, whenever you're ready."

Mathias rises, and I know I shouldn't have said anything.

"Yeah," he says, walking over to Pandora. He stops before her, and she takes his hand and squeezes it. If he says something to her, I can't hear it, then he continues past her, out the door. To my surprise, she doesn't leave with him.

"I can go, or . . . I mean, you don't have to stay here with me," I say as I stand up, unsure I want to get to know this girl. "I only came for a stroll. I didn't realize anyone would be in here."

"We star-readers are creatures of the night," she says, her amethyst eyes practically glowing in the dark, reflecting the constellations.

"How is Mathias really doing?" My throat closes on his name.

"Better. I probably won't be here much longer," she adds in a lower register.

Even though I'm not displeased by this news, I can't help but hear the disappointment in her voice. Her feelings for Mathias—and her fear that he might not need her anymore—are as obvious on her as they've probably always been on me.

But does he love her back?

"How . . . what's he like? Now that he's . . . been away for so long?" My greedy heart can't help itself—I miss him more than I can let myself feel. For five years, he's taken up so much space in my mind, but the past few months he's lodged himself in so deep, I don't think I can uproot him without leaving a permanent scar.

"He's quiet," she says in her normal, airy voice. "He mostly holds my hand and thinks. He used to wake up every night, screaming, but he doesn't anymore. Sometimes he'll speak in his sleep, though. Those nights, he only says one word." Her eyes flash to mine. *"Rho."*

My heart feels like a carafe that's close to overspilling. I have to turn away, pretending to study the lights of the Ephemeris while my pulse slows. "If you're a Nightwing . . . have you seen anything in your reads about what's coming?"

"No . . . but I have seen something . . ."

Her voice trails off, and she orbits the holographic Helios, turning her face away from mine. A cloud drifts past the full Taurian moon above us, and the map glows brighter in the deepening dark, dappling the glossy floor with its lights and shadowing her profile with mystery. I survey the ground for an Astralator or another mathematical tool, but there's nothing, and Pandora didn't seem to bring any supplies.

"How do you do your reads?"

"I'm different, like you." She looks at me, semi-smiling, but there aren't enough stars out to be certain.

"On Aquarius, we use astrogeometry instead of astroalgebra. We make predictions based on the new shapes formed by the stars shifting in the sky." She paints invisible lines with her finger connecting the moons of Sagittarius and shows how they form an unevenly five-sided shape. "Most Aquarian Acolytes measure the movement with an Astralator to decode the new patterns, but I solve the degree differences between the old and new shapes in my head."

I nod. She's a natural, like me, only her instincts lean more toward the math than the stars.

"My instructors disapprove of my methods," she says, her words gathering speed and energy, "even though my reads are right eighty-six percent of the time. Then I heard about you, how you didn't use an Astralator and were predicting something nobody else could see . . . like I was. Then Mallie told me about you, and she believed in you so much that I signed up for the armada. I realized I could keep trying to fit in at the Academy, or I could leave and search for where I belong."

My insides freeze.

The crystal room has transformed into a Snow Globe, filling up with an icy memory. I press my head into the wall to steady myself as images from the worst day from my childhood resurface. Pandora just reminded me of the last words Mom spoke to me.

"Rho? Is everything okay?" she asks, walking over to me.

"Yeah, just . . . déjà vu," I say vaguely, still pressing my forehead to the cold crystal.

"On Aquarius, we have another name for déjà vu," she says, her voice dipping to a whisper. Her breath forms puffs of vapor on the crystal wall next to our faces. "We call it *starstruck*. We believe the sensation comes from the stars picking out a moment in your life to highlight, and it's up to you to discover the reason."

I stare into her wide amethyst eyes, and I realize she still hasn't answered my question. "Pandora . . . what have you Seen?"

"I still See it," she whispers. "When I Center myself as deeply as I can . . . I feel this *heaviness*. My predictions show . . . something awful." Her waterfall of hair swallows her face, but I can still see her orb-like eyes, which have grown larger and rounder. "I've Seen that Helios is going to go dark . . . and then the rest of the Houses will follow."

A chill ripples through me as I picture the moons of Cancer flickering and their eventual turn to darkness, then I imagine that same thing happening across the entire Zodiac.

"Someone's going to turn off the sun," she whispers. "Have you ever seen an omen like that?"

I shake my head, and for a moment, I know what it must be like to listen to my warnings of Ochus. Staring into Pandora's terrified face, all I can think to myself is *please let her be wrong*.

When I'm back in my room minutes later, I'm still contemplating her vision. I don't know what to make of it; all I know is if someone is going to turn off the Zodiac's light, the best way for an *everlasting flame* to fight back is by burning even brighter.

30

I WAKE UP TO MY own screams.

Footsteps pound the floor, and I hear my door opening in the darkness. "Rho?"

"Stan . . . sorry," I blurt between breaths. *"Nightmare."*

As I say the word, I catch a glimpse of the dream. *Every House in our galaxy going dark, every planet being consumed by Dark Matter, our galactic sun burning into ashes . . . Pandora's omen.*

My vision adjusts to the night's blackness as my brother sits down across from me on the bed. Cross-legged, the way he used to do when we were kids. "Want to hear a story?"

I nod and close my eyes, eager for Stanton's voice to fill my head and drive out everything else.

"There once was a little girl whose name I can't remember, so let's call her Rho." That's how he often used to start his stories, and the familiar detail makes me smile in the dark.

"Rho carried within her a light so bright that it outshined those around her. At first, she was afraid to stand out, so she tried to muffle that light by stuffing it deep within her hard Cancrian shell. While Rho managed to fool most, a few people still caught glimpses of that light—in the passion behind her stare, or the sweetness of her smile, or the purity of her soul. So bright was that light that it soon burned right through her shell, and *everyone* noticed.

"The world was so blinded by Rho's brightness that they didn't know how to react. Some were attracted to her light and wanted her to lead them. Some were scared of it and wanted her to shut it off. And two fell in love with her and wanted to make her light theirs."

My eyes fly open, and I stare at my brother in mortified alarm. But he keeps narrating.

"Rho thought she didn't have anyone to talk to, that even her brother wouldn't understand. Until she gave him a chance, and he swore he'd trust her judgment. He also, however, imparted some humble advice of his own—because if he didn't, he wouldn't be doing his job as the older sibling."

I grin with nervous relief. The final obstacle standing between Stanton and me isn't actually there at all. "This is one of your better stories," I tell him.

"His advice to her was this: Forget everyone else for a moment and all their claims to your light. You've always done things for other people. Moving to Elara, accepting the Guardianship, leading the armada, coming here . . . but tomorrow, do what's best for you."

His story now at an end, Stanton takes my hand. "For once, don't worry about the rest of us, Rho. There'll be time to save the Zodiac, to choose a path, and a partner, and a home planet—but before your light can guide others, you have to let it illuminate *you*."

I lean forward and hug him. "When'd you get so wise?"

"Must've been all the brainberries I ate on Capricorn," he says into my ear.

When we pull apart, I rest my back against the headboard and exhale deeply. "I'm sorry I didn't say anything about Hysan or Mathias."

"It's okay. Your attempts at lying are too funny to be upsetting."

"Thanks. Hey, can I trade you in for the brother from your story?"

"No, but you can take over as storyteller." He leans back on his elbows and stretches out his legs, his feet next to me and pressing into the headboard. "Tell me, what did Rho say to her brother after he gave her such sage advice?"

"She thanked him . . . and she admitted that while she has no clue how she feels about the two guys, she's starting to understand how she feels about herself and her place in the Zodiac. And she thinks he's right—that might be enough for now."

"I'm glad for her," he says soothingly. "But remember, we can't stop until we've arrived at a death or a wedding." That's how we always concluded our tales as kids—weddings for comedies, deaths for tragedies.

"So for the story's sake, at least," he says, "and just between us—which guy's it gonna be? The Cancrian or the Libran?"

"I think this one's going to have to end on a cliffhanger."

I push his feet off the headboard, slide lower beneath the covers, and rest my head on a pillow. At the other end of the bed, Stanton snaps up to sitting. "Rho, you know that's not how we end our—"

"*Good night.*"

I roll over and pull the sheets across my head, and I feel Stanton's weight lift off the mattress. "Fine," he says indignantly. "*To be continued.*"

✦ ✦ ✦

Next morning I wake up to the rustling sounds of someone in my room. I crack an eye open to find Sirna bustling around the vanity and setting out beauty supplies. There's a white dress laid out on the hammock.

"What's going—?"

Before I can finish my question, the door opens and a couple of redheads walk in, carrying baskets filled with even more cosmetic supplies. I shriek and leap across the room, pulling Lola and Leyla in for a hug. *"I've missed you both so much!"*

"We're so happy you're well, Wandering Star!" says the elder sister, Lola, her big red curls framing her gleeful face. "Mother Agatha gave us leave to dress you for today's festivities."

Beside her, Leyla's sapphire gaze is as direct as always, her mind full of thoughts she doesn't share. In all of yesterday's excitement, I'd forgotten that before ending the Plenum session, Ambassador Crompton announced that today would be a holiday at the village.

"Lola and Leyla will take care of you," says Sirna, handing me a plush blue robe.

"Thanks," I say, pulling it on. "Would you mind if I invited Nishi, too?"

"Not at all."

I sprint next door and knock. "Come in," she calls.

Nishi's sitting upright on the side of the bed, facing away from me. She's wearing her traveling space suit, and her suitcase is beside her on the floor.

"What's going on?" I ask.

She doesn't turn to face me, and when I walk around to look at her, I see that she's only just stopped crying. "I'm going home, Rho." She stares out the window as she speaks. "My parents are back from Libra, and they have no idea where I am or where I've been. I need to see them . . . and get away from everything here. I need to find somewhere quiet."

"I know," I say, sitting down and taking her hand.

She looks up at me. "I've loved him since we were twelve, Rho. I don't know who I am without him."

"I'm sorry I haven't been here for you," I say, squeezing her fingers, "but I already testified, I'm done here—I can come with you to Sagittarius. Or we can go somewhere else if you want, anywhere—"

"No . . . you can't." The sudden steadiness in her stare takes me aback.

"You have to stay here and finish this. Otherwise Deke died for nothing."

I crush my best friend—my *sister*—to me, and she cries onto my shoulder. She only pulls away when there's a knock on the door.

"It's probably Hysan," she says, sitting up. At the sound of his name, my heart beats harder. "He's taking me to the spaceport. He booked me passage on a Libran ship. Will you talk to him while I wash my face?"

She slips into the small bathroom, and my hand trembles a little as I open the door. Hysan's green eyes flash with surprise. "My lady," he says, bowing.

"Nishi will be right out," I say awkwardly.

"You were spectacular yesterday." The wornness of his expression makes me want to reach out and stroke his cheek, but it'd be unfair to do when I don't know what that kind of touch would mean.

"You left midway through," I say. It sounds like an accusation, and I wish I hadn't said it.

"I've had a lot of work to do on Neith."

Everything I discussed with Neith on the ship comes flying back to me, and I swallow it back with difficulty. "Are you any closer to figuring out what happened to him?"

Hysan shakes his head. "I think it might have been a fluke, just a temporary misfire in his wiring." He's speaking in a different decibel than normal, like he doesn't believe his own words.

"If you need help, I'm here," I say. "Or if you just want to talk or anything . . ."

"I always want to talk, Rho," he says softly. "It's you I'm still waiting on."

Nishi comes out just then, and Hysan brushes past me to lift her bag before she can reach for it. He carries it out into the hallway and waits for her there.

"Wave me when you get home," I say, wrapping Nishi in my arms. "I love you, Nish."

"I love you, too," she says into my ear. "Stay safe. And tell your brother I said bye."

✦ ✦ ✦

When I return to my room, Sirna's gone, and Lola and Leyla start their work. While they wash my hair, shave my legs, and clip my nails, Lola fills me in on what they've been up to. I learn that they stayed on Oceon 6 after I left, and when Agatha was named the new Guardian, they were dispatched to Gemini to meet her there. When I landed on Hydragyr, I had only a moment to greet Agatha because she was embarking on a tour of the Cancrian settlements on the other Houses, so I didn't get to see the sisters.

"We were visiting Libra when this emergency session was called," concludes Lola.

"What's it like on each settlement?"

"Hard," she admits. "On every House, Cancrians are trying to re-create Cancer . . . but they can't. That's why Gemini is so popular. People can still see their home and loved ones in the Imaginariums."

I grow quiet as I picture what it would be like to see Dad again. Or Mom. I'm so lost in my own Imaginarium that by the time I focus on my reflection again, my hair is glossy and wavy like it was for my swearing-in ceremony. Sirna chose a single-shoulder dress for me to wear, its pure white color also reminding me of that night. The airy material gently hugs my figure, and I look a little like the warrior Rho from the Ophiuchus glyph. Except that one of my arms is still fully bandaged.

Lola paints my face with subtle, natural makeup suitable for daytime, and my lips are a glossy pink that shines and sparkles. When Lola leaves to help Agatha get ready, Leyla stays with me longer to add a final touch to my hair. She braids the two front sections and pulls them back so that the style resembles a coronet. "You look older," she says, only venturing to speak now that we're alone. "Like someone who's grown too much in too short a time—but only on the inside."

Immediately I'm reminded of what Jewel said about Stanton the morning Mom abandoned us. "Leyla . . . have you ever thought about becoming a Lodestar?"

She shares with me a rare smile. "Mother Agatha secured me a place in the Geminin Academy. I start next year."

"That's great! And Lola?"

"Serving our Holy Mother has always been her dream. She's going to stay with Agatha."

After she's packed up her supplies and is about to go, I tell her, "You and Lola mean a lot to me." I've never blessed someone before, but something compels me to touch her forehead, the way Agatha touched mine the night I was made Guardian.

"May your sight always be this clear, may your soul always be this pure, and may your heart always lead you to happiness."

Leyla bows deeply, for the first time seeming moved. "Thank you, Wandering Star."

There's a sudden hammering on the door. "Your escorts, Rho!"

Leyla opens it to reveal Stanton and Aryll, who are sporting matching baby blue silk suits they must have purchased at the stores in the Taurian embassy. "It was Aryll's idea," says Stanton, seeing the smirk that must be on my face.

"Liar!" shouts Aryll, shoving my brother.

Leyla turns to me and says, "I should help Lola." As she's shutting the door, I notice a funny look come over her features, as if she's seen something troubling.

I look to the guys. Aryll is trying to spray Stanton's curls with my glossing spray. "Let's go!" I reach for the Wave on my bed, all the while wondering what was wrong with Leyla, but my fingers stop just shy of the golden clamshell. Tonight, for the first time in forever, I want to disconnect—if only for a few hours.

So I follow the guys out of the room and try to leave everything else behind.

✦ ✦ ✦

When we cross the plank into the village, the three of us exchange looks of awe. The place has been completely transformed.

Representatives from the Houses have constructed simulation games, food stands, cultural booths, and gift stores on the front lawns of each embassy. The doors to every single building are open, and citizens of every House are visiting each other. Holographic wildlife from every constellation roams the village streets, the animals so lifelike that people in their paths are dodging out of their way. Above the embassies float the House glyphs, and the center of the sky reads ZODIAC.

"Look," says Stanton, pointing to the Plenum building in the middle of the village. "The Thirteenth House."

Stanton leads the way toward a makeshift spot for House Ophiuchus that someone has cobbled together. Groups of people cluster the area, trading Ophiuchus stories, superstitions, and suspicions, as well as fictions and facts from their own Houses. Holographic screens depict the Ophiuchus myths from each world, and the new glyph that shows me wrangling the Snake is projected throughout.

At the very back of the improvised embassy, a panel of five people takes questions from a growing crowd. The panelists are all from different Houses, but they're each dressed in identical white suits that make me think of the Marad. A hologram hovering by their heads reveals them to be representatives of the group 13.

Once dismissed as conspiracy theorists, their knowledge is now in high demand by even the Chroniclers in the audience, and hands are shooting up with questions from the continuously expanding crowd. The Zodiac believes in Ophiuchus at last—right when I have to convince them that Ochus is not the master, that a far more elusive, intelligent, and *dangerous* threat exists, about whom we know nothing.

A teenage panelist abruptly abandons his seat at the table. "Rho!" he calls with familiarity in his voice. I squint, wondering how I might know him.

He smiles widely as he approaches, revealing two rows of perfect, sharp teeth. He's a Leo—I can tell by the broad face, multiple eyebrow piercings, and striped sideburns. "I was hoping you'd come. I've wanted to meet you for so long. I'm Traxon Harwing, but friends call me Trax."

We trade the hand touch. His skin is rough and calloused, most definitely from the adventuring life on Leo. His eyes travel down to my dress, and he smiles even wider. "You're wearing his color, too."

"Whose?"

"Ophiuchus—white was the Thirteenth House's color. It's the hue that contains all others. There's a ton of lore I'd love to share with you whenever you have time. In exchange, maybe you could address some of our members—you know, tell us what it was like facing him?"

"Right now the Marad and the master are more pressing."

I bite back my annoyance by reminding myself that *of course* people are more interested in a new House—a whole new constellation—that's been hidden from us for ages. Of course they want to learn as much as possible about that lost world and its people. Of course they're more concerned with an immortal, invincible Guardian who can crush planets with Dark Matter than some unknown master who couldn't possibly be scarier than a children's book monster come to life.

"Ophiuchus warned you before the last attack," says Traxon. I'm not sure, but it almost sounds as if he's *defending* the butcher. "If you give him a chance, he could lead you right to the Marad."

"I did give him a chance. And he did lead me to them, and two of my friends got killed," I snap. "He can't help us. Ophiuchus is violent and unfeeling. His ways aren't ours."

"All the more reason you should learn as much as you can about him," argues Trax, his tan face flushed with red. "He might know how to defeat the army—"

"We defeat the master and the Marad by bringing the Houses together and forming a unified plan," I cut in. Even if this Leo has a point, I don't like his pushiness or his unwavering fascination with Ophiuchus. "Ophiuchus is a *murderer*. He destroyed my House."

"But you can't shut him out, Rho!" he says almost pleadingly, pronouncing my name as if saying it is an old habit. "He's chosen *you* to be his connection to our world. You have a responsibility—"

"I don't need you to tell me about responsibility—"

"I think you do, actually—"

"Excuse us," says Stanton, clapping his hand on my shoulder and pulling me back from a red-faced and disappointed Traxon. "We're late for an appointment."

When we've walked far enough away, Stanton lets go of me, and he and Aryll burst into barks of laughter.

"You should've seen your face, Rho!" says Stanton. "I didn't think anyone could make you that angry, but I should have known getting a Leo on your back would do the trick—"

"'*I don't need you to tell me about responsibility!*'" says Aryll in an unflattering caricature.

"I am *not* that shrill!" I protest. Once the guys have calmed down, we make our way past the Ophiuchus crowds and emerge near the Aquarian embassy, a majestic royal palace with turrets shooting high into the air. It's the tallest structure in the village.

Stanton goes straight to the simulation games. He and Aryll line up to try an aural tonic, a small vial of highly concentrated Abyssthe that wears off almost instantly, but the moment its hits your system, it projects a glimpse of your soul. The glimpse—a mix of images and words, like a freeze-frame of your brain in a single moment in time—is fleeting, and it appears on a huge wallscreen hanging over the stand.

While we're in line, Gyzer and Ezra come up to greet us. "Hey, Aryll!" says Ezra, trading the hand touch with him.

"Ezra, this is Stanton. Rho's brother." She looks from Aryll to Stan and trades the hand touch with him, too. When she finally turns to me, she nods a subtle greeting but keeps her distance. Either she hasn't forgiven me, or she's not sure how to make amends.

Gyzer trades the hand touch with me. "I'm glad you're safe," he says in his mournful tone.

"Thank you."

"Do you still believe you're not ready to lead?" he asks, and I think I spy a smile in his deep eyes.

"I don't think anyone ever is." I think of Vecily and Hysan and Brynda and so many other young leaders like us who weren't expecting the stars' call. "I think the most any of us can do is try," I add, shrugging. "What have you and Ezra been up to?"

"A Stargazer discovered one of Ezra's inventions, and next thing we knew, we were guests on Guardian Brynda's ship to the Plenum session. Ezra's device helped track part of the signal of the Marad's universal transmission. It might be the key to breaking the code the army is hiding behind and capturing them."

We all look at her, and I can't help but be impressed. Aryll asks, "How did you do it?"

"Sometimes, when you get too clever, you overlook the simple stuff," says Ezra, shrugging so casually it's as if she's unaware that she's a Hysan-level genius. "The Marad is so technologically advanced, I thought there was a good chance its soldiers had forgotten the old ways. So I started looking at old wartime strategies in history texts. I read up on this ancient spy language that used basic sound waves to ping a location, which gave me the idea for a more primitive kind of Tracker."

"Brilliant," I say.

Ezra tilts her chin up. "Thank you."

The line moves up, and Stanton and Aryll go with it, while Gyzer trails away a little, leaving us girls alone. I'm not sure what to say, since I don't want to take all the blame for our argument in Starry City when I think Ezra was also in the wrong, but before my brain can analyze the words, my mouth blurts out a question.

"Are you still mad at me?"

Ezra's proud expression melts into an impish smile. "Not what I was expecting you to say." She laughs a little. "You know, I think Sagittarius rubbed off on you."

"I'm glad," I say, smiling back. "I'm also glad you found your own way to fight the Marad. I have a feeling you're going to be a force." I hold out my hand, and at last, she gives me a fist bump.

"Not so weak yourself," she says to me, her wide eyes traveling down my bandaged arm. "I'm sorry for stepping out of line before. But I'm not sorry for fighting for my chance to fight. If that makes sense."

"It does. I respect that."

"Rho, I'm up!" shouts Stanton. I look over and realize he and Aryll have reached the head of the line. I say bye to Ezra and join my brother as he eagerly downs his aural tonic. His eyes are closed, brow furrowed with focus, and soon an image pops onto the wallscreen.

Four faces smile at me from the fog of time—Mom, Dad, Stanton, and me, at least ten years ago. There's also a jumble of words, but only a few of them are legible. *Cancer. Rho. Jewel.* Like a true Cancrian, Stanton thinks of his home and loved ones to Center himself.

My brother grins at the sight of the projection, then looks at me. When our eyes meet, his smile grows sad, and I know we're both thinking of home, in the days when it still was a home. The image dissolves.

Stanton steps aside and grabs another vial for Aryll. "Nah, I hate the way that stuff tastes. Let's check out holographic wrestling in the Aries tent instead."

"Oh, come on, we're already here," says Stanton. "It doesn't taste *that* bad, and it only takes a second."

Aryll seems on the verge of arguing, but when his eye lands on mine, a change comes over his expression. "*Fine*," he says, as if he's doing Stan a favor. "But I've told you before I have a hard time Centering."

He sounds more embarrassed than annoyed, and then he throws his head back and takes the aural tonic. He stares at the ground in a pose of great concentration for several moments, but nothing happens on the wallscreen.

"It's okay, sometimes we end up with weak batches," says the white-haired Aquarian running the stand. "Here, try this one." He hands Aryll another vial. The line grows longer behind us, and Aryll tosses back the new aural tonic. As his face grows redder with renewed effort, I start to feel bad that Stanton pressured him into this—if there's anything Cancrians don't like, it's the spotlight. Stanton seems to be thinking the same thing, because his face creases with concern, and he seems about to speak, when an image flashes out.

It's unintelligible. The screen is shaded with tones of gray and charcoal, which muffle a series of shapes and letters in the background, like a veil of interference on a transmission. The projection disappears too quickly to register much, but I do catch part of his name in it: *ARY.*

Aryll doesn't speak as we leave the Aquarian embassy and head to the First House. The line for holographic wrestling is so long it spills out onto the Taurian and Geminin embassy lawns, but Stanton and I still follow Aryll there without complaint.

"I'm not mad," he says when he finally turns to look at us, scratching at the skin under his eye patch. "It's just that Centering—concentrating on anything, really—has always been hard for me. That's why I didn't get into the Academy."

"I'm sorry," says Stanton, "I didn't mean to push—"

"I'm not mad," repeats Aryll, shoving my brother into the girls in line ahead of us. Two ticked-off Scorp teens turn around.

"Sorry," says Aryll to the Scorps.

"No, *I'm* sorry," says Stanton, slinging an arm around Aryll's neck. "We were just wondering whose suit you like better."

The girls giggle, giving Stanton a green light to keep flirting. "I'm Aryll, and he's Stanton," he says.

Aryll laughs. "He means *I'm* Aryll, and *he's* Stanton."

"What'd I say?" asks Stanton. He used to do that with me when we were kids all the time—talk to people as if he were Rho and I were Stanton.

"I'm Maura," says one of the girls.

"Hayden," says the taller of the two. She has red eyes, like a Maw—she must be from one of the deeper waterworlds of Scorpio. Like most Scorps, they're both thin and wiry, and their skin is so pale it's nearly translucent. Since their populations live in underwater cities, they don't get a lot of sun.

While Aryll and Stanton flirt, my mind drifts off, and I start to wonder what Hysan and Mathias are up to. "Think I'll wander," I tell Stanton.

"We'll be here," he says, gesturing at the hopelessly long line.

I walk past a band performing from the balcony of the elevated theater that is the Leonine embassy, and people from every House are dancing on the front lawn. When the song ends, the musicians take a break, but the singer stays onstage and starts to belt out a slow ballad. A pack of rowdy teenage boys groan loudly with displeasure, but I stop to listen to the sad melody.

A familiar husky voice speaks in my ear. "Never did get that dance on Starry City."

Hysan holds out his hand, and I gaze into his lively green eyes as I rest my palm against his. We step onto the Leonine playhouse lawn, and he slides his other hand around my waist, pulling me toward him until our chests are touching.

"Thanks for being there for Nishi today," I say, my bandaged arm draped around his neck.

"No need to thank me, Rho. I like being helpful." He pulls me into the crook of his neck, where I can't see his eyes, and speaks into my ear. "But these past few days, I've been at a loss. I couldn't help Twain. I can't truly help Nishi. And I don't know how to help you."

"That's not true," I say, raising my face to look at him. "You rescued us—"

"That's not what I mean." We're so close that all I can smell is the cedary scent of his hair. "Maybe it's because a robot raised me, but I've always been ruled by my mind. I don't react to feelings—I think first, feel later. Except ever since meeting you, all I want to do is be near you, even when it goes against my better judgment."

I stare into his eyes, and everything around his face fades out of focus. "Rho, even though I've been alone all my life, I'd never been lonely . . . not until I met you."

Twain was right: Hysan is so outwardly focused that no one can ever look in. This is the first time he's let me see past his golden reflection . . . and the first time I've seen he's just as breakable as I am.

"I'm really happy Mathias is alive," continues Hysan, skating our joined hands along my jawline and tipping my face up to his. "But you've barely looked at me since we rescued him."

"It's just . . . I can't think about anything other than the Marad right now."

"There's been someone trying to kill us since the night we met," he argues, pushing away my excuse. "I haven't proposed marriage—all I asked for was a date. *If* we survived our mission, which we did. So why do I feel like I'm getting brushed off again?"

Shame torches my cheeks, and I murmur, "I know it's not fair to you, it's just bad timing—"

"It'll never be good timing." His eyes stare determinedly into mine. "Just tell me how you really feel. I can't keep doing this."

My heart is so loud that its beat feels like part of the song. "I don't know what to say that won't sound cruel and selfish."

"Then be cruel and selfish."

"The truth is I love you; you already know I do. But I love Mathias, too." Swallowing my scorching shame, I admit the rest. "And now that he's back, the only thing I'm sure of is I don't want to lose him again."

Hysan's stopped swaying, and now we're just holding each other in place. A vivid holographic lion drifts across him, making his eyes glint like emeralds and his hair glimmer like threads of gold. From the look on his face, I can't tell if he's ever going to speak to me again.

"I fell for you at first sight," he says at last, his tone filled with tension. "Not just for your beauty, which is considerable, but you. I could *feel* your emotions when you stood in front of us at your swearing-in ceremony. I saw the pain you were in, the horrors you'd seen, the crushing loneliness you felt . . . and yet you seemed so brave, and your voice held this wonderful warmth that transmitted to the whole room. Anyone could feel how much you cared for your people."

He caresses my palm with his thumb. "But this whole time, you've been too scared to let yourself fall in love with me. I hoped your feelings would grow stronger than your fears . . . but they haven't."

"What are you—"

"You're holding on to old feelings for Mathias because he's always been the easier path. Rho, the things that make you so deeply Cancrian are the very reasons I love you. But the fact that I'm not Cancrian is the reason you can't truly love me."

"That's ridiculous." I let go of him, my heart still too loud, my skin suddenly searing not with shame but fury. "I'm not in the mood for your games, Hysan."

He lets go of me, too. "That's just it, my lady. I never played games with you." The hardness in his voice has melted away. "I never regarded you so lightly."

31

OUR DANCE IS OVER, AND Hysan has walked away. I wander around
the village on my own, furious with him for expecting so much from me.
Good for him that he's so in control of his emotions, but I'm so ruled by
mine that sometimes it's hard to think at all.

I head back to the holographic wrestling line to find Stanton, until
I realize he's not the person I'm looking for. I turn around and cross the
plank to the Cancrian embassy, and I don't stop moving until I'm outside
Mathias's parents' door.

Somehow, I doubt he's out among the crowds, and even if he's inside,
I don't know that he'll want to see me. I knock softly, half-hoping no one
heard me, then turn to go.

I hear the door opening and spin around to see Mathias. "Hi," I say. "I
was just . . . checking on you."

After a beat, he says, "Come in."

He's in bed clothes—wrinkled shirt and comfy pants—and looking more
like himself than he has since he's been back. I couldn't tell last night in

the dark, but his hair has been trimmed—not Zodai short, but it's no longer covering his eyes, and the bruises on his face have faded after a few sessions with healers. There's light stubble in the barely noticeable cleft in his chin, like he used to have when he attended the university. The only scar that stands out is the one that slices down his neck.

I follow him into the den. "Where's Pandora?"

"Outside, with my parents." Knowing we're alone makes the air in the room feel charged. He gestures for me to sit on the couch. I take one end, and he takes the other.

"How are you?" I ask.

"Well, I don't need to cling to Pandora to feel real anymore." His words sound almost aggressive, which he must realize, because now he adds in a lower voice, "When I saw my parents . . . something changed. I wanted to be strong for them, so I became stronger."

I nod, thinking of the strength Deke mustered for his family the day we met, even though he was heartbroken inside. "You're Cancrian through and through," I whisper, echoing words Mathias once said to me.

He turns away and pours us water from a carafe. He hasn't looked me in the eyes yet. I probably shouldn't have forced my presence on him when he's already made it clear he isn't ready.

"I shouldn't have come here," I say suddenly, rising so quickly that I spill the glass of water Mathias set on the table. "Oh, sorry—"

I whirl around, searching for a towel to dry the mess. Mathias gets to his feet, too, and I keep my head lowered, willing a towel to appear, *unwilling* to look at him—

"I clung on for you." His voice is musical again, and I look up.

"I held on so I could see you. I fought for you even after I forgot myself, and your name was the only word I remembered." His pale face is cracked with pain. "But when I saw you . . . you saw me, too. Like this. And I wasn't ready for that."

He takes my hand. Touching him again restores something I hadn't realized I'd lost: my faith in the stars.

"When I thought you died, I stopped living, too," I say into his shirt, my cheeks flushing with nervousness. "I wished I could have told you so many things . . . but mostly I wanted to tell you that I love you, too."

He pulls me into his chest and pins me there with his strong arms, his chin on my head as he holds me tightly to him. Inside his embrace, I feel my soul releasing a heavy weight, at last letting my heart rise higher.

I look up at him, and he presses his mouth to mine. A tingling, sleepy sensation spreads through my nerve endings—it's the way I feel after sitting on my legs for too long, only it's happening to my whole body. I'm not sure my feet can hold me up for much longer, but they don't have to.

Mathias lays me down on the couch, and as our kiss grows more urgent, I let my hands wander across his muscles and start lifting the hem of his shirt. He stops me.

"What's wrong?" I whisper.

He shakes his head. "I don't want you to see."

I look again at the scar on his neck, at how it disappears into the neckline of his shirt, and I understand. "I'll show you mine," I say, sitting up and tugging at the bandage Hysan tied on. Leyla and Lola offered to replace it with a prettier fabric, but I didn't want them to see the scars.

When I finish rolling off the long, white bandage, I don't look. I just watch Mathias's indigo eyes as they survey the twelve symbols that were crudely carved into me. He gingerly touches my raw skin, and I feel a jolt of shock from the contact.

"Does it hurt?"

I shake my head. Then, slowly, I peer down. The sight is gruesome. My arm is blue and black, and each symbol is just a series of ugly and jagged red lines.

Mathias leans over and kisses the Cancrian scar.

"Can I see yours?" I ask softly.

He sighs and clenches his hands into fists, as if he's fighting a force of memories. I rest my hands on his until, gradually, he relaxes and looks into my face. Then, slowly, he moves his hands away, and I gently remove his shirt.

The gasp leaves my lips before I can stop it.

The straight line on his neck doesn't end. It weaves across his chest and abdomen, then cuts into his back, forming a tangle of intersecting lines. It's one long, intricate design that someone must have cut over and over and over again into his skin, giving it no chance to heal properly. "Was this . . . *her?*" I breathe.

He doesn't answer, but his jaw clenches with anger again.

"I'm sorry, we don't have to talk—"

"I know the whole Zodiac knows this now, but I haven't said it to you yet. You were right, Rho. About Ophiuchus. About everything."

He swallows and takes my hand, staring at the scars on my arm as he speaks. "They were waiting for me when I left *Firebird* on my Skiff. I was the last one to take off. As soon as I was in the air, something felt wrong. I didn't have control of the ship, and I couldn't access the Psy or use my radio. Something was pulling me.

"I entered a veiled space station that was invisible to my scanners. I was taken into a cell filled with men, and when they came through identifying us and discovered who I was, they moved me to a private cell where their senior officers interrogated me." He says *interrogated* in such a way that I know what he really means.

"Do you remember anything about where they were holding you?" I whisper. "Or where their base may be?"

He shakes his head. "But Pandora is right. They're organized, and more powerful than you could imagine."

"I believe her. I spoke with Chief Executive Purcell yesterday." I recount everything Fernanda's former correspondent told her about the activist group that recruited the Risers. "This plan has been in the works for years. That means *none* of this is random. The master has a goal, and I don't think it's chaos for its own sake."

Mathias's face furrows in thought, and the familiar sight plunges me into nostalgia. I've missed these conversations. I've missed my Guide.

"I'm sure my memories could give us some clues; I just can't access them." He sighs. "I can't Center. I'm not even sure if I want to."

I take his hands and pull him up. "Let's go upstairs."

✦   ✦   ✦

Mathias puts his shirt back on and replaces my bandage, and then we head up to the crystal reading room. We look through the windows out onto the celebration, watching the setting sun cast an amber glow over the festival. Holograms of every kind and color twinkle in the golden light.

"What are we doing here?" he asks. His lower lip glints with my glossy pink lipstick, but I'm too embarrassed to say anything.

"Yarrot."

I lie on the floor and wait for him to join me. I can tell he wants to resist, but he complies. Together, we cycle through all twelve poses. He's still weak and sore from his ordeal, but I don't let him give up. I push him, the way he pushed me on Oceon 6 when, like him, I thought I had nothing left to give.

The moon is shining over us by the time we've completed a full cycle. We lie back and stare up at the stars, breathing heavily.

"Close your eyes," I murmur. "Find home inside you. Picture the whirlpools of blending blues of the Cancer Sea, the sand-and-seashell bungalow homes, the pod cities that from high up looked like lily pads cradling small civilizations . . ."

I feel my mind drifting away, inadvertently casting my spell on myself, too, and I flit closer to my Center. The Abyssthe in my Ring buzzes against my finger, activated by the sudden absorption of Psynergy.

Tapped into my soul, I feel a peace with my place in the universe that I've never known before. I understand myself, my impact on the Zodiac, and what I want to do with my life. The uncertainty is no longer within— it's solely without.

The Psy's instability intensifies every time I access it. Even now, the Psynergy I've pulled into myself is so erratic that it's hard to keep Centered. I may be at peace, but the Zodiac is going to war. I can feel it here, in the deepest recess of my being: This war will be as devastating as the Trinary Axis. And just as the Axis did a millennium ago, it will change the Zodiac forever.

"Squary."

I open my eyes, and it takes me a few moments to return to the present. I look at Mathias. He's still lying beside me, staring into my face, the moonlight shining in his midnight eyes. "I remembered something," he says. "They said something . . . a name. They must have thought I was unconscious from the pain. I think it was the name of a place. *Squary.*"

"Squary . . ." I pull up my interminable catalogue of Zodiac locations, the ones Mom spent years drilling into me. Squary, I know this one. "Isn't that a military base? On Aries . . . ?" But on saying it, I know it's not. Squary is a testing zone for new weapons, but it's not on Aries.

It's on Scorpio.

I sit bolt upright. "Squary is on Sconcion," I say, scrambling to my feet. "One of their above-ground testing zones. It was shut down decades ago after someone fired an experimental nuclear weapon. The damage was total, and the Stridents declared it wouldn't be usable again until the next millennium. But the Marad obviously found a way—"

Something else is bothering me, though, another memory. Not anything I learned from Mom. It's more recent than that. Squary . . . squ-*ary*.

The letters in the projection of Aryll's soul.

I run from the room, Mathias at my heels. "Rho, what's wrong?"

I have to find him—I have to find *them*. Hysan was right—he could tell that—

I freeze in the horror of my newest realization. Hysan planted evidence claiming he has the Thirteenth Talisman.

Aryll's coming after him.

32

I'M RUNNING SO FAST I don't know if Mathias is following, or where I'm going, or what I'll do when I find Aryll. I can't hear or think or breathe—all I can do is run as if my heart depends on it. Because it does.

Outside, the village is illuminated only by the lit-up embassies and the colorful holograms flitting between people. I close my eyes and touch my Ring.

Hysan.

No response, and I don't have my Wave. I run to House Aries and search the wrestling line, which is even longer now than it was during the day. "Stan!" I call out, running alongside the line.

Finally I spot his baby blue suit, only two people away from the front. "Stan!"

"Rho! Can you believe we're still in line?" The two Scorps from earlier stand with him, but I don't see Aryll.

"Where's Aryll?"

"I don't know—he left a while ago to get us something to drink. If he doesn't hurry, I won't have a partner—"

"Stan, Aryll's Marad."

My brother's face grows stern. "Rho, I don't care what that Libran says—"

"That Libran is likely the best judge of character in the Zodiac," says a voice behind me.

If not for the familiar baritone, I wouldn't have believed it was Mathias speaking. I turn to see him barefoot and still in bed clothes, staring at me. "If he said Aryll was duplicitous, you should have listened."

I never thought I'd hear Mathias praise Hysan, especially not in front of me.

"Hysan planted false information so Aryll would come after him," I say brusquely, scanning the heads of the crowd in search of his familiar golden crown.

"The Libran embassy," says Mathias, urging us in that direction.

"Wait." I close my eyes and touch my Ring. *Sirna.*

Rho—what is it?

A member of my crew—the redhead with the eye patch, Aryll—he's Marad. He might have Hysan; they could be anywhere. Can you alert the Royal Guard at every embassy to do an immediate search?

Helios! I'll give the order right away. Where are you? I'll send you a guard.

Don't worry about me. But if anything happens, you know how to track my location. Just let me know what you find. I open my eyes and meet Mathias and Stanton's waiting stares.

"Sirna is alerting the Royal Guard of every House." A mere moment passes before we're watching people begin to pour out of the surrounding buildings as the Zodai shut each embassy down for a search.

"Rho . . ." Mathias furrows his brow, a light sheen of sweat beading his forehead. "We had our most advanced ships in the area of Space where the Marad captured me, and none of them sensed the army's presence. If Aryll wants to stay hidden, they won't find him."

I close my eyes and concentrate. If I'm going to save Hysan, I have to think my way through this the way Aryll would. "We have to assume the worst—that Aryll already has him. Aryll's smart. He knows us. He won't take Hysan to his home turf, he'll bring him where he can have the upper hand." I look pleadingly at my brother. "Stan, you know him best. Where do you think he would be most in his element?"

Stanton looks at me blankly, and I recognize the expression because I'm feeling the same way. Neither of us knew the true Aryll. He wasn't the baby Stanton saved. He's not the hurt, heroic Cancrian we took him for. I can barely process it myself, but I don't have the luxury of doubt or disbelief any longer. Hysan's life is on the line.

"You said Squary is on Scorpio," says Mathias. "I wouldn't be surprised if Charon is Marad—he's corrupt enough. Maybe that's where Aryll went."

It feels too easy. Aryll didn't just act the part of family; he really became it. He knew things about us, understood *exactly* who he had to be for us to take him in and defend him with our lives. To do that, he had to really mine our heads and hearts and understand us from the inside out. He's thought through what we're most likely to do in this scenario. He knows we'd go to Libra first, and then we'd denounce Charon and demand to search Scorpio. *So where is he really?*

"Gemini," whispers Stanton.

I survey my brother's pallid face. "Why?"

"It's the only place I've ever seen him really connect with. Every Cancrian on that settlement spent most of their time in the Imaginarium to see their loved ones. Most of us couldn't stay too long before the bad thoughts warped the good ones, but Aryll would stay in there for hours. I thought he must miss Cancer more than anyone to endure it that long."

Mathias looks at me. "Every moment we stand here, Hysan's . . ."

He doesn't finish, but I know what comes next. In the normal world, a few seconds is nothing, but every second of torture feels like a lifetime.

We race toward the orange Geminin embassy. Elaborate cupolas encircle the top of the globe-shaped building, like a fanciful coronet, and windows bubble outward, reflecting the silver moonlight. Orange-suited Dreamcasters patrol the front steps, still ushering people out onto the village pathways.

"Thank you for visiting," I hear a prepubescent centenarian tell a group of veiled Piscenes as each hands him back a pair of heavyset glasses. We hug the round outer wall as everyone files out, and then we wait. Gemini's embassy is one of the smaller ones, so the platoon of Dreamcasters finishes its search quickly and marches back outside.

But it's enough time for me to cast every doubt I can think of on our plan. What if Aryll's taken Hysan away from the village? What if they're at the spaceport? What if the price of having Mathias back is losing Hysan?

I snap back into the present as Mathias tries the double doors. They're locked. He looks at my hair. "Do you have a pin in there?"

I dig into my hair and pull out the long pin Leyla used to fasten my braid. Whittled from a nar-clam shell, it's smooth and sturdy. Mathias fits its pointy end into the lock.

Rho, Sirna chirps in through the Ring. *Where are you?*

I twist the band around my finger. *Searching the Geminin embassy with Stanton and Mathias.*

We've already searched it, she says shortly. *You need to get to safety.*

Any sign of them?

Not yet. Rho, please, let me get you a guard—

Listen, Sirna, I think the Marad's headquarters are in Squary, the former weapons-testing site on House Scorpio. I need you to check it out, but discreetly. Don't trust Charon.

She pauses for a moment, then says, *I have other contacts on Scorpio. But I won't reach out until you meet me and explain—*

Sirna, I know you're concerned for me, and I'm grateful. But I need you to trust me again. I need you to look into this lead and get back to me as soon as there's news.

I let go of the Ring and focus back on the task at hand. Mathias is holding the door open for us, and I think back to when he, Hysan, and I visited planet Argyr, and how defenseless its capital city was, just like planet Cancer. The Geminin people only protect one thing: their regenerative formula.

We slip inside the building into velvety blackness. "Where's the light?" I whisper.

"I don't feel any switches or controls on the wall," says Mathias.

"I found a crate of eyeglasses," says Stanton. "People were handing these to the Dreamcaster out front." I feel my way toward him and take the pair he hands me. I slip them on, and suddenly I can see.

We're surrounded by a maze of orange walls that sparkle and flicker like flames. The fiery images make me think of the color-changing changelings, and suddenly the room cools to the blue tones of the Cancer Sea. The colors start to drip off the walls like paint and pool on the floor, until the ground is flooded with water. I scream.

A weight lifts off my face, and everything vanishes. I'm back in velvety darkness. "The glasses," I hear Mathias say. "This whole place is an Imaginarium. The orange maze is real—everything else is only in your mind. Focus on the weight of the glasses to stay present."

He slips them back on my face for me, and I keep my eyes closed until I'm focused enough to face this. *I'm in the Imaginarium. This isn't real. We need to find Hysan.*

When I open my eyes, the walls are orange again, and I see Mathias and Stanton beside me, both wearing the same thick-rimmed glasses. I feel their weight on the bridge of my nose, and it helps me anchor myself.

There are a dozen directions we could take, and each pathway is named for a different House. Stanton and I start toward Cancer, but Mathias says, "Rho, turn around."

Behind me is a nameless thirteenth path.

"Thanks," I say as the three of us head into the unknown, until we come upon a fork in the road. One way says *Infinite*; the other, *Finite*. "Should we split up?"

"*No*," says Stanton, and Mathias shakes his head.

"Fine." I think of Aryll. As an unbalanced Riser and a liar, there's nothing finite about him. "We'll take *Infinite*."

The guys follow me, and soon we come upon another choice: *Fate* or *Free Will*. This one's obvious—Risers have no control over their transformations, so they probably despise Fate. I know I would.

We take *Free Will*. As we run down the next hall, the orange walls ripple in the periphery of my vision, as if my imagination is itching to generate more distractions. I press the glasses down against my nose until they cut into my skin. Then I hear Stanton scream.

Mathias and I whip around to see my brother cowering before an invisible monster. Mathias reaches across and rips the glasses off his face, and Stanton stops shaking. Mathias waits a moment for his breathing to slow before giving them back.

"Fear is bringing out the worst in our imagination," says Mathias. He's broken into a full sweat, and beyond the tinted lenses his eyes are growing cloudy again, regaining that lost, dazed quality I noticed on the trip to Taurus. This place isn't good for him.

"Do you want to take a moment without your glasses, too?" I offer him.

"No. Let's keep moving. If we don't find him soon, we should try another House. We don't know for sure that he's here."

"Agreed," I say, even though instinct is whispering to me that we're going the right way. We come to the intersection of *Star* and *Constellation*. Since Risers are loners, we take *Star*. Every time we turn, we speed up, so by now we're running.

We come to the end of the maze and stop in front of our final decision. Our choices have led us to three doors: *Yes*, *No*, and *I Don't Know*.

"We're splitting up," I say decisively. "There's no time to search them together. Each of us chooses a door, scouts the room, then we meet out here to report. Whoever isn't back in three minutes, the others go in to find them. Ready?" Without giving them a chance to answer, I say, "Let's go."

Mathias takes *Yes*, Stanton takes *No*, and I take *I Don't Know*. This room is dark, even with the glasses on, so I decide to try something. I picture Helios as I saw it from 'Nox's nose, and I imagine a miniature version of the sun floating beside me and lighting my way.

Immediately, a small galactic sun pops into existence. I smile at the mini Helios, a red corona glowing around it and tiny jets of vapor bursting all across its surface. With the sun's light, I see I'm in a white room, similar to the ones on Sagittarius. Only the walls here have the same sparkly, shimmery quality of the orange ones from the maze, and it's very possible they were painted with the pearlescent paint Deke's family produced that's so prized on Gemini.

A distant melody—birdsong, only low-pitched, like a bird singing underwater—plays softly in my ears.

My skin crawls with an eerie sense of recognition.

Mom's black seashell.

I press the glasses into my nose again. *I'm in the Imaginarium. I'm in the Imaginarium. I'm in the Imaginari—*

"I don't remember where I came from, but I think if I had to choose a House, it'd be Gemini."

Aryll materializes out of thin air. I know he's real and not imagined because when I'm not looking directly at mini Helios, the projection retains its light but loses its details. Yet this Aryll appears as precise and intricate as the real thing.

Just as Mathias suspected, he's been veiled this whole time. "Where's Hysan?"

"When I got to the Cancrian refuge on Hydragyr, I'd expected Gemini to be a bit more like Sagittarius: busy, colorful, diverse in landscape and style.

Instead, it felt barren and stark." He walks around the room's perimeter, giving me a wide berth, taking his time with each step. He sounds completely different from the Aryll I thought I knew—older, smarter, meaner. "I didn't realize that curiosity and imagination were completely different things."

I can't feel the Abyssthe in my Ring; Aryll must have put up a hyperlocal Psy shield. I know I'm too far in to make it to the door before he catches me. I'll have to keep him busy until it's time for Stanton and Mathias to check on me. "Is Hysan alive?"

"The difference is, curiosity must be piqued. It's something that gets ignited, like a fire. It requires outside stimuli." Though his voice has changed, his cadence is friendly, as if he's actually conversing with me and not delivering a monologue. "But imagination is like Space—it's always there, always a mystery, always expanding."

Aryll continues his slow pacing around me, in no rush to be anywhere. "I've never had trouble withdrawing to the deep recesses in my mind. Maybe it's a defensive mechanism left over from when the changes began—probably a good thing I can't remember."

"*Please*. I'll do whatever you want. Just don't hurt him—"

"Back on Hydragyr, I used to spend hours in the Imaginarium. I always felt powerful in here. You, though . . . you might not like it so much. You don't know the joys of amnesia." He stops moving and stares at me. "I bet you remember perfectly how Ophiuchus's icy fingers felt when he wrapped them around your neck."

My throat grows sore as a glacial grip closes in on my neck, and I feel like I'm fighting for breath. *It's not real, it's not real, it's not real.*

"Or Corinthe sticking that knife into your arm." Again, actual pain blazes through me, a memory made real, and I clutch my bandaged arm to be sure it's not really happening. "Or your dead father, what must he have looked like when he kicked it . . . ." To my horror, a shadowy form begins to take shape in front of me. "Let's see, he drowned in the sea, so his corpse would be bloated—"

"Stop it!" I shriek as Dad's features begin to fill in, only deformed, colorless, dead—and I take off the glasses.

The room is dark again. Dad is gone. So is my little Helios.

In the blackness, Aryll looms larger. I feel a chill in my chest, and I thrust the glasses back on, more afraid of what I can't see.

The dark lifts only a little. Quickly, I picture Helios again, and the small sun materializes.

A cold hand covers my mouth, and another grips my waist. "Imagine all the ways I could kill you," whispers Aryll in my ear. "I could stab you in the back right now." I feel a knife dig into me, and the pain is so blinding that for a moment I think he actually did it. "Or I could crush you from the inside. Destroy all your reasons for living."

I brace for the worst pain of all, but instead he lets go of me. He's taking his time. He doesn't seem afraid that he'll get caught. Or that I'll escape. "After all, what's the point of killing you if you don't know you're dead?"

"But you saved Stanton."

"The price of admission into your heart, *my lady*." He mocks Hysan's centaur smile, only on Aryll it's a delirious grin.

"Why wait until now to show yourself?"

"At first I was only supposed to get close to you and collect information," he says, resuming his orbit of the room. "But when Corinthe failed, I decided to carry out my master's plan in her stead. I was going to kill everyone on the ship that night, then broadcast your deaths to the Zodiac. But then I discovered Hysan knew something—a secret that would make me invaluable to my master."

I stifle a gasp. Hysan's lie about the Thirteenth Talisman—his deception saved all our lives.

"The Libran was smart," says Aryll. "I had to be smarter. He already disliked me, so I had to be careful not to give myself away. That meant refraining from killing everyone who came over from the Marad ship, even though their knowledge could pose a threat."

I turn in a slow circle to keep my eyes on him as he paces. "You mean the hostages we rescued?"

"And the Risers you took hostage."

I frown. "Why would you kill your fellow soldiers?"

"Corinthe is no soldier. She disrespected my master. Showing you her face, trying to kill you ahead of schedule—she's just as much a liability as the others."

"Why didn't she recognize you if you're both Marad?"

"Nobody knows I'm Marad. For a month now I've been working for my master on a secret mission." He stops walking when he's in front of me, standing just a few paces away. "*You.*"

He whips off the eye patch, and I scream. His eye isn't missing—it's in a state of transformation. It's grown into an oversized orb, and the skin around it is drooping and flaking off. He's beginning the molting process— the sunburn, his peeling nose, they're all signs of the shift.

My muscles quiver, and I dig the nails of my right hand into my palm until pain overpowers my fear. Aryll is more of a psychopath than Corinthe. He's one of the Marad's top men. He's been close to us. He knows me.

"We loved you," I whisper.

"And love overpowers hate, right?" he says excitedly, as if he's eager to trade philosophies. "Only that's a lie you Cancrians made up. I never felt the love. I could tell that you and your idiot brother felt it, but being around you two only made me feel my emptiness. It filled me with hate. And I think that if I've ever loved anything, it's *hate.*"

The space between us has shrunk to arm's length. My fists are still clenched at my sides. "Who is your master?" I demand.

"You really do have a deluded sense of self. And yes, I know I'm not one to talk." His leering smile unnerves me. "You're just a teenage girl who's seen a few visions—you're not a *star*. While you're off predicting tomorrow, my master's foreseeing the next age of man. Didn't you ever wonder how I knew exactly what to say and do? How to make you and your brother love me enough for you to throw aside the Libran's warnings? How I knew about the White Dove?"

"You studied our family."

"I studied *you*. My master has long seen your coming. Why do you think you grew up motherless?"

No. I refuse to believe his words. He's using this place as a weapon, trying to mess with my mind, to unravel my imagination—

The heavy door bangs open as Mathias and Stanton burst into the room, halting as soon as they cross the threshold. "Imagine light!" I shout.

"I underestimated you," says Aryll, who's now slowly backing away from me. "I thought after getting two of your friends killed, you wouldn't risk the lives of more. Now you'll have their heads on your conscience, too."

As threatening as Aryll sounds, I know he also feels threatened. I can tell from the tight, clipped nature of his new tone that he wasn't counting on my bringing friends. He thinks he understands the concept of selflessness because he knows its definition, but he doesn't have the emotions to feel it.

Aryll has assumed that my guilt over having defended him to Hysan would consume me, driving me to reckless measures—like meeting him here on my own. And if this were last month, he would have been right about me.

But operating alone, in secrecy, was what got Mathias taken hostage. Deke was right: If I'm going to unite our worlds, I have to start by trusting the people fighting beside me. I have to accept help. I have to allow my friends to choose their own fates.

Stanton and Mathias must have been able to manifest light, because I see them running over to me. Their faces freeze with revulsion at the sight of Aryll's oversized eye.

"Aryll—what's going on?"

Stanton's question frightens me. That's my brother's voice, but it also isn't. He's only sounded like this once before.

"Come on, big guy," says Aryll. "Don't go projecting your abandonment issues on me. I saved your life—I think we can all agree that pretty much gives me immunity for any sins I commit against you. Or maybe it doesn't. I know who we could ask! The Libran. He's a good judge, isn't he?" Aryll's asymmetrical gaze jumps back to me. "Too bad he's in love with you. That can't be good for his health."

"Where is he?" I growl.

"Tied to an explosive somewhere in this room, hidden under one of my Veils. There's a shield preventing all communication in this building, so he can't use his Scan to send messages. Are you listening now?"

None of us says a word.

"I could have wasted time torturing him, but I already know there's only one thing that will break him. That's why you're here." He looks at me. "He dies no matter what, but he has a chance to save you if he tells me what I want to know. And since I'm prepared to go down with this building, your time is his to waste."

Aryll turns around. The next moment, Hysan materializes. His hands are chained to a heavy device that's bolted to the floor. Red numbers count down on a screen: We have three and a half minutes before it blows.

"I told you there was no need to involve her," says Hysan, his voice groggy, as if he's just waking up—or he's been drugged. The moment his face is free, he flashes golden light into the room from his Scan, and we all lose the glasses.

"I thought I'd bring a little incentive," says Aryll, "to keep you honest. So, tell me where the Talisman is, and she and I will leave the rest of you to die."

Mathias darts forward to attack, but Aryll hurriedly backs away, holding up a white pearl. The one he's kept in his locket the whole time. "Don't move," he warns, edging closer to me. "I can activate the bomb this instant if I drop this pearl."

Mathias freezes in his place, right above where Hysan sits. "Fine," says Mathias, backing away slowly—but before he does, I spot the glint of something dropping from his hand onto the floor.

Suddenly my brother lets out a ferocious growl and jumps at Aryll.

None of us expect it, least of all Aryll. He hesitates a moment, staring at my brother in bewilderment, and I use his distraction to reach out and swipe the pearl from his hand. I toss it to Mathias, who catches it. Behind him, Hysan is using my hairpin to try to undo his chains. Aryll thrusts Stanton into me, and we both fall backward.

"*Trust Only What You Can Touch*, Rho!" Aryll launches something at me, and it bounces off my shoulder onto the floor next to my face. Stanton's already rolled off me and is rising to his feet as I stretch my hand out for the object.

I gasp.

It's Mom's black seashell.

33

I SHOOT TO MY FEET, the seashell in my hand, and start chasing after my brother, who's chasing after Aryll, when a hard, urgent voice stops my muscles.

"Can you deactivate it?"

I spin around, and in the fringe of my vision I see Stanton turn, too. Mathias has taken over trying to unlock the chains binding Hysan to the bomb, but he's not making progress. Hysan is examining the explosive and trying to disarm it—there are forty-five seconds left on the timer.

As though he feels the gravity of my gaze on him, Hysan looks up, and his green eyes meet mine. "Rho, GO!" he shouts before refocusing on the bomb.

Mathias stops working on Hysan's chains and springs over to Stanton and me. "You have to get out of here!" He's practically pushing us toward the door. "Take your brother—"

"Help Hysan!" I shout back at him, and Mathias ducks back down to the chains. Hysan's Scan is rifling through a variety of devices, searching for the right deactivation schematics. Every time he finds a potential match, he attempts to sync the hologram with the device, but the timer keeps ticking. By his fifth attempt, he looks up at me again, his face pale with perspiration.

Eighteen seconds.

"RHO!" Hysan yells at me. *"Please—there's nothing you can do!"*

Mathias suddenly stands and lifts me over his shoulder.

"NO—MATHIAS—NO!" I scream, kicking at his chest as he rushes me out of the room. Stanton takes my hand and runs alongside us.

My brother looks as wretched as me, but he doesn't slow down or stop Mathias. "Rho, there's nothing we can do," he says over my punching and shrieking.

We're halfway out the door when Hysan triumphantly shouts.

"GOT IT!"

Mathias sets me down on the floor, and I fly back inside the room and throw my arms around Hysan. Both our faces are drenched with sweat, but I don't care.

"I'm sorry, Rho, I didn't think about how planting that lie would affect you—"

"I'm the one who's sorry," I cut in, holding him tighter. "You were right. I should have listened to you. This is my fault—"

"No, it's *mine*." He pulls back to look me in the eye. "He came up to me in the village and goaded me into a fight. I just lost my objectivity—and the moment I got close, he injected me with a sedative. I woke up here."

Heavy, hurried footsteps fill the hall, and Hysan and I look over at Mathias and Stanton, who are standing by the door.

Suddenly the room's overhead lights blast on, and two dozen Lodestars spill inside, led by Ambassador Sirna and Lord Neith. "Thank Helios you're all right!" she says, surveying the four of us. "We came as soon as I realized our line of communication was cut."

Lord Neith's face fills with relief when he sees Hysan. He pulls out what looks like a long, thin lighter, only when he flicks it on, the red flame that blazes out isn't fire but a powerful laser. It slices through the metal chains binding Hysan's wrists. The moment Hysan is upright, Lord Neith bends down and gives him a father's hug.

I know now more than ever that Hysan will never consent to destroy Neith. He's too human.

"You were attacked," says Sirna, looking to me to fill her in on the details. The cavalry of Lodestars stands ramrod straight around us, awaiting orders.

I nod. "Aryll had an explosive. Hysan deactivated it."

Neith's chest puffs with pride.

"He got away," says Mathias, "but we could still catch him."

Sirna nods and turns to the Zodai. "We search the grounds for Aryll. Red hair, one eye, sunburn. Spread the word through the Psy." She looks at me while the Lodestars touch their Rings and start speaking soundlessly. "Do you have a holographic capture of him?"

I shake my head.

"I can describe him to a Chronicler, and we can create one," says Stanton from where he's standing, off to the side and apart from the group. His voice still sounds too fragile. I'm about to suggest he head back to the embassy, but then his expression reminds me of the guilt that so weighed me down after the armada, immobilizing me to the point where I lost all trust in myself.

Thinking back on that feeling of helplessness, I know I have to let Stanton contribute what he can right now. Not because he did anything wrong that he needs to make up for, but because it's the only way he'll feel right.

"Thank you," says Sirna to my brother. "The other Zodai are gathering. Let's join them and not lose more time."

"Did you find anything on Squary?" I ask her as we walk briskly through the embassy to the exit.

"Nothing yet. A group of my most trusted Stridents are looking into it. I'll check in with them again tonight, but first we must deal with Aryll."

Outside, platoons of Zodai from every House are gathered on the Geminin embassy's lawn. Stanton approaches the brown-suited Chroniclers, while Sirna meets with the leaders of the other troops and updates them on what's happening. I turn around to look for Hysan and Mathias and find them standing together on the building's front steps, set back from all the activity.

"Where'd Lord Neith go?" I ask, joining them.

"He's searching the forest for Aryll. Superspeed mode," says Hysan. Deep dimples dig into his cheeks—I haven't seen him smile since Sagittarius. "Thanks for the rescue, Thais," he says, looking from me to Mathias.

"I owed you one," Mathias says back to him.

Hysan's still smiling, but something changes as he looks into Mathias's face in this brighter light. I look, too, and I notice it. Mathias's lower lip is still shiny and glossy pink.

I watch Hysan's gaze lower to Mathias's bed clothes and bare feet, and my heart starts thrumming louder.

He looks up only when we hear Pandora and Mathias's parents call out. They're racing toward us from the Cancrian embassy. As Mathias climbs down the steps to greet and reassure them, Hysan turns to me. There's no trace of light left anywhere on his face.

"I'm sorry that I was right about Aryll," he says, his voice hard.

"Hysan, I apologized for not believing you—"

"I'm even sorrier I was right about you."

"What you saw doesn't mean what you think it means—"

"It means you only spent the night with me because we were about to die. But in a world with a tomorrow, I'm not even an option," he says in a flat tone. "Even if I did everything right, it would never be enough. You will always choose a Cancrian over me."

My whole face goes slack, as if I've been slapped. "Hysan, this has *nothing* to do with our Houses—"

"Wake up! It's *all* to do with our Houses." His face is so close to mine that under different circumstances, my mouth would be pressed into his and not pursed in a scowl. "You like the *idea* of inter-House relationships because you like the fairness of the freedom of choice, but it's not *your* choice. You proved it when you trusted a fake Cancrian over me, and again tonight, when you chose Mathias."

He backs away from me, his eyes growing more distant with every step. "In theory, you're enlightened, but you have a long way to go before you're really thinking with an open mind. I wish you luck with that."

I watch him walk away from me, too stupefied to react.

"Are you okay?" asks Mathias's baritone behind me.

I turn to face him. His parents and Pandora are climbing back down the stairs. Pandora sneaks a glance back at us, and I wonder if she saw the lipstick, too.

"I'm . . . I'm just sorry," I blurt, my emotions rising up within me and refusing to stay down. "That's all I ever say anymore, but I am. I'm sorry for having feelings for both of you, I'm sorry for leading us into danger again, I'm sorry for getting both of you kidnapped, *I'm sorry*—"

Mathias pulls me into his chest and holds me there, but I try to push him away. "No—don't forgive me, because you don't even know what I've done. Back on Aries, I was with Hysan, we—"

"Rho, I don't care."

His hold tightens, and I stop resisting. "At Helios's Halo, you told me that surviving is harder than dying. Because the person you were before the attack *does* die, and then you have to figure yourself out all over again. Remember?" I nod against his chest. "Whatever happened before, we were different people then. We need to figure out who we are now. I think maybe that's something we each do alone."

Before I can respond, Stanton and Sirna approach with news, and we pull apart. "Rho, I'm going to help look for Aryll," says my brother. Around us, only the Zodai from Cancer and Capricorn still linger; everyone else is already searching.

"I'm coming with you."

"I'm sorry, Rho, but you can't," says Sirna, holding up a hand to delay my protest. "I'm under strict orders from the Guardians to keep you safe. You must return to the embassy."

"But they can't—"

"Actually, they can," she says, her voice dipping to a whisper so that the Zodai can't eavesdrop. "Rho, you accepted the role of Wandering Star. Even though you're not in an official position of power, you're very much back in the public spotlight. You're the face of our unity. The Guardians will always want you protected."

"I'll swing by your room later," says Stanton, interrupting before I can fully process Sirna's meaning. They set off, followed by the two teams of Zodai, until only Mathias and I are left.

Mathias grabs my arm before I can chase after them. "Rho, don't." My foot is already on the next step down. "The most they might do is capture Aryll tonight, and even then they won't let you question him. Just wait until tomorrow. There's nothing you can do."

I want to argue, but my body is past exhaustion. My feet are so numb I can't feel them. So I let Mathias guide me to the Cancrian embassy. "Are you going to stay on Taurus with your parents?"

"For a little. Just until I decide what to do next. What about you?"

"I'm going back to Capricorn—*if the Guardians allow it.*"

I'm still reeling from Sirna's words. How much control did I just give the Guardians over me? And how come nobody mentioned it earlier, like *before* I accepted this title?

We stop walking when we're outside my room at the Cancrian embassy, one floor beneath the Thaises' place. Mathias brushes the side of my face with the tips of his fingers. "When will you leave?"

"Depends on whether or not they find Aryll," I say, my skin sensitive from his touch. "If he's caught, I'm sticking around. If not . . . maybe tomorrow."

"So soon?"

"If Aryll makes it back to his master, who knows what his next move might be? I need to talk to Ferez. We need a real plan this time."

Mathias nods, and he leans down, until his mouth meets mine. The force of his kiss presses me into the doorframe, sapping my muscles of their final stores of strength. "I know I just said we should be on our own," he whispers when he pulls away, "but I don't know if I can part with you now that I've found you again."

"There's always a place for you at the Fluffy Giraffe Resort . . . in fact, a vacancy just opened up in our suite."

His lips land on mine for a final soft kiss. "Don't be surprised when I actually show up."

34

ALONE IN MY ROOM, I sit down on my bed and try to unwind. We stopped Aryll before he could hurt any of us. The Zodai are out in full force right now searching for him. We might have located the Marad's headquarters, which could finally put a stop to their attacks. The Zodiac believes in Ophiuchus, and House Cancer's reputation has been restored.

Yet all I see is Hysan's face as he turned away from me.

I know what my heart is telling me to do is stupid, but I can't help it. I somehow muster enough strength to leave my room again and head to the Libran embassy. It's late, so there's no jury in the courtroom, just a judge. "I'm looking for Hysan Dax," I tell him.

He points a lazy finger to the back door, and I race into the black-and-white checkered lobby and up in one of the bedroom-sized elevators. "Penthouse suite, please," I tell the operator.

When I get there, I pound hard on the door until I hear Hysan's approaching footsteps. The door swings open, and instead of Hysan, I see a buxom blonde, wearing only a bathrobe.

"Rho, lovely to see you again."

"And you, Miss Trii." I look past her at the workstation. "Is Hysan here?"

"No."

"Oh." I turn my gaze back to her. "Where can I find him?"

"You've just missed him. He and Lord Neith are taking off on *Equinox*."

I close my eyes and twist my Ring. *Hysan.*

No response. Maybe he's not wearing his Ring—but it's more likely he's avoiding me.

"Would you like to come in?" asks Miss Trii pleasantly.

"No thanks," I say, completely drained and devastated. "I think I'll just get some sleep."

"Rho, Lord Neith told me he spoke with you about his fears of falling into the wrong hands. You understand how important it is that Hysan take precautions now, before the master uncovers his true identity and turns Neith's knowledge into a weapon." Her crystallized quartz eyes pierce into me. "It's time Hysan takes his rightful place. He's the leader Libra needs now."

"Hysan will never destroy Lord Neith," I say forcefully. "He loves him."

She looks at me almost pityingly. "Of all the lessons your species has failed to learn, this one is the most tragic. Sometimes the best way to love someone is to let them go."

✦ ✦ ✦

I sleep fitfully. At dawn I finally send Sirna a message asking about Aryll, and a little while later, she, Rubi, and Brynda show up at my door. It's clear from their half-lidded eyes and messy hair that they've been up all night.

"Did you find him?" I ask as soon as they walk in.

"No," says Brynda, crossing the room and sitting on the vanity. "Bastard got away."

"You were right about Squary, though," says Sirna, settling into the hammock while Rubi perches at the end of my bed. "Stridents found a group of Risers who'd been secretly living there, building what appears to be a nuclear weapon, a device more powerful than what even Scorpio's Stridents are familiar with. They're studying it now. The Risers' transformations must nullify the radiation's effect, because it appears they've been there at least a year, with enough food and supplies to keep them going for five more. They've been brainwashed and refuse to speak at all."

Sirna pauses for breath, and her severe face softens. "Rho, if you hadn't found out about this place, they would have completed their weapon, and who knows how much damage they could have caused."

"How'd you figure it out?" Brynda asks me.

I tell them how Mathias was able to remember the word, part of which I'd seen earlier when Aryll took the aural tonic. "It was all pretty lucky," I admit.

But even as I say it, I know it wasn't. If I could have heard Hysan over the sound of my stubborn heart, we would have known about Aryll earlier. Even now, looking back, I don't know how I could have ignored his warnings. Mathias is right: Hysan is the best judge in the Zodiac.

So is he right about me? Am I pushing him away out of fear?

Am I not as open-minded as I like to think I am?

"How's Nishi?" asks Brynda gently.

I shake my head. "She went home. I'll probably visit soon." I turn to Sirna. "What happens now?"

"The Guardians must decide how to deal with the Marad soldiers that have been captured. They will face judgment on either House Libra or Aries, depending on the vote. We will continue searching for Aryll and the rest of the army, and also study their technology from the ship you captured to the weapon on Squary. As for Ophiuchus and the master . . . we're all looking to you for the next clue."

"I'm going back to Capricorn," I say firmly. "I'm going to consult Sage Ferez and read my Ephemeris, and when I have new leads, I'll share them. But please, keep me updated on Aryll and what happens to the other Risers."

Sirna nods and stands. "I'm happy the Houses have rectified their mistake. I'll be in touch with updates soon. There are still too many dark spots in the Zodiac, and we could use your leadership."

I get to my feet, too. "Thank you, Sirna."

She bows to me. "Good fortune, Wandering Star."

Brynda slides off the vanity. "You'd better not come to the Capital without seeing me, or I'll come for you." As she did the first time we met, she gives me a hug and whispers in my ear. "And go easy on Hysan's heart. We're going to need his brains if we want to win this war."

Guilt sizzles like acid in my stomach, but I don't say anything. Sirna and Brynda leave, but Rubi stays.

"Sirna told me what happened in the Geminin embassy," she says when we're alone. "You okay?"

"Yeah," I say, sitting down again next to her. "Rubi . . . what's the point of the maze and the words in the Imaginarium?"

"They're prompts." She smiles and perks up. "Imagination isn't a reliable constant. It's different for each of us, and we can never know what it's like inside anyone else's head. As it is with what we See in the Psy, one's imagination exists only inside one's mind. The words are prompts to deepen your exploration, and the maze is a destinationless journey to give your thoughts space to wander."

On Gemini, every new set of Guardians has carte blanche to reimagine a new government. In Acolyte studies, we learned that, last century, Rubi and Caasy ran their House as a dictatorship—he took charge of Hydragyr, and she ruled over Argyr—but this century they opted for a democracy.

"Do you think it's good to keep reinventing the Geminin government over and over again?"

She shrugs. "I think we Geminin get bored easily, and we thrive on challenges and complexity and the unknown. So it works for us. Why do you ask?"

I shake my head absentmindedly, unsure I'm ready to vocalize my ideas. I don't even know if they're ideas quite yet—just thoughts. "No reason. Just curious."

"Rho . . ." Rubi looks into me with her tunnel-like eyes, her gaze so intense I feel like I'm falling into them. "In more than three centuries of life, I've seen many people rise to power and prominence and then pass their legacies on to the rest of the galaxy. I've seen firsthand how influential figures can change the course of history. But no one's ever united the Zodiac the way you have. I predict you will live on in Zodiac lore forever."

"How can you know that?"

"You've brought the Zodiac back to its natural state. We were always supposed to be united; that's why we've each been given one piece of the puzzle of survival. Your actions have reminded us of something we once knew but had forgotten, and as long as we remember your legacy, we won't lose our way again. You've become universally unforgettable."

35

TWO DAYS LATER, STANTON AND I are back on Tierre at the Fluffy Giraffe Resort. We ignore the empty third bedroom as though it doesn't exist, and neither of us breathes a word about Aryll or dares to say his name.

The newsfeeds are reporting on the discovery on Squary, and since every Marad soldier captured so far has been a Riser, everyone is speculating whether the army is *all* Risers. Riser hate crimes are growing commonplace on every House, and every time I see a new report, I think of Fernanda's warning.

The fair treatment of Risers has become a renewed subject of debate across the Houses. Fernanda is the only Guardian who's stepped forward to defend Risers, saying that extreme imbalance among them is rare and calling for empathy rather than rage. So, naturally, some Houses are now accusing her of Marad involvement.

Meanwhile, we're all awaiting the Guardians' decision on where the soldiers will face trial. With no boogeyman to hide behind, the master is staying silent. But I know this peace won't last long.

I message Ferez as soon as I land on Tierre, but I don't hear from him until the morning of my second day back. I check my Wave from bed, eager for any news, and I find a new note from the Sage.

Wandering Star Rhoma Grace, would you care to join me for tea in my office?

I jump out of bed and get dressed. When I walk into the common area, it's empty. Stanton's not in his room either. He must already be on the surface helping out at the settlement. Anything to avoid being down here, where the memories are too loud.

I zip through the Zodiax until the Vein deposits me at the Guardian's chambers. I press my thumb where I saw Tavia press hers weeks ago, and the whole wall slides open into the crystallized cave of amber agate, revealing the centenarian with eleven technologies.

Sage Ferez smiles kindly at me from behind the broad wooden desk. "You've had quite an adventure."

"I feel like I've lived three lives since we last spoke," I say, sinking down into the chair across from him. A teapot and two ceramic cups and saucers sit on a tray between us. "I'm so sorry I didn't tell you about Ophiuchus's warning sooner—"

"You have nothing to apologize for," he says, pouring hot brainberry tea into both saucers. He passes one to me. "Your testimony at the Plenum was magnificent."

"Thank you. And thank you for speaking on my behalf to the other Guardians." I withdraw Vecily's Ephemeris from my pocket. "And for this," I add, setting it on the desktop.

"What did you make of Guardian Vecily?" he asks, taking a small sip of his tea.

"I feel sorry for her. I think she was a talented seer and could have been a good leader if anyone had followed her. But she also frustrates me. I'm mad she gave up so easily. When she joined the Axis, she was taking on this uphill fight that she *had* to know would be incredibly difficult to win—and then at the first failure, she just gave up."

"Like you did by coming to Capricorn after the armada?"

"*No.*" I stare at Ferez, taken aback by the comparison. "I went to every Guardian, pleaded my case to the Plenum, and I was rejected by the whole Zodiac—"

But that's as far as I get before I fall silent, because I realize he's right.

Vecily was cast out by her House, just as I was by the Plenum. At first, like her, I chose not to use my voice again. I came to Capricorn and buried my head in its pink sand. Even though I was still secretly searching for Ochus, I abandoned people like Candela and Imogen and Numen and Twain—and all the others who'd rallied at my cry—to pursue my own obsessive agenda. If I hadn't gone to Sagittarius, I would have turned into another Vecily—a once-powerful memory trapped inside a forgotten Snow Globe.

A calm smile comes over Ferez's wrinkled features. "When we pass judgment, we hit a dead end. When we analyze something with an open mind, we can explore a concept into infinity." He gives me a moment to think about that before he continues. "If you dismiss Vecily, she remains forgotten. But if her experiences can guide you, then she still has the chance to lead someone."

I feel awakened by his words, and I sit up straighter. "Is that why there's such a weight placed on memory here on Capricorn?"

"Precisely. Wisdom lies not in facts themselves but in our understanding of them. Memory is the unseen fabric of our universe, the force behind intelligent life, and the way we train our senses. And it can either be an enemy you fear or a weapon you wield."

My confusion must show on my face because he leans in and says, "Consider this. How can we know about Ophiuchus, even after he's been written out of our history? He survives in children's tales so old that we remember the words long after we've forgotten their authors. You're our Zodiac's new Wandering Star—how do you suppose that title originated?"

A thirteenth place at the Guardians' table . . .

Ferez nods along with me, as if he can see my brain working it out. "Was this tie-breaker's seat perhaps the very place where the Thirteenth Guardian once sat?" he prompts.

As understanding dawns on me, the newfound wisdom makes me feel like I've accessed a larger universe. Memories ripple: Change the meaning of the thirteenth seat for one generation, and you've changed it for every generation that comes after it.

I used to think I had my past under lock and key, submerged behind the impenetrable wall of my shell. That I recalled Mom's memories when I wanted to, plucking them at will like reviewing Snow Globes in a Membrex. But the memories are always in me, and they shape me in ways I'm not even aware of.

Memories aren't the same as Snow Globes. We don't get to close them up and store them somewhere they can't hurt us. Aryll used a memory of Mom to manipulate Stanton and me. Mathias held on to his sanity by clinging to memories of who he was and the people he loved. The same thing that makes Lord Neith so human is what could turn him into a dangerous weapon in the wrong hands. The last words Deke said to us were *Don't forget me.*

Our memories aren't finite and containable. They're part of us, and they're so enmeshed in us that they're constantly evolving. They're more like Psynergy signatures, ephemeral and ever changing, and we don't have the luxury of shelving them. They stay with us. Always.

It's the reason why, in a universe obsessed with tomorrow, the wisest people turn to yesterday for guidance.

"I hear you met Fernanda," says Ferez, pulling me from this rush of revelations. "What did you think of her?"

I consider what I'm going to say before speaking, not wanting to sound judgmental, as I did with my comments on Vecily. "I think her heart is in the right place . . . but she's a little like I was before—so focused on her version of the truth that she's hurting her own cause."

"That is a wise assessment," he says, and I can't help but grin. "For Fernanda, the Risers' plight is personal. Just like Ophiuchus was for you."

I nod, thinking of Nishi's theory about Guardian Sagittarius and the possibility that Ophiuchus was betrayed. "Sage Ferez, do you think that maybe Ophiuchus truly was wronged by the original Guardians?"

"It's entirely possible. That would account for the intensity of his hatred." The Sage's inky black eyes glisten, and he leans toward me. "I have a new clue to add to this growing mystery. I've not yet made this knowledge public, but when the Marad attacked us, they smashed every Snow Globe in Membrex 1206."

"*1206?*" I grip my end of the desk forcefully. "But that's the one I was in the day we first met!"

"It is my belief," he says, nodding, "that they were only after one Globe, but they destroyed them all so we wouldn't know which one."

I take a sip of my tea and think back to the memories I reviewed. What could the Marad have found? I searched that room for weeks and didn't come across anything useful.

"I know I have kept you long enough already, but if you would gift me a little more of your time, I would like to show you something I believe will be worthy of it."

I nod and clink my cup into its saucer, eager to hear his theories about the master and see evidence of what the Marad did. If I was in the right Membrex, I must have been close to the right clue. Maybe I even found it without realizing—

The cave dissolves to complete blackness. "It's okay," says Ferez's gentle voice in the dark. "This room is a Membrex. I've just activated a Snow Globe."

A small light pops up in the center of the cave. It slowly expands, and the air around us looks like a black curtain lifting up to reveal a scene.

When the place is fully lit, we're still in a cave, only it's not underground. It's somewhere within the Capricorn woods. I can see the giant, gnarled tree trunks just beyond its mouth. In the center of the cave sits a boy no older than thirteen.

He has pale skin and obsidian eyes. His head is completely bald, and there's a small patch of skin over his ear that looks burned. Even though I've never seen him before, there's something familiar about him.

He's tinkering with his Sensethyser, either unaware or unconcerned that his recording has already started. When he finally looks up, I notice something peeking out from the neckline of his black robe, a pendant I immediately recognize.

"Aryll?"

"He's only thirteen here," says Ferez softly. "He'd already discovered how to record a Snow Globe. He probably learned more of the Zodiax's secrets by that age than most advanced Chroniclers."

I shake my head disbelievingly. "How did you find this?"

"When I learned he had betrayed you, I had my Advisors look into his astrological fingerprint. There was a second record buried beneath the first, which showed his birthplace. He was born here, on House Capricorn, seventeen years ago. At age thirteen, not long after this was recorded, he disappeared."

No wonder Aryll never liked it here. He might not have realized it on a conscious level, but some part of him must have known he was home.

Aryll suddenly looks at me, and I bite back my gasp. His black stare is so intense, I think he might actually be able to see me. Then he speaks.

"My name is Grey Gowan. Two weeks ago, I saw a warning in the stars when I was reading my Ephemeris. I saw myself changing Houses, to Scorpio."

An icy bolt cuts through me as I flash to the image of the Aquarian face in my own stars, and I clench my hands on my lap to keep them from shaking.

"Last week, my scalp started to itch," the Snow Globe boy goes on. "Today, I shaved my head and found tangible proof that the shift has begun. I'm becoming a Riser."

Aryll—Grey—pauses, his eyes still staring straight through me. "I've always loved my House. I love the power of memory so much, I taught myself to record Snow Globes. I know more about the Zodiax than even my parents. I don't understand what I did wrong. Why this is happening to me . . ."

His voice cracks, and he takes another, longer pause. "I'm leaving this recording to explain why I'm running. I hope I'm a balanced Riser and that I fit into my new home . . . but if the worst should happen . . ." Tears fall from the corners of his eyes. "Mom and Dad, I can't stay, because I won't stigmatize our family. I don't want to be a burden on you. If I'm balanced and get to keep my memories, I'll come back for you. But if I lose myself, and you never hear from me again . . . you know what happened. I'm sorry."

He nervously runs the pendant of his necklace between his fingers. It's strange how, even though he forgot everything else about himself, that habit still stuck with him.

"If I become a monster . . . and if I end up hurting anyone . . ." His voice is a low murmur. "Please forgive me."

✦ ✦ ✦

The light returns to the cave, but I feel like I'm still in the dark.

"Each of us is made up of millions of memories," says Ferez slowly, his tone tender. "In any given moment, a person is only showing one fleeting side of themselves. No matter how much we think we might know or love or be able to predict someone's actions, we will never see them clearly unless we appreciate their full potential, their many sides. Even the sides we're afraid we won't like."

I can't help thinking of Hysan. I've completely messed things up between us. Maybe he's right, and I was too afraid to love him. It was Mom's last lesson, after all. She taught me to believe in my fears.

"I'd like to record a Snow Globe of my experiences," I hear myself announce.

Sage Ferez smiles. "It would be an honor to house your memories, Wandering Star."

36

AFTER MY MEETING WITH FEREZ, I join Stanton on Verity's shore, and we look out at the ocean. In the distance, we hear hammering as Capricorns fix the part of the Zodiax that was destroyed.

The Cancrians on our settlement pass me with nods, bows, and smiles. So far, they've given my brother and me our space, but I can tell that won't last long. Ever since we've returned, there's been a new energy here. Something's happening . . . the onset of change.

But while the rest of the Zodiac seems ready to move forward, Stanton has reverted to his moody ways from a month ago. The only times he ever pulls out of it are when Jewel's around. "Stan, talk to me," I say after a long silence.

"I just can't believe how blind I was," he says with a sigh.

"We *both* were."

"I miss him, Rho." He won't meet my eyes.

"I miss him, too. But it's not really him we miss . . . it's the mask he was wearing. We never knew him, Stan." I think of the pale-faced, dark-eyed boy in his cave. Whoever Grey was, he doesn't exist anymore. Neither does red-haired, sunburnt Aryll.

"I need to show you something," I tell my brother, keeping my voice low so none of the Cancrians on the settlement behind us will overhear.

Stanton's gaze finally breaks away from the water, and he looks at me, his eyebrows pulled together. "What is it?"

"I wasn't sure if you'd noticed at the Geminin embassy, but Aryll threw something at me before running away." I produce the black seashell from my pocket and hold it out on my palm.

Stanton stares from me to the shell and back to me with wide, glassy eyes. He doesn't seem to know how to react. Finally he just whispers, "*How,* Rho?"

"Before you and Mathias arrived, Aryll told me that you and I grew up motherless for a reason. Made it sound like the master saw me coming even then."

"But does that mean—is she—?"

"*Alive?*" I shrug. "I don't know. But if we find the master—"

The sunny day suddenly darkens, the way it does when the House-wide lunch call blares, except that's not for another hour.

We look up at the slivers of light in the sky. They turn into letters, which spell:

NEWS.

Stanton and I jump up and join the Cancrians who are now gathering around a holographic newscast in the middle of the settlement. Jewel runs up and joins us, her frizzy curls and chestnut skin shining in the sun. Stanton rests a comforting hand on her shoulder.

A somber Capricorn newscaster in black robes is reporting from deep within the Zodiax, the brown Seagoat symbol suspended behind him. "We have just received word of a massive explosion on the Piscene planetoid Alamar. All Piscene communications have been knocked out."

Everything within me feels jittery and unsteady, as if I've inhaled a breath of Psynergy rather than air. This is the Marad's payback for Squary.

Ochus was right: The master has found a loophole to escape our galaxy's forecast. As long as only *he* knows what's coming, the future can't be predicted. He isn't just killing our planets and our people; he's also destroying the astral plane. No realm is safe from his reach. Every day he stays out there, the bonds holding the Zodiac together break further apart. Every moment we're not searching for the master is a moment he's using to plot more murders.

We have to act.

Now.

The reporter is talking about the army and recounting all the latest news stories: the discovery of the weapon on Squary, the captured Riser soldiers, and my return to the Plenum on Taurus. I pull out my Wave and start making a list of every person I've met on every House since leaving the Crab constellation, from those I spoke to for only a moment to those who have fought beside me since day one.

I'm following my own advice and opening my lines of communication with people from every House—because our universe is going to war. After I've run out of names, I compose a new message, just to Hysan and Mathias:

Whatever else you might mean to me, you are my best friends and allies. I know I've made mistakes, and I'll face them when this is over. But if we want to have a future at all, our present needs to be about stopping the master. Our problems can wait—but the Zodiac's won't. Please meet me on Tierre so we can finish this together.

✦ ✦ ✦

Once Stanton's gone to sleep, late into the night I sit up in bed and turn on Vecily's Ephemeris. I was going to get myself a new one in the Zodiax, but Ferez insisted I hold on to Vecily's for now. As I stare into the star map's pinpricks of light, I feel a frosty wind of warning seconds before Ochus's full form blooms into being before me.

You survived.

I glare at his hulking body as it looms larger, until he's three times my size. *Barely.*

You made me a promise, he reminds me. The coldness emanating from him is so strong that goose bumps sprout on my skin.

Yes. First I find the master, I say, keeping my frigid breaths shallow. *Then I set you free.*

He begins to shrink down, and I'm relieved to see time taking its toll on him—until I realize it isn't. The move is deliberate.

When we're face to face, his black-hole eyes latch onto mine with icy intensity. *Now I want another promise from you.*

What? I snap. *You want* another *favor, after getting my friends killed—*

Tell the Zodiac to show the Marad mercy.

I blink. My anger gets swallowed in my confusion, and I don't know what to say.

They are only brainwashed children, after all, he adds, as if the explanation helps. But it only confuses me further.

Since when do you care about anyone but yourself?

Ophiuchus grows bigger again. *I care about my House.*

What does that have to do with the army?

You can't really be this closed-minded, can you, crab? Where do you think Risers came from?

What are you—

They are descendants of the Thirteenth House.

The cold realization spikes my blood, freezing me from within, until everything about me is bitter and raw and stinging.

Most Ophiuchans went down with our world, but some assimilated into other Houses when ours was taken from us. His form begins to fracture and fade, like millions of ice particles breaking off in slow motion, getting sucked into a vortex. *Look after my children, Cancrian.* His voice echoes as he vanishes. *And I will help you look after yours.*

When he disappears, warmth returns to the air, but it doesn't penetrate my skin. I pull away from my Center and start settling back into my own body, when another vision appears.

I steady myself in the jittery Psy once more, trying to hang on for another moment, long enough to read this new omen.

It's my face in the stars again. I gasp, thinking of Grey or Aryll or whoever he is now. Am I destined to repeat his fate? *Am I a descendant of House Ophiuchus?*

But before my features shift from Cancrian to Aquarian, I notice something new in the lines of my brow, the curve of my nose. Something I hadn't noticed in any of the other visions.

It *isn't* my face. Not exactly.

The cheekbones rise a little higher, and her hair is a lighter shade of blond. When the shift begins, I notice that the woman seems to be about twenty years older than me.

As she morphs into an alabaster-white Aquarian, her lips part as if she wants to speak, but no sound comes out.

I pull the black seashell from my pocket, the force of my pulse bruising my chest, and I stretch my hand toward the holographic vision.

Mom?

✦ ✦ ✦

THE END OF BOOK TWO

✦ ✦ ✦

ACKNOWLEDGMENTS

WHEN THE STARS KNOCK US down, we rise up and defy them. And when we can't lift ourselves, we lean on our friends and family. Thank you:

To Liz Tingue, that wondrously wonderful Sagittarian who is the Nishi to my Rho, and the Rho to my Nishi: *Thank you* is a gross understatement. I owe you too much gold for this friendship to be a fair trade.

To Ben Schrank, Casey McIntyre, Marissa Grossman, Kristin Smith, and the rest of the Razorbill team: The stars smiled upon this Virgo when you welcomed her into your magical universe. Thank you for two stellar adventures—I can't wait for our third.

To her Excellency, the goddess Vanessa Han, for the best covers in thirteen universes. You, my lady, are an inspiration.

To Laura Rennert, my perfect literary partner and magnificent mentor: I am so happy to be working with you and so grateful for your warmth, wisdom, and brilliant guidance.

To Jay Asher, a friend to all: Thank you for existing. (Signed, everybody.)

To the many magic makers at Penguin Random House: Felicia Frazier,

Jackie Engel, and the sales team; Emily Romero, Erin Berger, and the marketing team; Kim Ryan and Tony Lutkus; Melinda Quick; and everyone else I've had the honor of meeting—you are the best, and I am so, so grateful.

Para Tomás Lambré, Vanesa Florio, y Del Nuevo Extremo: Gracias por hacerme sentir como parte del equipo aunque estemos en países distintos. ¡Espero vernos pronto!

To Scribblers: Lizzie Andrews, who's about to blow the literary world away; Will Frank, without whom I would've given up writing by now; Anne Van, whose wisdom we sorely miss in LA; and Nicole Maggi, my other brain and CP, a writer whose words I always devour, and a master at defying the stars.

To my friends and family across the globe, for your unending stores of love, advice, and encouragement. Cat, Ashley, Robin, Sungmi, Scribblers, Russ, Meli, and especially Mom—I'm so sorry for making you read through every draft of everything I've ever finished.

To Desirae, Erin, Tika, Melissa, Julia, Regina, Alyssa, Pavi, and, of course, first fandom founder Nat: You are out-of-this-world spectacular, and I adore our fangirling sessions.

To Andy Garber-Browne, my immeasurably creative and generous Geminin brother: I could fill every page of this book with the words *Thank you*, and it still wouldn't be enough.

To Russell Chadwick of House Libra: You are my best friend, my greatest inspiration, and an unknowable universe whose worlds I could spend eternity exploring.

Para mis abuelas, la Baba y la Beba: Dos mujeres más maravillosas serían imposible encontrar. Gracias por cuidarnos, querernos, e inspirarnos. Baba, lo que más felicidad me traería es poder leerte estas palabras en persona.

To Meli, my sister and my heart: You're the best person I know, the brightest light wherever you go, and I love you more than everything.

Para Papá: Te quiero tanto y te extraño todos los días. Gracias por siempre apoyarme en todo. Cuando Meli y yo éramos chicas, nos decías que todo lo material se puede perder—la plata, las posesiones, las propiedades—pero que nadie nos puede quitar lo que llevamos en la cabeza y en el corazón. Gracias por esa enseñanza tan sabia—nunca la olvidé.

To Mom, the strongest, smartest, and most beautiful woman in my galaxy: Your lifelong love, loyalty, faith, friendship, and support makes me brave enough to face my fears every day. I love you. Thank you for keeping our family together through everything and for being the universe's most incredible super-parent. You are, and always have been, my muse.

And, of course, to you—Rho's readers. I've loved getting to know so many of you at signings and on social media. You are absolutely the best part of being an author. We read books to know we're not alone, but I found that out by writing one.

✦ ✦ ✦

I've dedicated *Wandering Star* to my grandfather, Berek Ladowski, who passed away while I was working on the story. A true Capricorn, he chronicled his whole life in journals: eighty-seven years of memories that I've now inherited.

Like Rho, I was grieving through every page of this novel. Writing *Wandering Star* became an exploration into what my grandfather left behind—a collection of Snow Globes I hope I'm one day wise enough to unlock.